# The Safe Tree

*Friendship Triumphs*

## *Also from John D. Beatty*

*Crop Duster: A Novel of World War II*
*Sergeant's Business and Other Stories*

### The Stella's Game Trilogy
*Stella's Game: A Story of Friendship*
*Tideline: Friendship Abides*
*The Safe Tree: Friendship Triumphs*

# The Safe Tree

## *Friendship Triumphs*

## Part Three of the Stella's Game Trilogy

## John D. Beatty

•JDB•COMMUNICATIONS,•LLC•

JDB COMMUNICATIONS, LLC
WEST ALLIS, WISCONSIN

*For Evelyne;*
*My Ann;*
*The Girl of My Dreams*
*who fills my heart with joy*

# *Apologia*

The Stella's Game Trilogy—of which this is the *last* part—is a story told through four narrators; many other characters come and go like wraiths. Since the *whole* story takes place over the course of nearly a quarter-century and starts with young children, this is a narrative necessity.

Historical events punctuate our lives. The characters in this story saw remarkable history unfold in the mid and late 20th century. Some of those events anchor their stories and their lives.

\*\*\*

Once again, apologies to Metro Detroit and Key West, Florida, for twisting your geography. Bloomfield Hills, Bloomfield, and Birmingham city and township lines were redrawn three times in the twenty-four years I lived there, so I drew the borders *my* way for simplicity.

To Pilgrim Congregational Church at Adams and Big Beaver: We *were* members; my father, mother, and grandmother *were* eulogized there; and one sister *was* married there—but no, *I* wasn't married there. I wish I'd had the courage. That little limestone church will always be meaningful to me.

To my fellow alum and friends of the *real* Brookfield/Greenbrier: I had to bend our stories *more* than a little. Thanks for the beautiful memories and for our Brown-Eyed Girl, Clare, whose family saved me from *me*.

To the US Army, especially the Military Police branch: Women didn't wear the MP brassard until 1975, but for the story, I moved that up a couple of years to make Leigh's career more dynamic. And I know that the jurisdictional lines between CID, CI, and the civilians are a *lot* harder than I'm making them, but just bear with me and enjoy the story. And, thanks for the quarter-century that *you* put up with *me*.

To the US Navy: I became aware of the pioneering Petty Officer First Class Donna Tobias (1952-2010), whose diving career in the Navy began in 1975, just before the publication of *The Safe Tree*. Thanks to *her*, I know that the mermaid's naval careers *started* as something else—a brain bucket tip to Donna and the other *real* first mermaids. My apologies to the memory of Donna, earlier knowledge of whom would have changed this Trilogy. I had to make up the first female divers in naval service based on *not* much information.

To my family, who I dearly love, my sincere apologies for the liberties I take with our story, but *our real* story is nobody's damn business. We all know that the original "Charlie" had elements of truth *and* fiction as I have here.

And finally, to the *original* Wolverine…*get bent.*

# *Cast of Characters*

## The Narrators

John Jacob "JJ" Elrath—*Army intelligence analyst*
Claudia Ann Mueller—*Navy diver/storekeeper/hull technician*
Mike Dietz—*Army counterintelligence agent*
Leigh Taylor—*Army criminal investigator*

## JJ's Family

Stella Elrath Parkinson—*mother*
Brenda Elrath Jones—*sister*
Lois Laura McHenry—*sister*
Charlie Parkinson Junior—*stepbrother*

Kurt Parkinson—*stepbrother*

Will Parkinson—*stepbrother*

Charlie Parkinson—*stepfather*
Roy Jones—*brother-in-law*
Simon McHenry—*brother-in-law*
Dorothy Parkinson—*sister-in-law*
Julia Parkinson Addison—*stepniece*
Mary Parkinson—*sister-in-law*
Josephine Parkinson—*stepniece*
Anita Parkinson—*sister-in-law*

## JJ's Unit

Tom Merrill—*boss*

Gary Semitone—*fellow NCO*
Wendy Corey—*supply sergeant*

Nancy Anvers—*Spanish linguist*
Liz Devens—*Spanish linguist*
Alice Semitone—*Gary's wife*
Dennis Oakes—*Wendy's friend*

## Ann's Family

Howard Mueller—*father*

George Mueller—*brother*
Jim Mueller—*brother*
Jenna Savio—*stepsister*
Alex Savio—*stepbrother*

Claudia Mueller—*mother*
Barbara Savio Mueller—*stepmother*
Holly Cresto Mueller—*sister-in-law*
Carol Bell Mueller—*sister-in-law*
Billy Reidy—*Jenna's friend*
Brianna Gorgas—*Alex's friend*

## Ann's Unit

Kristin Collins—*dive buddy*

Betty Sadowski—*mermaid*
Laura Gutierrez—*mermaid*

## Mike's Family

Ben Dietz—*father*
Sara Dietz Halliwell—*sister*
Kiera Dietz Grun—*sister*
Mordechai Dietz—*uncle*

Monica Dietz—*mother*
Oliver Halliwell—*brother-in-law*
Nathan Grun—*brother-in-law*

## Leigh's Family

Ed Taylor—*father*

Cathy Taylor—*mother*

## Mike and JJ's High School

Dave DeHaven—*JJ's former housemaster*

Marie DeHaven—*Dave's wife*
Karen DeHaven Watson—*friend*
Clare DeHaven Alton—*friend*

Ramdas Brahmaputra-Reynolds—*classmate*

Sarah Silverman Simonetti—*classmate*

## Other Dramatis Personae

Jenny Jacobs Kent—*friend*
Donna Hammerfest—*friend*
Evan Hammerfest—*Donna' father*
Debbie Ford-Bell—*friend*

Jesse Kent—*Jenny's husband*
Nick Paulson—*Donna's friend*

Bob Bell—*Debbie's husband*

Randy Newhouse III (RF)—*Leigh's ex-father-in-law*
Randy Newhouse IV—*Leigh's ex-husband*

Joe Dryden—*minion*
Dave Harriman—*minion*
Herman Jimenez—*minion*

Sid Jackwell—*purveyor of services*
Gabe Knowles—*friend*

Adam Block—*chauffeur and more*
Bobbi Eldon—*friend*

Ingrid Torgensen—*bookkeeper*

Chuck Weir—*barkeep*

Mary Newhouse—*bookkeeper*

Lizzie Newhouse—*dramatis personae*

Randy Newhouse V—*dramatis personae*
Renée Newhouse—*dramatis personae*

## The Special Projects Division (SPD)

Dewitt Harris—*SAIC, SPD*

Dave Clawson—*Special Agent*
Frank Hitchcock—*Special Agent*
Tom Greenowitz—*Special Agent*

Ernie Packard—*SAIC, Wolverine Working Group*
Ellen Drew— *Special Agent*
Morgan Towne— *Special Agent*

9

# *January 1986*

## *Monday*

"*This* place is *some* reward, huh," JJ mused, holding his fiancée's hand on the penthouse suite's sofa. The fire they fought for a few *terrifying* moments was still fresh—the stench of burned carpet lingered. John Jacob Elrath went by *JJ*.

"Reward for *what*," Ann coughed, wrapped in her big fuzzy robe. Her *full* name was Claudia Ann Mueller.

"Putting the *fire* out, on *our* side, anyway." Roused by a blast of hot air as gasoline outside their door caught fire, he threw their quilt on them as she threw a champagne ice bucket's ice—a celebration of their two-day-old engagement—on the flames that shot under the door.

"For *that,* they put us up on the 5th Deck?"

"Fifth *Level*, dear. You can't get up here without a room key."

"Great," she harrumphed. "Remind me to *thank* your brother. Who *told* the hotel about us?"

"*Your* dad, probably." He twisted his neck stiffly. "Another week before we have to head back."

"They'll be glad to have *me* back. I'm the best O-ring counter in the fleet." She was a Navy storekeeper, hull technician, and diver

"Cloud, *you're* getting to be as cynical as *I* am," he murmured.

"*Not* possible, Johnny," she purred. "Let's *finish* the bubbly." They sat quietly in front of the *faux* fire, absorbing its scant heat, drinking warmish champagne. It had been a *very* long journey to that night. Friends since infancy, they lost touch as teenagers. After fifteen years apart, they ran into each other just months before, in a Navy dining facility in Key West, Florida. She was a Navy Petty Officer First Class; he an Army Staff Sergeant.

"Are you *trying* to get me drunk so you can have your *way* with me," he asked as she poured the last of the wine into their glasses.

"Forget *that*," she coughed, finishing hers in a long gulp. "*Not* tonight." She patted his leg. "*Nudge* me in the morning."

\*\*\*

"So, *that's* what all the fuss was about," Bob Bell asked. They were at breakfast in the atrium—the Northwestern Inn and Suites' hollow core—as they gazed at the charred door. Bob was one of those unlucky men who would go to his grave looking like a little kid—apple-cheeked and fair, smooth skin and bright

10

eyes, but close to six feet tall.

"Sorry," JJ mumbled. "Woke up the whole building."

"Were you *hurt*," Debbie Bell asked, her soft voice barely audible. Debbie was a small woman who didn't come up to Ann's chin. Since Ann was six-feet-one, *few* women *did*.

"No," Ann smiled. "Scared out of our wits for a few moments, got some smoke, but otherwise none the worse for wear. Wake you up?"

"Not *really*," Debbie—Ann's oldest friend—answered with a small smile.

"Hi," a woman smiled at Ann, setting a loaded tray down. "We met yesterday in the pool."

"Yeah, *hi*," Ann said to the woman she knew as Nancy, introducing JJ and the Bells. "Sorry about the wake-up call…"

"What *was* all that," Nancy asked. After a brief explanation, Nancy smiled again…a *too* genuinely, like a cue. "Well, *I* have to get back to the new hubby."

"Honeymooners?" Ann smiled brightly but thought, *honeymooners my ass. What honeymooner hides his face?*

"Yes, from Virginia. Dave has *family* up here…"

"Ah," Ann answered, "maybe we'll see each other at dinner tonight?"

"Sure," Nancy declared, picking up her tray.

The Bells had to check out of the Honeymoon Suite that morning and return to their *real* lives. Ann and JJ had to make statements to the police. They also needed to plan the rest of their stay around the fact that *someone*—apparently—wanted them dead.

And Ann wondered if *Nancy* could be one of them.

# *Wednesday*

"First group," Southfield Detective Paul Griffith mumbled as JJ watched eight men troop in for the lineup. The Oakland County Sherriff's Department hosted the Southfield Police Department's lineup at the sheriff's headquarters in Pontiac.

"Take your *time*, JJ," a dark, older woman added. "*No* rush, *no* pressure. Just tell us if *any* of them look familiar." She was Undersheriff Dorothy Parkinson, JJ's stepsister-in-law.

*No pressure…sure, Dot.* "Number six," JJ declared.

"Where do you know *him* from," Paul replied, scratching down a note.

"I saw him at the hotel Sunday night." JJ flashed on a much older memory, and a sudden chill came over him, making him shiver in the overheated room. "And, when I busted his head at Wolverine Military Academy fifteen years ago, *that* SOB was Cadet Sergeant Herman Jimenez. That streak of grey hair is *probably* from the scar."

Paul cleared his throat. "Why did *you* assault *him*?"

"If I *hadn't*, he would have *killed* me. What's *his* connection?"

"He has burns on his hands and legs that he can't explain," Paul smiled. "Someone matching his description was seen on the second floor of the hotel—

*not* where he *worked*—about the time the fire started. *And*, he disappeared from his *job* at the hotel kitchen Sunday night." He grinned. "Trifecta: he fills the bill."

"That's enough for now, JJ," Dorothy intoned, leading JJ towards the door.

JJ paused and turned to gaze at two *shadows* in a corner of the observation room. "Work for *you*?"

"Just *fine*, Sergeant Elrath," a man's voice answered.

"I *know* you," JJ stated. "FBI?" A voice he'd talked to years before.

"Yes, *we've* met." Silence. "Don't worry about *Herman* anymore."

"How about Chuck Wier," JJ asked. "I *thought* I saw him at the hotel the other night." Chuck had been a roommate, a *malevolent* one.

"*Yeah*," a woman's voice asked. "*Thanks* for the tip."

"Let's go, JJ," Dorothy said, taking him by the arm. "*They've* got stuff to do."

All JJ knew about either Chuck or Herman was from Wolverine—that he was often in trouble and always, *somehow*, managed to get out of it. *Wiggle away this time.*

That, and the fact that Herman participated in—and Chuck *watched*—the most horrible thing JJ had *ever* witnessed.

**\*\*\***

"*Who* called you, again?" Mike Dietz, an Army counterintelligence agent, gazed at Herman through the observation mirror. As a *military* cop, he had *no lawful* business talking to him.

"*That* guy," Leigh Taylor, an Army-trained criminal investigator, hitched her thumb over her shoulder. Mike glanced behind him at a nondescript man with FBI credentials around his neck. She had as much business talking to Herman as Mike did. "I met him last spring. He wants us to take a crack at him."

"Remind me *why*," Mike grumbled. "We've gotta catch *flights* this afternoon." The FBI file on Herman was not thick, but thick enough. But Leigh had known JJ since the 8th Grade; Mike since high school.

"*He's* Herman….*JJ's* Herman Jimenez." "This will be a *brief, information-only* interview requested by *Someone Else*."

"Ah." They'd been in the Army long enough to know what *that* meant. *Someone* felt Herman still needed *cooking*, in interrogator parlance. Two of the finest chefs skilled in *that* cuisine—who had knowledge that was *not* in the file—could and would *sauté* him.

"How long has he been *in* there," Leigh asked Paul, next to them in the observation room.

"Few minutes," Paul shrugged. "Read him his rights again an hour ago."

"We'll start with *Silence*," Leigh mumbled to Mike. "Then, *We-Know-All*."

"Worth a shot," Mike agreed, opening the door. They sat down across from the handcuffed Herman without a word, placed their file folder quietly on the table, opened it…and began to read.

Professionals know that humans near each other naturally want to communicate—especially when they've been isolated as Herman had been…waiting…expecting to be questioned. The *Silence* technique denies that impulse.

Leigh looked up at Herman every few moments, smiled enigmatically, and went back to the file; Mike *never* looked up.

*Silence* is *also* hard on the interrogator. For *two* interrogators, it's like Chinese water torture. Rather than steady stimulation, there's *nothing* but screaming quiet. But the *most challenging* aspect of the *Silence* technique is that the interrogator must *visibly, patiently* wait until the source starts talking on his own. *That* took Herman a little more than five minutes. "What I *here* for?" He spoke with a distinct Hispanic accent, his tone bordering on panic. "*Why you…?*"

"*Just* a moment," Leigh spoke softly, raising a cautioning finger, her emerald-green eyes shining at him before she went back to the file, pointing out something to Mike. Mike nodded and grunted, "uh-huh," reinforcing the agonizing *silence*.

Herman, frustrated and frightened, kneed the heavy table noisily. "What you *doing?*" He was a big guy, strong enough to make the table jump.

"Just a *moment*, sir," Mike soothed, *not* looking up. "We *just* got your file, and we *don't* have a lot of time." He gestured at another sheet, making the stillness even louder.

"*HEY*," Herman shouted. "*I want…*"

"*Mr.* Jimenez, you have a *most interesting* resumé." Leigh looked up suddenly, smiled, and pulled her honey-brown hair back casually. She leaned forward *just* enough so that her chest bumped the tabletop.

"Why I *here?*"

"You're *here*, Mr. Jimenez," Mike answered blankly, finally looking at him, "because that door you lit up belonged to JJ Elrath. But you *knew* that."

"I…I *not*…"

"Where *did* those burns *come from*, Mr. Jimenez," Leigh smiled lightly, her voice honeyed and sultry. "Herman—*may* I call you Herman? *I* shall tell *you*. You left your job in the kitchen of the Northwestern Inn and Suites at about 10 Sunday night. You *followed* Mr. Elrath and his fiancée to their room. You then went out and bought a gallon of gas at the Standard station at Telegraph and Twelve Mile Road at 11:17. You then *went back* to the Northwestern, *poured* gas on Mr. Elrath's door, and *threw* a lit pack of matches at it just before midnight. How am I doing so far?"

The biggest risk with the *We-Know-All* technique is getting *any* part of the narrative wrong. If *that* happens, the source knows that the interviewer *doesn't know all* and becomes confident, even brazen.

"What you *want?*" Herman turned pale and started to sweat

"Who *sent* you?" Mike snapped, his steel-gray eyes penetrating.

"Who sent…*no* one. I not *know*…"

"You're a *clumsy* liar, Herman," Leigh smiled brightly. "You *know* Mr. Elrath from Wolverine. *Someone* found you and sent you to *that* door. *Who?*"

"*That* guy…*different* guy. He *not*…"

"He *is*, Herman," Leigh smiled again. "You *know* he is. Mr. Elrath *identified* you as his roommate from *Wolverine*."

"*That* guy," Herman complained loudly, pointing to a dent in his forehead. "He give me *this* for *no reason!*"

"He *had* a *reason*, Mr. Jimenez," Mike grinned. "*Eight months'* worth of *good reasons*. You clobbered him in his sleep from *October* to *May*."

"Where *did* your burns come from, Herman," Leigh soothed.

Herman blanched, swallowed hard. "The gas can…fire *so* fast…"

"*Who sent you*, Herman," Leigh smiled again, winking. "Arson; attempted murder—*two* counts; fifteen *years* minimum. But with a *little* cooperation…*who* knows? C'mon: *who sent you?*"

Herman breathed deep, gazing at Leigh's chest. "A guy come to Miami; say he know where this Elrath guy is. He pays, he says. I come to Detroit; he sends me to work in the kitchen, and I see that Elrath guy. The guy says 'five thousand if he *dies*,' so I torch that place. But something goes *wrong*…"

"*Who*, Mr. Jimenez?" Mike was persistent,…and now, *loud*.

"He say his name is Joe."

"What's he look like, this Joe?" Leigh purred.

"He about my height, dark eyes, long arms, dark head—*gordo*, like me."

*Hefty*…. "What *other* names did you hear, Herman," Leigh smiled winningly.

"Other names I hear are RF and Dave."

"OK, Herman, *thanks* for talking to us," Mike stood. "Somebody else will be along soon, I expect."

They met Dorothy and Paul in the observation room. "Get *that*," Leigh asked.

"Got *enough*," Dorothy smiled. "We can continue to talk to him based on that, ah, interview-that-*didn't*-happen. You're *good*, I'll say that."

"I've been teaching the *femme fatale* for the past few months," Leigh sighed. "*Always* works on the dense ones."

"But Joe *who*," Paul wondered.

"Joe *Dryden; Dave* is Dave Harriman," Mike answered. "Two Newhouse goons. *RF* is Randal Fred Newhouse III. Dryden has a *personal* grudge against JJ."

Leigh squinted. "But *how* would *they* know about *Jimenez*?" She glanced at the man in the shadows. "Any ideas?"

"Not that we can *talk* about," the man answered. "Thanks for the help."

"*Who* are *you*, again," Mike asked.

"Special Agent Clawson, Sergeant Dietz."

*Gotta catch flights… can't stop to chat.*

# *February 1986*

"*Congratula*tions to you *both*," Navy Lieutenant Steve Wycoff beamed. The affable little personnel section head found Ann and JJ filling out the requisite changes to her records. While a mere engagement didn't change their military *status*, it *did enable* some paperwork changes in their 201-files. Grotesquely, though they could *not* legally change their next-of-kin, they *could* change their emergency contacts. "Ms. *Morris* wants to see you *both* before you leave." Lieutenant Commander Susan Morris, the base undersea warfare systems officer, was the senior ranking woman on Key West and the self-appointed mentor to *all* the women stationed there.

Ann knocked on Susan's office door an hour later, pushing it open gently when she heard "come," shouted over the whine of the air conditioner in the hall. "They'll fix *that* damn thing someday," Susan smiled, pointing them to uncomfortable chairs. Susan stood about 5-foot-8 with square shoulders and had an uncanny resemblance to Doris Day. "*Sergeant* Elrath; Annie *said* you were a good guy when I first *heard* of you, and I've heard *nothing* to refute that assessment."

"I *try*, ma'am," he answered with a small smile. "Ann brings out the best in me." Even their light, touch-of-the-lips promise-kiss they shared in the dining facility that day was a military policy *no-no*. The ensuing officious imbroglio was the stuff of bureaucratic legend driven by creaking personnel policy machinery.

"All right; *enough* schmoozing," Susan continued, "and we needn't be so formal. So, Annie: What does *this* do to your career plans?"

"Nothing *yet*, Sue," Ann answered. "I sit for my board next week." Promotion boards for everyone aspiring to E-5 through E-8 on Key West would sit starting the next Monday: JJ's E-7 board was Wednesday; Ann's Thursday. Both would sit in judgment on E-5 boards on *other* days, brow-beating the E-4s wanting a promotion, assailing them with questions about their jobs, careers, and current events. "Master diver's *not* gonna happen. I may not be able to *stay* on dive status much longer, physically." *Just made that decision, too.*

"Bends?"

"Those too. I just hurt in too many places. Just *swimming* can be a trial."

"*That* happens." Susan switched her gaze to JJ. "So, JJ, I *read* your book. *Interesting* ideas, but I think a generation ahead of its time." He wrote a book— *Profiles in Leadership: Case Studies in Command, Leadership, and Military Management*—that was well-received in most military circles. "But your *career*,

I understand, has been, ah…"

"Stalled. Took a Silver Star to get to E-6. *Finally* passed a PT test last week." He passed his Physical Training test *mostly* because the requirements fell with age. "Getting better gradually, though," he lied. A dozen years earlier, neither parachute opened correctly one morning, and he hit the ground like a well-trained, *highly*-skilled sack of potatoes. That sudden *joint-jarring* stop was taking a *relentlessly* worsening toll on him.

"Whose idea *was* those newspaper articles?"

"My sister-in-law," Ann said. "We *didn't* expect the response they've gotten." Two articles spoke of in-service couples and the policies and brutal mathematics their relationships faced because of the military's need to have the *right* people in the *right* place at the *right* time with *no* considerations for military spousal connections.

Susan smiled. "Well, *they* hit the Pentagon like a skid of bricks. Some people there want your heads, but most want more *time* to fix the issues. Got them *talking*, anyway." She glanced back and forth. "Which I believe is what you *wanted*?"

"Ma'am; yes, *ma'am*," JJ answered—an NCO's emphatic response to officers.

"Good," Susan replied, standing up. "Good *luck* to *both* of you." She smiled after a light embrace with Ann. "Annie: I'm going to *kiss* your GI, OK?"

"Don't let *me* stop you, Sue."

"Ma'am; *yes*, *ma'am*."

* * *

"*Highly* irregular, Sergeant," Captain Malcom Hargraves declared tartly. "*Very* irregular indeed." Malcom was the 4th Battalion, 75th Infantry (Ranger) taciturn personnel officer. His *impossibly* thick glasses and squinty appearance earned him the nickname Captain Magoo. His response was a Magoo bobblehead on his desk and his West Point boxing trophy next to it.

"*Why*, sir," JJ asked. "I *can* change my home-of-record, my emergency contact…"

"That's just *it*, Sergeant. Making another *service member*—especially one in *another* service—your emergency contact would mean that the Army would have to find *them*. This is *highly* irregular…"

"Well, sir, I'd have to change if my *current* contact moves, which she *has*. Sir. My home-of-record *has* to change. What's irregular about *that*? Sir?"

"The Army has rules against *cohabitation*, as well, Sergeant," Malcom glared. "But, admittedly, they are *enforced* infrequently." He glanced at JJ and Ann in turn. "Petty Officer, you know the Army doesn't *have* to keep you together. In *some* cases, it would be impossible."

"Yessir," Ann answered. "We've discussed it. Together or apart, we *want* to do this."

16

Malcom gazed at JJ. "Did you *see* the Miami *Herald* Sunday?"

"Yessir, *we* did. Nice piece."

"Indeed. 'Sixty-Day Wonder.' Where did *they* get *that* nickname from?"

"Sounds like the story in the Detroit *Free Press* got around, sir," Ann answered. They both grinned at the slang sailors used to describe the for-now lovers that some took on. Every day started *another* sixty-day clock for *everyone* in uniform. Orders that could send them wherever Uncle Sam needed them two months later could come *any* morning.

"*In*deed." Malcom shuffled some papers on his desk before he leaned back in his chair. "Oh, *you're* not alone," he sighed before he grinned. "We can't *stop* you or *any* of the others. Sergeant Corey has fallen in love with a sergeant in operations; they, *too*, are engaged."

"*Yes*sir," Ann grinned. Wendy Corey was the ranking Army woman in JJ's unit.

"*All* right, *get* started," Malcom nodded. "The commander wishes to see you before you leave."

After an hour with two different clerks, they knocked on Lieutenant-Colonel Ned Bentham's office door. He was a battle-scarred, physically bent man with a permanently tanned, creased face and close-cropped, grey hair—and was barely fifty-one. JJ saluted in the requisite fashion. "Sergeant Elrath reporting as ordered, sir."

Ann saluted, adding, "Petty Officer Mueller, sir."

Ned grinned slightly and returned their salutes crisply. "Sergeant, Petty Officer, *thank* you for coming. *As* you were." He stood abruptly. Even bent as he was, he *was* six-feet-five with the shoulders of an (aging) linebacker *with* pads. "I wanted to congratulate you; have a little chat. Please, be seated."

Gesturing to a corner behind them—the walls festooned with pictures and plaques—Ned joined them. "I've been aware of *your* relationship for some *time*, as you know. I have discussed this *kind* of situation at length with senior NCOs and officers in *both* services. Two service members together is confusing enough for the Pentagon. The idea of two from *different* services has sent them into a *frenzy* of meetings and memos. When they start having *families*…God, I don't want to think about what *that* will do to the bureaucrats.

"But those articles have rattled some cages. 'All we want is to be treated as equals with the civilians, to *love* who we *want*,' I think *you* said, Petty Officer? In*deed*. Equality with civilians. A *radical* concept for the Pentagon."

"We *know* that, sir," JJ said, "but we can't deny…"

"And we can no longer *expect* you to, Sergeant…not if we want to *retain* you. Used to be you had to ask permission to get married: *Then* we could control it. *Now* we can't *stop* you, not for the most part." Ned sucked his teeth. "The military reflects the society it protects, eventually. Do you plan to tie the knot down here?"

"We haven't thought *that* far ahead, sir," JJ glanced at Ann. "Getting everyone *down* here…"

"Logistically difficult; yes, I hear you. I married my wife in San Francisco in '75. My family in Virginia and New York couldn't get there. Her mother was stuck in Thailand, her sisters marooned in the Philippines, and one brother's still in Vietnam. Even with *my* connections, we can't find her *other* brother we *think* is still alive." JJ knew what *connections* Ned likely *had*. Senior Special Operations officers often had CIA and *other* agency friends.

"Very well." Ned stood, extending his hand to JJ. "Congratulations, Sergeant, and good luck to you," he mumbled, taking Ann's hand with a grin. "Sergeant, *may* I?"

"That's up to *her*."

"*Fine*, sir." Ned pecked her cheek. "Highest ranking officer ever to kiss *me*." Walking out, they brushed hands lightly. "Want to set a date?"

She sighed. "*Where*?"

"Thought *that* should be *when*."

"Nearly everyone we care about is in Michigan. How *could* we...?"

"You're right...we wait for developments." *Which means...promotions and orders to wherever.* They brushed lips gently as they had done whenever they agreed on a joint course of action. Now, they decided on *minor* things like when and where to get married...and they *still* kissed on it the same way.

"Though I've pelted you and flayed you..." he mumbled.

"By the livin' *Gawd* that made you," she continued, leaning on his arm.

"You're a better man than *I* am, Gunga Din." When widely-read servicemembers got orders that they didn't *necessarily* like, they recited Rudyard Kipling's poem's last lines. It wryly *reminded* and *reassured* them that *these* were the sacrifices *they wanted* to make every time they reenlisted, just like the sepoy of literary lore.

*Because it's the life he wanted, and so do we, God help us.*

*** 

"When I go to work," the dark man at the podium began, "I walk past the Memorial Wall just inside the main entrance of CIA Headquarters in Langley." Military brass and civilians crowded the Beltway hotel ballroom platform; the audience was crammed with more. All were there to see Mike and another soldier receive the nation's fourth-highest medal.

"Last Monday, two *new* stars had been cut into the white marble and inset with black paint. That meant two *more* of my comrades—maybe *friends*—made the ultimate sacrifice *some*where, *some*time, hopefully *for something*." Mike knew the speaker as Special Agent Brown. Brown had *not* been introduced before he spoke that day. After a Deputy Secretary of the Army explained that what today's awardees had done was still so secret the citations could not say what they *did*, Brown just *appeared* at the microphone.

"There's no ceremony for those stars, no readings or eulogies: many of them don't even get their names in the Book of Honor. *Once* in a while, though, we *publicly* honor our comrades in our secret wars for freedom. I'm *proud* to see *these* two given more than just anonymous stars on a wall." In *this* case, Mike and the other soldier got a defector to tell the powers-that-were-*then* what they did *not* want to hear but that the powers-that-are-*now* wished to reward.

Emily Naris, the *other* soldier, sat next to him on the platform. Leigh—fetched from Missouri for the ceremony—studied her. *Pretty; green eyes. About my height—five-eleven—and 30 or 40 pounds heavier—LOT of work to meet height-and-weight, girl. She looks like a painting....*

Sitting beside Leigh, Emily's parents quietly held hands, as did Mike's parents, Ben and Monica, on the *other* side of her.

"For distinguished service in the finest traditions of the United States Armed Forces," the Deputy Secretary declared, "the Secretary bestows upon Sergeant First Class Michael Ethan Dietz the Defense Superior Service Medal for his intrepid and brilliant actions of 15 December 1979." When Mike and Emily stood up for their medals, Monica reached for *her* hand.

*I passed my board? I HAD a board?* Mike, standing at attention as the Secretary pinned the medal to his jacket, could only catch impressions of his family. He shook hands with the VIPs—*and* Brown—as they passed. As his battalion commander stopped and turned for his handshake, he mumbled, "I'll have orders for your new rocker before you get back." As Emily's commander stopped in front of Mike, he quickly glanced at Mike's sleeve and grinned. "Can't even get *that* right."

"Got the medal on the right side, though, sir; gotta give 'em *that*."

The colonel suppressed a chuckle. "Gotta get Naris another rocker, too."

Mike nudged Emily with an elbow. "Hear *that*, Venus? We're *both* gonna get bumped."

"I *heard*. Congratulations to us both. That's Leigh out there?"

"Yeah. I'll introduce you."

A photo-op/toothpick chow reception followed in the same room, but Brown did *not* stay. Politicians, civilian intelligence wonks, and senior military mugged for the cameras, lingered for *one* last round of on-the-taxpayer drinks, and left.

One of the last to leave was Special Agent Dave Clawson. He didn't speak to Mike or Leigh, but they nodded when he smiled and left. When Mike's parents headed off to lunch with Emily's parents, only Mike, Leigh, and Emily remained.

"Let's find some *real* food somewhere," Emily sighed.

"*I* could eat," Mike agreed.

"*Come* on, Leigh," Emily said, "let's make it a threesome."

They ordered food and shared light conversation in the hotel's nearly-empty lower level bar-and-grill. "*Tell* me, Emily," Leigh asked, "Why does Mike call you Venus?"

She smiled. "*Tell* her, Sandy."

"Somebody in interrogator school said she looked like Botticelli's *Birth of Venus*. Red hair, pale skin, and, um..."

"*Full* figure," Emily finished, grinning resignedly. "I've been called worse. *Still* can barely control my weight. I'm going to have to put in *two* miles a day for a *week* to get rid of this lunch."

As they sipped coffee, Mike excused himself, leaving Emily and Leigh alone. Emily reached for Leigh's hand on the table; Leigh took it briefly. "He and I had *one* long weekend in interrogator school. What *we* did was…"

*Making love isn't a mistake; it's a decision that is sometimes…* "Unwise." Leigh sighed. "I've known Mike since 7th Grade; *I* gave him his nickname; his family treats mine like their own. We made a pledge about a year ago; my family was introduced to *his* community at Christmastime. We have a…"

"Soul marriage."

"*Yeah.*"

"*I'm* thinking about starting a family. Not getting any younger."

"Oh, yeah? Can't do it single in the Green Machine."

"Got to get *him* to *ask*, and policy's *so* hazy."

"Why don't *you* ask *him*?"

Emily looked surprised. "Oh, I *could*…but, you *know* guys can be…here he comes again. Mike, we have a question for you: would you freak out if a *woman* asked *you* to marry *her*?"

*Leave two women-strangers alone for two minutes, and they either bond or brawl.* "Ah, well, I'd have to say…too many variables…"

"*What* did I *tell* you, Leigh? 'Too many variables' is guy-code for 'no *way* I'm going to answer *that*.'"

"*Who* are we talking about," Mike glanced at Leigh. "Not…"

"Sure. Let's get *married*, Sandy." *I SAID THAT OUT LOUD?*

"What…are you…*serious*, honey?"

"Sure. Will you *marry* me, Michael Ethan Dietz?" *I AM…*

"Go ahead," Emily declared. "If it's what you *want*, make it *work*, and make *the Army* make it work."

"Leigh Elizabeth Taylor, I *will* marry you." *GOTT IM HIMMEL, what did I just say?*

They stared at each other for several moments before Emily grabbed both their arms. "*Ah*, fer *Chrissakes*, are *you two* gonna *seal* the *deal* with a *humongous* smooch or *not*?"

Leigh smiled, "*Now*, Sandy," and they gave each other a *genuinely humongous* lip-lock so long and *involved* they didn't see the busboy clear their table.

# *April 1986*

"*When's* your flight, again, honey," Leigh's mother Cathy asked, pouring herself another cup of coffee in her Lathrop Village townhouse kitchen.

"Twenty hundred hours: eight tonight, Mom." Leigh stared blankly, tiredly at an odd-shaped refrigerator magnet. "First time to Europe."

"Didn't know there *were* American soldiers in Belgium," her father Ed intoned, spreading butter on his bagel.

"CID's there," Leigh answered. "Criminal Investigations is…" A knock on the door interrupted her.

"Who could *that* be," Ed grumbled, getting off his stool. "Some peddler."

*No, Dad; it's Mike…but how do I know he's even in town?* Leigh's private smile at hearing her dad and Mike exchange greetings in the little hall got *much* bigger as Mike rounded the corner into the kitchen. "Hi, *zeeskeit*," she whispered, embracing him.

"Hi, *oytzer*," he murmured into her neck. "Wanted to see you before you left the hemisphere."

"Hi, Mike," Cathy interrupted. "*Good* to see *you*, too. I appreciate that *I'm* not the reason you're here, but *can't* an old woman at least get a 'hi' from her future son-in-law?" To call Cathy Taylor an *old woman* would do her a disservice. Though she *was* 53, she didn't look a day over 30, with honey-brown hair like her daughter and the same haunting emerald eyes.

"Ah, sorry, Cathy," Mike smiled, pecking her cheek. "I didn't *want* to disrespect you, but I only *have* today here."

"Remind me *what* you two call each other. *Leigh* said…"

"*Zeeskeit*: Yiddish for sweetheart, among other things," Mike answered. "I call her my *oytzer*: my treasure. And she is." *But first…* "Cathy; Ed: we don't *really* know each other that well, but I'd like to…"

Cathy arched an eyebrow with a hand on her hip in an authoritarian manner. "Oh? *NOW* you ask *permission* to marry our *precious* daughter?"

Leigh saw him go pale. "Honey, Mom's being her usual *funny* self."

*What…unexpected delay in speech…* "Uh, OK. Yes, I'd…"

"What *are* your *prospects*, young man? Can you *support* our precious daughter in the *manner* in which she is accustomed?"

"Mom, please, just *let* him…"

*Can I…ho-boy.* "My…prospects?"

"We can't just *give* our only child away to *anyone*." Cathy purred, chuckled, and smiled before she stepped around the counter, swinging her hips saucily. "I *always* wanted to do that." She held his chin and pecked him on the cheek, glanced at Leigh, winked, and lightly embraced him. "Take her off our hands," she whispered in his ear before kissing it, "and you have *my* blessing. Ed; *your* turn."

Edward Taylor was a tall, somewhat cadaverous man who resembled Michael Rennie. His light-brown hair was like Leigh's—even in his mid-fifties. His prominent jaw was just like hers. Ed had a way of looking at people that put them in mind of a friendly undertaker. His voice was reminiscent of Alfred Hitchcock *and* Boris Karloff, with a little Bela Lugosi thrown in: heavy, measured, and deep. "Michael, you appear to be making a career of the Army, as Leigh is." He glanced at Leigh, who looked puzzled. "Her mother and I once gave Leigh to a young man who was *less* than savory." He paused. "And even then, I favored *you* over Randy, even though I knew *you* hardly at all. I'm convinced that you can make our daughter happier than he *ever* could, and that's all we can ask." He extended his hand. "Thank you for asking. You have *our* permission *and* my blessing."

Mike shook Ed's hand and pulled a small box out of his pants pocket. "I want to make us official."

Leigh stared at the small, old box. *I knew it would feel different the second time.* "Can I...?"

"You're *supposed* to, honey," Ed mumbled, pulling his jacket on.

"Go *ahead*," Cathy smiled. "Let's *see MOTHER OF GOD! WOW!*"

Leigh opened the box and gasped at the old and elaborate gold setting with a large round center diamond surrounded by six smaller diamonds. *I can't believe...ohmygod.* "Mike, it's..."

"*Old*-fashioned. Grandfather Mordechai gave it to Bubee Rachel as an anniversary present: her engagement diamond is the center stone." He got down on a knee. "Will you *accept* this ring in token of..."

"Oh, absolutely," Leigh whispered as he slipped it—almost—onto her little finger. *It doesn't fit, and it's a little ugly, but it's beautiful.* "Mike, I..."

"I know," Mike murmured. "It needs a new setting, but I just *had* to..."

"Kids," Cathy sighed, "just *don't*...OK, *get* carried away, but do it in *her* room: *I'm* not done with *my* breakfast."

At a late lunch—Mike's flight to Arizona was at 6:20—both sets of parents toasted the happy couple.

With the Detroit *Free Press* article about their friends JJ and Ann taped in their briefcases as a reminder, they knew they could be separated again for years.

*Though I've belted you and flayed you...*

# *May 1986*

Ann shuffled her shoes off...

Then, stopped. *Today* was when the promotion lists of *all* the E-7 through E-9 were published in the Army, Navy, and Air Force *Times*. She'd seen her name on the Navy list, and...

*We'll be apart soon enough. We knew THIS was coming...by the livin' Gawd that made you...Suck it up, kid.*

She had been in dungarees, glad that the denim didn't stick to everything in the early summer damp of the Lower Keys. Just as she was sliding into a skirt, she heard JJ clomping up the stairs outside. *Their* apartment was a 20-by-40 upper; there were two 20-by-30 lower units in back of the building. The lower *front* was occupied by the only Kosher deli on Key West.

"Staff Sergeant John Jacob Elrath reporting, Petty Officer First Class Claudia Ann Mueller. Number 314 on the *list* I am. A Sergeant First Class I *shall* be, come September."

"Hi, babe. *I'm* 298." Between May and September, the services determined just how *many* new E7 to E-9s they would *need* in the next three years. The Army typically needed somewhere between 500 and 600 E-7s; the Navy about the same. It was rarely *less* than 400 for either. Thus, the top 400 E-6 on those promotion lists were practically assured of promotion. And there was no slot for another E-7 intel analyst in Key West, meaning JJ would be sent elsewhere.

He plopped into a creaky gray vinyl kitchen chair and started unlacing his boots. "Did you see that *other* article, the one buried towards the back?"

"Uh-uh. Run it down for me." She started massaging his shoulders. *Their* flat had two bedrooms and a big living room with a galley-like kitchen at one end, indistinguishable but for a half-dozen rows of ceramic floor tiles in front of the appliances and sink. They had sort-of divided it with a well-worn Formica-and-steel table and three nearly-matching chairs.

"Headline reads 'Brass to Tackle Two-Service Marriages.' They're actually going to make policies to keep married or *engaged* servicemembers together if at *all* possible." He turned painfully to grin up at her. "They're starting with E-7s and above."

"Well, *I'll* be *damned*. You mean..."

"Yeah. *Us*; soon enough. Leigh, probably: she's 351." There was a knock on their door: two of their neighbors, Tom Merrill and Kristin Collins.

"Just saw the list myself," Tom, JJ's beefy, dark boss, beamed. "I'm Number 81 for E-8; they'll need the top 150, probably."

"*I finally* got orders for first-class diver school in July, after they canceled my *last* orders in January." Grey-eyed Kristin smiled. She was a pretty, dark-haired woman, five-feet-eight and solid. People said that Kristin's bright smile could light up a whole island: even her frown looked cheery.

"Hey, great," Ann laughed. "Looks like we're *all* getting a bump."

"We have to celebrate," JJ sighed, getting up. "Ladies, if you *don't* mind, Sergeant Merrill and I have a ritual to perform…on the *deck*, of course."

"*Of* course," Ann rolled her eyes. "We *mere* women…"

"We can't spare the wind, Ann," Kristin reminded her. "Who wants to stink like an ashtray, anyway."

On the broad roof deck over the building's western wing, JJ handed Tom a Cuban-seed Monte Cristo, who bit off the end and offered JJ a light. They leaned over the rusting steel rail in the shade of a palm tree, barely inhaling the rich smoke. Neither of them smoked more than two cigars a year, and usually less. It was a malodorous bonding experience, nothing more. When Anvers and Dustin—two women in their shop—came back from jump school the month before, they both took a drag on Tom's offered stogie. Key West was known for its hand-rolled cigars, which was the only industry *on* the island except for fishing, tourism, and smuggling.

"See that *other* article, Tom?"

"Kristin showed me. My divorce is final in September. Have to see what happens." Tom—an Army E-7—and Kristin—a Navy E-5—had been together for months. With the disparity in their pay grades, the military had taken a dimmer view of *their* relationship than they had JJ and Ann, who were the *same* pay grade.

"Does she *want* to stay with you?"

"We've *talked* about it."

"What about Dennis? He didn't board." SSG Dennis Oakes was Wendy's fiancée.

"I had the usual chat with him as company re-up NCO. He's reenlisting for the *Reserves* in July. They plan on *him* becoming the dependent. *Speak* of the devil…"

Dennis and Wendy both climbed up iron stairs to the deck. "*Hey* guys," Wendy smiled, "I got jump school orders for August, and I'm number 501 for E-7, so *maybe* by the end of the year. Give us a drag on that stogie, JJ, *just* in case I get it."

"Let's *hope* so, Red." JJ smiled, offering his to the red-blonde, spindly Wendy. "Dennis: you didn't board?"

Dennis shrugged. "The *unit* that wants me needs an E-6 *or* an E-7, but the *bank* that wants me doesn't want to lose me to ANOC right away." The four-week Advanced NCO Course (ANOC) was required of Army E-7s within the first year after promotion. Balancing civilian and military careers in the Reserves often required such painful decisions.

"*Please* take a shower, babe," Ann murmured as their friends left that night, winking slowly. "If you want to *complete* our celebration tonight…"

"*And* I've *got* to finish my British history."

"I really *should* work on…what am I, oh, yeah, ethics in the business world. Bunch of slogans, dull as dust."

"Not *much* more compelling than British Corn Laws. I *also* want to go through the latest box Mom sent."

After homework, they watched a "Cagney and Lacey" rerun while JJ shuffled through his mom's latest trash-and-treasure trove that included registrations for cars long since sent to the junkyard; originals of his father's birth and death certificates, and his discharge from the Army in 1944; a picture he'd never seen of *his* father and Ann's in uniform (*they'd* been friends for *ages*); a contest entry form from the '60s; a still-valid deed to the family cemetery plot, where his grandparents and his father were; an old Polaroid photo of their house on Birch Lake; a 1944 equivalent to a W2 form for his mother. Finally, there was the deed of conveyance for the family's old Round Lake property, signed and dated by his mom in 1967 *and* by Charlie Parkinson—who became JJ's stepfather in '70.

"What do *you* make of it," he asked Ann, showing her the deed.

"Didn't know he was in real estate, too."

"He was once…there's his old license number."

Newhouse Properties—the buyer of the land—was a large firm in Southeastern Michigan. The heir to the empire, Randy Newhouse IV, was married to Leigh…*very* briefly.

*And Parkinson Title and Trust did the title on BOTH houses.*

There was also a faded letter:

> *To whom it may concern:*
> *There are certain lies told about me and mine by my sister, Frieda. A woman from down there is claiming to have borne a child of mine. I never MET that tart, and I'll take any blood tests necessary to prove it. I never want anything to do with Freida or her family again. I disown them completely.*

"What do you make of *this*," he mumbled, passing it to her.

She held it up to the light. "Notarized; signed. Something *legal*."

If anyone ever asked just *why* JJ kept *that* letter in his briefcase, he couldn't answer. Like keeping bag ties on hand, it just *felt* like he *should*.

\*\*\*

*Don't know if you saw this…looks encouraging.*

Mike scanned the *Stars and Stripes* article Leigh had sent him entitled "An End to Sixty-Day Wonders?" with interest.

*The Joint Chiefs of Staff have announced an initiative to give uniform service members married or engaged to other service members more opportunities to stay together after Permanent Change of Station (PCS) arrive for one. The policies would extend to those who meet the following criteria:*

- *Minimum of ten years' service for both members;*
- *The rank of E-7, WO-3, or O-3 (promotable) for one member;*
- *Minimum of three years obligation remaining for both*

*The policies are meant to "foster careers and encourage mid-grade professionals to remain in uniform...extending and shortening tours should become routine, not exceptional." The Guard and Reserve components of all the uniform services will need to expand their Active Guard and Reserve (AGR) programs...*

The article went on in that general vein, with those supporting and deriding the new policies getting equal space while the general tenor *seemed* optimistic. Too, there was an interesting caveat:

*...Engaged two-service couples would be given some leeway in reassignment and tour extensions, providing sufficient evidence of intent to marry exists.*

Encouraging, but as a *policy* example, less than helpful. He wrote back in some confusion…and desperation.

*…Can't say what "sufficient evidence of intent" is in this case—and I work with it all the time. My boss said, "I'll find out." Still waiting...*

Frustrated by the 20-plus day delays inevitable with the mail between Korea and Belgium, Mike sent a teletype message to Leigh's unit, setting a time for an AUTOVON call. The Department of Defense Automatic Voice Network (AUTOVON) was ostensibly only for *business* use. Still, anyone with knowledge of the system *could* use it for more mundane toll-free long-distance calls.

"Hi, Leigh," Mike shouted.

"Hey, Mike," Leigh answered. "How do you get me?"

"Clear but quiet as always. I think I have an answer about *sufficient evidence of intent*: announced engagement; a ring; date set for a wedding not more than 12 months after the engagement. That means we've got nine months, and I'm supposed to be *here* until next April."

"I'm *here* until 1989."

"So, we wait to earn enough leave?"

"That or divine intervention."

# *July 1986*

## *Friday*

"*Also*," Mike asked in German, "*was machst du so?*" They stood by their cars in the busy parking lot (it was evening rush hour) of the Seven-Eleven near the Busan (AKA Pusan) commuter train's western terminal. Mike finished a Slurpee in the sandpapery heat; the little man smoked.

"*Grüss Gott, Mein Freund.*" Little Emil Gast was the line-crosser who Mike had interviewed in '79…the interview he got the medal for. Gast was now an occasional source for the West German Federal Intelligence Service—not unusual for defectors. *He* was the reason Mike was *in* Korea. "Someone who goes by either Pak Sung Nu or Park Do Nu in the Presidential Security Service is getting Russian pay." The Presidential Security Service is South Korea's version of the US Secret Service's Uniformed Division.

Mike nodded appreciably. "I'll pass it on. So, how have *you* been?"

"Fair, *danke*. I finally have *teeth* that fit." Gast defected—in part—for dental care. "I found a community of Jews here; we celebrated Passover this spring." Religious asylum was the *other* reason. "*Und du?* I trust *you* are well."

"I *am*. I have something *for* you." Mike reached into his car and handed Gast a small package.

Opening it, the little man smiled widely. "A *mezuzah!* How thoughtful!"

Mike waited; he could see in Gast's eyes there was something left unsaid. "There's something else?"

"The time has come to repay your kindness." Mike's family helped Gast land a job with a German shipping company. He pocketed his gift and lit another cigarette. "They're falling apart in the east, asking *me* for ways out."

"If someone wants *help* crossing…" Mike started. In their world, *the east* was shorthand for the Soviet Bloc.

"*You, Kamerad,* will be my first call." Gast looked wistful. "One of my KGB contacts says a big American real estate firm has contracted the Seo-Bang to *find* you." The Seo-Bang Faction was one of Korea's most prominent criminal gangs. "I thought it *might* have been the KGB themselves because of *me*—they're not above such tactics—but my *Stasi* contacts *also* say it's Seo-Bang; they add something about a blood debt. Take care, *Mein Freund.*"

"*Vielen danke, mein Freund.*"

*How would Newhouse even know I was here?*

### \*\*\*

"*That* way, JJ," the young petty officer he knew pointed into the dark warehouse. JJ hitched up his pants absently—in *this* heat, he didn't wear a belt—sauntering through the wide-open sliding-barn-style door.

"Thanks, Tina," he replied. NCOs addressing each other by their first names was considered *unprofessional*, but only officers and stodgier NCOs *really* cared. Soldiers, sailors, and Marines of both sexes worked in sweaty t-shirts in the heat. It was stuffy despite the huge fans blowing in every corner and window.

As he reached a wide shelf-free desk area, he was met by a young-looking lieutenant junior grade who broke into a wide grin. "*Sergeant* Elrath, *always* a pleasure. Storekeeper Mueller's around the corner."

"Thanks, sir." The officer knew *who* JJ was there for; he was a fellow volunteer for the Lower Keys Boy Scout troop. JJ looked down the H-shaped warehouse central corridor and saw Ann shrugging her dungaree shirt on twenty yards down. He had a too-brief moment to watch her without being distracted by *that* face and *those* eyes.

Then she turned and saw him and smiled, warmed by his half-grin. She checked herself as he walked towards her, dragging his right leg slightly and favoring his right side. "Hey," she smiled, "thought you were working *later* today."

"Wet-bulb fade-out." His HQ company had spent three weeks sleeping in tents at an old missile base, honing their combat skills. Today they went to fade-out—end of exercise—when the wet-bulb temperature topped 90 degrees.

"They're *ready*," he mumbled as they walked next to the boiling-hot asphalt street that led to the baked packed-sand parking lot. "Want to get them today or wait?"

"Let's get 'em now; it's kinda on the way."

And they kissed on it.

He drove to the stucco building on Flagler Avenue with the jeweler's shop next to a pawn shop. He knelt to put the three-diamond ring on her finger to the applause of the half-dozen others in the shop. Not to be outdone, she knelt to try his plain white gold band on *his* finger to the delight of many.

Most of their weekends were given to laundry, homework, and unwinding—*if* neither of them had to work. Saturday was his 31st birthday—she was eight days older than he—and they would celebrate *then* with their friends. But *this* evening was *theirs* alone.

And they celebrated in the time-honored-fashion…falling asleep in front of the TV during a Clint Eastwood marathon, a half-eaten bowl of popcorn on the sofa between them.

## Saturday

"*Vous desirez*," the man asked, gazing at her. They were in not-all-that-comfortable chaises on the hard sand of a crowded North Sea beach.

*Mid-twenties; blue eyes, brown hair, maybe five-nine, 150 pounds.* "Merci *non*, I was just looking at the pictures of *Titanic*." Leigh had been staring at pictures of the rusting remains on the front page of the paper he held.

"You are American," he answered with an odd accent. "You *look* French." The beach was *very* cosmopolitan and unofficially *apparel-optional* for the bold.

"Sorry to bother you: just looking at the pictures." She stretched on the chaise, making her *too*-tight outfit even tighter. *Take this bait, little fish; this getup's uncomfortable...*

"*No* bother," he answered. "Here on holiday? I'm Michael."

"Just a day trip. I'm Liz." *Luscious, ain't I...*

"Ah. So, do you work in Belgium? I work in Bruges."

"Yes, I work in Belgium. What is it you do, Michael?" *Smell good, little fish?*

"Oh, nothing important. A typical job moving paper from one pile to the next. What do you do, Liz? Something exciting, yes?"

"No. I make small piles out of big ones." *True, most of the time.*

"Would you like an ice? I shall go if you'd like."

*A giant ice cube in a paper cone.* "I'll go *with* you." *Need to get out of the sun...and set the hook.* They stood sweating in line for about ten minutes, not saying much of anything. Their treats were melting by the time they got under a big hotel awning. *Reminds me of ice cream with Mike behind the shopping center in the summer of '68...whoa, EIGHTEEN years ago. The Tigers were...*

"So, Liz, *where* do you do *what* you do," he asked, standing *much*-too-close. *Mouth open...* "The Hague," she answered quietly.

"Would you like to get out of this heat? I know a little café not far from here." *Took it!* "Sure." They hadn't walked more than a block before Michael brought a short club out of his pant leg. Leigh quickly blocked his swing, took down his left knee with a sweeping kick, and announced the bust on her wire.

"So, Mikey," Leigh smiled lightly, somewhat later, having changed out of her *too*-revealing beach outfit. "How many people *do* you work with?" *Michael's* real name was Bruno—he was Dutch—and was suspected in connection with several muggings on North Sea beaches.

Bruno was talkative but *inappropriately* interested in Leigh. "I have seen your photo," he said at the end of their interview. "I *thought* I had before, but the hair was different, and the photo lacked your *distracting* figure. *Another* American— I don't recall his name—said you were a man's wife who had run away. He was offering a reward."

*Uh-huh. Pull the other one, Bunkie...* "Where and when was this?"

"Perhaps two months ago; in Bruges. Yes...it *was* you. I am certain..."

*MAY...what the...?*

# Monday

"You're *certain* of your source?" Chief Warrant Officer Fourth Class Willie Taft, Mike's commanding officer, scanned his after-action reports.

"As sure as I *can* be, sir." Mike thought his commander's name ironic because *this* Willie Taft was skinny as a rail, unlike the portly president. "Not gonna lie about being blown, sir." In the vernacular, *Blown* meant his true identity was known to people who weren't *supposed* to know it.

"Well, *nuts*," Willie grimaced. "This'll take you out of the field while we verify it."

"Yessir. Paperwork to…"

"And, Sergeant?"

"Sir?"

"If you *are* blown, you're of very *little* use to me *here*. Be prepared for *that*."

"Yessir."

"You should think *harder* about becoming a warrant officer. This *would* be a *splendid* time to work on your packet. Consider it *compelling career advice*, Sergeant."

"Yessir."

***

"Huh," Major Leslie Harris declared. "Well, so much for undercover in Belgium, Taylor." Leslie was a small man, a Peter Sellars lookalike *sans* glasses. Everyone in CID knew that he was *the* driving force behind the Army's part of the Walker spy ring investigation. Leigh arrived in Belgium just *after* Leslie was awarded his Defense Distinguished Service Medal.

"Yessir," Leigh sighed. "I haven't done a *lot* of that here, anyway…"

"You've done *enough*," Leslie declared, "and as a new face, you *were* useful. Now…" he shrugged. "Any ideas as to *who* this nosy bugger might be?"

"My ex-husband's family, maybe," she said. "Haven't heard from *them* for *years*, but…" she shrugged.

"Any *criminal* connections we need to know about?"

"Nossir; they're mostly obnoxious, not criminal or violent."

"Said you ran away?"

"In a way, yessir. I bolted on our wedding night after I broke his jaw."

"I've *had* wives I've *wanted* to…" Leslie had been married five times, a well-publicized CID record. "OK, but I'm going to have to report this up the chain. So, you're on investigations support for a while, I'm afraid." He gestured to a chair behind her. "You *should* put in for a warrant."

"I've *thought* of that, sir. I can work on my packet while I'm 9-to-5 for a while."

"Don't think about it: *do* it."

"Sir, yes, *sir*."

# *October 1986*

## *Monday*

"*Staff* Sergeant Elrath," Captain Wallace called, "*front* and center." JJ dutifully marched from the rear of the company formation, his boots crunching in the coral fill. He winked at Ann as she, too, made her way to the front.

"The Secretary, having been informed of..." and on and on the executive officer droned, reading JJ's promotion orders as Captain Wallace and Ann affixed the new insignia of a Sergeant First Class on his collar. The orders sending him to Alaska to organize an intelligence shop for the reconstituted 6th Infantry Division (Light) came the week before.

The week before, JJ had done the same for Ann. Just that morning, *she* was handed transfer orders—effective a week *after* his—for a storekeeper billet in Anchorage. She won it by dint of her sunny personality, her many accomplishments in the Navy, and by drawing attention to *her* needs as a role model (and an *actual* model, occasionally) in Today's Navy.

They would have three weeks at home before Thanksgiving. Long enough to get married among friends and family and to ensure—as much as *possible*—that they wouldn't be separated again.

## *Friday*

"Sergeant Dietz reporting, sir," Mike said, saluting. His unit had *just* ended the morning briefing.

"*Sit*, Sarge," Willie whipped off a salute and pointed to a side chair, handing Mike a stack of orders, still warm off the copier. "This has got to be *the* damnedest thing I *ever*..."

Mike scanned the orders quickly, half-expecting to see the "Permanent Change of Station," but *not* the "Assigned" block, which read:

*SFC DIETZ, Military Intelligence Support Command, Frasier, MI.*

*And my terminal date here: FIVE DAYS? Who's kidding who?*

"In fifteen minutes, we're making an AUTOVON call to Brussels. *Be* here."

\*\*\*

"Sergeant Taylor, sir," Leigh said, coming to attention but not saluting. The timing was odd—after regular duty hours. She was told to report *within five minutes, in uniform or out*. Baggy slacks and a sweatshirt with flip-flops were the best she could manage *that* fast.

Leslie nodded curtly. "Sarge, *have* a seat," he mumbled, distracted. "Here." He handed her a freshly-copied stack of orders. She scanned quickly, frowning at "Permanent Change of Station," and on to the "Assigned" block:

*SFC TAYOR, CID (Frauds), Troy, MI.*

*TROY? Next door to home? What the...?* Then she saw her terminal date: five days hence.

"*In twenty years of service,*" Leslie moaned, "I have *never* seen or *heard* of such orders, nor have I seen or heard of two service members simultaneously transferred to the same geographic area on such short notice—short of wartime needs."

"*Two* members...sir?"

"Your fiancée, Sergeant Dietz, got *his* orders just now. Be in here for an AUTOVON call in fifteen minutes."

"Why would...?"

"I only know that *he* got similar orders."

***

"Army CID Brussels; CW-2 Mahoney speaking...*wait* one." It was 1715 when the distinctive AUTOVON phone rang, and Jill, the duty officer and Leigh's CID school classmate, answered. She handed Leigh the phone.

"Sergeant Taylor speaking."

"Leigh? I *just* got orders for Detroit."

"So did *I. Something's* in the wind."

"Why does my intuition say it involves that FBI friend of yours?"

"*Could* be. I'll telegram when I get my flight information."

"Yeah, I'll *call* as soon as I've got *mine.*" There was a pause. "*What's* going on?"

"I dunno, *zeeskeit. Barely* time to clear post. You?" *Clearing post* usually took about three weeks; they had five *calendar* days that included a weekend.

"Same. Gotta pack up my hold-baggage, too. See you in Detroit, *oytzer.*"

"Yeah; *fabulous.* But *why?*"

# *November 1986*

## *Monday*

Ann searched around the flat for that ever-errant *something* that needed packing. An open box of JJ's books, another of binders and papers were all that was left on the stack of boxes, and they'd be taped up that night.

She smiled when she heard him clomping up the steel stairs. He opened the door and came in, gazing at her as he always did with his brave half-grin, and she gave him her warm smile back. "Hi, honey," he called. "I *sign out* Wednesday morning."

"Yeah, great, babe. Here." She handed him a slip of paper as she pecked his cheek. "Next Wednesday morning at the Oakland County clerk's office, we get the license."

"OK, great." He stared at her. "We're *really* doing this?"

"We *really* getting married in front of God and everybody in Detroit."

"Are you *sure* you don't want a Mass?"

"Your little church is fine, babe."

## *Tuesday*

> *Coming in from London from over the pole; flyin' in a big airliner!*
> *Chickens flyin' everywhere around the plane...*

*Fifteen hours from there to here, and WHY did Arlo talk about chickens?* Leigh arrived at Atlanta International after dark. She looped her overnight bag and purse over one shoulder, her attaché/backpack over the other, and scanned flight monitors as she started to walk to the pavilion.

> *I don't know; still we got to go; from here to there, eventually*

*Like Steppenwolf says...Twenty HOURS on airplanes. I should put in for flight pay.* Mike pulled his attaché/backpack and his overnight bag over his shoulder. As he trudged to the pavilion, he saw a familiar profile not far ahead. *Light brown hair, prominent chin, five-eleven and maybe 150, well-proportioned...*"Leigh!"

She turned to look. *Male Caucasian, light-but-rough complexion, short chestnut hair, six feet, and 190 pounds, solid jaw, shoulders like a bull, drop-dead good-looking and deadly grey eyes...* "hey, Mike!" As they drew together, they dropped their bags at the same time, exchanging hugs and light kisses as small crowds flowed around them.

"*So* good to…*so* good," he mumbled.

"Let's *get*." They picked up their bags and walked into the vast emptiness of the main concourse. The gift shops and food vendors slammed their gates shut as they walked by while loudspeakers blared with random urgency…

*Attention: 410, please report to security.*

She shook her hair loose of her hat as they walked, then stuffed the ugly headgear unceremoniously into her overnight bag. "OK. where *were* we?"

*Attention: 441, please report to security.*

"We were going home."

"Yeah," she sniffed, "*why?*"

*Attention please: Arriving Braniff passenger Nordstrom, please pick up a yellow courtesy phone.*

"Ours *not* to reason *why*…"

"*Ours* but to *ossify*." She rolled her bad shoulder. "*This* damn…*let's* get some chow." The last open burger stand was closing and overgenerous with French fries. They moved to a standing table by a glass wall that overlooked the apron between gates. They could see taxiways not far off and runways, where lights blinked blue, red, and amber in the isolated blue-black darkness. The white glow of buildings in the distance seemed incongruous. Airplanes rolled this way and that—some quiet, some noisy.

*Attention: 445, please report to security.*

He glanced at a TV screen. "Looks like Reagan's got himself into a mess."

*TWA Flight 41 from San Francisco now arriving at gate B 8.*

"Yeah."

*Attention: 445, please report to security.*

"Want to sit down?"

"I *really* want 445 to report to security so they'd shut the *hell* up."

An airliner rolled noisily along the apron outside the windows, lit by the building lights' glare, turning onto the end of a runway.

*Final boarding call for Pan Am flight 901 to Athens now at Gate E 19. Final boarding call…*

"*These* orders," he sighed.

"*Too* tired…."

*Attention please: Arriving TWA passenger Perry, please pick up a blue courtesy phone.*

"To *hell* with it." He reached out and put his hand behind her head, gently turning it towards him. She resisted for only a moment, turning to face him. Their kiss was tender, brief, and committed, tasted of salt and catsup from her French fries, with a hint of pickle and mustard from his burger.

*Attention please: 441 contact the security office immediately.*

"Thanks," she sighed. "I *needed* that."

"Me, too. Pops is meeting us at the airport."

"That *lounge* is mostly deserted. Maybe *that* guy over there's got the right idea." She nodded to a sleeping traveler.

"*Yeah.* Let's get to our gate and catch up on our sack drill. *My* internal clock went haywire somewhere between the mid-Pacific and Nebraska."

# Wednesday

"Ben, *thanks* again for the ride." Leigh mentally—reflexively—sized Mike's father up with professional care between flashes of street lights. The journey to Lathrup Village seemed shorter than she remembered; landmarks were often invisible from inside the freeway's concrete valleys. The signs were the same, but somehow everything *looked* different. "I didn't want Mom to have to pick me up in the dead of night. We were just lucky the airlines brought us both to Atlanta at the same time."

"*Quite* welcome, my dear. And how *are* your parents? We haven't *seen* them since June."

"They're fine. Dad's in New York; Mom said he'd be back next week."

It was nearly two in the morning when they reached the Southfield Expressway's transition from a limited-access expressway to a divided highway. Ahead of them, they could see the flashing lights of a line of emergency vehicles that started a block south of California Circle—where Leigh's parents lived. Roils of smoke and occasional mists of water wafted grey in the cold and clear night air.

Adam Block, the driver, got out to enquire of a policewoman on the street and knocked on the rear door. "A fire involved several buildings and an electrical substation. The Taylor's building has been evacuated."

Everyone quickly piled out of the limo and into the brisk night. The acrid stenches of ash and flame, ozone, and fire-fighting foam-filled their noses as cold mist and smoke occasionally pelted them. Police, firefighters, paramedics, and Red Cross volunteers held, consoled, and herded lightly-clad figures. On the southbound side of Southfield Road, a line of taxicabs waited, arrived, and departed; two sheriff's deputies directed the traffic. Long queues waited for their turn at a mobile phone van. Steam rose from their breath while frightened, cold, shaking hands clutched cups of hot liquid.

*Where's Mom? Damn mud; these shoes ain't made for this.* It took Leigh half an hour to find Cathy—clad only in a Red Cross blanket and a robe—amid knots of refugees. She sat on a folding stool, getting oxygen through a mask and clutching a bundle of forms. Her face was smudged with smoke; tears rolled down her cheeks, leaving streaks of white. "It was at the *other* end of us," she sighed, hugging Leigh, "but we got *lots* of smoke."

Mike studied Cathy's triage tag. "Smoke inhalation, Pops." He spoke to the harried paramedic in her ambulance. "Can *this* one go?"

The paramedic emerged and glanced at Cathy's tag. "Anytime," she announced. "One *less* patient on *my* hands."

"They need a place to stay, Pops," Mike rasped, throat raw from the smoke.

"Of course." Ben was a large man but limber. He stepped in front of Cathy and squatted down. "Accept the hospitality of my home, Cathy. I'm sure *this* is a humanitarian exception to the canon of legal ethics."

Mike and Leigh stood Cathy up and guided her to the car. As they passed a queue waiting for cabs, Mike saw a face he *thought* he remembered...

✻✻✻

Ann stumbled out of the bedroom to answer the phone in the kitchen, glancing at the clock. *0434...damn...better NOT be a wrong number...* "MUELLER! ...uh, *Jenny?* What...?" She suppressed a shiver in the clammy night chill, wrapping herself in a blanket. "Jenny, um, yeah. What's... OK, honey, slow *down*. Just...take a breath and start over, Jen. Where *are* you *now*?"

"*Who's*...?" JJ murmured, leaning on the door jam.

"Jenny! There's been a fire; her husband was shot." Jenny Jacobs Kent was one of *their* oldest friends.

"OK." he inhaled deeply, trying to shake the cobwebs out of his head. *Like I need THAT.* "I'll calm her down."

"I'm *sure* she's safe now," Ann mumbled as she handed over the receiver.

"Hi, sweetie ...yeah, OK, slow *down*...so how *is* he...OK; good...where's he *now*...and the kids? Uh-huh...OK, good. Listen, Jen, I'll be *up* there tomorrow... no, Ann's coming *next* week...yeah. OK, Jen. Be safe, OK? *This* number, then? OK. Just *hang in there*, sweetie?" He hung up. "Shot Jesse through a window. Not dangerous, just a .22 through the shoulder. The police *know* it was arson."

✻✻✻

Mike awoke in the dark, his bedroom alive with rolling shadows from a tree outside, waving in a stiff breeze. The curtains fluttered in the quiet drafts of the heat duct as he remembered helping Leigh and her mother to the cottage and kissing both good-night.

He stared at the photos that surrounded the mirror over his dresser: his parents and his uncles in their uniforms—two uncles had been in the Army, his father and an uncle in the Army Air Force, an uncle in the Navy, and his mom with her USO sash. They seemed out-of-place on the same wall as that first photo of him in *his* uniform. He remembered when the Army took *that* picture, his second *day* in uniform. In the West Texas June heat, they stuffed him into *that* Class-A uniform *just* for the photo, moments after they handed him his plastic nameplate. *Mama had it framed and hanging on the wall before I got my first leave.*

The sheets felt comforting, but he swung out of bed, stretching his stiff back. His luggage was neatly lined up along the wall next to his closet. He remembered bringing *some* of it in, but the rest must have been Adam's doing. Mechanically, he opened his backpack, making sure his records were there—medical, JUMPS, 201-file...all in order. *Lose them, and everything stops.* Pulling on a sweatsuit, he stumbled downstairs.

"Morning, Mama," He bussed her on the cheek, poured coffee, and flopped into the breakfast room's booth. The view out the north wall's French doors *always* looked like morning. He blinked at the growing light, the eastern windows over the booth sprinkled with sunbeams.

"Sleep well, Michael?" Monica barely looked up, nursing coffee and writing notes on a pad—*so typical*. Dressed in a pantsuit with a high-neck sweater, she *looked* the part of the dutiful hostess.

"I *slept*." He coughed briefly, shivered, and stretched, watching sunbeams slowly sink on the west wall. *Damn back. Always stiff.* "When *did* we get in?"

"About five hours ago." She sipped coffee. "How *is* Cathy, Michael?"

"Frightened out of her wits." *And THAT takes some doing.*

Ben walked into the kitchen a few minutes later, kissing Monica's cheek, pouring coffee, and opening the newspaper. Dressed in an elegant suit and tie, he looked every inch the dapper, patrician host. "What a mess Reagan's made in this Iran-Contra disaster, eh, Michael? *Trash* day hasn't changed. Please take the barrels to the curb." As affluent as that part of the world was, someone *still* had to deal with the weekly garbage in the same old way.

"OK, but to the untrained eye, yes, Pops," Mike nodded. "Makes sense in power politics, though. This *meshuggeneh* Congress won't fund it, so he had to find another way. Hi, Carla," Mike smiled at the pleasant and round African-American woman as she came in the kitchen through a side door. "And how is *your* mother?"

"She's *well*, thank you, sir," she replied, a look of puzzlement on her open face.

"You don't remember me, do you?"

"No, sir."

"It would have been 1964 when we last saw each other. Pops and I came to your brother Roland's funeral."

She stopped, thoughtful. "My *goodness*. *That* was *you*?" She was the daughter of—and replacement for—the family's *first* cook/housekeeper. Carla started working for the family when her mother retired and had consistently missed seeing Mike ever since.

"The first Gentile funeral I ever went to."

"And you were the only *white* faces there," Carla smiled.

"We felt obliged," Ben offered. "He died *so* young." Lieutenant Roland Hall was one of the first American soldiers killed in Vietnam.

"Carla, *let's* make it tomorrow," Monica said. "We have unexpected guests in the cottage. Michael: trash." She cocked her head, listening to footfalls upstairs as Mike went to take the trash out.

\*\*\*

*Good outfit, good people.*

JJ breathed deep, taking a last look at the orderly room, staring at the company roster where he'd signed in fifteen months before. *It seems like a lifetime.* He exchanged glances with First Sergeant Noble Dix, a wiry, amiable man. *Just DO it.* He signed his name in the box: John J. Elrath.

"*Good* working with you, Sarge," Noble offered his hand. "Good luck with the legs."

"Thanks, Top. I'm going to *stay* a leg if I *can.*" JJ shook his head. "That *last* jump...." He stretched his ever-stiff back and neck. Like many older paratroopers (those over 30 or with more than 30 jumps), he had arthritis in all his heavy joints...and worse. "I'm *not* getting any better—or younger." *Leg* was paratrooper slang for non-airborne-qualified personnel. Rangers and Special Forces looked down on them as a rule. Still, the headquarters of special operations units were well-peopled with *legs* out of sheer necessity.

He said or waved goodbye to buddies as he left the building. He gave Liz Devens a brief and *unauthorized* hug. She was a petite, blonde Spanish linguist who he helped train as an intel analyst—she would get formal training next summer. He gave *another* to Nancy Anvers, a taller African-American Spanish linguist who, with *his* encouragement, was going to communications traffic analysis school in January. Both were reenlisting on the strength, *they* said, of JJ *and* Ann's counsel.

✳✳✳

Leigh woke up suddenly, trying to make sense of the kaleidoscope of the night before. *Flight after flight to Atlanta, meeting Mike, finding Mom chased out of the condo, coming here.*

The little bedroom was slightly bigger than her last barracks room. Pastoral landscape prints decorated the walls, joined by a nondescript photo of a farm scene in a desert—*Israel, maybe?* A small vase with painted copper-and-bronze flowers—*Mike's from junior high*—adorned a dresser; another empty vase sat on a desk. *If the last person I touched was Mike, how did I get naked? His girl-stripping skills ain't...no, I did it. I was rude to a woman offering a nightshirt.*

She stared dully at a snifter of brandy that she hadn't drunk, rolling her bad shoulder. She spotted her briefcase—*when did THAT get here*—and checked the contents: Medical records, JUMPS, 201-file. She rummaged in her B-4 bag, rejected the entire *idea* of underwear, pulled on a sweater and jeans, found her pumps in the closet—*when did I scrape all that mud off*—and opened the door.

In a living room just outside, she recognized a woman with pinned-back hair, Mike's coloring, and brown eyes. "*Hi,* Kiera."

"*Hi,* Leigh," Mike's sister grinned, standing up. "Did you sleep well?"

"Well enough, thanks," Leigh lied; she hardly remembered sleeping at all. Kiera guided her to a *very*-long sofa by the fireplace, sitting next to her and holding her wrist. "I was rude to you last night. Sorry." She *felt* genuinely sorry but was just too tired, her skin too irritated and her shoulder too stiff to *sound* sincere.

"I have a thick hide."

"How's my pulse?"

"OK. You've had a shock."

"Not like Mom."

"Talking about *you*."

"Where *is* Mom?"

"The other bedroom."

"Why is *this* called the cottage?"

"We treat *this* place as a guest suite…or a *retreat* when we get on each other's nerves. We *also* use it for emergencies." She shrugged. "The upstairs of the main house, *some* downstairs rooms, and *this* place can be closed off when we entertain the mobs."

The cottage's living room also had armchairs, a couple of small tables with unremarkable lamps, and a floor-to-ceiling sandstone fireplace. Little stone ledges bore a menorah and many pictures of people, *some* that Leigh had met. Windows on all four walls allowed in oceans of light with a brilliant view of the back yard—100 yards to the tree line. A small but complete kitchen with a counter/island separated it from the living room. "Meant to ask how married life's treating you. You're still an ER nurse?"

"Yes, and we're fine, dear. Nate and I are too *busy* to be unhappy. Let's look in on your mom." They opened the door of the dark room slowly. Cathy, curled up under the covers, had a flannel nightgown covering her shoulders. They listened to Cathy's steady breathing and went back out. "She needs to sleep off the sedative in her brandy. You didn't *take* yours."

"Smelled funny."

"I gave you too much, then. She *should* be down for at *least* another hour. Let's get *you* some coffee."

"Wait one." Leigh pulled a sweatsuit out of her B-4 bag and laid it on her mother's bed. Walking slowly down the short greenhouse-like corridor over the garage breezeway joining the main house, she was struck by the freshness of the air, courtesy of the thriving plants that lined the corridor.

The corridor—perhaps ten yards long—joined the main house on the second floor near the top of the stairs. They walked down the wide curved stairway that hugged the picture-lined, curved walls of the foyer. The palatial glass dome above the foyer let in brilliant light without shadows, illuminating the landscapes hanging on the walls and the sculptures flanking every door and portal. "*Beautiful* home, Kiera. I always loved it."

"Thanks. The others will be in the kitchen."

Mike and Ben stood when they came in; Monica smiled. Leigh sighed deeply, gazing into Monica's bright, steel-grey eyes. *Mike's eyes.* "Thanks for taking us in. We don't want to be a burden."

"Nonsense," Kiera murmured, guiding her to the booth with Mike. "It's a *mitzvah*. Here," she handed Leigh a small paper cup. "Aspirin. Nurse's orders, unless you want Tylenol. I'm going back."

"Hi," Mike smiled.

"Hi," she whispered—suddenly calm even as her skin crawled, and her bones ached, and *so* weary she couldn't think straight—popping the pills in her mouth.

"Coffee," Monica offered. "You take yours black as I remember?"

Leigh could barely answer before Ben spoke up. "Can I offer you anything?" He smiled. "You know we don't keep Kosher."

"Just coffee until my brain gets started, thanks."

"Sleep OK?" Mike squeezed her hand. "Kiera's here for you and your mom."

"We're causing you a *lot* of trouble."

"It's a *mitzvah*, *oytzer*." He smiled, a toothy grin she rarely saw.

She *painfully* leaned over to kiss him, murmuring, "thanks."

He held her face, kissing her deeply, wincing at his protesting back. "Any time, *oytzer*." Ben did a little shrug; Monica smiled.

They sat quietly, sipping coffee. "So," Monica spoke at last, "you're *both* going to be in town..."

"So it would *seem*," Leigh sighed, feeling better for the aspirin and the coffee chaser.

Ben arched an eyebrow. "Then?"

"Well," Mike squeezed her hand.

*Didn't think of that...today.* "Sure; let's *do* it."

Monica smiled. "*Mazel tov,* children!"

***

*How you Army guys do this EVERY day is beyond me.*

Unaccustomed to boots, Ann winced while cinching up the laces. Her promotion to Chief Petty Officer meant, among other things, a change in *fatigue* uniform: no more comfortable denim and deck shoes. Regulations dictated that chiefs wear a BDU—battle-dress utility—uniform and boots or steel-toed work shoes for *fatigue* work. Today, she was teaching a heavy-plate welding class. She looked up at JJ, who was just checking his bags one last time. "*When's* your flight?"

"They want me there before 9. Just enough time to..." The telephone interrupted him. "Hello? *Hi*, Mom. What's...? Oh, no, *no. MOM*, calm down. I'll be up there in a few hours. Where *is* he?...OK, Mom...*OK*, Mom; *OK*." He hung up, his face grim. "Please call your dad, honey: Charlie's had a stroke; he's at Beaumont." JJ's stepfather had just turned 78.

She dialed quickly. "Hello, Dad; Charlie Parkinson's had a stroke; he's at Beaumont...*I'm* here till Monday. JJ's on his way out the door...OK." She handed JJ the phone.

"Elrath...Hi, Howard...Mom's like you'd expect...I'd sure appreciate it, Howard. Yeah, see you tonight." He hung up the phone, sighed deeply. "Not that

I give a rat's ass about *Charlie*, but *Mom...*"

Ann put her chin on his shoulder. "I *know*, babe, I *know*."

***

Clad in Monica's nightgown, Leigh's sweatsuit, *and* Monica's fleece robe, Cathy *still* looked cold as Kiera guided her into the breakfast room. Wordlessly, Cathy took the offered aspirin and water, sat on a stool, and placed her elbows on the counter, chin in hand. It was a few minutes before she said anything, glancing at a clock. "I'm *supposed* to be in *court* right now."

"I took the liberty of contacting your office this morning," Ben smiled.

Cathy blinked several times, looked at Ben blankly, muttered "thanks," and went back to her stare, downing her coffee in one gulp.

Leigh watched her mother slumped on the stool, got up, and quietly sat next to her, gently massaging her back. "Hi, Mom. How doing?"

It took a few moments for the words to register, but as if a shade snapped up, Cathy sat straight, looked at Leigh, looked around the room, and made a face. "There was a *fire*. Was that *last* night?"

"Yeah."

"And *you* came in last night?"

"And *we* came *here*."

Cathy inhaled deeply, shook her head a little, and gazed at Monica. "Thanks for putting us up. Monica."

"My pleasure, Cathy. *Our* pleasure."

"Of course; your hospitality is unmatched. Thank you *so* much." Color returned to her face as she looked around at the dazzling morning and finally spotted Mike. "Oh, *hello*, Mike."

"*Good* morning, Cathy."

"Oh, *Christ*, boy: I may as well be *Mom*."

"Cathy," Ben muttered, "the children have an announcement."

"Yeah, Mom," Leigh muttered as Mike walked to her side. "We're going to get married. Here. Soon."

Cathy blinked hard before she smiled broadly. "Mike, you *do* realize that you will be increasing the size of *our* family by a *zillion* percent when you *finally* make an honest woman of my precious daughter?"

Leigh gave her a hug. "Mom, I'm *honest* enough." But her math was correct. The largest family gathering in Leigh's memory was when they visited her mother's maiden aunt just before she died: Leigh was nine.

"I'll take good care of her, um, *shviger*." Mike bussed her cheek.

Monica groaned. "*Ugh!* I *never* liked that word."

"What is it?" Leigh asked. "Yiddish, yeah?"

"For mother-in-law," Ben replied.

"Just *Cathy's* fine, Mike," Cathy grunted. "Don't want to need a Berlitz just to *talk* to you. I'll...son-in-law...that ain't sunk in yet." She blew out her cheeks

41

tiredly. "*I* need to call *Ed*."

"Certainly," Monica answered. "The little office; come."

Breakfast was served amid quiet chatter. Kiera excused herself as the omelets hit the island.

Ben was in and out several times, returning and whispering to Monica. "The fire never reached *your* townhouse," he announced at last. "You can get in to look around, gather some belongings, but they don't want anyone to *move* back in or clean up until the police are done."

"*Police*," Cathy asked, puzzled.

"It was arson and attempted murder. It involved an electrical substation and four buildings. *Your* building, Cathy, lost a unit. Two other buildings lost three; one building was completely gutted. A man was shot."

Leigh's first thought was, "Newhouse."

Cathy was suddenly angry. "Maybe they didn't like my response to their last interrogatory, but that was *months* ago."

Ben looked curious. "On that *maternity* matter? *Still?*"

"They've *never* stopped. At least twice a year, we get something from Fischer and Ally wanting to know what Leigh was doing on this date or that in 1970 and '71. *Nothing* seems to mollify them. The *last* one I answered with copies of her 3.75 GPA report cards."

Leigh groaned, "I've submitted to exams *more* than once."

"I *think* your father and I would have noticed if you were pregnant at fifteen."

"*I* probably would have, too," Mike mumbled.

"Fischer and Ally," Ben muttered. "Haven't done much business with *them*. I've offered *before*, Cathy, and I *repeat*: My firm *can* represent you…"

"*No*, Ben. I *can't* ask you to involve *your* firm in this mess."

"Cathy, when our children *do* get married, I shall *have* to *make it* my *family firm's* business."

"You're right, Ben. Didn't *think* of that."

"I'll take it up with the firm today; *now*." Ben got off his stool. "My dears, forgive me, but I *must* take my leave of you. Stay for as long as you wish. I extend to you my best offices and my home. Anything you need, you need only ask. Adam will take you wherever you want to go."

"Well," Cathy said, picking at the sweatsuit, "I *could* use some other clothes."

"You're a size 10 or 12?" Monica smiled.

"Or so, yes," Cathy nodded.

When Cathy and Monica went upstairs, Leigh and Mike were alone in the kitchen. After luxuriating in the silence and the calm of each other's company for a few minutes, Leigh quietly asked, "Sandy, is there someplace I can work out a little?"

"Ah, sure." He led her to the foyer and through a hidden door under the stairs that opened onto a landing. Another door led to the garage's breezeway and to stairs leading down to the basement rec room. Following him down the steps, she remembered the well-finished basement from the Thanksgivings that she celebrated with many Dietz cousins at the big gaming table.

Moving a ping-pong table out of the way, he tried to sound apologetic. "No padding, but will this do?"

"I just need to *move*." She kicked off her shoes, rolled her shoulder once again, and took a solid *Moto Daichi* starting position. As she moved slowly through a routine *he'd* only seen in movies, he began to leave when she called out, "babe, *please* stay. I don't want to be alone."

He sat on a big sofa to watch, stuffing a pillow behind his back. *Can't say how dangerous she is, but I sure as HELL wouldn't want to find out.*

Her clothes were restrictive, but as she worked the knots and tensions out, her mind could run free while counting her workout. *ONE damnit to hell Randy TWO leave us alone THREE get FOUR off FIVE our SIX back or I swear I'll SEVEN break you in EIGHT half you asshole NINE eunuch TEN sonofaBITCH.* She tried some rolling kicks but didn't have room or energy for more than two or three. *FIFTEEN how can SIXTEEN one family SEVENTEEN be so Goddamn EIGHTEEN vindictive about NINETEEN one unconsummated marriage TWENTY between TWO CHILDREN?* She concluded with a lightning-fast block-and-strike combination that looked to the untutored like an explosion of arms and legs.

When she finished, she was facing a large painting of an ocean beach. *Wish I was on that beach now*, but her reverie was interrupted by polite applause. She turned to see Cathy and Mike clapping appreciatively. She bowed politely.

"Some performance," he said. "What was I watching?"

"Just basic stuff," she answered, "nothing special."

"Where are you with that now," Cathy asked, in a wool pantsuit and silk blouse that fit remarkably well. Hair clips kept her long hair out of her face. The resemblance of Leigh's eyes to her mother's struck Mike once again.

"Third-*dan* black belt in *taekwondo*." She pushed her shoes back on. "I do it for exercise, mostly."

"I'd hate to get on your bad side," he muttered.

"*You've* got a Ranger tab," Leigh grinned. "Don't *you* get hand-to-hand combat training?"

"They don't emphasize it for us non-infantry types."

Cathy smiled. "Did I ever tell you that my *father* was a Ranger? Dad joined the Army after Pearl Harbor. Mom wanted to kill him if the enemy didn't; he *was* killed in Germany. I'm going over and have a look at the mess, Leigh. Come with?"

\*\*\*

"OK, kid, I'll bite: *how* do *you* rate a private jet?" Kurt Parkinson had watched JJ exit a Lear 35 on the terminal apron at Pontiac International Airport…alone, as blood freezer and organ chests were hauled out of the cargo compartment.

43

Pontiac was a small non-commercial airfield with a handful of hangers and a one-story, one-gate terminal with a CUSTOMS sign over a counter crowded with snack racks.

"I know the operators," JJ answered. While *true*, it wasn't the *whole* truth: He was on the firm's board of directors that leased the aircraft.

"If you say so. How was your flight?"

"*Two* stops; *three* passengers off and on; just over six hours. Not *that* bad." In Chattanooga, they boarded a young litter patient, her mother, and an EMT/nurse. The three got off in Toledo—the girl was to get a heart/lung transplant there. It was there they took on the coolers.

"*Heads* up: keys. This's yours as long as you're here," Kurt told JJ as they reached an older *passenger truck* in the parking lot.

JJ caught them. "Suburban. This is a, uh…" JJ couldn't quite place the model year of *this* example of GM's early contribution to the SUV craze.

"A '75." They loaded JJ's luggage in the back.

*Huh: four-wheel drive with lockout hubs.* "What are you *asking* for it?"

"Depends who's buying."

"Me."

Kurt grinned widely. "For *you*: $4,500."

*Probably what it cost him.* "I'll ask the boss. So, what's the old man's status, Kurt? How bad is he?"

"Not bad enough and *too* bad both," Kurt grimaced, his large and open face showing both dread and weariness. "He's *stable*, but they've knocked him out."

"How's my *mom*?"

"She's with Mary and some of *her* friends over at *our* place." He grinned. "I gotta say, JJ, your mom's something of a rock."

"She *can* be. Kurt; shift gears. I'm gonna need a best man in the next couple of weeks…"

***

"I think the foyer got the worst of it," Cathy declared. "A *little* in the downstairs." Leigh followed Cathy into their two-story English faux-row house. A fine layer of soot met them in the entry foyer but faded as they ascended the short stairs into the living room. They felt the tops of *everything* in each room.

"Soot gets *everywhere*, Mom." Leigh angled her flashlight on the upstairs hall ceiling. "Where there's *any* air current, you'll see *some*. Smoke *is* airborne soot." She remembered spending hours looking for scorch marks and smoke trails while investigating a structure fire in Korea where three people died.

As she checked the guest/her room, the bathroom that joined it, and the den/office, she saw familiar photographs speckled with soot. Her room still had her high-school furniture as if suspended in time, with most of her clothes and other stuff boxed up in anticipation of her move to Boston. Four boxes had *been* to New England and took years of haggling to get back. Cathy had hung some of

Leigh's watercolors on the walls to keep it from looking completely un-lived-in.

*No smudges; clean if musty, but I need clothes.* She went through her closet and drawers swiftly, stuffing the contents into two suitcases *intended* for her honeymoon. The haul included a couple Speedos and some underwear, a pair of running shoes she'd left behind in April, and a dress she didn't remember. There were also a couple blouses, a sweater, and some dress slacks of unclear origins.

In the den, she stared at the fading photo of her grandfather in an Army uniform—with incongruously hand-painted flowers in one corner—when Cathy came and stood with her. "Dad."

"You have *his* hair, *his* eyes."

"Ingle green. Mom said *you* had our eyes, but you don't remember *her*."

"No—*sorry*, Mom." Cathy's mother passed when Leigh was two.

Cathy shined her flashlight around the room. "Not sure I see a lot here—just around the vents. But cleaning is all or nothing." She made a face, running a finger on a bookshelf and coming up with a *hint* of soot. "Not sure it's worth it."

"Gotta get it out of the vents; not a lot of *choice*. How long will they take?"

"It could be two *weeks* just for a crew to *get here*, and they'll be done a week *later*." She shrugged. "I'll meet you downstairs."

When Leigh got to the main floor with her suitcases, Adam was waiting. Unintentionally, she slipped into MP-mode, looking him up and down quickly. *Male Caucasian, 50 to 60, five-eight, 180, athletic build, hard brown eyes, probably blonde hair but a shaved head...* and was startled when Adam smiled, "I've gotten a *little* older, Miss Leigh."

"Adam, we've known each other since, what, 7th or 8th Grade?"

"*Sounds* right."

"Since we're *old* friends, if there's no one *else* around, will you *please* just call me Leigh? I've *asked* you *before*...."

"As I *said* before, it's what my *firm* allows. I look forward to the pleasure of calling you *Mrs*. Leigh."

"I tried. You serve in the military?"

"In Israel, with the forerunner to *Shabak*."

"We had an Israeli *Shin Bet* officer with us one summer."

"*Shabak* is the Hebrew pronunciation for the two characters that stand for *security service*. *Shin Bet* is the pronunciation for the *Arabic* characters; it's sort of Anglicized."

"Are you an Israeli national?"

"Dual. My parents moved to a *kibbutz* from New York *after* I was born and *before* the war. I grew up there; met my wife there; our oldest was born there."

"Ah. Have you worked for the Dietz's long?"

"Twenty years. I work *with* Dietz, O'Bannon and Associates now; *my* business—Block Associates—*is* one of the *associates*."

"Your 'diverse services' business?"

"*Yes*, miss." Adam's firm conducted investigations and performed other

45

*related* services—including security—for firm and family…a fact *known* but not *openly* discussed.

Cathy came down the stairs, carrying a suitcase and Monica's wool suit over her arm. "Don't want to borrow *too* much; wear out our welcome. It's one thing to be generous in a pinch, but *quite another* to extend that hospitality for much more than a night or two."

"If I *may*, ma'am…"

"Adam, *please* just call me Cathy. Ye *gods*, I feel like I'm in court, you calling me *ma'am* all the time."

"*Mrs.* Cathy is what my firm allows. I took the liberty of finding some things out. The storage level got *a lot* of smoke, and, as you can see from the vents, it got into your HVAC. The fire department is forbidding residents from *moving* back *in* until *all* the power's back up—Friday, according to Detroit Edison—and the investigation's finished—probably *not* before then. Resident cleanup is to start Saturday."

"Well, thanks for finding *all* that out, Adam. I'll be taking *my* car back, and Leigh can drive my husband's *if* I get them out of the garage…"

"I can *get* them out for you, ma'am."

"Fabulous." Cathy looked around the living room as if looking for something. "*Saturday.* After *that*, we can either *impose* on the Dietz's or…?"

"If I *may*, the Dietz's *don't* think of *you* as an imposition," Adam said. "Mrs. Monica told us to treat you as family *years* ago. You staying with them will *not* be a problem."

Leigh stared out the glass doors at the patio, wet from when the fire hoses sprayed all the roofs the night before. "*Mishpachah*, Adam?"

"Her instructions *were* in English, miss: just *family*."

"Adam," Cathy sighed, "we *appreciate* your candor *and* your sentiment."

"Yes," Leigh added. "And, of course, *this* part of our conversation never took place."

"*What* part would *that* be, Miss Leigh?"

***

"*This* is yours, too, soon-to-be newlywed," Kurt grinned, handing JJ two keys as they dropped his bags in the honeymoon suite. Kurt owned the Northwestern Inn and Suites at Telegraph and Northwestern Highway. JJ got a better price *there* than he could have gotten *anywhere* else.

"Thanks, Kurt," JJ smiled. "Give me a few minutes; gotta make a couple calls." He sat at a small desk just off the full, small kitchen, which also had a round table and four chairs. The suite also had a sofa, two chairs, a recliner, a jacuzzi just big enough for four adults, a bathroom off the bedroom with a walk-in shower easily big enough for two, and skylights over the jacuzzi *and* the bed.

"Jenny…hi, Jen…yeah, *just* got in…" And… "Ms. Alton, please…hi, Ware…" He *had* to talk to Clare—who he'd known since they were teenagers—

because *she* always *just knew* when something happened to him.

"Let's *get*," JJ nodded to Kurt in the lobby and headed out to the Suburban. "*You've* lost weight…"

***

Ann looked around the apartment filled with her shipmate's stuff—two of her fellow divers were taking their upper and smiled wistfully. *Seems alien…*

Betty Sadowski, a large woman with a flat face, came in the door, followed by Wendy and Dennis. "Hey," Wendy called, "what's your schedule for Detroit?"

"*I* get up there Monday; we get the license Wednesday, and it's effective Saturday…"

"My father is a circuit court judge in Oakland County," Dennis said, "I *could* ask about a waiver…"

"You're from *Michigan*," Ann frowned.

"Yep: Pontiac. *Wendy's* from…"

"The UP; yeah." Michiganders referred to the Upper Peninsula as the UP—pronounced *ewe-pee*. Ann regarded her neighbors. "You two making it *legal*…?"

Wendy smiled. "Two *weeks*."

"You didn't *say* anything *before*…"

"Didn't *know* we *had* to before this morning. *Have* to now."

"Oh! *That* kind of fast?"

"The *we'll-know-which-in-seven-months* kind."

"Well, congratulations! When are you going up?"

"That's the *other* reason we came up," Wendy said. "We're flying into Detroit *Friday*—*pregnancy* qualifies for emergency leave. We'll get married the Friday before Thanksgiving in Iron Mountain, then fly back *here* that Sunday."

"Hey, great! We'll get together while you're there."

***

"Hi, Mom," JJ embraced Stella tenderly, unsteady on her feet and weeping a little. Kurt and Mary lived on Baroque Circle, an eighth-mile-diameter cul-de-sac with a wooded park in the center that whispered *wealth* at the top of its well-groomed fescue-and-bluegrass lungs.

Ann's father Howard and his wife Barbara—Ann's stepmother—were also there. "So," Howard smiled, sitting down after saying hello, "good flight?"

"Was OK, but on top of *Charlie*, a friend suffered a personal disaster last night."

"*Who*, Johnny," Stella asked.

"Jenny Jacobs, Mom. She was a neighbor over on Round Lake."

"A blonde, husky girl," Stella declared.

*She hasn't seen Jen in nearly twenty years.* "Yeah, Mom." As they sat on the big sectional sofa in the living room, JJ asked, "how *are* you, Mom? Are you alone in the apartment?"

"I'm in the guest room, JJ; *she's* OK." Barbara—a pleasant, slim woman in her mid-40s who greatly resembled the mom in the *Family Circus* comic strip— had been a nurse her entire adult life. Something about the way she said *OK*, also said *maybe*.

As dinner was getting ready, JJ excused himself. "I need just a *few* minutes. Buddy of mine happens to live next door; want to check in with his folks."

***

*What are YOU...oh, that's...so...oh! You're so...OH!*

Mike awoke from a long nap in the library, startled by the strange, erotic dream. He heard voices elsewhere in the house and entered the breakfast room blinking, seeing Kiera and Monica in the booth while his sister Sara was in the kitchen preparing dinner.

"Hi, sleepyhead," Kiera smiled. "Have a nice nap?"

"Ugh, guess I needed it." He looked around cautiously. "Has Pops come home yet?"

"Living room with your guests," Sara said.

"*My* guests," Mike mumbled. "Why aren't they *our* guests?"

"Her family first entered our home for *your* Bar Mitzva, Michael," Monica said. According to family tradition, Leigh, her family, and anyone *with* her would forever be *his* guests. Leigh's brother (if she *had* one) could marry one of his sisters, and he would still be *his* guest. Quaint and often awkward, but a tradition was a tradition. Whatever was wrong with *Fiddler on the Roof*, the insistence on such traditions ran deep even in ultra-liberal Jewish families. "*Invite* them to stay in the cottage until their home is habitable, Michael."

He shambled numbly into the living room, flopping down in a big armchair just when Ben noticed him come in. "You sleep in the afternoon, Michael, and the fields don't get planted."

"And *hello* to you, too, Pops." Mike sighed plaintively, squinting at Leigh and Cathy. "Sorry I'm remiss in my duties as host, but I was tired."

"Uh-huh," Leigh smiled. "Better that than fall asleep in your dinner. We were just talking about getting our place cleaned up."

Mike inhaled deeply. "I'm obliged by duty and affection to invite your family to stay in the cottage until your home is habitable. So saith your host—me—and your hostess, my mother." Leigh and Cathy looked at each other. "*Please* don't argue," he pleaded, "the *matter* is *settled*."

"So it would seem," Ben agreed. "Stay as long as you wish."

"*I* need to get to the office tomorrow," Cathy muttered. "Have to deal with the continuance I was *supposed* to be arguing *today*."

Just then, the doorbell rang.

\*\*\*

It was a hundred yards from Kurt's front door to Mike's, and answering the door was a *shocked* Mike. "*Holy…JJ Elrath,*" he exclaimed. "Of *all* the…*you're* about the *last…*"

"*I* expected anybody *but* you. And, *ho…*"

Leigh suddenly and *madly* embraced JJ. "*Oh,* am *I* glad to see *you,*" she whispered in his ear before kissing it.

"*Shh,* now…*shh,*" JJ soothed, glancing at a bemused Mike. "It's *OK,* whatever it is."

"Well, bring him in before we all catch a cold," Ben boomed.

"Gorgeous place," JJ sighed. "I'm in between Florida and Alaska."

"*Oh,*" Leigh exclaimed, "you *wrote* about that in your last letter; I didn't get a chance to write back."

"*Who's* here now?" Monica came in from the kitchen.

"*John Elrath,*" Ben pointed at JJ.

"Now…ah…*where* was…I?" JJ started to tremble. "I just wanted to…*ho*-boy," he got weak in the knees, "I've *gotta* sit down." Mike and Leigh hustled him to the big sectional sofa while Monica called for Kiera. It was several anxious moments before he could speak. "Just…so much to take in. I wasn't *expecting…*"

"A *lot* at once, brother," Mike declared. "What's goin' on?"

"Pulse strong, steady, rapid." Kiera smiled. "You'll be OK. Take it *easy* tonight."

"Um…you're *Kiera,* yeah? You went to nursing school…"

"You're not *that* bad, JJ," Kiera mock-sneered, pecking his cheek. "Just take it *easy* tonight."

"While we're all *here*: Ann will be here Monday night. We're getting married in the next few…"

"*Mazel tov,*" Ben exclaimed, grabbing JJ's hand. The next few moments were of hugs, handshakes, and kisses…the last from Cathy.

"*Mrs.* Taylor: *good* to see *you,* too," JJ smiled.

"Call me *Cathy.* Now, *you're* getting married to…"

"Ann Mueller; you met her last Christmas."

"I knew *her* before *that,* young man. Prom-dress shopping with Leigh."

"If you say so. On top of *that,* my *stepfather* had a stroke last night."

"Oh, *my,*" Monica exclaimed, "so sad! Please, *let* us…"

"As *soon* as we know more, Monica. We're to talk to the doctors tomorrow. And if you'll excuse me again, they're waiting for me over by my brother's. Everyone: I'd *love* to catch up, but I *just* wanted to…"

"Yes," Ben smiled. "If there's *anything we* can do, *please* don't hesitate…"

"Thank you, sir. I *must* be off. We're at the Northwestern."

Mike and Leigh glanced at each other as their friend left. "*Wired.*"

"Our John-Zilla *may* need help," Ben mused.

They glanced at Ben. *The name the firm gave him while they were suing Wolverine. "That's* affirm."

∗∗∗

"There's a whole *catalog* of stuff you don't usually think of that needs cleaning," Cathy sighed in the kitchen after dinner, "*besides* the ductwork. The walls *and* ceilings; knick-knacks; chandeliers dismantled and scrubbed; furniture and carpeting shampooed. They dismantle everything that *moves* air: the blowers, refrigerator, *and* freezer will be replaced. And we can send *all* our clothes out for cleaning on the insurance company's dime. The stuff in the foyer closet is *hopeless…*"

"Then I *have* to go coat-shopping," Leigh complained. "I don't have anything *that* warm here. My hold-baggage will take *months* to get here."

"You'll be doing us a *mitzvah* by making this place look and sound busy," Monica declared. "Seven bedrooms, four *full* bathrooms, two powder rooms, a library to rival a university, an indoor pool we use once a week this time of year, and three people to use them all. We rattle about like three beans in a can. You can sleep in the cottage and have the run of the house."

Cathy glanced at Leigh, then back at Monica. "Ed will be here tomorrow night." Cathy blushed, side-glanced at Leigh again, and mumbled, "If it's *not* too much of an imposition, can Leigh stay in the *house*? Ed and I…we, ah…and *that* place is *so* small…"

Monica raised an eyebrow with a sly grin. "*Do* you *indeed*?"

"We *tend* to." Cathy shrugged; Leigh nodded and rolled her eyes with a grin.

Monica grinned puckishly. "*Not* so loud as to wake the *neighbors*, eh?"

∗∗∗

"*Hate* to cut this short, folks, but I've slept about four hours in the past twenty-four." Dinner at the Parkinson's had been quiet, joined late by Kurt's daughter Jo. With meatloaf and mashed potatoes in his belly, JJ was ready for the rack.

"So, thirty days from next Saturday…" Mary frowned.

"Between now and Thanksgiving," JJ agreed, glancing at Stella. "That OK?"

"Oh, sure," she waved dismissively. "Don't let *Charlie* slow you down."

"*Hardly* time to find a dress," Mary went on. "Better start *this* weekend, Jo."

"We should be getting you *home*, Stella," Barbara smiled.

"OK, Mom," JJ told her, bussing both their cheeks. "I'll pick you up in the morning; we'll see Charlie, talk to the doctors."

"The *finance* people started asking for information when the bill hit $10,000. Don't know *where his* money is: all *I've* got is the household account, and that *won't* cover it."

After Barbara and Stella left, JJ spoke with Howard. "So how *is* he, really?"

"*Not* good," Howard grimaced. "His hemorrhagic stroke left an aneurism the size of a walnut in his head. The top neurosurgeon in town is treating him, as is

50

the head of vascular surgery at Beaumont. I'm just a GP, but in my *professional* opinion, it *doesn't* look hopeful."

"Sorry, Kurt," JJ murmured.

"Couldn't happen to a nicer bastard," Kurt replied, blinking. "Been waiting for him to drop dead for years, and now that it's *here...happening...*the only thing *I* can think about is your mom."

"Yeah. Poor Mom." *Couldn't croak all at once; has to do it like an opera fat lady.*

Howard stood; his 6-foot frame still strong despite his 63 years. "If I can bum a ride since Barb just took the car..."

"Sure," JJ yawned. "Kurt," he clapped his brother on the back, "I'll catch you *when*. Mary, darlin'," he grinned at her open face before smacking a cheek, "always a pleasure. And, *Jo,*" she smiled; "later." Once in the car, JJ asked, "how *is* Mom, Howard? She *seems* a little shaky..."

"I think that's about it, Johnny. She took the death of your father better than I had expected, even if it *wasn't* a surprise. But, since Charlie's..."

"*Huh?* Dad *wasn't* a surprise?" JJ's voice got involuntarily louder.

"I suppose she never told you. Remember when he was really sick in '65? That *may* have been a strep infection that went untreated, developed into a rheumatic heart. When your Uncle Murph first noticed his murmur—when he consulted *me* more than a year later—it had already done its damage. It was only going to get worse, not better."

"Huh. Never heard that. May have been why he was home for most of '68."

***

"I appreciate that the Army and the Navy don't see eye-to-eye..." Ann began, "but, surely..." Ann's and JJ's reporting dates were a week apart—it didn't matter because they could report any time *before* that. No, it was the *principle* behind the dates: no one *tried* to coordinate them.

They were friends of a particular kind—the close bonds that military members make when they work together for a day that gets stronger after a month and becomes unbreakable after a year. Kristen, Betty, Laura Gutteriez, and Ann were four of the first women in the US Navy's dive community and had lived and worked together since 1982. But now, as the expression goes, the band was breaking up.

"Ann, be thankful you got stationed in the same *state*," Betty told her, "and *stop* calling *me* Shirley. This two-service business is new to them, too. But you'll be the first woman *ever* assigned to a SEAL team." Their 20-person diving unit in Key West was mostly men, and five guys had joined the move-in party.

"*That* joke was dumb *then*, Sadowski, but yeah," a flat-headed, big-armed guy named Leon answered. "You *won't* be a SEAL, but..."

"Yeah, it's in *Alaska*. Count what blessings I get."

"So, SEAL Team Twelve," Kristin said. "You'll be on dive status?"

"Doubt it," Ann replied. "I'm filling the lead storekeeper billet up there. Still not training women as SEALs, and I wouldn't *want* to go to BUD/S at 31."

"It was brutal enough at 22," Leon agreed. "Hell, *I* barely made it, and I could dead-lift 200 pounds when I got there."

"It's not just strength; it's *will*," Laura declared. "You've got to *really* want it." Laura, her blonde braids reaching nearly to her waist, could dead-lift 180 pounds. She once considered suing the Navy to be able to *be* a SEAL—Basic Underwater Demolition School was the first step. She was dissuaded by her fellow divers, who pointed out that she had to be careful what she asked for because she just might *get* it—and *not* be able to cut it. "Between the sleep deprivation, the cold, the psychological abuse, and the rest of it, I wasn't sure I really *needed* it *that* bad."

"That's why only about 30% graduate every cycle," Leon mused. "But how did Ann get into a SEAL team?"

"Dive *community*," Kristen muttered. "We *were* the first."

"Had a lot to do with it," Ann agreed. "That and…excuse me," she went to the ringing phone. "Mueller…oh, *hi*, honey." She motioned for quiet. "Yeah? *How's* your *mom*…uh-huh…yeah, the *party's* here, but *you* ain't…OK, everybody: say 'hi, JJ'" She held the phone out for a cacophony of shouted greetings. "Yeah, OK, babe. Talk to the Red Cross about an extension…oh, *really*? Both? …great! How about Jen…good…a Suburban *sounds* OK, but I'd want to drive it first…OK, babe, 'night…Love *you* too."

## *Thursday*

"Cathy, you look *quite* fetching this morning," Mike smiled. The noisily pelting rain they heard that morning threatened to turn to sleet.

"*Thank* you *very* much, Mike." In a figure-flattering tailored suit, Cathy munched on toast in the cottage's kitchen. "*That* means a *lot* to a fifty-something woman. *Why* does Leigh call you Sandy?"

"My hair used to bleach out in the sun…"

"I see. So, *now* you're *here* because…?"

*There's that little smirk, the half-closed eyes, the head cocked back.* "Mom, c'mon, just *let* him…"

"Just saying good morning to my fiancée…"

"*Nothing* to do with your future mother-in-law."

"We don't *see* each other very often, Cathy, so I don't *presume*…"

"*Quaint*, Mike, but unconvincing." Cathy grinned widely before she hugged him. "You'll get used to *me*, my dear." She put on a curious face. "You *are* a handsome devil, but remember: Leigh's father has guns and *knows* how—and *likes*—to *use* them…and *I've* been known to *join* him." A little louder, she announced, "I'll pick your father up this afternoon." She gathered her valise and was out the door moments later.

Leigh smiled, watching her leave while she flexed her shoulder. "She *can* take some getting *used* to, babe. Are you going to seduce me now?" She winked slowly, inching her sweatshirt up. "I've *been waiting...*"

"I...*ho-boy*," he gasped as she pulled her sweatshirt off. "Gently, OK?"

"*Very* gently, babe; my shoulder's *killing* me," she winked, leading him into her room.

\*\*\*

"Mr. Elrath," the woman in a business suit and holding a clipboard began. She was maybe ten years older than he, with a warm face and well-worn hair tied in a bun. "I'm Callie, the concierge. How are *you* this morning?"

"Upright and able to take punishment. If I remember from last time, *you* want to..."

"...coordinate your penthouse stay, Mr. Elrath."

"Call *me* JJ. The last *Mr.* Elrath died in '68, OK?"

"OK, JJ. I understand your fiancée will be flying in on Monday? We can send a car for her if you'd like."

"OK, maybe. *When* would you *have* to know?"

"Sunday. I'll have your other luggage brought up this morning: they arrived last night. I *also* understand your scheduling is unclear at this time."

"How did you come to know all *this*?"

"Mr. Parkinson has given us instructions."

"Well, I appreciate that, Callie. Who's *us*?"

"Hotel staff. Your housekeeping service: what time works best for you?"

"Um...let's call it 10 AM?"

"Fine. How about breakfast? As early as 6, delivered to your door; groceries if you prefer to make your own." She handed him a four-page flyer/menu/checklist. "We'll provide *anything legal* with six hours' notice and room service from 5 AM to 9 PM. Your brother says, 'no charge *before* the wedding—*within reason*—and three days *after*.' Your wedding present."

"Callie, just between you and me, what's the *reason* got to be *within*?"

Callie put on a disarming smile as though she were talking to a friend. "Don't order for any more than two *normal* people *most* of the time, and *easy* on the booze. Kurt's a great boss, and we're doing *very* well, but he *has* limits. If there's *anything* more we can do to make your stay more pleasant, leave a voice message for me."

"Thanks, Callie. I'll drop off the menu on my way out."

\*\*\*

"*Hello*," Leigh shouted upstairs as she let herself into Donna's house, across the lawn from the Dietz's garage.

"Come on up," Donna Hammerfest shouted from the top of the staircase. Donna was a pretty, tall blonde, though time had dulled her blue eyes. She was trying to get her mid-shoulder-blade-length hair to do what she wanted and was losing the fight. "*Hell*," she mumbled, "cut it *all* off next chance I…honey, do you *like* your collar-length hair?"

"Practical; I *have* to keep it *off* my collar for work." Leigh looked around Donna's suite while she waited. Donna's digs sported a kitchenette, bed, and living/working space crammed with work tables, clothes racks, bookshelves, a drawing board, three tailor's dummies, and clothes in various states of construction intermixed with books, notebooks, and *three* sewing machines. A whiteboard with a schedule chart hung on the bathroom door. Pictures on corkboards filled the space on walls that *didn't* have shelves, sharing space with patterns and sketches, charts and tables, and swatches. There was a photo of their old gang at senior prom; others of her family. A poster of Dik Young's signature cartoon character on the bathroom door looked *just like Donna* with curlier hair and bent knees—why *her* nickname was Blondie. One of Leigh's experiments with tempera paints—an undramatic landscape of Donna's back yard—hung in a fancy frame near the doorway. *Tempera is so unforgiving. Should do it again in watercolor.* "You still have *that?*"

"Yeah. I like it," Donna replied, touching up her lipstick in a mirror. "*You* don't?"

"Eh, I've done better since." An understatement: Leigh's watercolor-and-pastel landscape titled *Korea at Dawn* had hung in Korea's national gallery.

"But you gave me *this* one. *That's* what matters to *me*."

"How's your dad been?"

Donna inhaled deeply. "*One* day at a time. He went on a bender after Angie's birthday last spring."

"Sorry." Leigh glanced at a menorah on a nightstand. "Friends with Bill W. again?"

"*Twelve steps* and all. He's diligent about AA *most* of the time: even goes to temple twice a month, *most* months." She leaned against a shelf while she wedged her shoes on.

"Does he go with the Dietz's?"

"Sometimes we *both* go with them." She smiled as she wrapped her hair in a bandana and secured it with a scrunchy. "It'll *do*," she declared, pulling on a jacket. "Where *to?*"

"I need a warmer coat," Leigh declared. "Crowley's?"

"*That'll* do," Donna grinned, shooing Leigh out the door.

***

"Heard anything, Mom?" Stella—wan, but presentable—and Barbara had been waiting for JJ in her kitchen. Stella and Charlie's was a newer five-story condo building was at the edge of Birmingham near 14 Mile and Woodward.

"Haven't heard; *no* news is *good* news," Stella muttered. "I'll make breakfast," and before JJ and Barbara could intervene, they were watching helplessly as Stella turned a half-dozen eggs into a dry yellow powder. The eggs were soon joined by bacon strips that were *so* well done they shattered when they hit a plate. Only the dry toast and half-raw/half-burned potatoes were vaguely edible. In his youth, JJ considered *Mom's home cooking* to be cruel and unusual punishment.

After the breakfast ordeal, the one-mile trip down Woodward to Beaumont Hospital in Royal Oak took no time at all. The walk to the building from the far corner of the crowded lot took longer than it did to get from the front door to Charlie's room.

"Remember, Mom," JJ smiled in the elevator. "You brought me to the emergency room here, and I saw the on-call doctor?" JJ burned his hand on a hot grill while working at a church carnival.

"I remember your last visit to his *office*," she smiled. "All those expecting women..."

"What," Barbara asked, puzzled.

"The doctor on-call here that night was an OB-GYN," JJ answered. "Just another doctor in the hospital when I first saw him."

"*Those* were the days," Barbara said. "We don't staff like *that* anymore."

Charlie was unconscious, a cannula in his nose, his grey pallor contrasting with the white sheets. Stella took his hand, gazing at him briefly before she turned to leave. "Let's meet the doctors."

"Given your husband's age and cardiovascular condition, surgery is far too risky." Dr. Assad, the neurologist, was a large man with clear diction but a decided accent and was gentle but frank. "The aneurism may burst, which would merely hasten..." He stopped. "There *are* newer body-chilling techniques, but we are not equipped for them, and his age is a contraindication."

"Mr. Parkinson also has occlusions in his neck veins and arteries." The vascular surgeon, Dr. Secord, a young and fair-skinned woman, agreed. "Vascular intervention into the brain with catheters is new, and very few practitioners in the area are familiar with it. I've *seen* it done, but I've never *done* it. Ultimately, there is not a lot that surgery can do, so we must try to reduce the clots medically and hope for the best."

"But that big bubble will *probably* burst sooner than later." Stella grabbed JJ's hand to ask.

"*Likely*," Dr. Secord answered.

"*Will* he wake up?"

"He's mildly sedated," Dr. Secord said. "We want to take him off; see how he responds. He may *not* waken, or he *may*. We can't tell."

"At *this* point, Mrs. Parkinson," Dr. Assad said, "the *best* we can do is to keep him quiet. The aneurism *may* contract on its own, but we shouldn't *expect* it."

"How *long*?" Stella's voice was hollow, vacant of emotion.

Dr. Assad glanced at his colleague. "We don't *make* those predictions, but frankly, *not* long."

"Let's get some tea, Mom. Come on." JJ and Barbara led her to a small alcove near a vending area at the ward entrance. *Dad died in November '68; her father in March '52 and her mother in March '70. An awful pattern if Charlie doesn't last the month.* JJ held her hand tightly while Barbara got tea.

They sat quietly, sipping tea until Stella declared, "*hell*. He didn't have the *decency* to *just…aw, nuts!*"

Barbara started and grinned; JJ snorted. "*Don't* hold back, Mom. Tell us what you *really* think."

"Damned *albatross*," Stella muttered. "Since spring, he's been griping about a lawsuit from I-don't-*know*-when that *he* said cost him a *fortune*. Tuesday afternoon, he yelled that he would 'get *that rat* back,' whoever *that rat* is, for an *hour*, sat down and…*poof*. Silence. The best *I've* liked him for *years*. I had half a mind *not* to call 911." She glanced at Barbara and JJ, saying, "if you want to talk about *me*, just step over *there* and *do it*. I'm not *that* far gone, but I don't need to *hear* it."

Barbara and JJ walked across the vending area, keeping an eye on Stella. "How's she, really?"

"I *think* she's OK. She was all excited last night; wants to go dress shopping this weekend."

"She's *really* not bothered? I mean, he could take a turn for the worse, screw up *any* plans we make for our wedding…"

"Not that she *said*." Barbara smiled. "Are *you*?" Since they met not quite a year before, Barbara and JJ had been better friends than he thought he *would* be with a future mother-in-law. They shared an antipathy to Charlie, as well.

He grinned mischievously. "What do *you* think?"

She touched his arm. "*Keep* it that way, Johnny. I *will have* my dance with the groom." But she had an *odd* sense of humor…

"I don't *dance* well…"

"What the hell difference does *that* make?" She winked. "You and I *will* be cheek-to-cheek at *least* once."

***

"*Why* are *you* here *now*?" Leigh told of her sudden orders and about the fire and forced exile. Donna, usually expressive, stared blankly. "Huh. You don't know *why* you're *here*, and you're bunking with Sandy at his parent's house? Sounds…interesting."

Leigh made a mock-disgusted face. "*And* my parents *and* his parents. Ever been in *there*," she asked as they drove past Birmingham's Section 36 Club—an unassuming three-story, 140,000-square-foot Victorian Revival mansion behind City Hall. *Only in a place like Birmingham could that place exist.* Section 36 took on new members only as old members died, moved, or went broke. Only those who managed *not* to get food on their shirts during the interview luncheon—and could afford the dues—got in. Prospective members could wait decades for that interview.

"Me? No. You?"

"No. Not even the Newhouses are members. By the way, I saw JJ Elrath last night. He and Ann are getting married on their way to Alaska, but his stepfather's ill in Beaumont."

"Oh? I'll look him up. The name's…?"

"Parkinson. Since *we're going* to be around, *we'll* pull *our* trigger sooner than later. Will you stand up for *me?*"

"I get to kiss the groom?"

"He *was* your boyfriend."

"*Not quite,* honey. I was his Girl-Next-Door. We made out when *either* of us *needed to.* We got to second base *once,* but *that* was *too weird,* so we never did it again." She smiled. "To answer your question: I'll be *proud* to."

Department store chains like Demery's/Crowley's first catered to women who had a membership to a club *like* Section 36, where she met friends for *luncheon* once or twice a month. By the '80s, these stores had shifted their emphasis to the *working* woman who had *less* leisure time than her mother had. Still, she *likely* had at least part-time help if she shopped in Birmingham.

Leigh *felt* the change rather than *saw* it, having been in few department stores since her enlistment—and the PX hardly counted. "More business wear than *I* remember."

Donna squinted. "Yeah. *Most* of what I *buy* is uniforms and casual wear."

"Me too. When was *your* last date?"

"Three weeks ago; got one Saturday." Donna checked the tag on a vee-neck dress cut practically to the mannequins' navel. "Wow; *look* at *that* cut."

"How's Nick and that relationship *doing?*" Nick Paulson had been a school classmate.

"*Good,* honey. We're *casual,* except when we're *not.*" She gave a bright but secretly sad smile.

"*Casual* sex?"

"*Not* casual, my dear; *non-committal.* We take each other's *edge* off, not *much* more," Donna sighed. "We *like* each other too much to say 'love' only to have one of us screw it up. But the other night, he said, 'I want *more* out of *us,*' and *I* didn't know what to say. I *just*…you *know?*" She shrugged. "But we've *both* said we don't want to be alone."

*Change the subject.* "*You* still make your own stuff. I thought about making my paycheck stretch more, but I'm in *uniforms* so much…" Leigh checked the plunge-neck's price tag idly. *WOW.*

"I could make *that* dress for a tenth of what they're asking, and in polished satin, not polyester." Donna made a face. "And shoulder pads on *everything?* *What* the *hell?* Like I *need* to look like a Lion's center."

They browsed around several racks until Leigh declared, "*This* one," holding up a black nylon-shell parka with a removable liner.

"*You* need a shot of estrogen: shopping is an *experience.* Go look at the faux furs rack."

"Shopping is a *chore*. You *know* I've never been a big fan." Leigh tried the parka on, waving her arms and twisting. "This *works*. I don't *need* to look anymore. I just wanted to get together with *you* today."

"Well, if *that's* what this is all about," Donna grinned, blue eyes gleaming, "then *that's* OK. How's the Army treating you?"

"Up until these *last* orders, just fine," Leigh declared, folding the parka over an arm. "Let's find some real coffee." Out in the chill breeze, they started walking across Woodward Avenue. Most of Birmingham's structures were—or *looked*— newer; the fast-food joints had tony facades; most advertising was tastefully subdued. That said, the huge Dietz, O'Bannon, and Associates sign on the largest office building in town was said to be visible from orbit.

They stopped at a corner coffee *shoppe* on the corner of *Old* Woodward Avenue and Maple with a wide sidewalk outside meant for little tables and uncomfortable chairs in the summer. "Didn't this used to be a Rexall?"

"The owner died, and this coffee outfit moved in," Donna explained. Inside, the *shoppe* was clean and utilitarian, and the coffee ground and roasted before the patron's very eyes before being dispensed in small foam cups. The place sported blown fiberglass and plastic furniture with tables too small to lean on and worn Naugahyde benches along the stucco walls.

"You've been dating *Nick* for how long now?"

"Wouldn't call it *dating*, but we've been *hanging out* off and on...mostly *off*...twelve years."

"And in between, you've had *how many* 'real' boyfriends who *all* broke your heart?" Leigh supplied helpful air quotes.

"*Four. Yeah*, but I *like Nick so much*."

"*Yeah*...he *is* the *one* who *never* disappoints, who *always* understands, and who would *never* do what you fear most."

Donna nodded; wiped a tear. "So I want to get really-serious-beyond-sex with my *best-guy*-friend until we *maybe* come to *hate* each other?"

"Would one *have* to follow the other?"

"Do we *have* to *try* to find out?"

"Could you do better than the *one* guy you've known for half your life?"

Donna stopped, stared. "*Yeesh!* We've known each other *that* long?"

Leigh smiled. "Yeah, *we have*."

***

"Can I *help* you, sir?" A young sergeant in BDUs whose name tag read *Knelling* gazed at Mike curiously. He had entered the building by the front door, which he guessed no one used except strangers and first-time delivery guys. He was also taking a chance by just showing up at his new unit early—*and* out-of-uniform—to find out why he was sent there *so* suddenly.

The T-shaped, three-story drill hall was a Cold-War-designed-and-built, brick-and-cinder-block structure. It had fenced-in asphalt-and-gravel parking lots crammed with camouflage-painted vehicles on one side and in the back and *non-fenced-in* parking lots on the other. An illuminated sign out front, visible to any terrorist or rubbernecking interloper to see, announced *US Army Reserve Center*.

"You *can*, Sarge" Mike flashed his military ID. "I'm looking for the NISC office."

"*Oh*, OK," Sergeant Knelling answered brightly. "Down this way." She led him down the long linoleum-lined hall that ran from the building's parking lot to the fire door end. Despite the names on the buildings, Active Army units *not* on bases wedged themselves into Reserve Centers when they *could* because they were cheap space. This one housed a Reserve engineer company, a Ranger company, an armored cavalry troop, a military intelligence detachment, *and* Mike's Active Component unit. They passed posted announcements for holiday parties and annual training, EEO action and reenlistment, and other informally-passed information to the building's unit members.

Knelling pointed Mike to a door down the hall with a sign that read *NISC Detachment A16*. Inside, a small man with a bare wisp of hair in a civilian suit sat at a grey-steel desk. "Sergeant *Dietz*," he grinned, rising and extending his hand. "Ivan Thomas. Close the door and have a seat. I *heard* Jessica's voice out there."

"I know you're not expecting me for another three weeks, but I get nervous with my records hanging out." Mike sat on a standard-issue, barely comfortable sofa opposite the desk.

Ivan smiled. "You *want* to sign in?" A name plaque on the desk announced him as a major. "You won't be *in* uniform *or in* the *office* for a *while*."

"All right, sir. Ah, my fiancée was posted to Troy CID the same day I was posted here…a week ago. Cut *both* our tours short. Know anything about *that*, sir?"

Ivan smiled slightly. "A *little*. We meet with the FBI next Monday. Meanwhile, let's read you on." In their world, being *read-on* meant signing all the requisite paperwork for the credentials—badge, ID card, *and* a sidearm—that his work would *require*. "You're to be an integral part of a joint law enforcement project. Have your fiancée call into *her* unit immediately, if not sooner. That's all I can say right now."

*What…the…?*

***

"D/4/75, Captain Marsh: this line is not secure. How may I help you, *sir*?" JJ called *this* number—Co. D, 4th Battalion, 75th Infantry—out of the phone book.

"Sir, I'm SFC Elrath, just separated from HHC in Key West. I've got…"

"*JJ* Elrath? Roger Marsh here. Were you in Ranger school when I was an instructor in '74?"

"Oh, *yeah*! You were a buck sergeant then."

"Yeah, but time flies. Went OCS then got hurt a few years back, and they sent me to *this* job."

"*What* job?"

"Company commander. Sounds like *you've* done well."

"Well enough, sir. I *just* called the Red Cross for a leave extension because…" JJ went through the litany of Charlie's poor prognosis. "I'd *like* to contact my new outfit directly if I can find an AUTOVON line…"

"There's one in the building. Where are you staying, at home?"

"No, sir. I'm at the Northwestern Inn and Suites."

"If you're *interested*…should it *come* to that…I *could* make you my training NCO."

"But I'm *not* infantry…"

"Most of the *unit* isn't, either. Most lack even *basic* combat arms skills. There's plenty *gung* around here but not much *ho*. They see *Ranger* and start thinking of James Garner in *Darby's Rangers*. I've got thirteen school-trained Rangers and sixty-five other guys." Roger cleared his throat. "If you've *got* some *time*, we drill on the first weekend of the month. We can swap lies about the old days, scare the *shit* out of the rookies."

### ✳✳✳

"Let's make lunch *quick*, guys," Donna asked as she walked into Alban's with Mike and Leigh, "I've got a *double*-shift at four." Alban's was sometimes mistakenly called the Wagon Wheel, which *was*, in fact, their signature sandwich prominently advertised on their garish neon sign.

"This table is from the Wigwam." Mike declared it as a fact when he sat down, not a question. The Wigwam cafeteria was a Woodward Avenue hot-spot when Alban's was just another deli. By 1986, the Wigwam was gone, and Alban's was a sit-down restaurant with a wine shop.

Leigh looked carefully at the shellac-filled cut-log section. "*Never* went there, Mike."

"No, Sandy," Donna answered. "*I* was there every Sunday from 3rd Grade until they closed, and *their* tables were glass with stuff underneath, like bugs and bottlecaps."

"Why 3rd Grade," Leigh asked.

"When my mom died," Donna replied, "the day before JFK was shot."

"Sorry," Leigh whispered.

"Sorry, Blondie," Mike said, "didn't mean to…You have *more* family?"

"*Oh*, yeah." They chatted for a while before Donna smiled—she could charm an executioner—looking over Leigh's shoulder. "*Megan* over there *might* still be on the Newhouse payroll."

"Who?" Mike struggled not to look.

"Megan Woods. She was working for RF last I knew."

"She had a Randy Band." In school, girls most favored by Randy were awarded ribbon chokers—Randy Bands. "Think *she...*"

"*Oh*, yeah. She's been staring at you and Mike for a while." Megan had been a fetching light-brunette in school—Randy's type. But years of hair treatments had not been kind, leaving her hair like weathered straw that she cut to shoulder-length and pinned back. Her round face looked older than her thirty-one years but still showed some spark of a vivacious youth, and her brown eyes still had some fire.

"Let's see what her interest is in *us*." Mike got up just before their food arrived, pulled a chair around to Megan's table, and sat backward on it, chin in hand. "*Hi*, Megan. Remember me?"

Megan regarded Mike as she might the sudden appearance of a delivery driver. "Mike Dietz."

"Yup. You remember Leigh and Donna?"

She glanced in their direction. "Haven't seen any of *you* since graduation."

"Eh, we could say the same. Want to join us? Old time's sake?"

She gazed at Mike, then Leigh, then back to Mike. "I'm about done here."

"What do you hear from Randy these days?"

"Randy?" Megan started, tried to look baffled, but it was too late. "What makes you think I've heard *anything*?"

*That look of trapped desperation you just flashed.* "Just wondered. Listen," he pulled a pencil out of his jacket and scratched his phone number on a napkin. "Give me a call sometime. We can catch up." He winked and went back to his table. Leigh and Donna looked in her direction, nodded, and smiled.

"Anything," Leigh whispered after Mike sat down again.

He smiled and winked before he whispered, "plenty. Watch till she leaves." He bit into his sandwich, marveling at the delicately-seasoned beef pastrami and rich Swiss cheese on light rye.

"Gone," Donna mumbled after a few minutes. "Spill."

"She took the napkin with her?"

Leigh looked. "Yep."

"She'll report to them this afternoon." He glanced at Leigh. "*Maybe* we'll get some answers about that fire."

***

"Jenny Kent, please; JJ Elrath," he asked the receptionist. Jenny's office building was a blend of concrete flying buttresses, opposite-angled roofs, and blue-and-white steel-and-glass walls gleaming in the thin sunshine. He admired the style shots of properties that lined the reception hall before Jenny came out smiling, if a little weary, and embraced him warmly without a word. "Hi, sweetheart," he mumbled. "Hi."

She pulled away, quickly wiping a tear. "*So* glad you're here." She swung her thin blonde hair gently. She had never been shapely but *curvy* and athletic.

"*Anything* for my sweetheart. Where's your husband?"

61

"My brother's. The first thing he said when he was hit was 'not again!' He already *has* two Purple Hearts!" She smiled, a pleasing look on her fair face. "How long are you *here* for?"

"Good question." He told her about Charlie. "I've got at *least* three weeks."

"Well, come on in; I want you to meet some people." She *introduced* her stepbrothers, Leon and Thomas Nickell. The young men didn't remember him, but it had been nearly two decades since they'd last met. Jenny's *father*, Brian Jacobs, remembered JJ's *name*, but not much else.

"So, you're going to tie the knot? When?" They had gone down the street to a cafe.

"Next three weeks," he answered. "Um…where are you staying *now*?"

"Holiday Inn. We're going to look at the townhouse on Saturday. The damage... we got a *list* of hotels…"

"I can get you a *rate* at my brother Kurt's place. *We're* in the honeymoon suite." He shrugged. "I can get *you* a suite."

"Let me talk to Jesse." She smiled, the bright-eyed grin he'd always loved. "I'll talk him *into* it." She looked puzzled, "*Ram* called. We weren't friends, but he offered his help. Then Clare, then *Sarah*. Hadn't heard from *them* in *ages*. They wanted to know what *they* could do. And Julie in Indianapolis—did you *know* she was a builder? And *Lucy* out in San Francisco…" She smiled again. "The jungle drums of Brookfield alerted them, I guess. *Thanks*, sweetie."

"Anything for my sweetheart." *That thunder started when I called Clare.*

"You said *that* when we were closer."

"Just because we're not skinny-dipping anymore doesn't mean we can't still be there for each other."

"You're the only guy I *ever wanted* to swim naked with."

"I'll leave word with the desk; we'll go swimming with something *on*."

### ✳✳✳

"*Good* afternoon; Army CID Detroit, Ms. Armor speaking; this line is *not* secure. How may I help you, *sir?*" With orders in hand, Leigh framed what to say. *I'm getting married, and my family home is smoked out. Sounds entirely plausible.*

"*This* is Sergeant Taylor. I'm *supposed* to…"

"Leigh! Amy Armor!"

"Amy! *Wow!* I didn't know *you* were up here." They were the first female patrol MPs in Korea. "You got a warrant?"

"Five years ago. I've been up here two years. How long's it *been*?"

"Let's see…end of our first Korea tour, so, '75—eleven years. I need to tell the boss…"

"*That* would be me. Leigh, I *can't* tell you *why*, but *you need* to *report here most* Rikki-tick."

"Tomorrow?"

"Make it 0900. We clear?"

"Roger, out here." *Why the all-fired hurry?* "I called my unit…" Leigh sighed to Ben a few minutes later in the kitchen. "I need my *own* wheels to report."

"We *know* people," Ben winked and casually tossed a set of car keys on the island.

Leigh stared at the nondescript GM keys. "What's *this*?"

"It's the car next to your mother's in front of the garage." Ben sipped coffee. "One of my clients is *selling* or *leasing* it. Here's the paperwork."

*Hard to say 'no' when he puts it like that.* "Thank you, Ben."

Ben cleared his throat theatrically. "I *observe*, my dear, that things with your service are moving with extraordinary swiftness. As an attorney and an Army Air Force veteran, I know *enough* about military service to know that *this* situation is *not* normal. I realize that there are many things you can't tell either your friend or your father-in-law, but there are *few* things that you *cannot* tell your attorney. Are we *clear*?"

"We *are*, Ben," Leigh said. "And as soon as *I* know anything *you* need to know—as my *attorney*…"

"Then, we *are* clear, my dear."

***

*Take care of the girls for me when I'm gone.*

From time to time, JJ could still hear his father saying *that* out-of-the-blue one sweltering July afternoon. Jake passed away four months later.

*He knew he didn't have much time left.* He thought about that as he munched toothpick chow with a beer during happy hour at the hotel. *Who's…?* "*Jules*," he called, waving.

Julia Addison, his niece, stopped and gaped. "*Hi*," she waved, "be *there* in a minute." Following her were a man and two teenage boys…and a couple of faces among several others that he dimly remembered.

After a while, Julia and one remembered face came up to his table. After a brief hug, Julia nodded to her companion. "JJ, this is…"

"Clawson," JJ interrupted, offering his hand. "Sorry, but your *first* name…"

"Dave," he replied. Dave was 5-foot-11, perhaps 180 pounds, with a round face and doe-brown eyes. His voice was of an unusual timbre, something between a tenor and a baritone. "*We* met in Panama in '81 and *here* in January."

"We *did*," JJ said. "Talked about Wolverine. How's all that *going*, anyway?"

"That's one thing we're *here* for," Julia answered. "We're both official and *un*official this trip. Mom said you were headed for Alaska?"

"Yeah," JJ said, watching *more* people come out of the elevator and head for his general area, including the two boys.

"This is *Tony Junior—TJ*," Julia smiled, holding her hand out to the older boy, "and his brother *Kevin*. My *step*-sons and their father, Tony. Boys, this is my step-uncle, JJ Elrath."

All three solemnly shook JJ's hand as the boys marveled at the wonders of the atrium and, of course, the glass-enclosed pool. Tony was a dark man about Julia's height, with seemingly glassy light-green eyes; his boys looked like him. "Heard about you from Jules," he said, his voice deeper than JJ expected.

Three women exited the elevator soon after, joining JJ and Julia. "*This* one's my wife, Beth," Dave declared, putting his arm around a small woman with light-colored hair and a sleepy toddler on her hip, "and my *other* partner..."

"Nancy," JJ interrupted. "*We* met in January..."

"*Ellen* Drew," she said. Ellen was a little shorter than Julia with a somewhat angular face, short and wiry brown hair, blue-green eyes, and a *spare* figure. She looked athletic in a 30-something way—though not as *centerfold*-worthy as Julia.

"*Ignore* him," the third woman declared, "like *he* just did *me*. Morgan Towne," she offered her hand. "I'm with *them*." Morgan was not much shorter than Ellen but not *heavier* than Beth, with lighter brown hair and a dulcet voice to Beth's soprano. "My Jerry will be around soon enough."

"*Pushy* as usual," Dave sighed. "Yeah, *she's* with *us*. Busman's holiday."

"Well, glad to meet you all," JJ sighed. "Chow's over there," he pointed.

"Let's put on the *feed* bag," Tony announced, leading the boys and most of the others.

Beth and Julia sat at his little table; Beth sat the toddler in another chair. "He'll be *out* in a minute," Beth declared...and she was right. "*Most* predictable kid."

"Good thing," JJ nodded. "If you're in town, Jules, Ann and I are tying the knot between now and Thanksgiving."

"*Yeah*," Julia smiled. "We *should* be here. We've got a *thing* for a while here. You've been to see Gramps?"

"Yeah, he's circling the drain. Well," JJ declared, finishing his beer and toothpick chow, "see you around. I've got *phone calls* to make."

JJ called his sisters; Brenda first. "Hey, Roy: JJ...I'm *OK*; how's it by you...can I *just*...yeah, later, Roy... *Hey*, Bren. I'm in Detroit, on my way to Alaska, but the old man's had a stroke...hemorrhagic; there's an aneurism...he's off sedation, but he's *not* waking up...Mom's more OK *now* than she was when she called me. Just getting to you on the list...*three* weeks, *maybe* more. Listen, I'm gonna get married soon...*yeah*, Claudia, who do...OK, *wise*-ass. *Very* funny...no, she's not due up here until Monday. *Typical* military, *can't* get their acts together...Saturday? OK, see you then." *Brenda will call Mom in a few minutes, be here Saturday.*

Talking to Lois, younger than Brenda by a year and a half, took a *different* touch. "Hi, Lo; JJ. How's Chicagoland these days? I'm in Detroit on my way to Alaska...yeah, I *heard* you were up there a few years back...Listen, the old man's had a stroke...no, a *real* one. The doctors don't think he's *going* to wake up. There's an aneurism, and they can't operate...*Mom's* OK...we're at the Northwestern Inn and Suites at Telegraph and Northwestern. *Kurt* Parkinson owns it...you *don't* know him, but he's *nothing like* Charlie...*Tonight?* OK; I'll leave word downstairs; I'll let Mom…OK, *you* tell Mom. See you *tonight*, then." *Geez…I didn't see THAT coming. Lois doesn't give two shits about either Charlie OR Mom. I expected her to CALL, but…huh. Both sisters in town at once. This'll be interesting.*

His family had been doing this ritual for decades, pretending affection for each other when it suited them. Ann's family (even her institutionalized mother) was close-knit, sharing joys and tragedies and holidays like a Norman Rockwell painting in comparison to his.

*Why not mine?*

* * *

They were just finishing their dinner when the phone rang. Monica got up to answer and, unexpectedly… "Leigh, dear: it's for *you*."

"Taylor."

"Leigh Taylor Newhouse?" The voice was muffled. "This is the law office of Fischer and Ally. We are serving you with notice that you *shall* appear…"

"Hold on," Leigh motioned for Ben to pick up another phone. "OK, let's start simple. That's *not* my name."

"*You* are *required* to appear in the 48th District Court tomorrow morning at 10 to show just cause…"

"Wait, what? *When* was the petition filed?"

"Petition? This is an *order* from the *court*…"

"No, it isn't," Ben's voice was clear, firm, and smooth as silk. "This is Benjamin Dietz, representing Miss Taylor. To w*hom* am I speaking, please?"

"*This* is your *daddy*, asshole," followed by a loud click.

Leigh hung up, glancing at Mike and Ed, but made a face. "*Not* Randy, but *someone* I can't quite place."

Ben shook his head. "No Michigan court can demand appearance with less than five business days' notice, *always* in writing and *never* through a third party. Remember *that*, my dear."

"I *will*." Leigh looked bleak. "I'm sorry I—we—dragged you into this."

Ben waved a hand. "My dear, you are a part of *us*. If I don't miss my guess, *that* was an attempt to get you somewhere you didn't *want* to be. Clumsy, amateurish: what a non-attorney might do."

Monica, ever the attentive hostess, led both women to the living room. "Brandy, ladies. *Come* now, no protests. Leigh, dear, you had lunch with Donna? Lovely girl."

Mike, Ed, and Ben cleaned up the dining room and kitchen silently. As the last plate went into the dishwasher, Mike stared at his reflection in the breakfast room window. "*I* screwed up, Pops."

"You did what *I* would have: brought them out in the open. Come." Ben nudged his son with a bottle of beer and led Mike and Ed to the pool enclosure, steamy yet chilled after sundown.

They sat in still-warm chairs, not speaking, sipping beer. "Pops, *when* did you *know* when you loved Mama?"

"When your sister Sara was born."

"Not before?"

"No. Not the way it worked then."

"It *was different* then, Mike," Ed added. "I was dating Cathy's roommate, not *her*, for six months." He finished his beer. "I had tickets to a play around Christmas '53, and her roommate got sick. *Cathy* and I went. Our first date turned into a dozen, then…well…"

Ben smiled. "You couldn't imagine life without her."

Ed chuckled—a hollow-yet-rich sound in that resonant space. "Yep, that's it. Mike, before Leigh's wedding, everyone urged her to walk away if she thought she *should*. Everyone but *you*. If *YOU* had told her to walk away, I believe she would have."

"I told her to follow her heart because I wanted to be her friend if it *did* work out with Randy. I think she would always have wondered but never have *known for sure* if she *hadn't* gone through with it."

"Ben, your son certainly knows my daughter better than *I* do." The silence of the next several minutes was broken only by the sound of the pool filters cycling. "We care *so* much for *your* family, all the family the three of us *have*. With *your* family, I've always felt we belong. With the Newhouse's, I always felt Leigh was more a trophy than a wife, and her mother and I were just *there*." Silence. "Mike, *please* be sure."

"Sir: *I'm* sure. I'm confident *Leigh* is. *Please* trust us."

"I shall *have* to, young man."

**\*\*\***

The knock on the door was strong, brilliant, opinionated, confident, and beautiful…*everything* that described Lois Laura McHenry. JJ opened the door to see a younger and smaller *female* version of their father, with his oval face and brown eyes but longer and browner hair. Brother and sister embraced briefly before they sat, and he offered a beer. "You look *fabulous*, Lo…" *And what brought YOU here so damn fast?*

"Well, *you* look great. *What* kind of a rate did I *get* here? This place *has* to be worth more than what *I'm* paying." Lois preferred rapid-fire interrogations and dense oratory to measured chatting. "And what's *the asshole's* prognosis?" She had not referred to Charlie by his name for years.

"You got a family rate here for ten days, which means taxes and fees. And Charlie's *not* good. He…"

"I need to get with Rockland, see what Stella's going to be *able* to *do* with Gramma's money…" For reasons surpassing human understanding, Lois had referred to their mother as *Stella* since her wedding. Lew Rockland was Charlie's—and thus *Stella's*—attorney.

66

"*Gramma's* money? That's *long* gone…"

She looked at him as if he were a child who said something amusingly naughty. "*Gramma* paid *her own* bills. You *know*…"

"No, Lo: Gramma's money was gone before *Dad* died." The only way to get a word in edgewise when talking with Lois was to interrupt, allowing only *certain* people to do so.

"But *she* paid for *my wedding*," she protested.

"No: *Dad* did. 17th Airborne Division Fund. Ever heard of *that*?"

"We got a fat check from *them* as a wedding present. Paid for nearly *all* the…"

"The 17th Airborne Division was Dad's outfit before he went to the 101st and is *long* extinct. Howard Mueller set up *that* ruse with *Dad's* money, paid *all* our bills with it—*and* sent you that check at *Mom's* behest."

Lois's mind didn't change often or easily, but careful observers could see wheels turning and steam rising when it did. "But…*why*?" She stared, blinking.

"Dad didn't *trust* Mom with *his* money—you *know* how she *can* be. He made Howard his trustee with Mom as the cosigner. Dad paid not just for our educations, but for *both* yours and Brenda's weddings *and* paid off the mortgage on Birch Lake in '68."

"Then, when *that bastard* wanted *us* to *pay rent*…?"

"Charlie made Brenda and I pay rent in a *home we owned*."

She glared—an accomplishment for Lois through her thick glasses. She was so nearsighted she had trouble seeing the eye chart and the *wall* it was on. "Got anything stronger than beer?"

"Some wine that Ann likes; schnapps that *I* like."

"Who's *Ann*?"

"*Claudia* Ann. She's been going by Ann for years."

She made a hard-to-describe face—a curious mix of resignation, fury, and amusement. "Let's have some of both."

\*\*\*

"I'm for bed," Monica declared, casting a glance at Mike. "Leigh, dear; you'll share a room with the washer and dryer. The *other* bedrooms are in a *state*." She cleared her throat. "You'll share a *bathroom* with Michael."

"That's fine, Monica," Leigh smiled, finishing a note to herself. *Subject expressed surprise to have been called out by Attorney DIETZ and ended call.* "I'll be up in a few minutes." *I'm drafting an After-Action Report?*

Cathy finished her brandy and stretched, yawning. "Me, too; Ed's already gone over there." She side-glanced at Leigh and made a face. "Honey, don't abuse Monica's hospitality."

"*Mom*," Leigh rolled her eyes. *You'll make a passion-racket in another twenty minutes, and you want US to…?*

"*This* is their *home*." Cathy kissed Leigh's head, whispering, "don't get *caught*."

67

"*OK*, Mom." *Why do I WANT to draft an AAR?*

As Leigh ascended the stairs a few minutes later, she saw Mike and Ben conversing quietly. She kissed both goodnight as she passed and rolled into bed as the house went to sleep. She had just dropped off when Mike quietly slid between the sheets behind her, wrapping an arm around her. "Huh?"

"Hi. Just wanted to cuddle."

"*Fine*: cuddle." They were quiet for some minutes, but she knew he wasn't sleeping. "What were you talking about with your dad?"

He chuckled. "He reminded me that *we* are not yet married."

"So…you're *here* now…?"

"It's the *way* he said it; a little German and a little Yiddish. The Yiddish was for Mama. He was saying, in *his* way, don't get *caught*." He paused. "Are we running our own investigation?"

"*Feels* like it." She rolled to face him. "Come laundry day, *this* room *would* be crowded."

"That's *Tuesday*." He gasped as she reached for him. "Thought we were just *cuddling*."

"I *changed* my *mind*. Just…don't *make* me…make …*noise*."

## Friday

"So, Lo, what's on *your* schedule for today?" At 6 AM, brother and sister lounged in the gym-sized atrium, watching the clouds through the glass roof.

Lois sipped coffee. "*Mother* needs access to that SOB's money, and *fast*, and Rockland won't answer her calls. *I'll* get to see him if I have to wait all day."

*She's 'Mother' now, huh?* "Well, good luck to you. I'm taking her to see Charlie after I do a few laps and eat something. There's a dinner at the Mueller's this evening. You *should*…"

"Mom mentioned it last night. I haven't *seen* a Mueller since we moved."

*And 'Mom' now?* "*Not* so; you saw Ann in '68 after Dad's funeral. I gotta get going. One more thing: Mom's cooking hasn't improved any."

She grinned. "*Didn't* think so. See you tonight."

When he got back to the suite to get ready for PT, there was a message on the phone: "Sergeant Elrath, this is Colonel McCann, G2 for the 6$^{th}$ ID. I'm authorizing an additional 14 days delay en route. Good luck, JJ." *Captain* Hal McCann had been his boss in Germany; he'd made time for JJ to write his book.

*One LESS thing I've got to think about.*

\*\*\*

"Dietz, O'Bannon and Associates; how may I help you?" A woman answered on the third ring.

"May I speak with Nick Paulson, please? This is Leigh Taylor."

"One moment…Mr. Paulson is in; I'll connect you."

She watched the roiling clouds and slashing rain outside before… "Dominic

Paulson: *how* may I help you?"

"Nick? Leigh Taylor."

"Oh, *hi*, Ms. Taylor, Mr. Ben said you'd call."

"What's with '*Ms.*?' I've *seen* you *naked*, big guy."

"Yeah." He giggled for a few moments. The girl's early-morning boxer raid was the stuff of legend. "Sorry, old habits die hard. How are *you*, Leigh?"

"I'm *OK*. Nick. Ben thought it would be a good idea for my family to retain *you*. The first business-day availability we *all* have to get together is next Wednesday."

"Ah…what about…lunch at Old Alexander's on Woodward, south of 14 Mile at about one?"

"1300 at Old Alexander's."

Watching his coffee cup studiously, Mike waited for her to hang up. "So, that *towel*—the one blocking us off—*was* pulled, wasn't it?"

"*Bobbi* did it."

"But the towel was in *your* hand when *I* turned around."

"Gravity *has* mysterious ways."

**\*\*\***

"After today, Johnny, I'll just come every *other* day unless something changes." The weather was wet and windy when he picked up Stella and Barbara. She sighed. "*Brenda* called last night; Lois, this morning." She made a face. "Brenda says she'll come down tomorrow. I asked her to leave the kids someplace else. They're *too* much for me right now. Did you *know Lois* was in town? She's going to see Lew Rockland," She screwed her face up in a disgusted look. "He won't answer *my* calls, but he's Johnny-on-the-spot for *her*."

"*Not* exactly, Mom." They found a parking space within visual range of the side door, unlike the day before.

"Mrs. Parkinson," cardiologist Dr. Chen-Winston intoned in Charlie's room, "your husband *may* have suffered a mild heart attack. We want to…"

*UGH.* JJ tuned the rest of it out, went out to clear his head. He chose a chair at the end of the corridor, head in hands.

After several moments, a pair of white shoes faced him; a gentle hand touched his shoulder. *I KNOW that touch...* He looked up and grinned, finding himself standing up and embracing Donna so fast—and lifting her off her feet—she didn't have time to react.

"*Cutie-Pie*," she grunted, "*thanks* for the *spinal* adjustment, but *put me down!*" She had once sent teenage *Cutie-Pie* to bed with *that* touch.

"Sorry," he mumbled, setting her down but *not* letting go. "I just…"

"Yeah. Happens to me *all* the time." Her bright-eyed smile made *him* smile as she pecked his cheek, and he let go.

"My stepfather…"

"*Why* do you think I'm *here*, buddy? C'mon." The doctor had left Charlie's

69

room; two more IV bags were hanging; two nurses set up monitors around the bed. Donna spoke with the nurses while JJ sat near Stella and Barbara. After a few minutes, Donna crouched beside Stella and grasped her hand gently. "Donna Hammerfest, nurse-practitioner, Mrs. Parkinson..."

"You brought Ann's Christmas present to the house last December."

"Yes, ma'am. May I look in on your husband when I can?"

"*Thank* you, dear. That would be *so* kind."

Donna cocked her head towards the door, leading Barbara and JJ just outside. Even in baggy scrubs, her crossed-arms posture could stop rush-hour traffic. "He's a drunk, isn't he?"

"Functional," Barbara nodded. "*You* work for Sally Donne in the NP ward?"

"Yes, ma'am."

"Been a lush since I've *known* him," JJ grunted. "How would *you* know?"

"I can *smell* it. In a deep rest, DTs *can* look like a coronary. *Seen* it before."

"*Could* be." Barbara nodded. "Let me talk to Stella."

Donna took his arm. "I'll hang with *Cutie-Pie*, ma'am..."

"*Cutie-pie?*" Barbara made a face. "*I* should tell *Ann* about your secret life, Johnny. But you don't work for *me*, Donna. Just call me Barbara. Go down and get some coffee."

Donna led JJ to the break niche. "Are *you* OK, honey?"

"Yeah, I *will* be. Lot on my plate right now."

"*You* need to take it easy."

"If you should *see* Deb down in physical therapy, tell her that we're getting married before Thanksgiving *if* she doesn't already know."

"I'll pass it along *only* if you promise I can kiss the groom...and *you* take the afternoon off."

"*Too much stuff* to *do,* but for *you,* I'll *try*."

### ***

"You're in *uniform*?" Amy Armor was a small, somewhat stocky woman dressed in a black civilian suit. She met Leigh just inside the office door—a full glass affair emblazoned with *US Army Criminal Investigations—Detroit.*

"Thought I *should*. Sounded official."

"Well, it *is*, but first: *just* to make *us* official." Amy flashed her credentials, showing that she was *Chief Warrant Officer Third Class* Armor.

They walked around a short wall and into a big room that was filled with desks and tables. Few had anything personal on them like photos or even coffee mugs; *some* had computer monitors; nearly all had telephone headsets. Military Police history milestone posters lined the walls, from the Revolution's provosts to Grenada, where MPs alongside the Rangers were in a *short* firefight with Cuban combat engineers. Leigh had been a bit player there. "How many people are assigned here?"

"Twenty-two, *including* you. They don't spend a lot of time *here*—there are satellites in Dearborn and Lansing—and rarely on Fridays; *I'm* here doing the paperwork more than most of *them* are here working. And now we've got *this*…whatever the *hell* it is."

"What's…?"

"The reason you're *here*," Amy sighed. "Are you ready?"

"For *what?*"

"Sorry: credentials first." Leigh signed into the unit and for her badge and ID card, then completed all the paperwork standard with CID units. Finally, she signed for a pistol and hip holster. "You *should* carry it for safety. The *details* of our role in a joint FBI operation will *hopefully* be made clear more at the Troy FBI agency at 1000 Monday." She smiled. "Tell *no one* what's going on."

*Hell, that's easy…I haven't the faintest IDEA what's going on.* "How long *is* this assignment?"

"At *least* six months; probably a year."

"And Sergeant Dietz?"

"He'll be at the briefing. So, what *have* you been *doing* with yourself, girl? I *heard* you were in Grenada…*Rod* ditched me in '76, but I married a *great* guy; his name's *Phil*…"

\*\*\*

"He has no partners, and he never incorporated," Kurt grumbled. JJ's lunch with his brothers at *God's Bar*—the Knights of Columbus hall in Royal Oak—*felt* like a summit meeting. "Can't say how well the dealership's doing."

"Not *too* bad, Kurt," Thin, urbane Will muttered, spreading mustard on his sandwich. Charlie's youngest son owned two car dealerships in the Detroit area and had only ten years on JJ. "His 90-day-overs are at like 30%." *90-day-overs* was vehicle-dealer-speak for the percentage of unsold new vehicles on hand for more than three months, costing the dealer more in interest.

"Huh. Better than *my* shop," Kurt, the owner of a custom car and truck shop, mused. "Good salesmen, then."

"Yeah. *Great* salesmen. But without the owning *dealer*…?"

Will asked, "does your mom *want* to *find* someone to run the place…?"

"I *doubt* it," JJ said. "Mom hasn't worked for wages since she had Brenda. She *has* a diploma from a *business school for young ladies. That* means she can read a balance sheet, but *she* wouldn't know a 90-day-over from third base."

"OK," Will grinned as he glanced at Charlie Junior, the tall and stoic oldest son who was but ten years younger than Stella. "That land's worth *a lot*: thirty acres, seven buildings. A new dealer would buy what GM *doesn't* own—the new truck inventory and the parts—and slide in, as *I* understand it. I'll get with dealer relations about the details."

"Good." While Charlie Junior worked for GM as an engineer, the dealer side was alien to him. "Will, can *you* look after the place for now?" Will shrugged and nodded as he took another swig of his beer. "How do you think your mom's fixed for money, JJ? Is she OK?"

"She only has a household account, doesn't know where *his* money is. The hospital's *looking* for money."

"Of *course,* that *bastard* has accounts he doesn't share," Kurt declared. "Jo's looking around..."

"Yeah, OK. My sister Lois is downtown with Lew Rockland..."

"*That* nuisance?" Kurt seemed surprised. "What's *he* got to do with..."

"He's the old man's lawyer *and* Mom's."

"*Christ* on his *cross,*" Kurt grimaced. "*She* needs a new lawyer."

"Guys, you *do* appreciate that he's not leaving there alive, right?"

"Yeah," Charlie Junior sighed; Will and Kurt nodded.

"Charlie, you're supposed to come to the Mueller's this evening, last I heard. Yea or nay?"

"Yea. Dot's made a point to get the evening off."

"OK, we'll talk about the business with Mom *then*." JJ gobbled the last of his brisket sandwich. "The *other* business, real estate and title. Any ideas?"

"He got rid of *that* years ago," Kurt mumbled.

"What about what Mom won't *want* to talk about."

"*He* wants to go into *his* family plot in Berryville, Indiana." Will spoke to his plate. "I've argued about it with him until I'm blue in the face, and he won't budge."

"I'm missing something," JJ said.

"Our mother is buried here in Detroit," Charlie sighed, "and the old man wants to be buried with *his* family."

Kurt looked vaguely angry. "Mom was *never* in favor with *his* family."

"Dad got a letter from Aunt Frieda years ago; she griped about 'your idolatrous, bigamous ways," Will said.

"*Bigamy,*" Charlie mumbled. "*Never* figured that out. They're members of a little church affiliated with nobody: Church of the Living Apostles of Christ the Son. For *them*, marriage *survives* death. Aunt Frieda used to say that Mom was a *harlot* for marrying Dad."

"They *were* pissed off most of the time," Kurt frowned. "Aunt Frieda wrote a letter; sent us all copies. Something about a *wife and child* in Berryville..."

"I've got a hand-written, witnessed, and notarized version of his reply, disowning them," JJ said.

The boys all looked at him, surprised. "Hang onto that," Kurt declared. "*Might* come in handy. *You* spent summers on Uncle Newt's farm down there, Charlie; *I* went down there during the war. All contact with them ended in '45."

"Never figured *that* out, either," Charlie said, finishing his beer. "Haven't seen or heard from our cousins since."

"The old man's Catholic, though, yeah?" JJ stretched his back.

"*Mom* was." Kurt frowned. "Sometimes, he'd get a snootful and yell at Mom for dragging him into Popery. He still went to Mass, even after she passed. Habit,

I guess."

Charlie wiped his mouth. "I've gotta get back. I'll look in on him tomorrow. Will; Sunday? Kurt; Monday? JJ, whenever your mom wants, OK?"

"Guys: one more thing." JJ grinned. "I want you to come to my wedding before Thanksgiving."

The three looked at each other, Will with a diabolical, impish grin. *"Well,"* he breathed, "know what *that* means?"

"Yeah. *SMOKER!*" Charlie shouted. "Hey, everybody: our baby brother's getting hitched!" This was met by general applause in the half-filled hall and a quick smack from their matronly waitress.

Charlie's boys always treated JJ like *he* imagined a brother *should* be treated—pain-in-the-ass little brother, sometimes, but a brother nonetheless.

*I can't wait to find out just what a smoker is...*

***

*"We* need a gun safe," Mike mused. "How much ammo did they give you?"

"Two boxes, you *romantic* devil," Leigh replied sardonically. "First thing we *jointly* need."

"Other than a ring setting." He glanced at a card stuck behind the wall phone and punched the numbers on the phone. "Hi, this is Mike Dietz. I have a sudden and urgent need for a gun safe for two small-frame handguns, four magazines, and four boxes of ammunition. The Army doesn't issue one, but *we're* responsible for the weapons...Tonight? I'd appreciate it." He side-glanced at Leigh as he hung up. "That's..."

"Block Associates." She made a face. "*I* should get to a range."

"I'll get some range time."

"Are you on leave?"

"No. You?"

"No."

"Ring?"

"Next week, maybe? Church? I'll go on Sunday; try to schedule it."

"License next week?"

"Let's..."

She was interrupted when Donna came into the kitchen; she was such a fixture at the Dietz's she could just walk in. "I ran into JJ at work this morning. He's worried about his mom and a *shitload* of other things."

"Yeah," Mike replied, "he was here last night. He was in and out *so* fast."

"He's *gonna* crash and burn soon; need to get him unloaded." Donna thought for a moment. "I've been invited to dinner tonight. *I* can get him so he can rest later." She glanced at Leigh. "He *should* be ready to unload with someone he knows and trusts in the morning, but *I* have a VA shift. Leigh, can *you* be there for him?"

Leigh sighed. "Yeah, *but*..." Leigh and Mike looked at each other, knowingly, as both friends and lovers. "*WE* know who'd be *better*…"

***

*Boy, I AM beat…I should lie down for a few hours…next time anyone needs me to be anywhere is 1700…three hours.*

The telephone on the little desk had a message light. "Hi, JJ," Wendy's voice said, "I *know* it's a surprise, but we *just* got here. We're staying with Dennis's parents in Pontiac. Call sometime, and we'll get together before we head to the UP. *See* ya!"

He scratched down the number she left, reclined in the suite's big chair, and closed his eyes, trying to think of nothing. *Just close my eyes…I thought Wendy was from Iowa…no, Nebraska…who pulled the plug?*

The unbidden question roused him: *who pulled the plug?* On Christmas morning 1970, he found his Wolverine classmate Jason Samson in a bathtub, both arms slashed from wrist to elbow and completely drained of blood. But the tub was empty, just a tinge of red coating the porcelain almost up to the rim. *Someone had to have…*

He glanced at the clock: 1445, *a half-hour. But…who DID pull that plug?* What disturbed him wasn't the *answer* but the *question.* In all his Wolverine nightmares—and they *were* fading—he hadn't thought of it. *Why now?*

Once again, he relaxed in the recliner, closed his eyes, and tried to clear his mind with Billy Joel:

> *Maybe this won't last very long*
> *But you feel so right*
> *And I could be wrong*
> *Maybe I've been hoping too hard*
> *But I've gone this far*
> *And it's more than I hoped for*

He went through that song until he dropped…off…

He awoke to the phone ringing and a vague image in his mind; *who's that walking away from Jason's room?* A glance at the clock: 1625. *An hour or so.* "Elrath," he grunted into the phone.

"*Hi,* John," Lois answered. "Back from my exercise in futility downtown. Come on down, and we'll talk about it."

"Sure." Lois greeted him at her 3rd Level room—surprisingly—with a peck and a hug. "So, how's Rockland and them?"

"*Much* too *busy* for the likes of *us,*" she answered in her the-*staff*-is-*uppity* tone. Lois was brilliant but couldn't relate to those who were merely smart or intelligent. "I sat in their lobby for maybe fifteen minutes before I was shown to a conference room. *There* I sat for about *two hours.* Every half hour or so, a secretary would ask if I wanted coffee. I repeated that I *had* to see Mr. Rockland. 'Oh, he'll be in as soon as he's free,' she kept saying. Finally, I went looking and found him and a half dozen cronies in a lounge yucking it up. 'Oh, I'm *terribly* sorry,' the greaseball croaked. *'No* one *told* me *you* were *here.'*

"It went *downhill* from there. I asked how Mom could get some money to pay the medical bills. He said, 'oh, *that* needs to be arranged by *Mr.* Parkinson.' I explained *once more—I already told him he was ill—*and *he* said, 'oh, *my*; that's *terrible.* What's his...?' And I went through it *again.* He acted as if it were new to him *the second time.'* We went around *this* circle twice. At *first,* I thought he didn't *understand* the *gravity....*

"Then he said, 'well, perhaps Mr. Sherith can help. Let me just *call.'* He picks up the phone, says 'can you get August Sherith on the phone?' We wait a minute; he tries small talk like how Mom is, then the phone buzzes. This voice answers and Rockland lays it all out on the speaker, then says, *'Mrs.* Parkinson needs some financial information for the hospital.' The line goes dead for a few seconds, with Rockland flashing his fake smile, then the phone says, 'you *know* I *can't* do *that.'"*

Lois had a bottle of something brown; she swigged a jigger or so down. "Rockland grabs the receiver and says, 'her daughter, Ms. McHenry, is *here* in *front* of me.' He listens, mumbles *yes* a couple of times, then hangs up. *Then* he says, *'Mr.* Parkinson's financial affairs are separate from *Mrs.* Parkinson's by pre-nuptial agreement. His bills will be paid, but only a maintenance allowance will be available to your mother. That's the way *they* agreed it *should* be. Now that he's been made *aware* of the situation, Mr. Sherith will take *care* of it.'"

"I find *that* incredible," JJ sniffed.

"I *told* this imbecile that she'd never *willingly* cut herself off like that, and he just shrugged and said, 'my *hands* are *tied'* over and over again. *This* took about *another* hour before I gave up. He handed me a business card and blathered the usual BS about *'anything* we can *do.'* It was all I could do to keep from strangling the weasel with his own *tie.*"

"I know some lawyers myself." He grabbed the phone book, glanced, and dialed. "Afternoon. JJ Elrath for Mr. Ben Dietz. It's *urgent...thank* you...Ben, sir, my *mom* needs help..."

When he hung up after several minutes, Lois stared at her brother, blinking. "That *big* sign in B'ham; Dietz and something...?" B'ham was what local sophisticates called *Birmingham.* If you *lived* there, you just *knew.*

"That's the one."

"Holy..." she whispered and was quiet.

*First time Lo has EVER been speechless.*

***

"They're bringing this safe over tonight?" Monica asked. The fish-and-chips dinner was being consumed amidst happy chatter.

"Yes, Mama."

"Mike, it's *time* you *knew.*" Ben got up and opened a cabinet across the room,

75

taking out a shotgun. "*I've* never used it, but *Adam* felt better because we *had* it."

"Huh," Leigh sniffed. "Remington 870 Express. Laser pointer and everything. *We* carry Mossbergs or Ithacas on-post, but they're pretty much the same." She took the weapon from Ben, opened the breach, pointed it across the room, and pressed the switch so that a red dot appeared on the wall. "They use these up on the DMZ to bug North Korean sentries."

"Allow me," Ed mumbled, taking the weapon from his daughter. "Prefer a Browning, myself, and unlike Leigh, I *do* find a distinction." He shouldered the piece swiftly, tracking it across the room. "The laser wouldn't help on field clays at *all*. If *you* would *feel* safer, *I'll* keep it *loaded* in the cottage."

"You haven't done *that* for a while, Ed," Cathy declared. "Your shotguns..."

"Still a couple in the storage space, Cath."

"Those *trophies*, Dad..."

"Second place for field clays at the Nationals in '66. First in skeet; third in trap. Haven't been *that* high since, though I *still* shoot from time to time."

* * *

"*Hey*, Donna," JJ grinned. "Didn't know *you* were coming." She was in the Mueller's kitchen when he entered, bright-eyed, and rested in a fuzzy sweater.

"*I* invited her, Johnny," Howard announced. "Wanted to get her perspective on...hey, *Lois*? Jeez, *when* was the last time...?"

"*Been* a while." Lois affected her simulacrum of sincerity that she wore when her sardonic-and-cynical self would be *just too* off-putting. "*Hi*, Mom." Stella hugged her daughter for a *bit* longer than JJ thought was *normal* for them. Jo was also there. Lois had *never met* the reserved woman, who was six months younger than JJ.

Ann's stepbrother Alex Savio was there; so was Brianna Gorgas, his rail-thin girlfriend. As JJ shook Alex's hand and introduced his sister, he introduced Brianna as "my dance partner last New Year's."

When the teenagers went to a movie after dinner, the adults had a chance to discuss the *serious* business in the sunken living room. "First, Stella," Charlie Junior started, "do you *want* to keep the business?"

"If I can get out of the automotive business for the first time in my life, I'll be a happy gal," Stella declared. Her father and first husband were manufacturer's representatives who, in southeastern Michigan, had little choice but to sell their small-factory client's capacities to the carmakers.

"That may *not* be an *option*, Mom," Lois smiled. "I *tried* to get some money from Lew Rockland today, but *he* says your pre-nuptial agreement..."

"My *what*?" Stella was genuinely stunned as the telephone rang in the kitchen, and Barbara went to answer it.

"Your pre-nuptial agreement. *He* says it stipulates..."

"We *never had* a pre-nup..." Stella said.

Lois smiled genuinely, glancing at JJ. "We *thought* not, Mom, but he's *waving*

76

one."

"Johnny," Barbara interrupted, "the *phone's* for *you*. A Mr. Dietz?"

"Elrath...*yessir*; *we* met at your father's *Shiva*...." The living room—open to the kitchen—fell silent, listening for several minutes. "...Oh, *thank you so* much, Mr. Dietz. *One* more question, sir: will *you* represent my mother? Oh, *thank* you, sir."

JJ returned to the living room, grinning. "*That* was Mr. Mordechai Dietz. *He's encountered* Lew Rockland *more* than *once*. *He* says, if I get this right, 'no Michigan pre-nuptial agreement can freeze finances while both parties live as long as they are still married to each other and there are no pending domestic legal actions between them.' So even if there *is* a pre-nup, it *can't* do what Rockland says. He also says that *this* is a typical Rockland/Sherith stunt."

Donna smiled. "Mrs. Parkinson, I can *personally* assure you that the law firm of Dietz, O'Bannon, and Associates will *only* act in *your* best interests."

"I've never *heard* of them," Stella declared, smiling at Donna. "And *please* call me Stella."

"*I* have, Stella," Dorothy grinned. "As a law enforcement officer, I will say that the Dietz firm *completely* overshadows Rockland, Atkins, Terrance, and Schumpeter. We call the latter the *RATS* firm: the kind of lawyers with stacks of business cards in ambulances and bail bond shops, despite having former governors as partners."

"So," Lois asked, "*then* what?"

"Dad asked *me* to look around in Grampa's truck shop," Jo spoke quietly...the first time she'd said anything substantial all night. "It's doing *well*, but something just isn't *right*. There are account books there that don't make sense, some under different *company* names. I'm going to consult my business partner."

Lois stared blankly. "What is it *you* do?"

"Forensic accounting. BA, accounting, Eastern Michigan, '77; MBA, University of Chicago, '79; JD, Michigan State, '83; Michigan CPA and bar the same year. Now, a PI license from the state."

"*Julia's* used her," Charlie added.

"Julia?" Lois asked.

JJ stared. "Our stepniece, Charlie and Dorothy's daughter. She's in the FBI."

Lois did that thing with her eyes that expressed both puzzlement and confusion. "*I* have a *niece* in the *FBI?*"

"*Yes*, Lois," Stella smiled. "You've known *that* since she graduated from the FBI Academy. I *sent* you that announcement."

"She and her team arrived in Detroit last night," Charlie declared. "They're staying at Kurt's place."

Lois looked pensive—briefly—before she sighed, "*I* suppose," but still asked, "wouldn't *most* of the bastard's money be with Sherith's firm?"

"*No*," Charlie declared. "He set aside *some* of his money with Sherith, but *he* still keeps *most* of it handy, expecting to make *more*."

"*Or* hiding it," Jo added, "but I can't say *why*."

"Ultimately," Howard intoned, "Stella, dear, you have to find *where* he's got *what* he's got. I *don't* believe he's *ever* going to be able to handle his own affairs again."

"Dr. Mueller's right," Donna agreed. "I've had patients similar to Mr. Parkinson, and they follow *his* pattern after a brain attack. He *may* waken briefly, but his response to outside input...?" She shrugged. "Years of booze just does too much damage..."

"You're a..." Lois asked—surprisingly—sincerely, without her who-do-*you*-think-*you*-are sneer.

"Neuro-psychiatric nurse-practitioner specializing in illness caused by substance abuse. I could *ask* Dr. Byington to consult—he's the head of my department, but..."

"I believe Donna's qualified to render an opinion,' Howard declared. "She's been working with substance abuse health issues for some time."

Donna sighed. "I treated my *Dad* since I was a kid. But Dr. Byington *could* look if..."

"We'll see, children," Stella sighed. "I should be getting home. Thanks *so* much for all the help."

"And, Mom, Mr. Dietz will represent you if you want. Just call his firm and ask."

"I'll think about it."

JJ and Lois took their mother home, then went back to the hotel. "So, what's *your* weekend like, Lo?"

"Simon's driving over tomorrow. We'll be here until next Sunday or so; I've got some *work*, and he has a genealogy conference. Just worked out that *you* were here."

They had just walked into the atrium when Julia and Morgan stepped out of the elevator. Lois hadn't *seen* Julia in sixteen years, but Julia recognized Lois, "Hey," Julia exclaimed, "I *know* you! This is my partner, Morgan Towne, and that over *there* is her Cousin Felix..."

"Guys," JJ declared, touching Lois' shoulder, "I've got a *thing* in the morning, so I'll say g'nite."

Lois looked...contrite? Hard to say about *what*, but, in a surprisingly small voice, she added, "I really *don't know* a lot about my family anymore. So, you're in the FBI? *Well*..."

***

He had been trying to rest when the phone... "Elrath...*who*...OK, let her up."

"Let's talk, *Cutie-Pie*." Donna appeared at the door.

"What can I do for *you*, Blondie?" They sat in uncomfortable chairs at the small kitchen table.

"*Talk* to me. You're a thousand miles from your *main* stress-reliever." She had a clinical-yet-compassionate expression and an odd smile while pulling little bottles of schnapps and of something *brown* out of her purse. "Have a snort."

"I don't believe in a social lubricant."

"*Don't* be such a smartass: it *doesn't* suit you. *I* believe in the stress-relieving power of alcohol in controlled doses…and in talking with friends."

He drained his bottle while she sipped hers. "So, how have you *been*, Blondie? I barely *know*…"

And everything went black.

He didn't know how *much* later it was when he found himself on his bed with his sweatshirt, shoes, and socks off, and the bedspread over him. Donna sat in the love seat to one side. His head hurt where he bumped it on the table, but he felt remarkably calm. "You slipped me a mickey?"

"*Just* enough to let you rest—deeply."

"Whose idea was the schnapps?"

"Dr. Mueller." She crossed her legs. "*Talk.*"

"I was in the infirmary at Wolverine when Charlie called to ask me what I'd done *now*. I'd *just* been *thrown* out a second-story *window*, and he acted like *I'd* done something wrong. He says, 'we're packed for our cruise; you're *not* getting out of there'…."

He couldn't remember anything after saying that, except it felt like a *very* long time before she got up to take his pulse and kiss his forehead. "*Sleep* now, Cutie-Pie."

## Saturday

*0138 on a Saturday morning?*

Ann stumbled to the phone. "*MUELLER! MAKE IT GOOD!*"

"Ann, it's your father."

"Charlie didn't make it?"

"*He's* still with us. Johnny's been pretty pent up."

"Yeah, I could *hear* that."

"Well, it *got* critical. I'm going to pass you to Donna Hammerfest, OK?"

"O…K."

"Hi, Ann. I met JJ at the hospital, *completely* wired. He needed to unload, and his *go-to* for *that* is…"

"Me."

"Uh-huh. I shared my concerns with your parents, and we agreed on a course of action. This evening I administered ten drops of chloral hydrate in 1.5 ounces of 100-proof peppermint schnapps. He went down *very* quickly, and Dr. Mueller and I wrestled him into bed. He was semi-conscious in 40 minutes and started venting. He talked about Wolverine and *you* a lot, the Army, his mom…and how much he *hates* his step-father for some *damn* good reasons. It was…how long, Doctor?"

"An hour," Howard added.

"Did he mention *Eddie*? Did he say he should have stopped it?"

"He *said*, 'poor Eddie,' and something about pulling a plug."

"How did you leave him?"

"Flat on his back under the bedspread, lights off, pulse regular and strong, just on the edge of sleep. Physically he's fine." There was a pause. "Ann, it was either *that* or watch him crash and burn by Sunday. I've *seen* it before; I *wasn't* going to let it happen to a buddy if I could help it."

"His PTSD *can* be hard to manage, Blondie. Dad, I take it this call was *your* idea?"

"No; Donna's," Howard answered. "She insisted."

*And after I get Johnny unwound, this will be one great liberty.*

＊＊＊

*What...where... what? Am I awake or...?*

At first, it was hard to focus on anything. *Donna at the door; then what?* He felt strangely relaxed, slightly numb. *What's this bump on my forehead? WHAT in the name of...?*

He answered the phone in a haze. *Who? Yeah, sure.* Then a knock on the door: soft, hesitant. He pulled a sweatshirt on and went to the door.

Clare looked up at him; he was both stunned and suddenly alert. "*Leigh* said you needed company." She smiled her sweet, dimpled smile that not only warmed his heart but had once preserved his soul.

He embraced her gently, her cheek on his shoulder. "*Hungry,* Ware?" The atrium's weekend breakfast buffet had all that *anyone* could want, from to-order eggs to kippers in oil and tofu pudding.

"You *feel* OK?" Her soft voice was soothing to his jangled nerves; the aroma of her tea soothing—Clare never drank coffee. "Leigh said you had a lot on your plate, and *we* know what *that* means." He had spent more than *one* night at the DeHaven's home; he'd wakened them with *more* than one nightmare. "She thought *I* could help this morning."

"Yeah." He rubbed his forehead. "Woman slipped me a mickey. I feel better for it."

"Good. I..." She stopped because he waved at Lois, wandering among the tables. "Somebody you know?"

"Yeah. You never *met* my sister Lois."

"Hi, John," Lois glanced at Clare. "Hello."

"Lois McHenry, Clare Alton; Ware, Lo," he smiled. "I went to Brookfield with Clare, Lo."

"Oh, *you* went to *Greenbrier*? I *so* wanted to go there, but Dad nixed *that*. I was *so* jealous of Johnny when he..." Lois burbled.

"I *lived* on campus: my parents still teach there."

"Oh, *faculty* brat. I graduated from Central with Peter Manhart."

"Our next-door neighbor..."

JJ listened to the exchange, somewhat baffled. Lois was *not* a social butterfly, but the easy way she took to one of his dearest friends was *cautiously* gratifying.

Gradually their conversation slowed down until, awkwardly, both women stared at him in silence, like he'd missed his cue to suggest a *new* topic. "Leigh said you'd want to talk, John." Clare waited, expectantly.

*What's the FIRST thing on my mind?* "Charlie's dying, and I *don't* regret it." He inhaled deeply. "As you *well* know, Ware, the goddamn bastard's been a pain in my ass since he moved in. I love his sons, but there was a time I prayed for his sudden demise. He probably *won't* wake up; Mom's ambivalent about it; I can't help but think I *should* feel more of…*something*."

Clare and Lois looked at each other and smiled slightly as Clare murmured, "a lot of guilt there."

"But, I *should*…"

"You *should* own up to what you *feel*, John," Clare grinned, bundling her wiry hair over her shoulder, her eyes smiling. "Feelings are *feelings, darlin'*. You need to be more honest about them; come to terms with them, so they don't eat you alive. I've been *trying* to get you to do *that* since we *met*."

Lois looked confused. "Do…what?"

"*Talk* about Wolverine *and* Charlie; get *angry* about them; *cry* about what they *did* to you."

"That *school* you…?" Lois looked back and forth between them—Clare with a to-*her* unintelligible smile; JJ with an odd grin. "*Oh*," she sniffed. "*OK*. John, I have *stuff*; Simon and I have dinner with friends this evening. Clare, *so* nice to meet you."

"Yeah: *see* ya, Lo." As Lois left, he breathed a deep sigh. "I *have* been talking about them. Ann knows *most* of it; my *sisters* know almost nothing about Wolverine *or* my life with Charlie. It's so *pointless* to talk about."

"Doesn't mean you *shouldn't* talk about them."

"Yeah," he sighed. "Ware, I *love* you, but…"

"Your heart belongs to Ann. I know…it always *has*. I've *never* been the girl of your dreams, but I've *always* cared for you…"

"*You* were there, and *she* wasn't."

"We *needed each other*, darlin'."

"I'll always be grateful to you *and* your family, Ware. I'll *always* love you."

"And *we'll* always love *you*, John." She reached for his hand; he took it idly.

*Old lovers can be the best of friends.* They sat for a few long moments, not *looking* but *knowing*. "Ware, *I* have Army business today. We can get together tonight?"

"If you promise to buy me more than appetizers at happy hour."

He smiled. "*Jenny's* here, you know."

"Yeah," she smiled, "*right* over there: *I'm* gonna go say hi."

\*\*\*

"*They're* here *already*?" Leigh was surprised at the dry-cleaning truck as they drove past the gutted, the merely damaged, and the smoked-out buildings. The complex was already busy with people loading down cars, trailers, and trucks with their worldly goods. "Loaded like the Joads coming across."

"*They're* not dawdling. 'Joads coming across'? *Steinbeck*? *Really*?" Cathy looked dubiously amused.

"Lit class. We had to watch *The Grapes of Wrath* movie, too."

The dry-cleaning van was nearly three-quarters full outside their building. Cathy rolled down her window. "*We'll* have *more...*" she shouted to the boy next to the nearly-full van.

"We'll be back," the bulky kid promised.

"Poor-man's Schwarzenegger," Leigh grinned. "*Looks* like one, too."

They pinned their hair while Cathy read from the cleaning company's checklist. "OK. *First*, we have to bundle everything that needs to be *conserved*, like photographs, works of art, jewelry, and rare books. *THEN* we collect everything that needs to be *washed* or *dry-cleaned*, including clothes, linens, towels, curtains, blinds, seat covers, and throw rugs. *Then* we empty *all* the drawers, closets, cabinets, and shelves of what *can* be cleaned, including silverware, dishes, glasses, cups, mugs, pots and pans, and durable containers. *And*, we box up any small electric appliances that are *not* in sealed containers *and* the contents of any *unsealed* containers with consumables so the insurance adjusters can inventory it."

"OK, what I'm *hearing*, is: if it *moves*, it *will* be moved. If it *can* be cleaned—somehow—it *will* be. If it cannot be cleaned in *any* manner...?"

"It *should be* discarded. And if it's *not* marked *or* stacked *or* piled *or* bundled one way or another, it WILL be pitched...but they'll write a check for it."

"*Piece* of cake, Mom."

They began by stacking and layering family photographs, paintings and pastels by Leigh and Cathy's mother, using rolls of brown paper placed on every sidewalk. They labeled each stack CONSERVE and put them on the living room sofa that had become too dirty to sit on anyway. Since Wednesday, *everything* had acquired another layer of soot.

They collected knick-knacks into the cardboard boxes stacked in front of every garage, left open on the floor. They left all the drawers and cabinets empty and slightly ajar. They threw the refrigerator's *and* the freezer's contents—packages and all—into a dumpster labeled FOOD WASTE.

It was *like* moving because they found things they hadn't seen in years: a collection of kitchen gadgets Cathy bought at the state fair and *maybe* used once (Salvation Army collection bin—the lot); a Polaroid camera that Leigh just *had* to have at Christmas in 7th Grade (no film available —trash); a pipe stand that Ed used during his brief pipe-smoking stint after college (joined the kitchen gadgets)—and *WHY DID WE MOVE ALL THIS JUNK THE LAST TIME*?

82

Leigh donned protective gear to venture into the soot-covered utility/storage space. Christmas tree ornaments, a few of which came from Ed's mother, were saved from those Stygian depths. So were Leigh's Donna-made senior winter-formal gown and Cathy's wedding dress. She wiped off the locked hard case that contained Ed's 12-gauge Browning A-5 and 16-gauge pump shotgun and put them in the car.

*** 

"Looking for Captain Marsh?" The trip to the Frasier Reserve Center wasn't far in *miles*, but it *was* cross-town Detroit—a half-hour one-way.

"Right," the woman in civilian clothes behind a desk pointed, "classroom three doors down on the right, *that* way. You're Sergeant Elrath?"

"Guilty." He'd decided to wear BDUs just-in-case.

"Roger was *hoping* you would come," she smiled, standing up with some effort. "I'm Sherry, his wife."

*VERY pregnant.* "Ma'am," he smiled. "Glad to meet you."

"No 'ma'am' to it, Sarge; I'm a Sergeant E-7. This outfit gets two clerk-typists and a personnel section NCO, and *I'm all three of 'em*." She stretched her back. "Even my *maternity* uniform doesn't fit anymore."

"When are you due if I *may*…?"

"*TOMORROW*," she shouted, "everybody *else* asks; why not you? And I'm not feeling a *twinge* from her either. Go on down and see Roger."

"Can I *help* you?" A lieutenant behind a podium teaching a land navigation subject voiced his annoyance when JJ opened the back door.

"Sergeant Elrath for Captain Marsh?" The mostly-full classroom had school desks in the center and plastic chairs lining the walls. All heads turned to look.

"Right," Roger answered from the back of the room. "Let's take this outside. *Carry on* with the class." He was shorter and darker than JJ, with a genuine smile and one brown eye and one blue eye, his most distinctive feature.

"Wanted to see how the Reserve component lives," JJ smiled. "I *got* a 14-day extension on my leave."

"*Out*standing. Listen: What I'd like *you* to do for *us* if you're *willing*…"

*** 

"You should think about joining the men's council, Mike. We could *use* a younger man's perspective." Mike and his parents went to a late lunch at the Bloomfield Hills Athletic Club after services. It was a tony New Money establishment that served a full menu only on weekends and holidays. More importantly, it had never restricted membership to white Gentiles.

"Maybe I will, Pops." The formally-informal, officially-unofficial gathering of men discussed community matters like the price of specific seats on high holy days, building repairs, and other issues outside the purview of more formal bodies. "I want to see some of the cousins outside the holidays; might take some doing."

"It would *that*," Monica said. "As of the first of this month, I have fifty-five nephews and sixty-four nieces. About *half* live in the 313-area code."

Suddenly Mike was seized by a curiosity that had never struck him before. "How did you two meet? Pops grew up here in Detroit, and *your* family was in Saginaw, Mama? And you were in the Jewish Relief?"

"Yes, and if Roosevelt's Treasury Secretary *hadn't* been named Morgenthau, we never would have existed. We worked *with* the USO: our Yiddish *felt* more like home for Jewish soldiers. We seven women and five men from western Michigan were sent to San Francisco when the boys came back from the Pacific."

"So, you met at a demobilization camp?"

"No, we met at a transit terminal in San Francisco," Ben said.

"You see any action?"

Ben grinned sagely. "Depends on what *you* call 'action.' I was assigned to the 1027$^{th}$ Air Material Squadron, in the 509$^{th}$ Composite Group, stationed at Tinian." He paused. "You *know* what…"

"Yeah, Pops."

*If people only know ONE UNIT in the whole of WWII, they know that the 509$^{th}$ dropped the A-bombs.*

*** * ***

"The cooks are glad for another name," Roger mumbled as JJ signed the mess roster. He shook hands with Roger's two lieutenants and senior Ranger-qualified NCO—a big Hispanic E-7 with a Combat Infantry Badge named Guevarra.

"How's *that*?" Enlisted people got a half-decent Thanksgiving-themed meal of turkey roll and canned gravy with *real* mashed potatoes for the cost of a signature on the meal card roster. Officers paid a pittance but signed anyway. Not having cooks assigned, the Rangers got *their* chow from the engineer company that drilled on the same weekend.

"If a unit's roster shows a hundred showing up for drill, they expect to *feed* a hundred. But not everyone *stays* for chow, so they're *always* short on signatures. If they *stay* short, the brass starts to wonder if it's worth it to feed the units or even *keep* 'em."

"Are they *that* cheap, even with the Reagan River?" The *Reagan River* was the sudden cornucopia of supplies, equipment, and training opportunities that began to appear not long after Ronald Reagan took office in '81.

"Was *worse* during the Carter Crunch." *This* started after Jimmy Carter announced that his administration would be known for *style rather than substance*. "Even in the Active, we couldn't get spare parts for gas masks."

"And *damn* little realistic training," one of the lieutenants mumbled. "But, we've wrangled a *very special* annual training this year: A challenge course down at Fort Benning with Ranger school instructors. Two weeks and we'll find out how many of *these* guys have what it takes."

"An afternoon in The Pit, and you'll *know*," JJ winced. The Pit was a gymnasium-sized cinder block enclosure floored with wood chips and sand. Twice a day, six days a week for the first week, Ranger wannabes did PT in The Pit.

"*Damn* straight," Guevarra grunted. In the afternoon session every day for the first month, they did pushups in The Pit until *someone* quit…no matter *how* long it took.

***

*I'm gonna miss this place…*

"Hey, Ann," Laura called in the door. "Just coming back with the laundry."

*But not THAT.* "Hey," Ann answered, trying to act as if it weren't her *last* Saturday in Key West. "Weekly chores just *don't* end."

"Nope," Betty said, coming in behind Laura with her basket. "Don't get *any*…"

The phone rang; Laura answered, said, "sure," and handed Ann the phone, shrugging, "*Claudia* Ann?"

*One person on God's Earth calls me that.* "Hi, Sid."

"*Hi*, Claudia Ann," Sid Jackwell answered in his deep, resonating voice. "I trust I find you well."

"*Very* well, thanks, about to go up by *you* soon…"

"Yes, I *know*."

"*How* did *you* know?"

"That's what I wanted to tell you. My source in the Newhouse organization says that it is *known* that you are going to Alaska in December."

"That's….*so*, but…how did *they* know?"

"I don't know. My *dear* friend, I must warn you that someone in the Newhouse organization who means John Elrath harm has decided that they will strike while you and he are in Detroit. My source thinks *something has* happened…not sure *what*, but somehow it's become more *urgent*."

"Well, I'm going to be up there Monday night. Do they know *that*?"

"No, they only know that you'll be around from before Thanksgiving to the end of the month. Claudia…contact *me*, of course. You have my number. Have Mr. Elrath call if he needs to."

"I'll do that, Sid."

***

"I'm SFC Elrath, and I just left HHC 4/75 in Key West Wednesday on PCS to Alaska. Captain Marsh asked me to tell *you guys* about a modern Ranger's life." The company gathered in the classroom after chow, with JJ at the podium.

"I'm a *summer* Ranger, an intel analyst by trade. *That* said, I've served with Rangers and Special Forces for *nearly* all my thirteen-year career, and it's *not* the kind of life that's at *all* good for the *rest* of your life. Here's a little ditty I

85

first heard at Fort Benning…to the tune of 'Pop Goes the Weasel:'

> *I don't go out with girls at night! I live a life of danger!*
> *I sit at home and play with myself! Whee! I'm a Ranger!*

He let the giggling die down. "There's a *lot more* truth to that than the *movies* tell you. Sure, Rangers lead the way, *and* we have a *stratospheric* divorce rate because we're *always* training, *always* tired when we get back, and *always* on the verge of being sick. *Sua Sponte*: of our own accord—that's our regimental motto. We're triple volunteers: we *volunteered* for the Army, we *volunteered* for jump school, and we *volunteered* to be Rangers. Since we did all that volunteering, Uncle Sam *also* expects us to do a metric *shit*-load more *of our own accord; far* more than you *ever have* done…including *living* on your own as a Ranger. As elites, we are *expected* to be *instantly* ready for deployments; *Reserves* or not; civilian *job* or not; *marriage problems* or not; *kid's ball games*…or *not*.

"Our lives are *not* our own; our futures are unclear except for *one more* mission as long as we're in the Army. Our training is expensive, and Uncle Sam *must* get his money's worth. We're military athletes who have to be prepared to *get* hurt, and *be* hurt, *all* the time, regardless of precautions or training. I've got health issues from jumping out of airplanes and being out in the weather that I'll have until I die. We live and work with people who kill quietly and anonymously, who take *no bullshit* from *anyone*. *One* false step, and you're on *their* bad side…and that's *not* a place you *want* to be.

"Like a priesthood, *many* are called to special ops, but *damn* few are chosen. The Green Berets figure about three percent makes it through all their training— yeah, like the song—which *includes* Ranger school. It can take a decade—from start to finish—to complete. The Navy's SEALs have a failure rate a lot like ours—a third in every cycle—but their in-service attrition's higher. Most are *never* in an operational team for more than one tour before they get out. That's one reason why their *complete* training takes as long as Special Forces. I know because I've partied with SEALs. The Air Force Pararescue, Coast Guard rescue swimmers: their training's a *little* easier, but their attrition is worse because *they* have a peacetime, continuing mission. Overall, about three percent of *all* special operators are still physically, mentally, and emotionally capable after twenty years of service. That includes us, the Brits, the Germans, the French, the Israelis. *One* percent of Soviet *Spetsnaz* operators make it to military retirement age these days…*alive*. Thank the *Mujahedeen* for *that* number." A ripple of laughter broke the gloom.

"Captain Marsh tells me he needs to recruit to 80% of his assigned strength by the end of next September: a little over a hundred twenty guys. He *also* needs to have no less than 60% of *those* to be tab-qualified within two years of joining. Of the first batch he sends to Ranger school, maybe 60% will pass the first time. He *also* tells me that you'll only get *one* recycle as a member of this unit. And you'll be a year *older* when you get that *second* crack at it; and, yeah, *that twelve months WILL matter, brother.* And there are no more *summer* Rangers: they scrapped *that* in '75.

"So: you either *love*…no, *crave* this *bullshit, ultra*-demanding, *screwed*-up-from-the-get-go goat-rope of a way of life to *death* or go find yourself a unit that's a *lot* easier on *you.* Questions?"

There followed a palpable, almost deafening, hush. The silence was broken when an airborne-qualified staff sergeant about JJ's age raised his hand. "Settle a bet: did *you* have Captain Marsh as an instructor?"

"I *did.* He *didn't* flunk me, and *now* he *probably* regrets it." Chuckles.

"You said you have health issues. Are you getting compensation for them?" This was one of the lieutenants.

"I *am.* VA tells me I'll get more after I leave the Active."

"When will women be allowed in the Rangers?" This was from a younger man with an Expert Infantry Badge.

"*Good* question. Be advised that there *are* women in Ranger *units*—airborne-qualified but *not* Rangers—who *go out with* them often enough." Some guffaws. "But there's no 'dating' between uniform personnel—you *know* that—but *that* don't stop hormones." A ripple of laughter. "You need to ask *Congress* when women are going to be going to Ranger school. Then ask God *not* to lower the standards so women can pass *more easily.*" More chuckles.

"Were you in Grenada?"

"Me and about seven thousand other guys."

"Sergeant, are *you* married?" This from a young man in civvies, probably still in high school.

"I *will* be soon."

"But, doesn't that divorce rate kinda make you think you *shouldn't?*"

"Special operations is the easiest kind of outfit to get *out* of: just terminate your special duty status. I *had* to terminate when I left Key West. I may *not* go back on it. I'll *keep* the qualification *and* the aches and pains."

"How did your special operator work affect your girlfriend?" This from the First Sergeant, who looked like an early Sergeant Rock.

"*Good* one, Top. I've been fortunate to love a Navy diver associated with special ops herself. We…"

"Oh! *You* were in the paper," another lieutenant exclaimed. "The soldier-scholar and the lady diver."

"Yessir, that's us."

"You wrote a book." This from a deep voice in the far back of the room.

"I did: *Profiles in Leadership. Some* folks like it…"

"And some of us *love* it," the voice replied. "Can I get an autograph?"

"Congratulations, Sergeant Elrath, and thank you." Roger interrupted. "Any more *relevant* questions? No? Out*standi*ng. Fall in on the drill floor for land navigation problems in one-five mikes. Smoke 'em if you've got 'em; bum from your buddy if you don't."

As the classroom cleared out, a bull-like colonel made his way forward; one of those full-chest types prevalent in special ops whose BDUs were running out of space for badges. "Jed Forester," he announced as he offered his hand, "commanding 10<sup>th</sup> Group in Chicago. I happen to agree with *everything* you said, and I *really do* like your book."

"Glad *someone* does," JJ smiled, scribbling in the battered, dog-eared book. "Took enough to write it."

"It *shows*, Sergeant. Hal McCann called me last night," Jed confided. "We'll work *something* out if your situation should *come* to that. I hope your family can ride out this storm." He handed JJ his military business card with a Chicago number scribbled on the back. "Call anytime, day or night."

Roger extended his hand after Jed left. "*Just about* what I was looking for, Sarge. We may lose *some*, but at least they will have been warned what they're in for."

"Your job offer: how long's it good for?"

"Until I fill the slot. *Sherry's* about to pop, so I'll have my hands too *full* to think about it for another few weeks."

***

"*Done* shuffling these boxes around," Leigh muttered to herself. She stripped off her sweatshirt and jeans while pondering the fact that the contents of the twenty-odd boxes in her bedroom represented the totality of her pre-Army life. "This stuff either *fits,* or it *doesn't*." One by one, she opened each box and flipped through its contents, making keep/toss decisions—*mostly* toss—before moving on to the next box. She kept a couple of T-shirts, three skirts, and two pairs of jeans that still fit. She held onto some art books and some *very* expensive pastels, brushes and watercolors, more than a *few* sketchbooks, canvases, palettes, a desktop easel, and a couple of nylon jackets.

The discard pile gained the girdle she just HAD to have in 8th Grade—that she wore for a half-hour, and never again—and heaps of other clothes. The last box contained her first *gi* and her yellow belt and a silk-lined brown leather jacket, hardly worn and too big on her.

"Do you remember *this*?" She showed Cathy. "It *didn't* go to Cambridge."

Cathy made a curious face, fingered the zippered cuffs, touched the butter-soft leather. "*Not* at all. Didn't Randy help pack those boxes?"

"*Some* of 'em." Leigh found a small black faux-leather address book with gilt edges and little metallic corners in an inner pocket. She studied the entries—*some in Randy's handwriting; some not.*

*Is THIS what he's after?*

***

"*Hey,* big guy," JJ smiled, "to what do I owe *this* honor?" Not expecting anything for a couple of hours, JJ was surprised to see Will in the hotel lobby.

"Just…something been weighing on my mind, buddy," Will answered. "Something I *should* have told you a while ago."

"OK, c'mon. I'll buy you a beer."

"You *know* that *I* went to Wolverine for high school." Will sipped his Stroh's gingerly.

"No, I *didn't* know that."

"Yeah. In '59…Christmas time…Dad came home and said, 'I've got this *great* place for *you* to go to *school* next year.'"

"Huh." *More polite than the "you're going" chat I got.*

"Mom went and looked around, said, 'if you *want*, go ahead.' I was on a military kick at the time, so I *went*. It was *different*, but I *liked* it."

"How many beatings did *you* take in your first year?"

"My first two years were *nothing* like what *you* saw—and I know a *little*. In my senior year, I was a cadet captain in command of B Company. Some of the guys *that* year were *animals*. One of 'em liked to keep his roommates awake by demanding they sing *his* favorite song all night. If they *didn't*, they'd get clobbered with a rolled-up towel."

"We called that a *crop*. What did *you* do about it?"

"I handed him demerits; he laughed and tore up the slips right in front of me. I went to the battalion commander like I was *supposed* to, and he went to the Commandant. He held a hearing and handed the kid fifteen demerits."

"Pretty stiff."

"*Would* have been, except those demerits disappeared because he had *merits*. No idea where *they* came from, but…" Will stopped, looked a little haunted. "But he *didn't stop doing it*. And he did *worse*. That was December, just before Christmas. That year, there were a dozen or so guys who stayed at Wolverine for Christmas break. Nobody *had* before.

"I came back in January, and we had a *new* battalion commander; some guy who came in in September. 'Henceforth,' he said, 'discipline is a *battalion* matter, not a *school* matter. You are *not* to trouble the school with disciplinary issues that do *not* affect school functions.'" Will shook his head. "Didn't make any *sense*. After that, we kept getting new guys; mean and messed-up guys, right up to April. Never *had* before.

"Understand that when I started there, about half the student body were legacy boys; sons and grandsons of graduates. Most of the rest were like me: guys who just wanted an education in that environment. But these *new* guys not only *didn't* want an education, but they also didn't want to be *there*. A lot of us who'd been there a while—some who'd been there longer—agreed something was screwed up, but…it *had* to have been the *school* changing something. Had a mandatory party with some girl's school on the other side of town…"

"Francis Hartmann School."

"Yeah! Half of 'em were pregnant; the other half had *razors* in their bras."

"Will, my brother; *you* need to talk to our *niece* and *her* people…"

89

\*\*\*

"If it's *his* property, it needs to be returned, but Randy hasn't *specifically* asked for it?" Ben looked at the notebook carefully for several minutes before speaking.

"Of all the legal actions, none mention *any* personal property," Cathy replied.

"Christ *Almighty*," Leigh groaned, "*Why* do I feel the need to write an after-action?" *Did I keep the box?* "*And* the need for evidence tags and bags?" *What else was in the box with it? What's driving my suspicion? Have I become a habitual cop?*

"I'll go see Dorothy; she *might have* bags and tags," Cathy mumbled, shrugging her coat on.

"I'll go *with*, Mom," Leigh sighed, grabbing her coat.

\*\*\*

"There's a difference between my cold dreams and my hot ones," Jesse Kent declared as the dinner dishes were cleared in the hotel restaurant. "*Cold* ones wake me up; *hot* ones wake me up *hard*." Jenny's husband was a five-foot-ten, 250-pound, blue-eyed African-American with a big round head and muscular arms.

"Which is worse," JJ asked while Clare and Jenny talked of old friends.

"Hot. I can get back to sleep after the cold. Can't after the hot."

"How's the shoulder?"

"*Ain't* that bad. *Something* grazed my right knee in '68 that ain't been right since, and another hot *something* gouged my forehead down to the bone a year later that *still* hurts worse than my *knee*, sometimes. After all *that...this* ain't nothin'."

"What was your rating?"

"Gunner's Mate: the *one* thing I couldn't do *anything* with on the street. I joined the Navy in '65, needing to do something my daddy *didn't* do and get out of the Everglades. I did an 11-month tour in the Mekong Delta '68-'69, and I was back in the swamps! But, *man*, that weren't nothin' but *aching* routine punctuated by rare terror. I re-upped for the money and did an 8-month bit turning boats over to the ARVNs in '71, got out in '73. The VA awarded me a 40% disability that meant I could get a free ride for my degree, where I met my Jen."

"*And* nightmares that he'd only *recently started* talking about," Jenny added.

"Sorry for that," JJ muttered. "I have flashes from time to time. There was a training accident in Germany; a bunch of guys burned up in a command vehicle. I was dumb enough to be the first to open the back door." He stopped, looked around. "Don't mean to play 'more miserable than thou.' Sorry."

Jesse looked blank for a moment before he spoke. "*Crispy critters* at *dinner*, man?"

Jenny giggled; Clare laughed. "Yeah, JJ. *Real* good dinner conversation."

"Well," JJ started, "at *least* I'm *not* talking about what we had to eat in jungle

90

school in Panama."

"Ah, good thing too," Jesse grinned. "Else, I'd have to talk 'bout some of the stuff my daddy used to bring home for supper."

"That book you talked about on our one *real* date, JJ," Jenny remembered. "Something that had all kinds of bodies in it."

"Stalingrad, maybe...no, it was Shiloh. I remember now: 'bodies so numerous one could walk across the field without touching the ground.'"

"*Lovely*, JJ." Clare frowned. "Let's talk about *sex* now. We've *had* the violence."

"*Ho*," Jesse exclaimed, "not with *Jen*, we don't. Skinny dippin' and all..."

"It was *dark*, and we were..."

"Teenagers," Jenny grinned.

"*Really*," Clare chuckled, a strange grin on her face. "*We* never went skinny dipping, JJ. You never even asked *me*."

"You *wouldn't* have...*would* you?"

"You never *asked*. I wanna try it *tonight*, Jen." *There* was apple-cheeked Clare's *infamous* grin.

"Here. Right *now*, Clare," Jenny loudly declared, getting out of her chair. "Come *on*."

"Jesse, this was *your* idea. You gotta stop 'em."

"Stop 'em, *hell*. *I'm* thinkin' maybe I should sell tickets." The back of the restaurant opened to the atrium, which led to the pool. The ladies, chattering and giggling, walked determinedly through the happy hour buffet to the glass-enclosed pool, kicking off their shoes. The men followed dutifully, with the occasional glance over their shoulders. To the gents' grateful surprise, *skinny-dipping* it was *not*...but *swimming* it was. Both ladies wore suits under their clothes and laughed at their dates as they stripped poolside and jumped in.

"Wonder whose idea *this* was," JJ muttered, watching them.

"My Jen's a free spirit; God bless her," Jesse mumbled. He glanced at JJ. "Clare's just a friend, yeah?"

"Yeah. *Good* friend, *sort of* like a sister."

*Now.*

## Sunday

"Green-Eyes, dear; *first* things *first*: *thanks* for calling Clare." In the little church's basement, where coffee and treats were served during the social hour after services, JJ and Leigh isolated themselves in an out-of-the-way corner after meeting *quite* coincidentally...*really*.

"My *dear* Blue-Eyes, you know *it should not* have been *me*." She chose *not* to wear the ugly tab tie with her old-style round-collar blouse.

"Yeah. Since we're getting *married* now, we *need* to..."

"After eighteen years, I gotta say this: I'd *love* to *make love* to you."

He smiled, puckered slightly. "*Seventeen* years, Green-Eyes. And *I've* wanted

91

to get *you naked between the sheets* since we first went swimming."

"We *were* half-naked *on top* of the sheets last August. Now, we *can't* do that to Ann *or* Mike."

"No. We *should* talk to the pastor."

"You *read* my *mind.*"

"As well as *you* read *mine*," They found bulbous-nosed, wispy-haired Pastor Lou Beckham near the coffee urn. "Padre," JJ started at length, "we need to talk about weddings."

"My office is upstairs." They followed him into a long hall that still smelled of drywall mud, paint, and carpet glue. Lengths of uninstalled shoe molding lay on the floor along the baseboards. "I remember *you*, young man. You donated the new furnace in your father's name."

"Yessir. We need a wedding," JJ began once they reached his office, noting that *this* pastor did not affect a clerical collar like some of his predecessors.

"*Two* weddings," Leigh added.

"Yes, you *had* different partners in January," Pastor Lou said. "Get Margaret, our secretary, to book..."

"Just a few details, though," Leigh interrupted. "My groom's Jewish. Will you hold a *joint* service with a rabbi here?"

Pastor Lou looked thoughtful but not surprised. "Never done *that* here. Will you want a canopy?"

"I'm sure he'd *like* one. *You* were a chaplain?"

"Lieutenant-Commander, USN. I retired and took *this* job. I'll speak to the deacons. I'm sure it will be all right." He smiled. "But *you two* knew each other *before*?"

"Youth group with Dr. Bull," JJ answered. "How would *you*...?"

Pastor Lou pointed to their photo in a gallery on the wall: there they were, grinning for the camera in 1970, standing closer together than any other two kids. "All I know of Howard Bull is his picture over there." He smiled at JJ. "Your family has a long history with this church, yes?"

"Since it was founded." JJ turned to Leigh. "My grandparents signed the church charter two years before Mom was born."

"Huh," she smiled. "You talk to the secretary *first*, JJ; *we've* got a bigger window."

✱✱✱

"Haven't been to River Hills since *last* Christmas." JJ declared as he pulled into the parking lot alongside the White House-like main building of the country club, one of the oldest in Michigan.

"Roy and I were at a wedding reception here maybe ten years ago," Brenda mused. She was a small woman, compact but not frail, with her father's oval face and dark coloring. "Hasn't changed a jot since."

"No," Stella muttered. "Let's not linger too long. I want to get to the hospital

92

this afternoon, see how his kidney infection's doing."

The main dining room with its old *fleur de lis* wallpaper, chandeliers, and sconce lighting suffered from an odd combination of a stuffy-air center and cold drafts along the sides. The Elraths and the Taylors sat at a large round eight-setting table. The dining room was a third full, but Cathy waved to someone just entering. "Harry Gordon, everyone." Harry was about six feet tall and 200 pounds, fair of face and hair, if coarse of beard, wearing a turtleneck with a tailored suit.

"Join us," Ed said, gesturing to an empty chair.

"Don't *mind* if I *do*." Harry's long legs slipped neatly under the table. His voice and eyes were clear; his grip sure and firm. "So, *you're* Leigh," Harry smiled, forking a piece of beef. The flow of conversation was naturally—briefly—interrupted by forays for food.

"Yes, I'm *her*."

"What is it you *do* in the Army, Leigh," Stella asked, savoring an omelet.

"Military police," Leigh replied, trying to get something in her mouth before she had to answer another question.

"Didn't know there *were* WAC MPs."

"Yes, ma'am, there *are* women MPs now; the WAC went away in 1978."

"How do you like it," Brenda asked, hacking into some hash browns.

"Oh, I *love* it," Leigh smiled between bacon strips. "Fun, travel, adventure. I'm in criminal investigations now."

"What do *you* do in the Army, JJ," Harry asked.

"Nothing as *exciting* as Leigh. I sort information into piles, then write about the piles."

"Where are you guys stationed?" Harry *seemed* innocuous enough.

"Alaska," JJ answered, sipping coffee. "I'm due there by December."

"*Here*," Leigh shrugged. "Criminal frauds in Troy."

"Where all have you guys *been*?" Brenda looked genuinely curious.

"Well," they both said before JJ mumbled, "go."

She listed her many assignments, ending with "…Top *that*," grinning at JJ.

He listed *his*, finishing with, "…How'd I *do*?"

"You two ever in the same place?" Brenda seemed *uncomfortably* curious.

"Grenada for a week," Leigh replied. "Surprised to *see* him, too."

"Dumbfounded *me*, but I could never forget her eyes," JJ grinned.

"Our green eyes are our trademark," Cathy smiled, "just like your *blue* eyes are."

"*Thank* you," Stella nodded. "There was something in the paper about their meeting at a banquet. But socializing wasn't what they were *there* for."

"No," Leigh sighed. "Me and the *other* dozen female MPs out of Fort Bragg were there for *photo-ops*, mostly…"

"They picked a bunch of *us* out of the infantry," Harry lamented, "gave us brassards and said 'you're now a military cop. Act like it.'"

"Korea, yeah?" Cathy glanced at Ed quickly.

"Yep. I started in the 2nd Infantry Division and ended up in the 55th MP Group."

"Huh," Leigh frowned. "I thought the MPs were formalized *before* Korea." She sensed that there was something *more* between Harry and Cathy than just being fellow club members.

"There were *never* enough of 'em," Harry said. "We did what the *real* MPs *told* us to do. It wasn't until I reenlisted and said I wanted to *be* an MP that I got formal training. After I left the Active Army, I joined the 46th MPs and retired two years ago."

During brunch, Leigh had been as personally warm as possible without using the fake sincerity and ersatz concern that *MP-mode* required. All that time, one of many eye-contacts Leigh could *not* pass off was that of a busboy, perhaps five-ten and 170 pounds…before she finally recognized Dave Harriman.

"*Pit* stop," Leigh announced. Glancing at JJ, she cocked her head ever-so-slightly. *Read my mind, Blue-Eyes: I know you can...*

*Like a book, Green-Eyes.* JJ made excuses himself, following Leigh until they were out of sight. Without looking at him, she whispered, "I need to ask this guy some questions. Make sure nobody gets curious?"

"Check."

***

Dave *politely* followed her down a long hall, stopping to loiter a discrete distance from the ladies' room door.

Inside…*OK; I can make myself hot enough for Dave. Let's see if this dim-bulb knows anything about fires…*

*Christ, Green-Eyes; THAT'S WORK?* JJ, better positioned between the dining room and Dave than she thought *he* knew how, couldn't hear *what* she said, but he *could* hear *how* she said it.

"*Hi*, Dave," she purred as she sauntered towards him in the long hall, her jacket folded over her arms. "Long time no *see*."

"Leigh," Dave grunted. "Didn't think *you'd* come back here."

*You've got something to say, little fish; now say it to ME.* "Why *not*?" She put on a saucy grin, sashaying towards him with her arms crossed, lifting her chest. "This is my *home*, Dave."

"Because Mr. Newhouse wants you *and* your old lady dead."

*Still in the fold.* "Yesterday's fish wrap, Dave."

"Huh?"

*Still stupid, too.* "Heard it before."

"After what she did *three weeks* ago, he's *serious*."

*HERE's the bait, little fish; SO luscious. You won't feel the hook when you swallow it, I promise.* "What *happened*, Dave?" She spoke in a low, saucy voice, pressing her arms against his chest with his back against the wall, spreading her

94

blouse open.

"Ask your old lady. She's messed with Mr. Newhouse's business for the *last time*. We'll *teach her...*"

*Just keep nibbling, little fish...* "Teach her *what*, Dave? Teach her *how*?"

"I know *who*, and I know *what* and *when...*" He went quiet.

*TAKE this bait, little fish. You KNOW you WANT it.* "Just *tell* me, Dave. *You* can tell *me anything*. I can keep *your* secret." *This draft is giving me goosebumps and your stare...* "Just *say* what's on your mind, Dave. You'll *feel* better."

He shook his overlarge head and sighed heavily. "Last Tuesday night..."

*You WHAT?*

***

"*So*, Charlie: *here* we are." JJ sat alone in Charlie's room, machines blinking and whirring. Stella and Brenda had gone out to talk with Charlie's regular doctor, who had been out of town all week.

*Green Eyes, if that poor SOB knew what happened to Hoffa, he'd have spilled then and there.* He could not shake the memory of Leigh's studied-and-slow hip-swinging stroll down that hallway. She left that poor busboy in her wake—leaning against the wall, stunned—gaping after her retreating figure. As she passed JJ and entered the dining room, she hastened to put her jacket back on before everyone *else* saw her. *Ever* the gent, JJ helped, struggling *not* to glance down her half-open blouse. He closed his eyes and smiled at the warm memory...until he remembered where he was.

"Why *should* I give a *damn* that you're here like this?" JJ took in the antiseptic-tainted, oxygenated air of the room, wincing at the bleach-funk of the sheets and the booze-sweat that Charlie still exuded. He looked around the mostly sterile room: a card from GM; another from Sherith's outfit and another from Rockland's; one from his dealership; photos of him and Stella. He was surprised to see that his mother *had* kept—and *framed*—newspaper articles about him that stood on a side table.

Then he noticed Charlie staring at him. For an instant, he thought he'd rush out and find his mom.... Then... "Nope: *not yet*, Charlie. You're not gettin' off *that* easy. I *do* hope you can *hear* me, 'cause you sure-as-*hell* can't interrupt me." He took a deep breath. "You may be a good businessman, but you're one sorry-assed, *rotten to the core, goat-rope of an excuse* for a human being. We never saw eye-to-eye on anything but my mother's need for support, and you've *done* that. My sisters and I thank you."

Charlie blinked—or *seemed* to—and turned his head slightly away. "I don't know *what* or *who* made you the drunken bully that you are, and *I don't care*. We *knew* you weren't Dad, but you were such an *anti*-Dad that it was impossible to even *start* to like you. God *knows* Brenda and I tried—Lois, *not* so much. Lois is the smartest person I know, and *she*, at least, knows when to *shut up*.

"You've got a bubble in your head that'll *probably* burst and kill you. If it wasn't for Mom, I *really* wouldn't care, and no one *else* does. Everyone dies alone among strangers; *your* death is the only experience you *can't* share. So here you *are*, you miserable sonofabitch. I just wish you'd hurry the hell up and *do* your Mortal-Coil-Shuffle so the rest of us can get on with our lives."

JJ stood up; Charlie turned his head again, his dull eyes tearing. "Thanks for providing a *perfect* example of how *not* to raise kids." He found Stella just down the hall. "Mom, his eyes are open."

Stella and the doctor hurried back into the room, leaving Brenda and JJ alone in the vending lobby when he Debbie and waved. "Hi, Johnny," she smiled. "And...Brenda? *Wow!* It's been..."

"Bren, *you* remember Debbie Ford from Round Lake?"

Brenda squinted. "Um, the *name* I remember, but it *has been* twenty years."

"Up here for work," Debbie said. "Your stepfather, Johnny."

"Yeah? He *may* be awake. And *congrats*, Deb! When are you due?"

"February," she sighed. "Not soon enough for *me*. Ann's due in tomorrow?"

"Yeah." He led her to Charlie's room, where Stella and the doctor were trying to get a response. "Mom, Debbie *Ford*..." he began.

"Oh, *hi* Debbie," Stella gushed, happily distracted. "*Bell*, now, isn't it?"

JJ shook his head in amazement. *Mom hasn't seen Deb in twenty years...*

"I hyphenated, Mrs. Parkinson," Debbie replied. "Too much trouble to change it everywhere. I'm up here for Mr. Parkinson's therapy."

"We need to clear out, then," the doctor muttered, ushering everyone else towards the door.

*Patient response to communications not noted, and nobody cared.*

✳✳✳

"So, let me get this straight. This Harriman character—what—just *flat-out admitted* that he drove some guys to our complex but got the *address* wrong?" It was dark when the Taylor's got back to the cottage; Cathy was *still* in disbelief.

"That's *about* the size of it," Leigh replied absently, outlining a report in her head. *I wish I had taken notes...*

"Huh." Ed glanced at his daughter as they got out of the car. "You take your *bra* off to do *that* kind of thing a lot?"

"*That* was an expedient that I knew would *work*. My techniques get results."

"Dorothy Parkinson was impressed, bra or *no* bra," Cathy mumbled as they climbed the stairs. "Newhouse didn't like something *I* did three weeks ago," She tossed her keys on the kitchen island. "Can't imagine *what*. As a prosecutor, I've never had *any* Newhouse-related cases. I hand 'em all off."

✳✳✳

"*Buy* you a drink, Bren. *No* ain't an option."

"Well, if you put it *that* way." The Fishin' Hole was a non-descript little saloon in Cass Lake on the way to Roy's family home, with mounted fish and old fishing gear on the walls and a TV on a shelf behind the bar. Since it was bow-deer-hunting season, it had maybe a half-dozen people inside. Regulars would have been either Up North (anywhere north or west of Detroit) or *said* they were.

"Strange, ain't it, Bren? The old man's dying, and all *I* can think of is that he's leaving Mom alone." Brother and sister sat on vinyl-covered steel stools at the ornate bar. The TV had the Bears game on: a radio by the pool table blared the Lion's Silverdome pummeling by the Vikings.

"Don't know how *strange* it is, Johnny. *We* never thought much of him, anyway." Never close as kids, the three were entirely different personality-wise and hadn't *had* many grown-up conversations.

"I told the bastard off, Bren. Don't know if he under*stood*, but..."

"Doesn't matter, Johnny," she muttered; her voice was so soft JJ could barely hear her. "What matters is that *you* heard it." They were intimate strangers in an overheated-yet-drafty neighborhood tavern. A brother and sister who barely knew each other discussing a mutual nemesis, trying to reconnect to a shared past while remembering that past only in unshared fragments.

"Not *especially* cathartic." He sighed, glancing around. "I never really *got* saloon culture. Sitting on a stool, chatting up strangers. Never did it much, never *saw* it much as a kid. I mean, how many are *in* Bloomfield Hills, anyway?"

"*Not* many," she admitted. "But Charlie found them."

"No; he mostly drank at the club or the living room. Dad never drank."

"Not like *that*. We still had the wet bar in the basement on Round Lake and one out in the shed." A building behind their home on Birch Lake was called *the shed*, even *after* half of it was furnished as a rec room.

"*That* was for the business," he muttered.

"How *often* was it *used* for business," she pressed.

"Once in a blue moon."

She smiled; he nodded. "How's the Army treating you these days?"

"Like beavers treat trees. But if it weren't for the Army, I'd never have found Ann again."

"Looking forward to seeing *her* again. What's it been—1968 since she came to the house with her dad; *eighteen* years."

"Eighteen years next Friday. Yeah: 21 November '68." The day they buried their father. "You *think* of it much?"

"Around this time of year." They were quiet. "Hope Charlie survives the month."

"Yeah. Bren ...tell me: *Did* Charlie offer Roy money to just walk away before the wedding?"

"*Nearly* took him up on it," she grinned. "If it weren't for Mom, we would have cashed his check and eloped."

"Would have served the bastard right," he chuckled. "Can't *buy* everything, Charlie."

97

"Was Wolverine *that* bad?"

"Worse than *you* probably heard. I *saw* Eddie Evans get *it*. I ratted *those* animals out, and their friends pitched me out a window, strung me up, beat me, marched me around in circles for hours at a time. Guys hanged themselves, cut their wrists just to get away." He stopped, shuddered at the memory.

"Huh. Heard from Lois?" Brenda stood up, seemingly oblivious to his revelation.

"She's *here*, at Kurt's hotel. She didn't...no, she *wouldn't*." For unclear reasons, Lois and Brenda didn't communicate either often or pleasantly. "She and Simon will be joining us for dinner at the Mueller's tomorrow."

"*Oh*, what *fun*," she sighed. "Poor Simon; has to put up with *her*."

"Eh, sixteen years in, they *seem* happy. I write to them about four times a year, call on birthdays."

"More than you write to *me*."

"You're two letters behind from *years* ago, Bren."

"Well, I'm *busy*..."

"Join the club. I haven't even got a birthday card from you in years."

"Yeah, well." She finished her wine. "Let's go."

"Wait." He drained his beer, waved off another round. "We're brother and sister, Bren. We *shouldn't*..."

"No," she patted his arm. "No, but we *do*."

Her brown eyes reminded him of his father's, an ever-fading memory. "So, let's *not* anymore. We're not in touch, OK. We're not particularly close, OK—never *have* been. But we *can* still communicate and *not* trade old hurts."

She pecked him on the cheek. "*Great* idea. Let's get."

*\*\*\**

When *Kramer Vs. Kramer* was a third of the way through, Leigh decided to...just *ask*. "What's with *Harry*, Mom?"

"We're friends."

"You're more than *that*, Mom."

"We *were*, for a while."

"She didn't *have* to be a nun while we were separated. She was *technically* single." Ed put his pen down, stuffed papers into his valise. "We agreed to *that*."

"What's 'technically single' mean?" *I HAD to ask?*

"We *were* legally separated." Ed moved to the big armchair by the fireplace.

Cathy cleared her throat. "Harry and I started *seeing each other*—that's the *polite* phrase—six months...no, *ten*...after your father and I separated. We were *involved*—that's *another*—for a couple years. We were very *adult* about our *affair*—that's two more."

Ed gazed at Cathy. "I *knew* about Harry, but *I* wasn't a monk, either."

"*He* had a friend in New York," Cathy shrugged. "I met her. She didn't look like me."

*And I never even suspected...* "But you got back together."

"*Oh, yes,*" Cathy grinned. "Your father and I couldn't find in *others* what we found in *each other*. Even when we were *sleeping*—*another* polite phrase—with other people, we couldn't *wait* to see each other again; have...."

"I *get* the *picture*, Mom." *Do I need THIS conversation with my parents?*

"Your mother and I were only physically and legally separated, honey," Ed smiled. "We were never *out of love...or* like. We gave—*give*—each other peace of heart."

*Peace of heart? Interesting.* "So, a soul-marriage." *So does Mike...and JJ ...*

"*Soul*-marriage?" Cathy and Ed looked at each other, surprised, before Cathy answered. "*Beautiful* phrase! Yes, that's *it.*"

"In the beginning, though, was Dad the *only* one?"

"My *only* boy? A second date didn't mean monogamy *then* like it does *now*. Our *fifth* date—a *little* second base, a first for *both* of us—*that* was it. She glanced at Leigh meaningfully. "You've had more than one boy at a time. While there was Randy, there was Mike *and* JJ."

*HO-boy...* "*Always* Mike; my *buddy* Mike. *We* have a soul-marriage. But *JJ?* He was a cute boy I *swam* with, but..." *Do I want to know more?*

"Hard to resist *that* temptation," Cathy smiled. "Wet, warm, a little out-of-breath, and *those* bumps, a *moment* or two from naked. That's how I *convinced* your *father*: *too-loose* bathing suit, *tepid* pool, *warm* day, *sexy* eyes..."

"Don't forget the *blanket*, Cath," Ed added. "JJ was *your* boy that got away but was still around to *remind* you that he got away."

*When did my father get so smart?* "Uh-huh."

They were quiet as the movie droned on until Ed mumbled, "now, *Mike*," thoughtfully.

"*Always* Mike," Leigh sighed. "I treated him like a doormat in school."

"*No*," Cathy said. "You treated him like the intimate friend that he's *always* been, the boy whose shoulder you *could* cry on when your parents separated." Cathy looked thoughtful. "*That* was what Ed and I missed. We *became* friends, but we *were not friends* at the beginning like you and Mike have been all along."

"Mike's been calling me *sweetheart* since 8th Grade."

"*Sweetheart* may *not* mean to *him* what it does to *you*."

"What?"

"He calls you 'sweetheart' because it's more endearing to him than *pal*. There are many *very* subtle levels of endearment, but in today's oh-so-sophisticated and *liberated* society, we recognize—*maybe*—three: friends, lovers, and spouses. Friends *can* be forever, but nowadays, people jump from *that* straight to bed because the stigma's been removed. Too often, *that* leads to confusing physical pleasure with affection. I sometimes wished *we* had put sex off a *little* longer."

"Why?"

"We barely knew each other," Ed added quickly. "We'd been dating for a little more than a semester, maybe once a week. Two or three hours a week for six months is hardly enough time to *really* know someone *even after* some groping."

"*That's* the function of the honeymoon…at least it *used* to be," Cathy interrupted.

Ed laughed briefly. "Even though I'd only ever *seen* naked women in stag films and biology books, I *thought* I was ready for *it* that afternoon."

Cathy pulled her knees up to her chest. "I *wasn't* sure, but *oh*, I *thought…*"

*Do I want to hear this?* "Um…"

"June 6th, 1954," Cathy smiled. "We swore eternal devotion to each other…"

"Right there on the blanket," Ed chuckled. "*I* hadn't caught my *breath* before I asked her to marry me."

"*I* was *still vibrating* when I said *yes*. We got married two months later."

"And I came along eight months later," Leigh smiled. "Honeymoon baby."

"We *said* you were, but you *had* to have been conceived a month *before*," Cathy laughed. "Happiest day of *our* lives when we found out I was pregnant. But don't think you weren't *wanted*…just *unexpected*. For us making love has always been a joy, *especially* with each other."

*I was an oops?* "Good to know, Mom. Well, this has been the most awkward conversation *I've* ever had with *my* parents."

"*Could* have been worse," Ed smiled. "*Could* have caught us *en flagrante delicto* right here in the living room."

Cathy smiled, lithely uncoiling, rising from the couch, unbuttoning her blouse… "*Sounds* like an invitation…"

Leigh rolled her eyes. "I'm *outta here…*"

\*\*\*

"Beer?" Jesse found JJ trying to relax in the atrium.

"No, thanks. Had my limit today."

"Me, too, now I think about it." He paused, looked around. "Jen told me pretty much everything about you and her back in the day. Everything except the answer to one question: was *she YOUR only one?*"

"The only one I was *physical* with. I *liked* other girls; *loved* one I couldn't find."

"Claudia?"

"Yeah. But Jenny and I were special."

"She didn't think *she* was good enough, but you *fixed* that." They were quiet again, listening to the fountains gurgling as the happy hour cleanup was finishing. "Curvy girls like her don't *think* much of themselves. You loved her like she *wanted*. The way she talks about you…if I were a different man, I'd be jealous."

"Before Brookfield, I spent a year in a school that nearly killed me, literally. I was scared *shitless* of everything, everyone, while I told myself I feared nothing because I had nothing left to *lose*. Then I got to Brookfield, and Jenny said 'hi' at a party, *talked* to me, kissed me 'bye, and *that* let all her friends know…"

"You were OK. Yeah. She did that for me, too. She was my math tutor at Notre Dame. I could barely think straight; I was so *pissed* at the world. But she always smiled, kept me on track. I finally said, 'look, sweet-cheeks: let's go out for some drinks and settle this.' *Man*, I gave her the *biggest* load of Black 'Nam Vet Psycho Boonie Rap *bullshit* you *never* heard—*every*thing but a dap and a power check. *Bless her*, she didn't even *blink*, had me walk her back to her dorm. Kissed me goodnight in front of all her friends." He suddenly turned serious. "*She* saved us both."

"Sounds like. Let's do Veteran's Day here. Toast our survival, swap lies to spook the civilians, hoist one for absent friends, and for life-saving women."

"Right *on*, brother. I'm for the rack."

JJ was about to retire himself when Lois waved from the lobby. "Hey, Lo."

"Hi, John. Can I get directions to the Mueller's?"

He sketched a map on a piece of lobby stationery. "About five?"

"Sure. A-*hem*," she cleared her throat theatrically as she sat, signaling a change of subject to something possibly unpleasant. Communicating with Lois was an art form mastered by few. "And *who*, may I ask, was *that woman* you were *with* yesterday morning?"

"Clare? I stayed with her family at Brookfield a lot. I went to her sister's wedding and *hers*. I sent her flowers when her daughter was born in '80, and she cried on my shoulder when she died in '82." He sighed...*why the hell not?* "I asked her to come with me then, but she said, 'I'm sorry.' She met Ann in January, and *they* say they hit it off. Lo, you're my sister, and I *love* ya, but *please* don't presume to know me *or* my life."

With that, for *just* a moment, JJ noticed that rare light, seen only when Lois dropped her façade of self-assurance and sardonic wit. She smiled, pecked him on the cheek. "See you tomorrow."

***

"Mueller." It was 11 at night when Ann came out of her room in her long shirt after Betty answered the phone.

"*Hey*, Legs, it's Sandy." A year before, Mike had dubbed Ann *Legs* after answering *her* Wolverine questions—JJ *hadn't* told her much—during a brief stay in Key West. *That* was a bonding moment seldom experienced.

"*Sandy? Hi!*" She ducked back into her room, closing the door softly on the long and *sorely*-abused cord. "Did *Charlie*...?"

"Still with us, as far as I know. Wanted to talk about *our* friends."

"Blue-Eyes and Green-Eyes?"

"Uh-huh. We *both* know there's a *lot* between them."

"Yeah." Silence. "How are *you* about *that*?"

"I trust them both with my *life*. I wanted to ask *you*..."

"I've loved and trusted *both* of them as long as I've known them, Sandy." Silence. "I'm going to tell you a secret: I had a *weird* dream a few months ago,

101

the only one of its kind I've *ever* had. It had you, Leigh, JJ, *and* me in the same room…the same *bed*…making love. *Very* erotic."

"*Sounds* like it. What *happened*?"

"Just *that*. Then I woke JJ up at two in the morning on a duty day to…." Silence. "There's a light in his eyes when he reads her letters."

"I've seen it in *hers*, too, sometimes, reading *his* letters. I *tried* to be jealous…"

"*You* have the most beautiful *grey* eyes I've *ever* seen." *WHERE* did that…?

"Legs: you've got the *prettiest* brown eyes on the *best* figure *I've* ever seen." *Ho-boy*…

"So, *Sandy*, *should* we *mind* that our spouses-to-be *lust* for each other?"

"Not as long as they don't try to *hide* it. They did some making out last year…"

"Yeah: lights-out, bare chest-to-bare-chest. A *wildly* unchaste-yet-chaste night of stress-*relieving* in a motel room, *he* said."

"*That's* what Leigh called it, yeah. 'I'll *share* my lips with JJ,' she told me, 'and *you* have the *rest* of me.'" Silence. "I've got no problem with *that*. You?"

"Like you *said*, if they don't try to *hide* it." Silence. "Sandy, *don't* answer if you don't *want* to. Every*one* and every*thing* else aside, would *you consider me*?"

"I'd give *a lot* for a guilt-free hour in *your* bed." *WHAT!!!???*

"So would *I*." *OHMYGOD!?* "Ya know, I've been a *little* jealous of Leigh *and* Donna since junior high. There: I *said* it…*we* said it. Having *said it, buddy*, what could we say to *them*?"

"*We can't* say *no* to *them* if *we* have *lust* in our *hearts*…"

"No, we *can't*, Jimmy Carter-ism aside. Let's keep *this one* between *us*…"

"*What* one?"

"*Yeah*." Silence. "See you soon." Silence. "You…gonna hang up?"

"Don't *want* to, Legs." He sighed. "Could *this* get any *more* awkward?"

"I'm in a *blazing red lace* teddy and *untying the*…"

"*'Night*, Legs."

"*'Night*, Sandy."

## *Monday*

*For this, I have to wear a dress mess uniform?*

"*Chief* Petty Officer *Mueller* on the deck," Chief Boatswain's Mate Al Parrish announced just inside the office door.

"*On* your *FEET*," Senior Chief Bert Dekker called as Ann marched in. All three clerks stood at parade rest. "Chief Petty Officer Mueller will sign the deck log and the unit roster."

Ann signed the boxes next to *CPO Claudia A. Mueller* and extended her hand. "Chief, see you on our *next* ship."

"*Good* luck, Ann," Bert smiled. "We extended your liberty to match Sergeant Elrath's emergency leave. Take it *easy* on that future husband of yours, eh? He's *just* a GI."

"Yeah, sure," Ann grinned. "Troy," she offered a hand to a petty officer who she had helped with his promotion packet. "Good *luck* to you. Garibaldi," she smiled at the petite personnel *technician*, "take care. And Junka," she smiled at the painfully shy young man, new to the unit, "*we don't bite*, OK? Sometimes we *nibble. Let's* go, Al." She marched bravely out of the office, though her hip was doing its *I'm getting older* thing. "Do I get piped and rung off, too?" This was the first duty station she was *leaving* as a senior NCO, but even *that* little ceremony seemed overdone. She had watched the base commander's departure ceremony—*after* the elaborate change-of-command—a bright-brass ritual of pipes and bells and flags.

"No, but I *do* announce your departure from the building and thus the unit," Al assured her. "*Tradition* only knows why, but E-7s and above..."

"Yeah, I get it. How long are *you* here for yet?"

"I'm back shipboard in January. USS *Stark* in the Persian Gulf."

"Well, *good* luck, Al," she shook his hand before she pecked his cheek—and he hers. "See you on our *next* ship."

***

"Elrath." He grabbed the phone on the third ring, barely winning the race with the voice-messaging service. Despite having been up for nearly an hour, he was stiff and inexplicably dopey. He shook his head to try to clear it, but that only made his neck burn.

"Yo, JJ! Mike Dietz!"

"Uh, hey, Mike, what be the haps on your end?"

"Ain't *no* haps here, brother. Leigh says, you want to get together *there* tomorrow tonight?"

"Yeah. Hoist one on Veterans Day."

"Roger that. How's your stepfather?"

"Not much change."

"Eh, my best to all."

"Yeah, thanks, buddy, but I've gotta get going."

He had barely hung up when the phone rang again. *Who? Why would she...?* Mystified, he went downstairs. *Why on Earth would...* "Jo," he mumbled when he saw her. "You have *business*?"

"*We* do," she pointed to a willowy man with very hard, very dark eyes. "May I introduce a business associate, Sid Jackwell?"

"Sid," JJ said flatly. "Long *time* no *see*. We were in Mrs. Marshall's 5th Grade class together. You *know* Ann.."

"Yes, *and* Miss Flack's 4th Grade. I look forward to seeing *Claudia Ann* again, Mr. Elrath," Sid was tall and thin with thin, fair hair but long arms that ended in overlarge hands that seemed to want to drag on the ground. "I trust you are well. My congratulations on your upcoming nuptials."

"Thanks," JJ grinned. "And *you* can call me *JJ* since we've known each other

103

for so long." They drifted into the atrium, finding seats in a quiet corner where a small woman with a seemingly permanent grin sat. "Can I ask *your* name?"

"Bobbi Eldon, Mr. Elrath. I work with Jo. I don't know Ann *well*, but she *might* remember me—there were over six hundred of us in the class. I've known Leigh and Mike since junior high; Donna since 3rd Grade."

"Now we all *know* each other; what can I do for you?"

"Other way around, JJ," Jo declared. "*We're* in the helping business. We provide financial research and recovery services."

"Ah, *hah*," JJ answered. "I know *your* credentials, Jo. What do *you* do, Bobbi?"

"Business intelligence," Bobbi smiled. "Much like *military* intelligence, but I work in the business and financial worlds. I figure out where, what, and how. Jo takes it from there."

"Ah. Mr. Jackwell, what do *you* bring to the party?"

Sid smiled. "My organization provides diverse services *for* the Bobbi/Jo Partnership."

"Uh-huh," JJ mused. "*Diverse services.*" *If you have to ask WHAT they are, you don't need them.* "And you guys want to…what…for *me*?"

"We want to help Gramma find Gramps Charlie's money," Jo smiled.

"Why ask *me*? Go to Mom directly…"

"I *did*, JJ," Jo answered. "She wanted us to talk to *you* before we did anything more than the scant work we've done already."

"And, ah, what are you *charging*?"

"*Ten* percent," Jo sighed.

"*Why? My* mom's *nothing* to *you.*"

"She was always nice to me, no matter how mean *I* was. She *defended* me when I came home." Jo had taken too many pills a year before; Mary brought her back, with Kurt's ambivalence.

"And Mr. Jackwell, why *you*?"

Sid smiled, one of those smiles you see on people who have deep secrets and tend to keep them. "*I* am in *your* debt, Mr. Elrath. Shall we leave it at that?"

*One you can never repay, right? Wish I knew what it was…* "Very well. Wait *here* for a minute." He went upstairs and called Stella, told her of the meeting, then added, "Jackwell's Ann's friend, Mom. You *know* Jo…"

"Yes. When can *we*…?"

"*This* doesn't involve me, Mom."

"It *does*, John. You and Ann *know* these people, and I *can't* trust *anyone* else."

*And how can I turn that down?* "Sooner than later, Mom. Tonight, at the Mueller's?"

***

"Chief Armor; SFC Dietz. Mike; Amy." The weather seemed unable to make up its mind between sunny and overcast, dry and drizzling that morning.

"Sarge," Amy, in uniform, beamed, "I *heard* about you from Leigh."

"Heard about *you*, too, Chief; you were *enlisted* then," Mike replied. He and Leigh entered the FBI Resident Agency's conference room, where another woman waited. Soon, a half-dozen people came in, led by an enormous man who took to the podium as easily as one might don a pair of slippers. Ivan Thomas soon joined them, followed by Dorothy, who added County Sherriff's cards to a pile by the door.

"Ladies and gents, I'm Senior Special Agent Ernest Packard—call me Ernie," the big man began. Ernie had teeth like bathroom tiles, hands like hams, "and I head the FBI Special Projects Division's Wolverine Working Group ..."

The room fell silent; Amy and Ivan nodded; Leigh muttered, "*explains* a *lot*." An FBI Working Group wielded tremendous, almost *legendary* authority. The Special Projects Division (known colloquially as SPD) had a reputation in law enforcement circles as a mysterious, perhaps mythical, organization. Depending on experience or rumor sources, it was either feared, respected, or ignored.

"It *does*," Ernie glanced at Leigh. "Now, *most* of us are strangers to each other, so let's start with the *round-the-table* game. Julia: *go*."

"Julia Addison; SPD;" "Dorothy Parkinson, Oakland County Sheriffs—*her* mother;" "Ellen Drew, SPD;" "Dave Clawson, SPD;" "Morgan Towne, SPD;" "Frank Hitchcock, SPD;" "Tom Greenowitz, SPD;" "Ivan Thomas, Army Counterintelligence;" "Amy Armor, Army CID;" "Leigh Taylor, Army CID;" "Mike Dietz, Army Counterintelligence;" "Paula Karris; this is *my* office."

Leigh and Mike, having met Dave, nodded; he grinned.

"Excellent," Ernie grinned. "Is everyone *clear* on FBI Working Groups?"

"I *think* so," Dorothy frowned. "Never *seen* one, but..."

"You're *in* one, Undersheriff." Ernie nodded. "We have rather broad authority from the Attorney General; new members will be given copies of our authorization. Now, Special Agent Clawson?"

Dave cleared his throat. "For some *time*, Sergeants Dietz and Taylor's duty stations, movements, and even *relationships* have been known to the Newhouse organization soon after they *happen*; in *some* cases, *before they arrived* at their stations. The *simplest* explanation for this is that *someone's* reading their mail." He glanced at them. "You're here on *such* short notice because the Chief of Counterintelligence *and* the Provost Marshal thought my cock-eyed theory had merit."

"Five days to clear post," Mike nodded, "not enough time for a letter to get from either Belgium *or* Korea. But how would *you* have known that the Newhouse's know...?"

"Mr. *Jackwell's* organization has a source," Dave replied.

"*Sid*," Leigh asked. Dave merely nodded...in a way that said, *shut up.*

"And the postal inspectors *have* been alerted," Ernie added. "*They* couldn't get someone here today. Now, we've been looking at Wolverine since January of '81. We found it is connected to several less-than-savory organizations. We've found more *since*." He paused as if for effect. "*And* to people in the Newhouse organization. Wolverine takes on guys who *should* be in juvenile detention. They *also* hide *younger* men to change their identities. Without knowing *who* owns it, *who's* paying the bills, *and* the bribes to hide the abuses *and* the crimes, we can't move ahead. We cast a wide net, but it's almost impossible for us to get a warrant to search either Wolverine or the Newhouse organization without a criminal referral. Unless and *until* we get referrals for everyone involved, the evidence *could* vanish. We believe, because of *your* relationship with the Newhouse family, *you* can be of some assistance."

"If they're as smart as we *think* they are," Julia added, "they're *hiding any* records related to Wolverine."

"*That's* our problem in a nutshell," Ernie said. "They're hiding something, and we barely know where all to look." He glanced at Leigh and Mike. "Now, as for you two: you are sources of both *information* and temptation: dangles."

"*Dangles*," Dorothy frowned, "what's *that?*"

"Bait, ma'am," Mike grunted.

"Because of the Posse Comitatus Act, you won't be able to *arrest* civilians," Amy announced.

"You shouldn't *have* to arrest," Ernie agreed, "but you *can detain*. You're *also* here to get into the Newhouse's head. We know from public records you were married to Randy Newhouse IV, but we don't know much else. Would you care to elaborate?"

"I was Randy Newhouse IV's girlfriend from 1967 to 1973, fiancée from January to June '73, and *technical* wife for nine days. On our wedding night, he told me that he had a two-year-old son in Bay City…"

"He *did*," the room blurted simultaneously.

"Yeah. We were in bed—our *first* time. *Then* he said *something* like, 'even if I *could* screw you *now*'…*you* get it." The room chortled loudly. "I broke his jaw and left; annulled him and enlisted. Since '74, they've been claiming that *I* bore Randy's child, harassing my family and me with the lie."

Ivan grinned; Amy chuckled; Dorothy smiled; the SPD grinned. "Most *entertaining* meeting I've *ever* been in," Ernie declared at last. "Certainly grounds for annulment—*and* a broken jaw."

Dave said, "*whoever* owns Wolverine *may* be using *you* as bait for John Elrath. You two are the common threads running through this case."

"Right," Julia said, "and NOTHING about *that leaves this room*." Julia glared at Leigh and Mike. "*Nothing*."

"Elrath cost Wolverine's owners millions," Frank added. Frank was an urbane-looking guy with a fresh haircut and manicure and sounded like he was in a boardroom. "Dave's theory makes sense from *that* perspective. The *maternity*, though, confuses the matter. Those kids up in Essexville…"

"Those…*those* kids," Leigh asked, puzzled.

"Yeah: *two* of 'em," Dave said. "*Both* named Newhouse, *both* living with a woman claiming to be their aunt. We saw them on surveillance a year ago, been trying to figure out *what* they are to each other ever since. One *is* named Randy; the other, Renée, according to their guardian's tax returns."

Leigh made a face. *TWO kids?* "Randy *has* four sisters. One of them...?"

"*No*," Dave declared. "Only two of his sisters have had children. None of them are named *Mary*..."

"*That's* who he *said* had his son," Leigh said. *Wonder who she is?*

"If you're in touch with Sid Jackwell," Mike added, "then you know that *they* believe it's the Newhouse *organization*, not the *family*, that's behind the harassment."

"Yes," Ellen smiled, "*and* the fire last week: *nice* interview, by the way, Leigh, Mrs. Parkinson. We're not *that* interested in an *apparent* internal conflict..."

"We *should* be," Leigh interrupted. "That outfit has *not* been violent before; we *should* want to know why it is *now*."

"Speaking of internal conflicts," Dorothy began, "the Oakland County Domestic Violence Unit got a partial domestic complaint from Phyllis Newhouse in March '73..."

"*Phyllis* filed a complaint," Leigh blurted. "Was she *sober*?"

"No mention of *that*," Dorothy mused. "Is *she*..."

"A drunk, yes," Leigh answered. "I can't *remember* seeing her sober."

"She *said* her husband wouldn't let her see her grandson," Dorothy continued, "wouldn't give her an address."

"So, the boy *isn't* a dirty little secret in the family..." Mike shrugged. "He's known *of*."

Leigh pulled the notebook—tagged and sealed in a plastic bag—out of her attaché. "I found *this* Saturday in with stuff I boxed up in '73. It was in the pocket of a leather jacket I'd never seen before. Randy helped pack some of it."

"OK. Was *your* name on *that* box," Ernie asked.

"Yes, sir."

"*Huh*," Ernie grunted. Somehow, his grunts all had specific meanings. This one said *very interesting*. "You *brought* it?" Leigh pointed at the large bags on a side table. "We *could* argue that putting it into a box of yours *before* you were married means he *gave* it to you."

"*Most* of it is in Randy's handwriting; the *rest* I don't know." They passed the notebook around the table, followed by blown-up copies of the pages.

"You think he forgot about it," Julia asked.

Leigh shrugged. "None of the legal actions mentions it."

"*You guys* made these copies," Ernie asked.

"We *did*," Mike answered. "If the Russians invent a Xerox-seeking missile, we'll lose the next war." Dave and Frank giggled. "I did some studying on it. *These* numbers under *B* are repeated under *M* and *P*: all three of them say *Mary*. If *B* is for *boy* or *Bay City*, and *M* is for *Mary*...can't say what *P* might be for."

"We'll need to have it analyzed by NSA," Ernie declared, "see if there's a code to the multiple entries."

"We also may have *traps* on many of these lines already," Ellen said.

"We can find *this one* out." Mike pulled the conference room phone towards him.

"That's *another* reason we have you," Ernie said. "*We* can't misrepresent ourselves. *You* can because you can't arrest civilians." Mike nodded, punched in the number, and turned on the speaker.

"Good morning," a woman's voice said after the second ring, "Parkinson Title and Trust; how may I help you?"

"Hello, ma'am. *This* is Michigan Bell. We're checking our subscriber lines. Can you tell me *your* name and the name of your *business*, please?"

"Michigan Bell? *This* is a GTE line..."

"Yes, ma'am, *that's* why we're calling. There's been some cross-wiring in the main exchange that has resulted in double-billing, so we're polling all the circuits to ensure that each subscriber line is connected and billed properly. Now, if I could have *your* name and the name of your business?"

"Well...*I'm* Mary Newhouse; the business is Parkinson Title and Trust."

"*Thank* you, Ms. Newhouse. I have you in Bay City?"

"The zip code—48732—comes up as either Bay City or Essexville in the computers."

"Yes, ma'am; *that's* what we have. And the GTE billing should remain uninterrupted. *Thank* you for your cooperation; *have* a *good* day." He hung up, grinning widely. "Well, that answers *that*. Mary Newhouse in Essexville, working for Parkinson Title and Trust on GTE phone lines."

"Major," Morgan grinned, "you don't *pay* this guy enough."

"Legally," Ernie mused, "*that* call may as well have been asking about Prince Albert in a can."

"And at one time, she *married* a Newhouse...*maybe*," Leigh mumbled. "A *Newhouse* working for a *Parkinson*; that *number* in a *private* Newhouse phone book..."

"But," Dorothy squinted, "Parkinson *Title and Trust* is defunct."

"We've been *aware* of that for a while," Dave said. "That one little office in the Hampton Center Mall...can't find it in *any* business registry."

"And the *other* two numbers," Ernie asked.

"Find *out*..." Mike punched in another number.

On the third ring... "You have reached...Leave a message for the Newhouse's at the beep."

"OK: residential voice line," Ivan declared. "Let's try the *third*."

Mike punched the *third* number...

And it rang...and rang...and *rang*...

"A *second* voice line without an answering machine," Ellen declared. "*We'll* find out if it's published..."

Ernie glanced at Mike and Leigh. "Have you *got* domestic legends in place?"

"Nothing *current*," Leigh admitted.

"Not in-CONUS," Mike frowned. "And my Korean legend's blown."

"We'll provide all *possible* support to create legends for you," Ernie nodded.

"We need to *plug that leak*," Ivan declared. "Your value as field agents is compromised by it."

"For what it's worth," Leigh sighed, "we've had two other contacts with Newhouse's since we got here."

"Tell us." Everyone listened; the SPD—*all* of them—took notes on their encounter with Megan and the phone call. Finally, Ernie sighed, "this is going to be messier than we thought. All right: scratch out reports. We work *out of* and get support *from* the Troy Resident Agency. The Detroit Division and the Lansing Resident Agency are *not* part of this Working Group; the *why* is office politics *you* don't need to know. All right: if Sergeants Taylor and Dietz, Chief Armor, Major Thomas, and Undersheriff Parkinson will *please* stand..."

*What the...?* Leigh glanced at Mike, puzzled, but did as did the rest.

"Hold up your right hand and repeat after me," Ernie intoned solemnly. Leigh glanced around, expecting to see at least a hidden smirk...but *nothing*. "I—state your name—solemnly swear that I shall never divulge anything of what I learn having to do with the Wolverine Working Group or the Special Projects Division, so *help* me, *Hanna*."

Mike gazed at Ivan, who shrugged slightly. Leigh glanced at Amy, who did the same. Dorothy looked to Julia, who smiled...but they swore, anyway.

***

"May I *help* you?" Margaret, the matronly church secretary with silver-streaked brown hair and lovely blue-grey eyes, looked up from her desk. The school—a secular pre-school that generated income for the chronically cash-strapped church—was noisily in session at the far end of the wing.

"Yes, ma'am," JJ answered, "I'd like to book the church for a wedding."

"Come on in, have a seat." She gestured to a small, worn love seat along one wall, surrounded by stacks of file boxes. "What's your name, young man? Are you a member? I don't recognize you, and my eyes aren't *that* bad."

"JJ Elrath, ma'am. I'm a member in absentia."

"Ah. A *wedding*? Who's the lucky girl?"

"Ann Mueller, she's *not* a member."

"Ann...Mueller," she mused, writing. "You've spoken to the pastor?

"Yes, ma'am."

"*When* were you thinking?"

"We have to be in Alaska in early December. We're in the military..."

"Oh, I see. Alaska? My word. Are you looking for a week*end* or week*day*?"

"Most friends and family work or go to school, ma'am, so let's try weekends."

"Week*end*." She perused a large calendar on the wall, dotted with sticky notes. "*This* Saturday is open."

"Um, *that* might be a little *too* soon, ma'am, but let's keep it in mind."

"The next weekend opening…December 6th."

"That sounds…OK. And, um, if you *could*, hold *this* Saturday open just in case? Ann's coming in tonight, and I need to ask *her*."

"I can. Good luck, young man, and if there's another booking, I'll let you know. Your phone number, please?"

As he pulled out of the parking lot, he wondered if the unilateral decision he just made would come back to bite him. *Could have done it during the week, but then school for the kids, work for everyone else…small, yes, but not microscopic, else we could go to the courthouse.*

Then he discovered that he'd turned around and found himself studying the front door of the church again. *Dad's was the first funeral here. Lois's wedding; Gramma Burgess funeral. No, not the courthouse.*

He looked around the parking lot that his family raised money for. He felt a slight tingle in his hand: a memory of the burns that haunted him, sometimes.

*I'll continue THIS ONE tradition of what's left of my family, if YOU don't mind, Cloud.*

✳✳✳

"Welcome to Dietz, O'Bannon and Associates. How may I help you?" The receptionist was about JJ's age; her nameplate read Naomi O'Bannon. She had dark hair and eyes and had an unattractive telephone headset clamped on her head.

"Stella Parkinson and JJ Elrath to see Mr. Mordechai Dietz."

She looked in an appointment book. "Yes. *You* were here last winter."

"I *was*; I'm a friend of the family.

She looked in her book again. "Yes, I *see* that." She spoke into her headset. "He'll be right with you. Please, be seated." The big office was airy, spread out on the ground level with hardwood paneling and solid wood furniture, and filled with natural light. Plush leather chairs—not the *typical* waiting-room/lobby fare—lined one wall, facing a gallery of paintings of historic Detroit.

"*Good* afternoon, John," Mike's Uncle Mordechai Dietz emerged from a door and grinned. He was a *bear* of a man with an enormous, tie-hiding beard and a deep, booming voice. The hand he extended—capable of swallowing both of JJ's at once—was surprisingly gentle. "It *has* been some years, yes?"

"It *has*, Mr. Dietz," JJ smiled. "May I introduce my mother, Stella Parkinson."

"*Mrs.* Parkinson," Mort smiled, speaking softly. "Mordechai Dietz. Please, *come* with me." He led them into a well-appointed office with a leather corner sofa and two giant chairs, a massive desk, and shelves packed with books. "Please," he gestured to the couch as he sat in a facing chair, "may I *offer* you anything? Coffee, tea?"

"Tea for Mom," JJ said, "coffee for me."

Mort pressed an intercom button on a speaker in front of him. "Cindy: two coffees and a tea, please. Now then: *how* may I *help* you?"

"As you *know*," Stella began, "my *current* attorney, Lew Rockland, is *not* cooperating and has lied *once* too many times to both my daughter and me."

"One lie *is* too many for an attorney, yes," Mort agreed. An older woman with a stiff perm arrived with a tray bearing a coffee pot, a hot water pot, three mugs, and all the usual accessories.

"And I *think* he's been lying to my husband for years," Stella went on, stirring her tea. "I believe we *both* need new representation."

"And your *husband*, I understand, is *unable* to communicate his wishes," Mort asked, sipping his coffee.

"That's right. The doctors don't think he'll *ever* be able to communicate again."

"I see," Mort said, setting his coffee down. "If you wish my firm to represent *him* as well, I shall have to get a judge to declare *you* as his guardian. Rockland *might* fight it, but he'll lose."

"There's also the *money*," JJ said. "He's hidden it behind that bogus pre-nuptial agreement."

"I know he has a great deal of money *somewhere*," Stella added, "he *spends* it like *water*."

"*Who* is his financial advisor," Mort asked, "*or* is it August Sherith?"

"Why, *yes*, it *is*," Stella said, surprised. "How would you know *that*?"

"He and the Rockland firm sell each other's services." Mort paused as if looking for words. "The combination of Rockland and Sherith is *not* good. *Sherith* in Hebrew means 'remnant,' and in many ways, that is what *they* thrive on: scraps. I'm not sure *how* your husband got tied up with them, but I am *confident* that *you* should get away from them." Mort sighed, then glanced at JJ. "John, your friend Edward Evans: He's still *your* financial advisor?"

"Yessir," JJ said, curious.

"Mrs. Parkinson, do you *know* the firm of Evans, Morgan, Shadrach, and Towne?"

"No, I don't think so," Stella answered. "What do *they* do?"

"They handle investments—*substantial* investments normally—for a *select* clientele. They provide *other* services as well. Nothing *shady*, mind you, simply *private*. While I do the legal work, allow me to ask Evans and Towne to do some financial planning—*and* research—for you. Since your son has invested there, it should be a simple matter for *you* to open an account. I shall speak to them on your behalf if you wish. Evans and Towne can open *many* doors."

"Can the Bobbi/Jo Partnership look into Charlie's money," JJ asked.

"Certainly," Mort said. "Roberta has a *brilliant* mind. We have used her for some years. Josephine has been an excellent investigator for the past year or so."

"Indeed," JJ smiled. "*Josephine* is my niece—Mom's granddaughter."

"*Indeed*," Mort declared. "Yes…Parkinson."

111

"We'll meet with *them* tonight," Stella said. "I'll tell them that *you* will be representing both my husband and me. How long will the guardianship take?"

"Well, tomorrow *is* a Federal holiday," Mort mused. "It's nearly two o'clock *now...and* I need to get the doctor's statements. I won't be ready to submit to the court until Wednesday at the earliest. I can justify emergency circumstances and expedite matters. Usually, it takes *about* a week, but I can *perhaps* get a ruling by Thursday if I get the right judge."

"I was in Judge Oakes's son's unit in Florida if that helps," JJ added.

Mort looked intrigued. "I play squash with him this evening; I'll *mention* your relationship."

"Then *that's* what we'll do, Mr. Dietz," Stella declared.

***

"Why *wait*, babe," Ann asked as they reached the Mueller's neighborhood on the way from the airport just after dark. "We've *had* the rings; the *license* will be valid; Saturday's *open*. The biggest problem is the out-of-town guests. How many are there? Your sisters..."

"They're both *in* town now. Wendy and Dennis are up here. The Florida gang...Julia's here with her family..."

"I'd *like* them *all* here. *Sweet Johnny*," she purred, "*let's* do it Saturday."

*You lost this argument before it started, Elrath.* "We meet Jo and them tonight: they want to help Mom find Charlie's money."

"OK." She squeezed his hand. "So, Saturday? Park in the forecourt here."

Her hand slid up his thigh. "Ah...?"

"*Saturday*, Johnny. These seats go *down*? Say *yes* to Saturday."

"OK, *yes*, to Saturday...*That's* why you wore a *skirt*?"

With steamy windows, they rolled into the Mueller's driveway twenty minutes later. Brenda, Roy, and their kids were at the Mueller condo; so was Brianna, who delighted in playing with the youngsters. Lois chatted amiably with Howard. Jenna's friend Billy Reidy, a rail-thin young man with dark and unruly hair, talked about football with Simon, Alex, and Charlie Junior. Jo chatted with Dorothy, Barbara, and Stella in the kitchen while Jenna and Brenda shared a laugh or two in their breakfast nook.

"OK, everyone," Ann announced after the *hellos*. "We *have* a date: *this* Saturday."

A stunned silence followed as everyone watched Stella until she cried "*wonderful*," with feeling. With that, they fell into an animated joy just as Sid and Bobbi arrived.

"The larger stone is from Gramma Burgess," Ann showed off her ring; "one of the smaller ones is from *you*, Stella. The matching smaller stone we got in Florida. *1911* was when the Burgesses were married; *1943* was when JJ's parents were. We'll engrave the wedding band with *1986*."

"I need a big and serious favor from you," JJ told Alex. "I'd like *you* to escort my mother. *That* means getting her to the church *and* the reception and making sure she gets home."

"*I* can help," Brianna offered, grabbing Alex's hand. "It'll be fun."

"OK, then: go on over and *offer* Mom your services." The couple spoke with her briefly before Stella smiled sweetly and hugged them (both were nearly a head taller than Stella).

"If you all will excuse me, I've got phone calls to make." JJ made his way to the den, suddenly realizing that he had less than 96 hours to pull together one of the most important events of his life.

*First things first.* "Margaret; JJ...yes, ma'am. The *bride* says we want Saturday...thank you, ma'am." *And...*"Yo, Kurt: Listen: she says *Saturday*...OK, thanks. Call *Will* for me, will ya?"

He put his battered phone book down, rubbing his head, but the taped picture of his father swinging a golf club somehow stuck out. It was the last photo that was ever taken of him, only developed after he died. *The girls are fine, Dad. It's MY turn now.*

*Reception.* "Hi, Callie; JJ Elrath...fine, thanks. We want our reception *there* this *Saturday*. I *know* it's short notice, but... you *can*? *Out*standing...a hundred...atrium at 0800 tomorrow? Thanks, Callie."

*Now: Florida.* "Tom? JJ. Wedding's Saturday, so everyone at the airport 0700 Thursday, bag-and-baggage for seven days...don't *ask*...roger; *out* here." *They'll need leave.* "Ram: that *list* I faxed you? Get their leaves and liberties to start Thursday for seven days. Thanks, brother." *Don't know how, but he said he can.* *Transportation.* "This is Mr. Elrath. My order is for Thursday morning 0700, Key West-Detroit, and the following Wednesday afternoon for return: nine adults and a toddler. *Thank* you."

He was just hanging up when Ann queried, "bridal party?"

"I asked Kurt to stand up for me. Alex and Mike?"

"I want Deb to stand up for *me*; Jenna, uh-huh, and Leigh to get the relay squad together again. I'll see about a dress tomorrow at Anita's." Will's wife owned a hard-to-fit ladies' boutique in Royal Oak.

"Gotta call Mike."

"Tell Leigh tomorrow morning." She bent over quickly...and they kissed on it all. "Hurry it *up*; I've *got* to call Deb. Dinner's in a half-hour."

***

"*Three* sets of *three*," Stella smiled, turning over the top card on what was left of the five-deck pile. This was *her* version of progressive rummy that the family called Stella's Game. *THIS* was how Stella *always* did business, made decisions, slowed *everyone* and *everything* down, silenced storms, and made friends. When *she* dealt cards, the world...simply...stopped.

Stella's Game is an easy rummy version: collect cards of the same value— three sets in the first hand. Set them down once you've got all three and keep playing until one player runs out of cards with their last discard—goes out. The first hand was quick: JJ was the first down with aces, threes, and jacks. Then Barbara went out just three rounds later.

"Jo, you think you *can* find Charlie's money," Stella mumbled as the points were tallied. Sid had the most with four wild cards—fifty points each.

"We *think* so, Gramma," Jo replied as Ann dealt the second hand: two sets of four. The game went around the table three times before Ann went down with sevens and nines.

"How does it work," Stella asked Bobbi, who hadn't gone down yet. "Jo, you looked at his papers in the den. Did you find all the keys you need? If *not…*"

"We *crossed* that bridge, Mrs. Parkinson," Sid declared. "One of the *services* I provide."

"We've studied the financial records you *have* and looked at the *accounts* you have, Mrs. Parkinson." Bobbi picked up a seven and went down with sevens and queens.

"Find *anything*," JJ asked. He passed a three, picked up and discarded a nine.

"We found *enough* to get the hospital off Gramma's back for now," Jo smiled, picking up the nine and going down with fives and eights, jacks, and queens. "Oh, *yeah*, I'm *out*," she exclaimed, discarding the nine.

JJ scowled, stuck with over a hundred points. "You sure you've *never* played this game?"

"No, *not* sure. *Seems* familiar, though." The deal passed to Lois.

"OK," Lois sighed. "*Run* of four and *set* of four." Round the table they went for the third hand, making light conversation and complaining about the cards until Howard finally went down with a heart run and fives.

"Who dealt this *foot*," Ann complained, picking up Simon's discarded queen and discarding an ace.

"Not *me*," Sid frowned, passing on the ace and discarding a seven.

JJ picked up the seven and went down with a club run and sevens, playing two hearts on Howard's run and unloading a five. "*Finally*," he groaned, trying to decide what to discard.

"By the way, you guys," Bobbi added, "Gabe and his band want to play a set for your reception if you're interested."

"*How much*," JJ asked.

"One set free for the class of '73," Bobbi answered.

"Huh," he glanced; Ann shrugged. "OK," he sighed, discarding an eight. "How long will you need, Jo?"

"We see a *pattern* now. We hope to find *more* resources with a more *thorough* search at the truck shop," Jo answered, passing on the eight and discarding a jack. "There's a *room* full of files that I *didn't…*" She frowned. "*Nuts*…shouldn't have done *that*."

"The way the game is played," Stella grinned, picking up the jack and going down with a spade run and jacks, unloading three clubs and two sevens before discarding a king. "What *else* do you need from me?"

"Just an agreement we can sign tonight," Sid replied, "authorizing *us*…"

"Who's *us*," Lois interrupted.

"S. Jackwell Associates and the Bobbi/Jo Partnership," Sid answered.

Silence followed until Stella asked, "John: what do *you* think?"

"Ann, *you* know Sid and Bobbi; *I* don't."

"I've known Sid since 1$^{st}$ Grade, and he hasn't got a *dishonest* bone in his body. Bobbi hung out with Leigh and Mike in high school."

Stella shifted her gaze. "Bren?"

"Mom, let's trust Johnny and Claudia."

Stella nodded. "Loie?" Brenda and JJ cringed. *Asking LOIS for advice?*

Suddenly, Lois stopped being stoic. "Mom, *I'm* with Brenda."

*Really?* JJ and Brenda blinked at each other, stunned.

Stella sighed, picked up a five, put *down* fives, played the rest of her cards on others, and smiled, "I'm *out*. Mr. Jackwell, show me where to sign."

*That's* how *Stella* did *business*.

***

"*Ugh! Eight* hours traveling, *seven* more socializing, a *quickie* in the *front seat!* I'm getting too *old* for all this!" It was after 11 when Ann dropped her briefcase on the kitchen table and flexed her bad hip.

"Age is just a number, Cloud." *The quickie was your…demand.*

"An ever-*growing* number, buddy. I need to swim. Come with?"

"Had my PT this morning. I'll see what's on the phone."

A moment later, from the bedroom, he heard, "*what* the…?" He walked in to see her marveling at the enormous adjustable bed (eight feet square and four feet high from floor to mattress top). It sported a smoked mirror ceiling surrounded by a motion-activated, low-intensity valence lighting that created *just enough* reflected light to bathe the room in a soft glow…the only light in the room when she entered. The tall, padded, sloped headboard was set a foot or so into the wall, with wrap-around arms like a sofa.

"Yeah," he chuckled, "that's what *I* said." He tapped the button for phone messages.

Minutes later, Ann stepped out of the bedroom in a neck-to-navel-to-elbow suit in thick Navy-blue Spandex; the bottoms reached from midriff to knees. "Anything *vital* on the phone?"

"Mike and Leigh are offering *their* services. I need to *call* Wendy. Donna says they'll be here by 9 tomorrow. You called Deb?"

"That's why *Donna* called; *she's* taking us to Anita's. I'm off."

The pool enclosure was long *officially* closed; Ann dove in, the pool lights the only illumination. She swam five quick laps and stopped, flexing her hip.

And she wasn't alone any longer. "Nancy, yeah?"

"Ah, well, yeah," the woman answered, seemingly embarrassed. "*Not* my name, though."

"And he *wasn't* your *groom*, either," Ann answered, pulling herself out of the water. Ann met this woman in this very pool in January after the *non*-couple suffered an *amorous accident* with a *groom* who—improbably—wouldn't show his face. "*You've* put some weight on since."

"Yes, I was sick last year. I'm Ellen Drew. *Nancy's* my Bureau nickname. We work with Julia Addison. We—*Dave* and I—were up here putting eyes on someone we've been looking for, for a *while*." Ellen stepped closer, her two-piece suit *not* hiding a nasty scar under her ribcage. "Dave had *met* both you *and* your fiancée, and we *weren't* ready *then* to let our surveillance targets know we were on them." She looked embarrassed. "*That* was expedient."

*Climaxing in a warm pool while standing up's expedient?* "*How* do you know who *I* am?"

"Dave and Julia, Miss..."

"Call me Ann, since *you* know *me* so well..."

## Veteran's Day

"*Oytzer*, honey, *get going!*" Mike awoke to the glaring reflection of the sun off the Hammerfest's windows, Leigh still sleeping beside him.

Leigh awoke suddenly, dimly remembering an odd dream. She walked lightly through the bathroom just as Monica knocked on her door.

"*Leigh*, dear: *laundry* day."

"Up and decent, Mama." *Mama?* "Sorry: Monica."

"Just *don't* call me late for services, dear. I'll be *your* Mama Monica soon enough; your wonderful mother will *always* be your Mom." She set her basket down on the washer in a closet, then stopped, sighing. "Leigh, dear, *please* be kind to my son."

"We *are* kind to *each other*, Mama." Leigh wrapped her arms around Monica from behind.

"That's *not* what I mean. Your bedrooms adjoin. Don't *not* get caught together at the expense of...your...of your..."

"Joy, Mama?"

Monica giggled. "Yes, *joy*. *His* bed *or* yours. We don't think it matters now. However," she turned, stood back, and took Leigh gently by the shoulders, "the night before your wedding, you'll stay with your parents, and you'll not *see* your groom until you are *both* under your *chuppah*. Understood?"

"Yes, Mama."

***

"First thing," Ann glanced pointedly at Callie, then JJ as they sat in a secluded, quiet corner of the atrium. "My *father* recognizes his traditional responsibilities and *will be substantially contributing* to this party." JJ spread his hands. "*I* know this is a *huge* undertaking for you, Callie. *Perfect* for us would be to have nearly everyone *well*-fed, *reasonably* comfortable, and *pleasantly* drunk."

"*Please*, Ann," Callie soothed, "As long as you *don't* want too many frills, you'll be *thrilled* with what we can pull together. You said a hundred? Ballpark?"

"That's a *big* ballpark," JJ muttered. "Between family, *near*-family, *step*family, friends, and others, we come up with just under eighty names, *less* kids. Add *kids*, the pastor, the band: it *could* hit a hundred."

"I'd recommend a brunch buffet; flexible enough that we can accommodate a dozen either way. We bill based on the champagne toast, which means minors and designated drivers eat free, but it's at a *premium* rate." They talked about cake, drinks, dance floor, flowers, decorations, prep time, and tipping. Callie herself would supervise.

"We're getting married, Cloud." The magnitude of the event suddenly struck them as they finished their coffee.

"We are *indeed*, Johnny. Second thoughts?"

"No. We've been *practically* married since February."

"But our services *could* still separate us any time."

*Don't remind me.* "I've been offered a job in the Reserves. Here."

She squinted. "I *know* what you feel about Alaska, but *that* solution doesn't address *my* job, the one I had to pull *many* strings to get."

"There's an E-7/8 slot for a supply rating at the Warren Navy Logistics Command."

"Huh. How hard would it be for *you* to get orders changed?"

"Don't *know*; never *tried*. It might depend on the circumstances." He squinted for a moment. "I *could* argue that Mom needs help, with Charlie like he is."

"Huh. Think *that* would work? Does she *need* help?"

He described the conversation between mother and son that included, for the first time, *I need you, Johnny.* "That waste of space might finally have some purpose in life."

\*\*\*

"Come *in*, ladies, come *in*," matronly Hillary gushed, greeting Ann like an old friend.

"I take it *you've* been here before?" Leigh gazed around Milady's Closet, aware of it only because Ann had described it.

"Once."

"Pretty high-end stuff, guys," Donna observed, perusing a rack. "*Good* but pricey."

"It's *for* the hard-to-fit woman," Ann replied, "and *I'm* hard to fit."

"*I* ain't easy, either," Donna sighed. "Why I make so much of my own."

They entered the opulently furnished Guest Suite, where refreshments were set out. "Guys, let me show you *this*." Ann pulled her mother's sateen low-flare dress with its four-foot-long train out of its bag, hanging it on a hook by a four-panel mirror. "Wish I *could* wear it, but we'd have to *butcher* it to get it to fit.

117

But that *flavor*, that…"

"*That* kind of *class*." Donna smiled.

Hillary and spindly Anita smiled. "Bring out *that* size 16, Hil," Anita mumbled. Hillary soon appeared with a slate-blue wool-poly backless dress with a *plunge-to-the-waist* neckline. "It comes with both a full jacket and a short cape. We thought of *you* when we saw it at a show."

"It's certainly for the long body," Leigh whispered. "Beautiful."

*Breathtaking*. Ann studied the dress on the hanger, fingered the delicately embroidered bodice.

"I think *you* could wear it, too." Anita grinned at Donna.

"We're not shopping for *me*," Donna muttered, checking the tag, "but I'd have to spend *WOW…three month's pay* on it. *Whew!* Or spend that long copying it *if* I could find this material…*and* match the needlework that I'm *not* good at. Elegant; *fabulous*. But where would *I* wear it? Inappropriate for the drunk ward."

"Go try it on, dear," Anita smiled at Ann.

After a few minutes, Ann was staring at herself in the mirror. *Wow! I LOVE it!* "A *little* tight in the hips…"

"We can let it out," both Hillary and Donna blurted before Hillary continued. "*Plenty* of time. The length…it's *made* long. Above or below the knee?"

*How the hell would I know?* "Ladies: how long *should* this dress be?"

"Um…" Leigh looked her friend up and down. "*At* the knee?"

"No," Donna declared. "*Mid-thigh* would wow 'em…"

"Would give *Dad* a *coronary*…"

Anita lifted the skirt nearly all the way up. "On *you*, dear, *this* dress would look good hemmed *anywhere*…"

"But I want to *wear* it again…maybe to *your* weddings, guys."

"Lets' go *below* the knee," Hillary suggested. "More *formal, and* save your father's heart. Then you can hem it up when and *where* you want. So, the jacket?"

Ann shrugged it on. "Do I really *need* shoulder pads…?"

"*We* don't," Donna agreed. After a few minutes… "yeah: the shoulders are good; the front closes fine. Hem the *sleeves*…"

"The jacket makes it look more…" Leigh struggled for the words.

"Like the office." Hillary looked thoughtful.

"Sure: a day in the weld shop, or maybe on a dive barge," Ann smirked.

"Try the *cape* instead," Leigh offered, placing it over Ann's shoulders. It fastened around the neck and reached to the mid-shoulder blade, rounded on the edges.

"*Much* better…in fact, perfect," Anita grinned at the nods of approval. "*Cape* it is."

"That's *it*, Ann." Leigh grinned into their reflections in the mirror. "You're a *bride*."

"Incredible," Anita muttered, walking up behind, placing a hand on Ann's shoulder. "The *first* time I saw you with JJ, I *knew* we'd end up fitting your wedding dress."

"Not the *first* time, Anita: we were half-asleep. Maybe the next morning." They met late one night when Ann and JJ stopped at Will's Florida condo.

Anita smiled broadly. "Does it *matter*, dear?"

*No.* Ann smiled and patted Anita's hand.

"Blouse?" Donna, barely an inch shorter than Ann, stood beside her. "Lace? Half-sleeves?"

"*No* blouse," Hillary offered. "Petals or backless bra."

"I *hate* wires in bras," Ann decided. "I *like* the half-sleeve idea." She turned to look at her mother's dress. "Like *that*." Though they tried several blouses, none quite matched Ann's vision until they pulled the new dress over the old one on a dress form.

"Yup," Hillary grinned.

"Perfect," Ann agreed.

"That's *it*," Leigh burbled.

"And...*nothing* like it here," Anita sighed.

"If *you've* got a few minutes, ladies," Hillary declared, "I've got something I can show the *bridesmaids*..."

"Oh, I'm *not*," Donna protested.

"I'm wearing my uniform, if *that's* OK, Ann," Leigh added.

"Sure."

"Well, *come* on, anyway."

Leigh and Donna left Ann alone with Anita, who was still pinning the dress. "*Sorry* about the blouse..."

"Don't worry about it," Ann sighed. "I'll find something...or nothing."

"We're the same size," Donna declared later. "I *might* have something you *could* use."

*New, blue, and borrowed in one fell swoop.*

***

"*You* should be attending to your details, John," Stella mumbled. "You don't *need* to be here." They sat in the vending lobby as Debbie finished with Charlie's daily dozen, and the aides changed sheets.

"Next thing the groom *has* to do is get the license with the bride tomorrow."

"Well, *Charlie* doesn't need you here."

*Charlie doesn't NEED me anywhere.* "I don't *mind*, Mom. Really. Is there anything else *you* need while we're out and about?"

"Brenda's doing some grocery shopping for me this morning. I *demand* the honor of hosting the rehearsal dinner Friday. *No* arguments."

"Wouldn't *think* of it, Mom."

"The *hell* you wouldn't. You're the *least* ostentatious guy I know."

"So I *don't* do *fancy*. Sue me. OK, bridal party's Kurt, Mike, Alex, Jenna, Leigh, and Deb; twelve with dates. Out-of-towners...Lois and Simon; Brenda and Roy, and kids. Our friends Wendy and Dennis; eight from Florida. Where?"

"River Hollow. *And* the McMullan's *and* the Barker's."

"Dad's family? OK. Call it *maybe* forty."

Debbie came out finally, smiling. "Mrs. Parkinson, he said your name."

They rushed to the room, not sure what they would find. "I've called the resident," one of the aides smiled. "It's *progress*."

Charlie's eyes were barely open, his lips moving, growling sounds coming out of him. He seemed somewhat agitated, eyes darting around, not focusing, moving his arms and legs as if trembling. The monitors showed increased heart rate and respiration.

"Mr. Parkinson, you're in the hospital," the resident said after a quick exam. "You've had a *stroke*. Do you *understand*?" She repeated this several times as Charlie seemed to calm down. Finally, he whispered, "Mary," before his eyes closed, and he was still. "Stroke patients sometimes do that." Dr. Hidalgo-Ruiz was a small and fair woman a little older than JJ.

Dr. Secord arrived, consulting with Dr. Hidalgo-Ruiz briefly. "I'm ordering another series of tests. We *may* have an opportunity here."

Stella stared at Charlie. "For what?"

"If there's more activity in the right places in the brain, it means he's rewiring himself, and the aneurism may be shrinking. Different parts of the brain…" JJ tuned her out. *Making yourself the center of attention again, Charlie?* He listened as Dr. Secord finished, "…so surgery *may* become an option. We'll have to see the results of the PET scan."

"How long will it take?"

"We should see the results this afternoon."

JJ and Stella sat once again in Charlie's room. Finally, Stella reached for JJ's hand, gripping it tightly. "I'll tell the club forty-five. I'm meeting Brenda and Lois for lunch." She took a deep breath. "No matter *what*, Johnny, he's *not* walking out of here. Even *if* he survives, he'll be in a nursing home. I *know* that; I *accept* that." She looked at him with an odd grimace. "And the last word I heard him say was *another* woman's name."

"Sorry, Mom."

"Let's just proceed with *our* lives and see what Charlie's will be like as it happens."

They waited until someone came to wheel Charlie to his tests. "Not sure I'm going to miss him, Mom, but I feel *bad* about *not* feeling bad."

"Sounds exhausting, Johnny." She patted his hand. "They'll call with any results. Can you take me home now? Lois said she'd pick me up there. I saw Claudia two months ago; we had a nice little visit. She seemed distracted, but she *knew* me. Is she going to be able to come? How many is the reception planned for?" They talked about wedding plans all the way back to Stella's apartment, plowing through enormous puddles on the road.

\*\*\*

"Think we could do the bachelorette party *here*?" Leigh studied the décor—and the security risks—at The Tavern on the Main, a renowned Clawson eatery where they stopped for lunch. It had a slightly underdone Olde Time motif, sporting barrel-like tables, cut-barrel chairs and stools, and saddle-like booth benches. "How many, Ann?"

They counted and calculated *certain* versus *possible* before Donna shrugged "twenty-six? OK…"

"Your mother," Leigh asked. "How's she these days?"

Ann smiled. "I *don't* think she'd do a party well."

"So, how is she?"

"*Stable* for the past few years. Good days and bad." Ann paused. "I want to thank you for helping Johnny. He internalizes so much, takes so much on himself, tries to turn his feelings into logic," she sighed. "He *loves* and gives *so* much…"

"*I* just helped him relax," Donna mused, "nothing special. I remembered his *adorable* eyes."

"Every woman I *know* talks about his eyes, even my *stepmother*." Ann gazed out at the dreary sky, the puddled parking lot. "Even if you'd *both* gotten naked with him *then* it wouldn't matter *now*."

"Bathing-suit naked," Leigh grinned, "we were *kids*."

"*Little* more than that, Leigh," Ann winked. "You were topless together in that motel room."

"*He* said my bra was scratchy, so *I* figured since the *lights* were off…"

"*The first* guy to *complain* about the feel of a *bra*," Donna grinned.

"*He* called it *erotically relaxing*," Ann patted Leigh's arm. "And *you're* uninhibited. I *know* that."

They were still chatting as Sid walked silently up to their table. "Hi, Sid," Ann smiled, "how…"

"Claudia Ann, please tell Mr. Elrath that Cliff Eyerdam is working for Newhouse. He should call me *right away* if he has *any* questions."

"Not familiar with *that* name…"

"*He* will be."

\*\*\*

"Hey, *Dad*," JJ grinned at Roger outside Sherry's room, "*got* something for ya." When he called the Reserve center, they said that Sherry's water broke just as they left their house for the drill hall Sunday morning. She delivered their daughter in the new obstetrics ward at the VA hospital in Allen Park that afternoon.

"Probably about two days' supply," Roger grinned and took the big box of disposable diapers.

"The best moms I know said it was better than flowers or even chocolate. More *needed*, anyway." JJ had never been *to* a VA hospital. However, he'd heard horror stories and remembered *Life* Magazine articles with half-naked amputees on gurneys and soiled sheets pathetically staring into the cameras. Inside this imposing colonial revival building, pastel-colored pastoral murals adorned the walls, lit by row after row of track and can lights, creating an atmosphere that belied the *Life* imagery.

"Got *that* right. How'd you find us?"

"I called the center. The woman who answered your number said she'd be *here*. So, here I am."

"Ask a simple question. Well, thanks. We got some of these," Roger hefted the box, "from the unit too. And with Sherry out for six weeks, they're *finally* sending us full-time clerks."

"How long can *you* be out for? I know the policy *says* six weeks, but it doesn't apply…"

"Since we're AGR, we get *some* of the protections that civilians get."

"I've *heard* of AGR, but…"

"Active Guard Reserve is just what it says. We're on active duty orders in a Reserve unit. It's a 9-to-5 gig most of the time, Active Army pay with a differential, benefits, and no night duty."

"Huh. Is that what you'd be offering *me*?"

"Yeah. How interested *are* you?"

"I've mentioned it to Ann—we're getting married Saturday. You can come to my smoker if you're so inclined."

"Yeah? Well, I…"

"Come on *in*, guys, lunchtime's over," Sherry called from inside the room. The baby was in a plastic bin; Sherry was pale but in good spirits. "Take him away for an evening with *men*, will ya? He'll be stuck with *girls* for the next eighteen years, at least."

"I've got my marching orders. Where and when?"

"Thursday night at the VFW hall on Maple in Bloomfield Hills. You can both come to the wedding too."

"We'll see…"

***

"I did an experiment a few years ago…yeah." Donna pulled a snow-white silk scoop-neck pullover top with half-sleeves off her rack. "Try *this* on."

Ann pulled the top on. *Long…almost to my thighs. A little loose. Textured like a handkerchief.* "What's the 'experiment' part?"

"I've done *this* neckline in everything from denim to canvas to macramé: dress, blouse, even a *crop* top somewhere. I thought I'd try it in silk as a long blouse." Donna pulled the slack out in the back. "*Some* cleavage but not a *lot;* sleeves are loose; shoulders neither sculpted nor restrained. Tighten it up?"

"It's beautiful, Ann," Leigh smiled. "Should fit right *with* that dress."

"I *like* the idea of gathering like that. *You* could be a designer." Ann stared at

122

a photo on the wall. "Who *is* that with my mother?"

"*Where?*"

"*There,*" Ann pointed.

"*That's* my *dad!* He *said* she was a neighbor."

"I've seen enough pictures of Mom right around the time she got married." She looked harder. "Yup. That's *Mom.*" She looked around her, pinched the sides of the blouse back. "How about a rope detail down the back?"

"What?" Donna snapped back. "Detail...*oh*, yeah. This silk is durable. A rope detail? Could do *that* in an hour."

"Even if they *don't* look right together, I still *could* go without anything at all." *Cold, but JJ wouldn't care...and who else is it for?*

"You *or* Donna could pull that dress off," Leigh assured her. "Me, no way."

"*That* dress *is* for us long-bodied women," Donna smiled, "but I'd bounce too much without a bra. So, I take an inch in. Guys, *I've* got a double shift tonight *and* tomorrow if I want *Thursday* and *Friday* off." Ann slid Donna's creation off over her head before they headed downstairs. "I'll see Deb this afternoon; let her know about the party," Donna waved as her friends left. "Call it thirty and three designated drivers?"

"Sounds right," Ann answered.

"Appetizers and drinks, no dinner."

"Right."

"G-string stripper or gorilla suit?"

"What?"

"*We'll* make it happen," Donna grinned, closing the door behind them.

***

"*That* was a Veteran's Day bash," she declared. "Ann's dad was in the Pacific at the same time as *your* dad; didn't *know* that." They stood across from each other over *his* bed, the door closed, rain softly beating on the windows.

"Neither did I. And JJ's brother was on Pork Chop Hill; his dad jumped into France on D-Day." He shook his head. "Kinda makes *our* service look pale." Leigh had followed Mike into *his* room directly after they came back from the hotel...and his parents had been right behind them on the stairs.

"*JJ* and *I* were on Grenada," she said, "and *you* got a medal for that interview you did in '79; not *that* pale."

"True," he sighed. "Did Ann find a dress?"

"Yes, and we found a place for a bachelorette party."

"Great." They stared at each other silently before Mike spoke. "Leigh: *about* you and JJ. *Ann and I know* you two have feelings for each other. If you *ever* want to...just *don't* try to *hide*..."

"We have a *lot* of feelings for each other, Mike. But, yeah, *sex* matters."

"I trust you *both* with my life, *oytzer*, but..." She started taking her blouse off...in *his* room. He stood in awe, tinged with alarm. "*Oytzer*, what...?"

123

"Mama told me this morning that it didn't matter."

"*My* Mama? No, *no, NO,* she *didn't. How* did Mama say *that?*"

"Well, it sounded like 'don't interrupt your lovemaking just to make us think you're not making love.'"

"No, *that's* not Mama. Try again."

"She said 'be kind to my son,' and I said 'we're kind to each other.' She came back with 'don't interrupt your joy just to make us think you're not…'"

"*THAT'S* Mama. And so, she said she and Pops…so," he whispered, pulling his shirt off, "no nightgown?"

"I can *get* it if you *want,* but it'll just…come…off…" She watched him close his bathroom door. "That means 'no?'"

"That *means, oytzer,* that you *can* get it if you *want*…but *please* not just now."

***

"*Some* Veteran's Day bash, Johnny," Ann sighed, spitting a stream of water. "Did you *know* Mike's Uncle Mort was a gunner's mate on USS *Savanna,* stuck with her through the war?"

"I did *not;* don't get to *shake* a hand that carried FDR up a gangplank very often. Nor did I know that Ben was in the 509th." JJ coughed. He submerged briefly as the rain beat on the atrium roof and the pool enclosure's glass walls. "Glad that Dave Clawson made captain. He was on the list when *I* met him."

"And his partner, Frank?" She flexed her hip. "An artilleryman in Vietnam."

"He was in the Mekong Delta at the same time as Jesse." He sighed. "And Cliff *Eyerdam.*" He grinned bitterly. "The First Horseman: the *first* name I gave the cops. I don't know *what* happened to *those* guys."

"Now, he's *here?*"

"Now, he's *here.*" *I'd sooner run through Hell in gasoline drawers than talk about this right now.*

*Change the subject.* "What's the latest on Charlie?"

"*Some* improvement, but not *much.* They'll look again on Friday." He hung on the pool wall, coughing. "You found a dress?"

"*You're* not *supposed* to ask, but Anita's *most* accommodating." She ambled toward him.

"Your mom was neighbors with Donna's *dad?*" He turned with his back to the wall.

She flexed her hip. "If he was *Mom's* neighbor, he was *Dad's.* The truth now: were you and Leigh ever an *item?*" She pinned him—smiling widely—against the pool wall.

"We made out. Personality-wise, she reminds me of *you:* sweet, kind, and generous." He sighed. "Even topless, she doesn't *feel* like you in my arms. How well did *you* know *Mike?*" He locked his hands behind her, pulling firmly.

*Her eyes ARE enchanting, but OH! so are yours.* "*You* made out half-*naked.* I know Mike a little; we've had some *chats.* You know *him* better." She leaned into him; he gave her his half-grin, closed his legs. "There's still a *lot* between you and Leigh."

"There *is*, but we *wouldn't*…"

"If you *do* go *that* far, just…"

"Tell *you*." Silence but for the lapping of the water. "I'll *still* love you; that'll *never* change. Even *that* time, we just…"

"*Yeah*," She sighed, leaned into him. "I tell myself that sex *should* be one person at a time—and *never* outside marriage—but *then* I think Roger…"

"But *you* were *hurt*…"

"I was hurt because I *might* have been a homewrecker. *Here*…in *our* case…" She breathed deep. "I love you both *so* much…"

"But sex *matters*, yeah?"

"So do *affection* and *honesty*." They looked deep into each other's eyes. "Tomorrow, we get the license." She spread her legs, gave him her warm smile. *I want THIS now…*

*She wants THIS now.* "Yeah. Do you *want* a Mass?" He pressed his hips forward gently.

*I'm gonna get THIS now.* "I can go to Mass every *day*. *That* church matters to *you*." She pivoted into him.

*THIS! NOW!* "*Had* to ask." He lifted her gently.

*Ooh!* "Remember, babe, I'm *not* changing my name." She shoved her hips into his, smiling brightly.

*Ahh!* "You *said* that before." He pushed…and…*pulled*.

*And…NOW!*

# *The Battle of Baroque Circle*

The morning came clear and bright, the wind and rain of the past several days were but a memory washing the fall leaves in the gutters. Leigh squinted in the glare before she opened the *unlocked* back door of the cottage. "*Good* morn— *OH SHIT!*" She did a *QUICK rear-march* outside as Ed and Cathy giggled inside.

"*Safe* now," Cathy called after a few moments.

"Not that it wasn't *safe* before," Ed mumbled, pulling a shirt on. "Just not something our *daughter* would want to…"

"*Yeah*, Dad," Leigh groused as he retreated to the bedroom. "I *get* it; *believe* me, I *get* it." Gazing out the window, she smiled. *Mom's THAT limber?*

"Joining us for breakfast, honey?" Cathy, her loose shirt unbuttoned and wearing *nothing* else, put a pot of water on the stove and popped some bread into the toaster.

"If I'm not *inconveniencing* anyone," Leigh replied, glancing around at the clothing strewn about. "Good thing I didn't bring Mike."

Cathy cocked an eye at her. "*That* would have been embarrassing for *you*?"

"Not *you*?" Leigh tossed a pair of tights at her mother as she sat at the island.

"Mike's a *cute* guy…" Cathy grinned, pulling them on.

"*MOTHER!*"

"Let me *finish*. If I were twenty years younger and *not* your mother, I'd be your competition…or ask you to join us."

"*What?*"

"You think *your* generation *invented* group sex?"

"*No*, but…"

"Well?"

"*Change* of *subject*. Ann and JJ want you guys to come to the wedding."

"Really?" Ed came out of the bedroom. "They barely know *me*."

"JJ *knows*…" They froze as the sounds reached them…then Leigh shouted, "*Dad: where's that 870?*"

***

"Michael, trash day," Ben declared. The golden morning was unseasonably warm for November. The light in the breakfast room streamed into the east windows, filtered through the ash trees along the lot line. Shadows played like feathered patterns of light wheeling and swaying across the wall.

"OK, Pops." *Something* told Mike to put his pistol in his pocket to perform the routine chore. *Load; lock; safety…why now?* He waved at Evan Hammerfest, fetching his morning paper out of the tube by the curb. Like Mike, Donna hauled *their* barrels out to the street, only she used the cart made for the purpose; he just picked them up by the handles. He also nodded to Kurt, taking out *his* trash as Mary fetched *their* paper.

Despite the irritating *something* that told him to take his weapon, Mike barely noticed the Crown Victoria rolling slowly around the broad, flat, and even Baroque Circle curve (which was, after all, *round*). It wasn't until the car stopped, engine revving and on the wrong side of the park …

*This don't look right…*

\*\*\*

"Huh. Your birthdays are only eight days apart." The marriage license application process had been relatively smooth and painless. However, *appointment* seemed to be more of a *guideline* than a *commitment*—they waited for an hour *after* their *appointed* time. The clerk—a frail-looking woman— grinned wryly. "My husband's lucky to remember what *month* I was born in. If I didn't put it on the kitchen calendar, I doubt he'd *ever* remember." She punched some keys on her computer. "Now…*oh*, yes. You're the Mueller/Elrath party?"

"We *are*," Ann smiled. "Did Dennis…?"

"Yes, you've been flagged. Take *this* down to Judge Oakes' chambers for your waiver."

They waited in more comfortable chairs in a paneled corridor. "We *are* doing this," Ann murmured.

"Pay our money and…" JJ started as a uniformed bailiff beckoned to them.

Inside, a large man in shirtsleeves and a tie held their application in front of him. "*Active* duty, are you," Judge Oakes boomed. "Did *my* bit in the Air National Guard. But, you're in different services. How will *that* work?"

"For the past year, your honor," Ann replied, "our services have failed to answer *that* question. The *advice* we're getting is 'do it and make *them* figure it out.'"

"I see. Dennis showed sound judgment, I believe, in leaving the Active before he and Wendy do it. But, if *you're* willing to risk Uncle Sam's indifference, *I* won't stop you." Judge Oakes handed Ann their application with his signed-and- stamped waiver. "Good *luck* to you."

After that, it was a check for $35 and a handoff, with the license effective immediately.

"We *have* done this, Cloud."

"We *have*, Johnny. You wanted to see Charlie?"

"Yeah."

\*\*\*

"YOU OK?" Leigh shouted into Mike's ear. "*AHHH SHIT, I'M HIT!*"

"I-don't-know," Mike huffed.

"*STAY DOWN,*" Donna yelled. "*STAY DOWN OW THAT HURTS!*"

\*\*\*

Ann studied the tubes and wires that were now a part of Charlie's life, thinking about the last time she saw him. *Can't get along with anyone.*

JJ noticed that *nothing* else had arrived. No *more* cards, photos, or notes. The flowers and balloons that brightened *other* rooms were conspicuous by their absence. *How drab your end shall be, Charlie. No one truly cares.* He found himself shedding a tear…or two.

Ann put an arm around him, whispering, "just let yourself *feel*, babe."

"Not *him*: *Mom*. Bastard's leaving her all alone."

"I *think* she'll be OK, Johnny."

"Yeah. Let's go see that florist." They had *just* started the Suburban when the news came on:

…*a shooting incident on Baroque Circle in Bloomfield Hills has left at least four dead and six injured…*

JJ didn't even *see* the traffic lights as he tore west on 13 Mile.

\*\*\*

Silence fell on Baroque Circle, save for an injured and noisily-annoyed goose. None of the three occupants of one car partially blocking Baroque Circle were moving. Four bodies lie around a second car, halfway up Kurt's driveway.

*Shots! Fired!* is *not* a radio call that Bloomfield Hills police officers often hear. *Two* minutes after that call, the first patrol car arrived. The officer—a young woman with less than a year on the job—called in what she saw, jumped out of her squad car, and shouted, "*are you hurt*" at three people lying on a lawn; a young woman waved her off. The officer drove off and blocked the access between Baroque Circle and 14 Mile Road.

After waving the officer away, Donna sprang up unsteadily, bleeding from an *inconvenient* place but strong enough to help both Leigh and Mike—who had been beneath her—to their feet.

*Three* minutes after that first call, two more squad cars and an incident van arrived with full lights and sirens. The squad cars blocked off 14 Mile between Telegraph and Inkster; the van rolled onto Baroque Circle. The supervisors and crime scene team glimpsed torn-up sod, oceans of glass, shell casings, and shotgun shells. With armed citizens standing around, it looked like a war zone.

*Four* minutes after the first call, there were flashing lights enough to dazzle even on that bright day. Fully half the Bloomfield Hills Police Department (of thirty total sworn officers) was present; more off-shift officers arrived every minute. Many Sheriff's cars and trucks also came to lend a hand. Then, the *state* police rolled in…*then* the FBI…

*Then* the questions began…

\*\*\*

"*Sergeant* Dietz, it would seem that *yours* was the *first* incident in this chain of events. Tell me, please, at your *own* pace, what *you saw* happened. Not what you *think* happened. What you *saw* and *did*." More shook up than hurt, the police led him to the incident van for a quick once-over...after disarming everyone in sight. Paramedics found a pencil-sized hole in his sweatshirt and a nick in his flesh under his left arm and moved him to an ambulance.

Mike glanced at the deputy—a clean-cut young man. Wincing at a stab of pain, he tried to put the blur of images into some rational order. "It *started*..."

The Crown Vic screeched into the driveway beside him as he threw both trash cans at the windshield. The cans cratered the glass, and the car careened onto the lawn, tearing up yards of sod when it came to an abrupt stop before a shotgun barrel peeked out of a rear window. Mike hit the ground, pulling *his* weapon out just before the shotgun exploded. He heard pellets *whir* around him as he squeezed his trigger, barely taking aim at a range of about five yards.

"It's the first time I *ever* pulled my duty weapon," Mike sighed. "I don't know if I *hit* anything but the ground with my chest. Did I *hit* anyone?"

"*Unknowable*," the deputy shrugged.

\*\*\*

"*You've* done this before, Ms. Taylor," the deputy sighed. "But, *best* as you can, put it together *again*."

Leigh remembered seeing Donna running towards her; she recalled aiming at the car's caved-in windshield as it rolled back across the street. She *also* recalled firing six shotgun rounds into the car when it gently bumped to a stop at the curb. However, she could *not* remember *how* she got to the driveway from the cottage...but she *had*, and her ankle and her bad shoulder hurt *A LOT*.

Moments after the first car was stopped, a *second* Crown Vic squealed around Baroque Circle, screamed in a ninety-degree drift, and stopped at the end of the Parkinson's driveway. Then, it roared halfway up...and stopped before what sounded like *hundreds* of firecrackers went off in *very* rapid succession.

Leigh—her shotgun empty—dropped on top of Mike as bullets buzzed around them, pushing him face-down on the ground. Then Donna dropped on top of them *both*.

"This is the *first* time I *ever* fired a weapon off the range. Did I *hit* anybody?"
"*Probably*."

\*\*\*

"Now, guys: get this straight," Dorothy admonished. "Get it in the right *order*. I'm pretty sure the prosecutor's *not* going to charge anyone here, but we need a *tight* story and a *right* story."

When the first car roared up the Dietz's driveway, Kurt had grabbed his loaded Ithaca Road-Blocker 10-gauge automatic shotgun from the dining room gun cabinet. At the same time, Mary pulled her mother's Browning Hi-Power pistol *and* her grandfather's Winchester trench gun out. From their front porch, the couple engaged four men emerging from the Crown Vic until they ran out of ammunition.

\*\*\*

"Mr. Taylor, Mrs. Taylor," the older detective sighed. "*One* more time for clarity."

Ed grabbed his Browning A-5 and went out after Leigh, loading on the run and aiming his weapon just as the second car stopped. He opened fire on it when the four men started shooting; one turned and fired at him. Much to his surprise, Cathy followed close behind him, shouldering his 16-gauge pump and blasting away.

\*\*\*

"Mr. Hammerfest," the small officer smiled winningly. "According to your statement…"

Evan used his prototype cell phone (he was a co-inventor of the system) to call 911 as the first car rolled back. Then he retreated to his front porch, where he gave the operator a running account of the raging battle.

\*\*\*

"Mr. Dietz; Mrs. Dietz," the chief of Bloomfield Hills police nodded, "I understand *your* participation was…"

"Late," Ben declared, rubbing his shoulder, "but we did our duty as neighbors."

By the time the second car stopped, Ben had grabbed his M1 carbine and Monica her 12-gauge over-under bird gun. Both fired at the second car as one of the passengers fired at their house.

"Father *insisted* I learn to shoot and gave me this gun," Monica declared. "Did we hit anyone?"

"*Hard* to tell."

\*\*\*

"All right, Ms. Hammerfest: *slowly*, now…" The older policewoman asked patiently as she sat next to Donna's gurney. "When the shooting *stopped*…"

"I heard dull moans from the *first* car, *nothing* else." Evan had carried Donna over his shoulder to a waiting ambulance. The bullet that grazed her derriere furrowed a welt about three painful inches long across each cheek.

\*\*\*

"Are you *sure*? Be *certain*, now: it's important. Who *was* it in that Lincoln?"

Before the smoke cleared, a Lincoln Continental *slowly* rolled around Baroque Circle, avoiding the first Crown Vic by rolling up on the curb.

*Everyone* who saw it remembered Joe Dryden smirking broadly from the passenger's side of the front seat. They saw his mouth move before the window rolled up, and the car drove away moments before the first police car arrived.

**\*\*\***

"Well, *fancy* meeting you here," JJ tried to grin. They had been waiting a *very* long half-hour, hearing rumors floating around among the hangers-on and rubberneckers at the barrier at 14 Mile and Inkster. Reporters among the crowd vied for *reactions* from onlookers. One seemed unusually interested in Ann but was glared away.

"Yeah, *real* fancy." Julia smiled from the other side of the barrier, bundling her hair into a ponytail as she approached.

They climbed into Julia's car and drove the half-mile to Baroque Circle while she filled them in. "Not *sure* yet *why*. Uncle Kurt and Aunt Mary are OK, but your friends Mike and Leigh *were* hurt—not *bad*, but they *were* hurt. So was another woman—*Donna* something. Jo woke up to the upstairs windows being shot out; she was *covered* in glass and debris and is in a *state*." They pulled up behind the sheriff's incident van nearest to Kurt and Mary's, where Julia hung badges around their necks.

Technicians were photographing bullet holes in the front of the Parkinson's home. Bullets had starred the heavy plate glass living and dining room windows. Several passed through the open door and hit the stairs. The porch pillars had been struck several times; the upstairs windows were destroyed; furrows gouged into the roof. In the living room, paramedics treated Jo with oxygen and an IV. Mary and a deputy sat with her. Kurt kept clearing his throat and coughing in the dining room.

"Anyone have *any* ideas as to *what* all this was about," Ann asked.

Julia shrugged. "We *had theories; now*, we need *facts*."

**\*\*\***

*Oh, Adam, you've got some 'splainin' to do.*

Adam and Kiera arrived, soon followed by Sara. Mike thought it odd that Adam flashed some sort of a credential that got him through the police barriers as if he were a sworn officer as they both headed towards him. Kiera spoke briefly to the EMT, glanced at the short chart, and went to see Leigh.

Adam pulled up a stool in front of Mike. "Newhouse." It was *not* a question. "We *saw* Joe Dryden."

"*Shit*," Adam snapped. "Sorry, Mike. Didn't *think* they'd turn *this* violent."

"*Nobody* did. You do what you've *gotta* do." Mike looked deep into Adam's face. "Secure the family."

Adam crouched by Leigh, an icepack on her ankle. "I'm *sorry*, but…"

"Adam, *we* had no idea that it would turn *this* ugly. But *this* is…"

"*Serious* firepower," Adam declared with finality. "Never *saw* so much 9 mm outside a range." He shook his head. "Is there anything *you* need?"

"I need *Mom* to calm down. Can you do *that*?"

"I can *try*." Cathy, nursing a sore shoulder, hectored everyone within earshot on criminal procedure and evidence preservation.

"Excuse me," Leigh called to an EMT inside the ambulance a few minutes later. "How long do *I* need to stay out here?"

The paramedic, an older-but-still-young woman with bangs that she struggled with every few minutes, glanced at her tag. "Go when you want. Your friend can go, too."

Leigh got up, still wrapped in the blanket (she wore a T-shirt and jeans but no shoes), and hobbled to Mike. "Sandy, we can go."

He nodded and discarded his blanket, feeling cold immediately. He grabbed her hand and started walking, but she limped painfully. He got her arm around his neck and hobbled towards the house. Adam, Sarah, and Kiera picked her up and carried her to the big sectional in the living room, ignoring the damage to the house's front and the starred living room windows.

Kiera studied Leigh's sore foot. "*Major* sprain," she murmured. "But *any* sprain hurts. I'll get you more ice now, a walking cast to use until at *least* Saturday." She nodded appreciatively at Mike's bandage, sniffed "paper cuts are deeper," then sat between them. "So, everyone feeling cold?"

"A little," Leigh replied. "My *feet* more than anything."

"Heavy socks," Kiera answered. "Just give your adrenaline a chance to wash out." She slapped Mike's leg. "Your *girlfriend hurt* herself saving *you*. You should be ashamed."

"Oh, I am," Mike grunted. "Infinitely. Now, see to Mama."

"Two slugs of brandy cure what ails *her*."

"Then, *get lost*." Mike smiled. "Let me do *this* on my own."

*Do what?* Leigh got her answer as Mike embraced her powerfully.

**✳✳✳**

"Kurt; Mary," Dorothy severely intoned, "all four men out of that second car were killed." The technicians were wrapping up their work, and the officers finishing the statements.

"Yeah, *then* what," Kurt snarled, pausing to cough. "Those guys were shooting at *us*."

"Do we know *who* they were; *why* they were shooting," Mary asked, bundling her hair once again; she'd *been* doing it over and over again for hours.

"The driver's ID was for Estavo Testa…"

"*Bullshit*," JJ shouted from across the room.

"That's the name on his license. Familiar to you?"

JJ chuckled. "Sure, like a wart on the back of my hand. A guy with that name was at Wolverine with me. I had him thrown out, along with Cliff Eyerdam, Nestor Boehlke, and Bruce Doyle."

The room was quiet. "Tell me *why*."

"Not...not *here*." There was still a half-dozen strangers in the house; technicians, police, and paramedics. "Back yard." Dorothy, Julia, and Dave followed JJ to a picnic table ten yards from the back door. "The Four Horsemen—Eyerdam, Boehlke, Doyle, and Testa—attacked a little guy named Evans one night. I ratted them out, and they were expelled."

"OK: attacked *how*? *What* was..."

"*Mom*," Julia interrupted with a *tiny* wink at JJ: he winked back—more a *tic* than a *wink*. "*Attacked*-attacked, OK?"

Recognition slowly crossed Dorothy's face. "*Oh*." She sighed. "So, then, when I say that Eyerdam was in the *first* car—*he's* dead—and Boehlke and Doyle were in the second, *that* wouldn't surprise you."

*Holy...* "No, Dot, it would *relieve* me. Let's go back in."

Dave, listening, shook his head slightly. "Whoever they *are*, *two* of them are *not* Doyle *or* Boehlke." He looked at all of them. "Take my *word* for it."

"All right, then," Dorothy resumed her narrative in the house. "*We* aren't sure why they were doing this, but I don't think it occurred to them that *anyone* would shoot back. We may *never* figure out *who* shot *who*."

"So, are *they* in trouble over there," JJ asked, distractedly looking out a living room window. *Something's in those shrubs there.*

"With three handguns in the first car, *and* the shotgun, and four submachine guns in the second?" Julia sighed. "*Don't* think so."

"JJ," he heard Jo's thin voice behind him. "Can I talk to you?"

"In a minute, Jo. Dot; Jules: come look at this."

Dorothy stood next to JJ. "What are we looking at?"

"Somebody in that hedge there; in that little park in the circle."

"We've *been over* it..."

"Steak dinner says there's *somebody* in there."

***

"Mr. Nick," Adam, the confident, clear-eyed island of calm cordially smiled, "*good* of you to come." As the news crews were leaving and law enforcement was wrapping up that afternoon, Nick Paulson knocked on the Dietz's door. Leigh wondered, *does Adam wear anything but blue/black suits and white shirts with conservative ties?*

"First, I need to make sure that everyone's all right," Nick began in a serious tone. "The firm is most concerned, and *I'm* concerned because we've been friends, Leigh; Mike." Nick was still the darkly handsome guy they remembered from high school, a little taller and a little more filled out.

"We *are*," Leigh smiled. "I don't know if you've met my mother, Cathy, and my father, Ed." Adam answered the phone in the kitchen—*all* calls, from the moment he arrived, went through him.

"Just call me Cathy, Nick," she smiled, offering her hand. "*Heard* about you at work."

"All the good stuff is true," Nick grinned, "and at least *some* of the bad. Mr. Taylor, pleased to meet you."

"Ed, please."

"I'm on my way to the hospital to be with Donna and her father. *She's* OK, they say, but she'll have a sore behind for a while. Mr. Avi and Mr. Michael have been asking but don't want to be in the way; Mr. Mordechai and Mr. Fabian have plans to come by tonight, *after* all the excitement."

"Well, *we're* a bit scratched up," Ben sighed, "but please tell the firm—*and* my brothers—we're otherwise safe."

"*So* glad to hear it, sir…"

"If I can interrupt, Mr. Nick," Adam said. "First, I *have* to apologize again…" Adam started.

"*Save* it, Mr. Block," Ben said sharply. "There was no way *anyone* could have predicted this morning."

Adam nodded. "The body count is seven; *three* in the first car and *four* in the second. We have IDs on them, but most are being withheld. However, the driver of the first car was David Harriman…"

"Poor *dumb* Dave," Leigh sighed. *Poor little fish…*

"Any relation to *Rob* Harriman," Ed asked.

"There's an uncashed paycheck in his wallet from Harriman Cartage."

"Rob owns a fleet of dump and cement trucks by that name; *we* use him from time to time." Ed shook his head quietly. "Had lunch with him a month ago."

Adam waited in the silence as Leigh shed some tears. "Mr. Block, *please* go on," Ben murmured.

"Sir, Estavo Testa, driving the second car, is—*was*—an *international terrorist*. Half the law enforcement agencies in the *world* will want to know *why* he died *in that second car* and *how* he *got* into this country."

"Any idea as to motives, Mr. Block?" Ben looked away. For the first time in a long time, Mike thought his father looked genuinely sad.

"What we *know* is that the first car had photos of the Dietz's *and* the Taylor's…"

"*US*," Cathy exclaimed. "They were after *US*? For *WHAT*?"

"*Easy*, Mom," Leigh warned. *The last time you got THAT look on your face was…*

"*AUGH*," Cathy exploded. "WHAT in the NAME of ALL that's HOLY are these…*AUGH*!" She left the room. A few moments later, a string of *distinctly* un-ladylike sounds emanated from the pool.

After several moments of unmitigated rage, Mike quietly asked, "does she do *this* often?"

"*Rarely*." Leigh grimaced at a string of words suggesting unnatural acts with forest friends.

Ed made a face. "*Ow, Cath: that* would *hurt*."

After several more moments, Adam observed, "she does it well."

"Haven't heard such a string of artful vulgarity since I left the Army," Ben agreed. "*Sailors* don't have that range."

"It sounds…healing." Monica cringed a moment later, looking questioningly at Ben. "I don't think *that's* anatomically possible."

"*Much* more eloquent than the hospital during a full moon," Kiera claimed.

"Haven't heard her repeat herself yet," Leigh muttered, wincing after an ear-piercing scream.

There followed a string of gibberish, ending with the loudest and most prolonged *"INTERCOURSE"* (the four-letter version) *screech* that any had *ever* heard. She came back to the living room, looking down. "Sorry. Just *had* to…"

"Vent," Monica offered. "Yes. Sometimes we do."

"Go on, Mr. Block," Ben prodded. "Is there *anything* else?"

"We'll be taking *active* measures from here on; I've started the outer cameras. No one can enter Baroque Circle without our knowing about it. There will be details on *everyone*.…"

"Details," Leigh interrupted. "Bodyguards?"

"*Not* like the movies, Miss Leigh. If you *see* us, we're doing something wrong."

"But when we leave the house, Mr. Block, what *then*?" Monica knitted her brows so tightly Mike thought they might hurt.

"We *have* enough people…"

"How *many*," Mike interrupted.

Adam smiled. "*Enough*, Mr. Mike. Sid Jackwell's organization will be working *with* us to safeguard you all."

"They know what they're doing, Michael," Ben murmured. "Mr. Block's people have guarded kings, prime ministers, popes, and presidents."

"Yessir. How much harder can it be to protect *you* if I can protect Mr. Sinatra?"

"*Frank* Sinatra," Cathy wondered.

"Some of our people were Secret Service; some, *other* services. Mr. Sinatra's employed some of them."

"So, we'll have to call someone before we…" Mike started.

"No. We'll *know* when you come and go. But for *my* own peace of mind, I'd appreciate it if we could drive you when there's more than just two."

"Um," Leigh looked disheveled and tired, "we have a wedding to go to Saturday; a couple of parties before…"

"No reason to change those plans, Miss Leigh."

"Folks: I gotta beat feet outta here," Nick declared. "Leigh, can I meet with *your* family tomorrow for lunch?"

Leigh glanced at her parents, who nodded. "Sure. Old Alexander's at 1300?"

Then they heard the gunshots outside; Adam reached into his coat.

\*\*\*

Dorothy spoke into her radio. "Sierra Two to all Sierra units: unknowns in Baroque Circle Park."

"Sierra Two." Moments later, two cars arrived, and five deputies emerged. One shouted into the hedge as two others went around to the park benches by the little pond. Once *again,* the waterfowl feeding on corn Monica had spread in the pond (the goose casualty had been carried to the humane society) were *noisily* disturbed. Moments later, there was an exchange of gunshots before three deputies rushed the hedge. More shots, some shouting, and deputies emerged with two prisoners.

"I owe *you* dinner," Dorothy smiled.

"Uh-huh." JJ peered carefully at the handcuffed men. "I'll be *damned;* Pale Face and The Hammer."

"You *know* them?"

"Yeah. The big one's Rick Stutz: we called him The Hammer because he's about as *bright* as a *bag* of hammers. The other one's Boniface Pale: called *him* Pale Face. He was the top marksman four years running. When I beat him in '70, I got eight demerits for insubordination."

"Oh, *shit,* I just *lost* another dinner," Dave grumbled.

"Why?"

"I *bet* that Stutz was still in *Oregon.*" JJ stared. "We've *been* tracking him."

\*\*\*

"Oh, *hello, Monica,*" Mary smiled at the door. The shadows were long on Baroque Circle as the barriers and bollards were being picked up. The second car had been flat-bedded away minutes before.

"*Hello,* Mary. You know Ben and Michael. You may *not* know his fiancée, Leigh Taylor, and her parents, Cathy and Ed. And you *probably* haven't met Adam Block." There commenced a round of handshakes and hugs amid the smiles and offers of refreshments.

"First, Kurt," Ben began as they sat in the dining room, "I want to thank you for intervening. If there are *any* legal complications…"

"Dorothy said *that* was unlikely," Mary said, with a slight cough. "Powder sticks in my throat …"

"*With* you *there,*" Ed agreed. "*Still* hacking it up, and my *ears* are ringing."

"Dotty's right," Cathy agreed. "Nobody in *my* office is gonna prosecute us."

"You were out in front of the garage," Kurt said to Ed. "They *did* shoot at you, but they missed."

Ed mumbled, "hit Donna Hammerfest, though, poor girl."

Monica asked, "what did they *want?*"

"*We* think…it's *complicated,*" Julia answered.

"I got *covered* with glass," Jo sighed.

"*Sergeant Tanner,*" Dorothy said sternly, glaring at the tall and fair deputy

136

sitting next to Jo. "*What's* your detail?"

"Front desk in Third Tour, ma'am."

Dorothy struggled *not* to grin. "You *realize* that Josephine's my *niece*."

"She's *also* my *friend*, ma'am. I heard the call on my scanner and came *machst schnell*."

Jo squeezed his hand. "I knew Dan in high school, Aunt Dot."

"Good German, Sarge," Mike said. "Use it much?"

"I was stationed in Germany—Butzbach—for a couple of years."

Dorothy seemed frozen for a moment. "I'm moving you to *this* stationary post tonight. You'll command the detail on Baroque Circle. Clear?"

"Yes, ma'am."

"All right, Sergeant; let's get your detail organized. Do you have anyone in *mind*...?" Dorothy and Dan left, followed by Dave and Morgan...who had seemed to blend into the background when they weren't actually speaking.

The parents moved off into legal territory in the dining room—getting repairs done and at whose expense. Their children had their *own* business in the living room as Mike asked Jo, "Do we *know* each other?"

"No, I was a grade behind." Jo sighed. "Sorry, I was such a bitch anyway."

"I don't remember..." Mike started.

"*I* do." She turned to Leigh. "I called you a tool of the patriarchy for wearing that choker in 8$^{th}$ Grade. Sorry."

"*Your* memory's better than mine..."

"Your eyes," Jo declared. "I remember your eyes."

"*Now,* I remember," Mike mumbled. "You called *me* a Neanderthal."

"No, *that* was my twin sister Mary's line. *Mine* was tool of the patriarchy."

"Well, *that* was *then*..."

Jo turned to Ann. "There was a time in high school when I was *supposed* to hate you because when you set that record in 10$^{th}$ Grade, you were competing as a *woman*, not a *swimmer*. My sister said that you should have *demanded* that the events be gender-neutral. She wanted you to boycott the state finals in protest."

Ann squinted. "Coach showed us that manifesto that was passed around. I remember thinking that just sitting it out would have been a forfeit. What good would *that* have done? We worked *so* hard to get there."

"I couldn't see the *point* of protesting," Jo finished. "I was *proud* you won; won for the *school*." She smiled sadly. "I never said *that* before."

Soon after, Kurt signaled for attention. "Gents: On a *less* gloomy subject, I am duty-bound to ask *all* of you to attend a *most* notorious smoker at the Amos Spalling VFW post tomorrow night. We shall send my baby brother JJ off to marital bliss with his most estimable bride, the *gorgeous* Ann Mueller."

"*Christ,* do I *blush* or *bow*," Ann muttered.

"Smile *demurely*, babe," JJ replied.

"Ladies," Leigh announced. "While *they're* exploring the depths of depravity that *smokers* fall to, *we* shall *tastefully* celebrate Ann's last hours of freedom at the Tavern on the Main in Clawson."

"Better not be *too* tasteful, or *I'll* leave early," Cathy grumbled.

"*Right!* No G-strings, no bachelorette party," Mary agreed.

"I've never *been* to one," Jo lamented, which was met with surprised looks. "I'm thirty, and I've never even been to a *wedding*, even my *brother's*. What goes on at a *bachelorette* party anyway?"

"Everything you've heard about bachelor parties is just, ah, *adapted* for a bachelorette party," Ann explained.

"Yeah, but the *guys* don't throw *their* underwear at the strippers," Leigh grinned.

## *Thursday*

"*Huh?* Elrath." Half-asleep, he answered the phone. "Yeah...OK; on my way." He grabbed sweats and his old green field jacket.

"*What uncouth* barbarian called *us* at the *ungodly* hour of...0619 while we're on liberty," Ann murmured.

"FBI Dave wants a *chat*." He shivered in the elevator and walking through the atrium to the lobby.

"JJ," Dave said; Morgan merely nodded.

"What ya got?"

"*One* of 'em's Testa," Dave said. "No *doubt* of it. Another's a local guy, Dave Harriman. The others we haven't ID'd yet."

"How'd you *know* it was Testa?"

"We've *been* looking for *him*," Morgan sighed, relating Testa's identifying marks. "Doyle's in New York; Boehlke's *elsewhere*."

"The only one of those IDs we *can't* say where they are is Eyerdam," Dave finished. "Just so's you *know*. Now," he glanced at Morgan, "*we* have waiting bed partners and some *sleep* to catch up on."

"Your *little* one," JJ asked.

"With my folks; his *grandparents*," Dave sighed.

JJ went back up to the penthouse to find Ann getting ready for morning PT when the phone rang.

"Hi, Ann," Mike said. "How goes it? Anything *you* guys need help with?"

"Yo, Mike. We've got it nailed. You guys make an appointment for the license?"

"Leigh's gonna call. Any pointers?"

"Appointment *times* are meaningless to them; bring a book."

"Will do. Listen, you guys busy this morning?"

"Sort of. We've got a plan to go over by Donna's. Turns out, my dad's an old neighbor of *her* dad's."

"Can you swing by *my* place after?"

"Yeah, sure. See you noon or so." As soon as she hung up, the phone rang again. "Mueller."

"Chief Petty Officer Claudia A. Mueller?"

*What the...? Navy mode on.* "Yes, *this* is Chief Mueller."

"Chief; this is Yeoman Striker First Class Art Peale calling for Lieutenant Brookhaven, commanding the Great Lakes Sea Frontier. Your orders for SEAL Team Twelve have been suspended..."

"They've been *what*?"

"*Suspended*, chief. Naval Military Personnel Command suspends until they can find another billet for you before they cancel orders."

"*Great*," she sighed. "What am I supposed to do *now*?"

"Since you're on liberty, you simply wait for orders."

"Yeoman, you *know* that the *first* signpost on the road to Hell reads '*simply*.'"

"Aye, chief. NAVMILPERSCOM doesn't *normally* do this when you're between stations. It's *probably* something budget-related, and they're just getting around to *you...yesterday*, the suspense date. I got *this* number from your father..."

"Ter*rif*ic. Wait, *how long*? I'm getting *married* on *Saturday*."

"Can't really *say*, chief. Week, *maybe* three. Your storekeeper rating is flexible, so probably not *that* long. If your liberty expires *before* you get orders, you're to report here."

"Where *are* you?"

"Downtown Detroit; the McNamara building." He was quiet before he spoke again. "You didn't hear *this* from *me*, chief, but Mr. Brookhaven *needs* a storekeeper."

"*Thanks* a *shitload*, yeoman." She sighed. "Sorry. You *need* a storekeeper?"

"The skipper doesn't *know* it yet. If you *want*, I'll make mention of *your* situation when I tell him *his* storekeeper ain't coming."

"I'll *act* surprised if he calls. You're striking for...?"

"I'm in a flag yeoman billet, chief...."

"That's an *admiral's* command?"

"*Captain's* with flag responsibilities. Can I do anything *else* for you?"

"No, you've done *quite enough*, yeoman. Out here."

JJ, having heard her end, stared. "So...Alaska's *off*?"

"*Looks* like. *Might* have a billet *here*." They stared at each other. "That Ranger company?" He shrugged. "Do you have any *Earthly* idea what a *Sea Frontier* is?"

"How would *I* know: it's *your* Navy."

\*\*\*

"Hi, guys," Donna smiled wearily, wearing a shirt-dress over baggy martial arts pants when she opened the door. "*Come* on *in. Dad!* We have *visitors*."

Evan came into the library/living room, took one look at Howard, and beamed widely. "*Howard Mueller*, as I live and breathe. My, my. Come *in*, please. And Stella! What's it been, *forty* years?"

139

They walked into the living room, crammed with books and furniture. "Can we *get* you anything," Donna asked. "Coffee; tea? Please excuse our clutter; we're a couple of packrats…"

"Eh, looks like my den," Howard declared. "Evan, I hadn't seen *you* since before you married Margie in '46."

Evan smiled. "*I* didn't marry Margie."

Donna grinned. "I have an *Aunt* Margie."

Howard went suddenly quiet. "*That's* why Donna doesn't even *vaguely* look like her."

"Margie married *Angus* after *you* married Claudia," Evan grinned. "*That's* why I went to MIT, where I met Donna's mother. Stella, *dear* Stella: you broke my heart when you married Jack Elrath."

"Evan, Jake died in '68. I'm remarried; I'm Stella *Parkinson* now."

"Huh." Evan looked thoughtful, glancing at Donna. "Jack *died* in '68? Did *we* see that somewhere, honey?"

"I dunno, Dad. It was in the fall, JJ…?"

"November," JJ offered. "But you mean 'Jake,' as in John *Jacob*."

"It was *Jake after* Angus started teasing him with *Jack*," Evan said. "There was a comic strip then with an ugly character called *Jackal*. Jack's father was known as *John*, so *Jack* took up *Jake* after busting Angus's lip."

"I *remember* that now," Howard grinned. "Nobody *ever* teased Jake again."

"Nobody but *me*," Stella added with a wry grin.

"I asked Dad about his father once," JJ mumbled. "He said, 'don't ever ask me again.' So, I didn't."

"*Safer* that way," Howard nodded, then turned serious. "Evan: we need a favor. Claudia's under care for dementia. Ann wants her mother around for her wedding on Saturday, but we *just* don't have enough people who she *might* know well enough to *help* her without *drugging* her. Claudia *might* remember you; you look *so much* like your brother. If you could go with Barbara to pick *her* up…"

Evan didn't hesitate. "*Certainly*, I'll do it."

"Dr. Mueller," Donna added, "*your* wife *should be* with your *daughter*. *I'll* help with Mrs. Mueller."

✳✳✳

"Mr. Elrath, Ms. Mueller, *please*, come in." Adam answered the door, urbane and quiet as ever.

Ann marveled at the marble floor of the foyer and the white ocean of the living room. "*Beautiful* place."

"The Dietz's will be with you presently, Ms. Mueller. May I offer you some refreshments?"

*Afraid I might stain the furniture.* "Not for me, thanks," JJ stared at the cathedral ceiling and the limestone fireplace that rose on two walls. "This place has *always* been…gorgeous."

"Funny, isn't it? I was *at* the Hammerfest's once—can't remember why—and Leigh and I were friends. *Never* thought to ask about you." Ann said. "Never occurred to me that you were *two*-timing me..."

"Now, now; *we* weren't in touch..."

JJ stood up when the Dietz's came into the living room. They exchanged pleasantries before Ben interrupted. "John, we have a wedding present for you."

"*Not* necessary, sir. We *don't*..."

"Block Associates will place three limousines and drivers at *your* disposal..."

"How *about*," Ann interrupted, "*two* limos and a medical transport van, My mother's at Pontiac State. She's *not* dangerous, but she tires easily. It's just easier to move *her* in a wheelchair..."

Adam grinned. "*Dangerous* is a relative term, Ms. Mueller. I have the man who drove Eichmann to the Buenos Ares airport on my payroll."

*It would not surprise me a bit if YOU were that man, Adam.* "Call me *Ms. Mueller* again, and *we'll* have a problem. I'm *Ann*."

"Honey," JJ frowned, "It's what..."

"It's what the *company* allows, Miss," Adam said. "My organization calls your future husband *Mr. Elrath* out of respect. You'll be *Mrs.* Elrath soon."

"I'll be *Chief Mueller-Elrath* pretty soon," Ann said, "how would *that* do?"

"You *will*," JJ asked. "You *said* you..."

"Well, it's *my* prerogative to change my *mind*. I'm simplifying *my* life and hyphenating."

"The Navy has some *fine* traditions, *Chief* Mueller."

"Kiera would like to offer *her* services for child care, John," Ben said. "She has two of her own, and I understand there's a toddler or two. She'll take them to the park, let them blow off as much steam as possible..."

"Before she puts them down for a nap...and she's *very* persuasive," Monica said.

"And two pre-teen children of my sister's," JJ nodded. "And Jenny has *three*."

"And Sara will help," Ben said. "*Her* children can calm *anyone's* down."

As they were leaving, JJ saw Jo waving at them from her house. He pulled up her driveway and rolled down his window.

"Hi, JJ. We've found an *old* physical address—before zip codes—for Parkinson Title and Trust at Nine Mile and Schoenherr. We'll check it out." She grinned, leaned into the car, and pecked him on the cheek. "Gotta *go*."

"She's working hard on this," Ann mused, watching her get into her car.

"Yeah. Can't decide if it's because she *likes* Mom or *hates* Charlie."

"Maybe both?" She nudged him in the ribs. "Or maybe because she likes *you*."

"What?"

She sighed. "You've never been *able* to see when a woman's interested in you."

"There haven't *been* many..."

She poked him harder. "*Half* the women you interact *with* are *interested* in you. You *never* saw it in Kristin's face when *she* saw you…"

"Well, she *did* try to *seduce* me…"

"*Twice, she* said. They have to *throw* themselves at you before *you* know that they *like* you. I think *that's* Asperger's Syndrome…"

"More like ass-*burner's*…"

"No *wonder* you didn't have any dates…"

"Not *many*."

"I *never* asked this before, but…how *long* did you go *between*…?"

He smiled wryly. "I'll put it *this* way: I had more sex the first *week we* were intimate than I'd had for the entirety of my *life before* that week *combined*."

She blinked; he nodded. "Should I be glad for *me* or sad for *you*?"

"Either/or, Cloud," he sighed, "either/or."

***

"*Hiya*, Nick," Leigh smiled. "Been waiting long?" Old Alexander's décor was a cross between a hunting lodge and a smoking parlor, with a pinch of old-style gentlemen's club. The waiters wore pseudo-tuxedo jackets; the waitresses were in high-waisted short skirts with dark stockings. Individually they looked a little silly; side-by-side, utterly ridiculous.

"*Not* long. Your parents are coming?"

"They'll be along. How've *you* been?" Nick wore a Brooks Brothers three-piece suit and a *tastefully* subdued tie and had *barely* opened his mouth before Leigh said, "*here* they are." With her parents dressed for the office, she felt slightly underdressed in civilian dress slacks and a sweater.

"OK," Nick started after they ordered. "All I *know* about Leigh's situation is that her marriage was annulled by reason of fraud default and that the Newhouse family has been harassing you ever since. Care to fill in some blanks?"

They told him all they could remember about all their contacts since '74. Nick scribbled notes on a pad before Leigh handed him a thick envelope. "Everything I received *and* copies of everything I sent back."

"Good," Nick replied, glancing at Cathy and Ed. "Can I get everything *you* received, too? If you *want* it back, I'll make copies…"

"I've got a whole drawer full," Cathy replied. "I'll have my acting attorney get in touch with you, and you can *keep* the crap."

"I still have *some* stuff at my office in New York," Ed admitted. "I'll *call* and get it to you by express. Nick, what's this going to *cost* us?" Ed looked stern, arms across his chest.

"Fees and expenses are being handled by a third party," Nick replied in a *most* business-like manner.

"That's the *script*, Nick," Leigh answered, smiling. "*Who*?"

"I'm not at liberty…"

"Are you *at liberty* to confirm that my family's legal fees and expenses are being paid by the Dietz family?" Cathy had asked in a *most* cross-examining tone as their meals arrived, crossing her arms. "Assume a like posture if affirmative."

He grinned and copied her pose.

"How did they pick *you*, Nick," Ed asked, slicing his beef.

"The firm likes my work, sir, and I'm familiar with some of the people," Nick grinned bashfully. "Out of *everyone* at Dietz, O'Bannon, no one else can say that. That my father *is* the US Attorney for Eastern Michigan *might* have something to do with it. And," he added, *sotto voce*, "if anyone finds out that *you know* who's covering this bill, *I'm* dead."

Cathy knitted her brows in mock concern. "Now, how on *Earth* would *we* know *that*?"

When the meal and the meeting were over, Cathy and Ed pled the press of business. Leigh and Nick were left in the nearly-deserted restaurant. Leigh sensed that Nick was thinking something that he wasn't *saying* and couldn't decide if he *should* say it...or *how*. "So, Nick, where did you go to law school if you don't mind my asking?"

"Wayne State," he replied, wiping his mouth. "Dad wanted me to go to *his* school—Columbia—but I couldn't afford it." He waited for a beat. "Does *that* matter?"

"Just to know what an old friend's been up to."

He grinned. "We weren't *exactly* friends, Leigh. A smooch at New Year's doesn't make us..."

"We weren't *intimate* friends, but..."

"You put up with me."

"That's not fair, Nick, and it's not *exactly* true."

"It *felt* true. Girls scare the bejesus out of me...always have."

"Do *I* scare you?"

"Your *gender* can make *mine* feel bad just by looking at us a certain way, and *that's* scary."

"I've *heard* of that." *Can't look at a women's magazine without seeing it denied, vehemently, and unconvincingly.*

"Once I, well, *talk* to a girl for a while—in Donna's case, for *years*—I can get a sense of whether or not she might be interested. Donna *never* gave me that look that asks, 'why do *you* exist;' neither did *you* or Bobbi." He sighed, a lonely, heart-rending sound. "I *have* to apologize, Leigh. I *was* kind of a shit in school."

"You *dismissed* us too quickly. We wanted to make up our own minds."

"I didn't want to embarrass myself by trying to get Donna's attention *or* yours. Besides, she was hanging with Mike up to 9th Grade, the *one* guy who *liked* me." He looked at her directly; his eyes were almost pleading. "I thought *she'd* never see anything in *me*. But then there was *you*. If it hadn't been for Randy, I might have gone for you."

"So why did you hang out with *us*, then?"

"Mike, then you and Bobbi. *Mike* listened. Not everyone did."

"He liked you because you're good at reading people. It's something he admires."

He looked briefly disdainful, putting his hands on the table. "Wow." He looked wistful for a moment. "Would *you* have given me a second look?"

"*Maybe*. You're a good-looking guy, but back then, you seemed to have been interested only in Bobbi." She reached for his hand, finding it cool to the touch before he withdrew it. "You and Donna have been cozy *lately*."

"I want to get more *involved* with Blondie than we've *been*." He frowned. "She called me out of the blue in '75. She'd *just* caught *her* guy with another girl." He looked puzzled. "I've never asked *why* she only calls *me* after every breakup." He shook his head. "I haven't had any other *serious* girls than *her*. We've *had* fun whenever we've got together, but it hasn't felt *personal*. I *want* more: I *asked* her for more the other day because I want a *future* with her. What if she says *no*?"

"She *still* sees that streetwise Brooklyn smart-ass who blew her off an hour after you met; part of your charm. But she *knows you* won't hurt her, that *your affection for her* has healed her time and again, sex or not. Do you imagine that *anyone else* in her life would have been *trusted* to bring her home from the hospital?"

"*You*, maybe, or Mike."

"She needed *YOUR kind of love,* buddy, *not* ours."

"Last I *knew*, we're…someone to be with so we're *not* alone. But *I asked*…" He looked at her strangely. "Why am *I* having *this* conversation with *you*?"

"Because, pal, you *had* to have it with *someone* you can trust *and* who knows *just* what you're talking about."

"*You?*"

"Why not?"

"Because I didn't think girls—*women*—had the same…"

*That sounds both familiar and sad.* "Trust me, buddy, *we feel like you do. Our* hormones just complicate things. Want *my* opinion on what makes relationships fail?" He stared. "Lack of intimate trust. Nick, my friend: Donna's had *that* for *you* for *years*. Come to Ann's wedding *with* her."

For a moment, he looked like a lost puppy that had found its mother. "I remember Ann Mueller from 11th Grade Government class. We did that trial project together. She was nice, convinced me to think about the law as a profession like my dad *couldn't*." He looked away. "JJ, I met last New Year's."

She smiled genuinely. "You can come to *my* wedding, too."

"*Can* I?"

"Donna's my maid of honor, but after the ceremony, she's all yours."

✳✳✳

"Now hear *this*," Ann announced in the atrium, soon after the Florida crew arrived from the airport. "*These* guys," she pointed to Mike and Leigh, "are old friends. *He's* one of my *oldest* friends," she glanced at Sid. "*Those* two," she gestured to Dave and Morgan off to the side, "are with the FBI, and collectively, *we've* got a problem."

"Ladies and gents," Sid smiled. "We're going to need your eyes and ears for the next few days. The simple truth is that someone here in town wants to do mayhem to Claudia Ann and Mr. Elrath and Miss Leigh and Mr. Mike. My security people and those of another organization are securing the events and the routes, but we can't *be* everywhere. The security details will be wearing either red ties or red scarves, but with nearly a hundred invited guests…"

"Our lives are over-compartmented," JJ interrupted. "We're relying on a few people who know certain elements of our lives to identify as many people as they can. My sisters can identify *my* family; my stepniece can ID my *step*family. *I* have friends from a private school who—except for Mike here—*no one* else would know. Most of my stepfamily are strangers to Ann's…"

"And *I* have friends and family *and step*family that JJ's family wouldn't know, either," Ann added. "And his *father's* family, who will be here, *we* haven't seen for more than a decade. So, the security guys are going to have their work cut out for them."

"But we're asking *you* guys to make sure that no one who just looks *wrong* will get too close," JJ finished. "I think you can appreciate *that*. Mike here—you guys met him in Florida—is in CI."

"The woman watering the plants over there with a red kerchief on her head…" Betty grumbled.

"One of mine," Sid smiled.

"Who's 'my,'" Gary quickly asked.

"S. Jackwell, Organizational Readiness," Sid replied, setting out a stack of cards.

"Organizational *Readiness*," Nancy giggled, picking one up. "You went looking for a name and settled on *that?*"

Meeting her gaze dead-pan, Sid said, "*superior security and unsurpassed business intelligence* seemed ostentatious. *And* was *way* too long for the letterhead *or* the cards."

"Red ties, scarves, kerchiefs…should we…?" Kristin scanned the glass-and-brick walls of the atrium, stopping at the pool enclosure.

"No," Mike answered. "*Those* people are armed." he nodded to Leigh, who pulled out her CID badge. "So are *we*."

Gary shrugged; Tom yawned; Liz and Nancy shared whispers; Betty and Laura studied the atrium's upper levels; Kristin's gaze didn't leave the pool. "That's a *heated* pool?"

"Yeah," JJ answered, waving at Wendy and Dennis coming in from the lobby, "and *it's three whole hours* before you guys have to be anywhere."

"Hey, guys," Wendy waved at the Florida gang as it broke up, who was as surprised to see *her* as *she* was to see them…but *not* as surprised as Dave and Morgan.

"What," Ann whispered as JJ chatted with Wendy.

"*They've* visited both the Newhouse home *and* offices this last week."

***

"Guys, thanks *so* much for coming," JJ smiled. Behind him was a single-story concrete block structure on Maple east of Lahser: The Veterans of Foreign Wars Post #669, known as the Amos T. Spalling Post.

"Well, thank *you* for inviting us," Ben replied. "I haven't been to one of these in so long I can't recall whether the girls were pretty or not." The building had a flat roof with overhanging and rusting eaves over an unruly hedge of sprawling yews.

"I remember mine," Ed grinned. "They had a girl jump out of a cardboard cake in a leotard: *she* was pretty but *older*." A WWI-era artillery piece and a flagpole flanked the recently-replaced, broad sidewalk that connected the disintegrating parking lot, the crumbling sidewalk to Maple Road, and the rusting mailbox. The post was marked by a garish back-lit painted glass sign firmly planted in an elevated bed of failing evergreens on the corner of the parking lot.

"*Feels* familiar," Mike mused to JJ as they went inside. The cheap paneled walls, the worn linoleum floors, and the slightly-cheesy stacking furniture were augmented by shabby hand-me-down upholstered chairs and sofas. The flags and patriotic posters made it look like every service club on every base they'd *ever* been in, including Fort Benning's legendarily opulent enlisted club.

***

"Whaddaya mean *no*," Leigh growled at a small man named Seth—according to his Tavern on the Main nametag—who began to sweat as Donna frowned, crossing her arms, scowling.

"We've got the Mueller party on the calendar *next* Thursday," he sputtered.

"But it *has* to be today," Deb moaned, sitting slowly on a stool. "It *has* to be. *Poor* Ann will be *so* disappointed. And *I* need a bathroom."

"The ladies' room is just around the bar, ma'am. We just *can't* make that many appetizers without a day or so notice, and it's on *our* calendar for *next*…"

"But you *can*," Lois purred loudly, "serve *that* many *drinks* until you *get* appetizers from *somewhere*, now *can't* you?" To emphasize her point, she opened her checkbook, pen poised in midair. "You have a *couple* hours before we consume *all* your peanuts and popcorn…"

"Well," Seth sighed, "I *suppose* we *could*…"

"Of *course,* you *can*," Leigh smiled broadly, watching Lois's pen descend.

***

"*Here* he is: the guest of honor," Kurt bellowed as JJ entered. "Last hours of freedom, eh? Whaddaya think, guys, is he gonna *run*?"

"No!" "Never!" "She'd hunt him down and kill him," were all replies shouted over the tinny jukebox music. The party—pulled together on 48 hours' notice—

was as festive as those occasions *ever* are.

Though he had only two beers all night, others tried to ply JJ with liquor as the dancer began her routine, gyrating to some Middle-Eastern tune on a boombox. "Traditional," Jim—Ann's older brother—slurred. "Groom should *never* leave his stag party sober."

\*\*\*

Brenda brought Stella to Tavern on the Main, who was most effusive and animated. JJ's aunts June McMullen and Brenda Barker spent much of the night catching up with JJ's sisters and getting to know Ann. Carol and Holly, Ann's sisters-in-law, shared laughs with JJ's surrogate mother from Brookfield, Marie DeHaven, and with Clare and Jenny. They arrived just before the well-made-up, delicate-looking dancer in an elaborate costume made his appearance.

"He *can't* be eighteen," Donna mumbled, watching his gyrations inches from Ann's bemused face.

"His 18th birthday was last month," Jenna grinned.

"*You* know this *how*," Leigh asked, watching Ann take a pair of (someone's) panties from a laughing Cathy...Ann was in jeans.

"We're in school with him," Brianna smiled as Ann threw the undergarment at the boy. He caught it deftly, hung it on his G-string. "Donnie does this in talent shows. Family business, he says. We got him to do this party; his *cousin* to do JJ's."

\*\*\*

"Pretty girl," Mike said to two younger men loudly over the boom-box music as the comely and smiling almond-eyed beauty swirled and twirled.

"She's in my 6th Hour Spanish class," one of them answered.

"Really?" *SHE'S in high school?*

"Yeah," the other one answered. "I've known Naomi since 5th Grade; Middle-Eastern dance is a family business. Her cousin Donnie does it, too."

"Who *are* you boys?" *She's in HIGH school...*

"I'm Ann's stepbrother Alex," the shorter one replied.

"Billy Reidy," the tall one said. "I'm friends with *his* sister. We got Naomi *here*."

"Oh," Mike sighed. *She's in HIGH SCHOOL?*

\*\*\*

Leigh watched the boy for a time before she realized that Jenna was talking to her. "Ann says *you're* getting married in a few weeks to a guy you've known forever. Why didn't you do it before?"

"Because, as much as we love our service, the Green Machine is a cruel bitch who, until recently, has insisted on Sixty-Day-Joes."

"What's Sixty-Day-Joes," Brianna asked. Leigh explained briefly. "Huh," Brianna mumbled. "But why do you stay with it? You don't *have* to."

"Because I *love* the job. It's challenging and interesting. I've done more real, important work than I *imagined* I'd do in high school."

"And the *money's* not bad. With the benefits, it's more than I could have made teaching language in Arizona," Liz added.

"*Or* Chicago," Nancy smiled. "And it's a *useful* skill; language analysis will come in handy."

"And manual salvage is dying," Betty complained. "That's how Starski and I got into *this* gig."

"Starski…" Jenna glanced at Laura, "*her*?"

Laura nodded. "And *she's* Hutch. We learned to dive in our family's salvage business: Betty in Missouri, me in Florida. But robots *are* taking over. We saw that the Navy allowed women to be divers at the salvage convention where we met, so *we* said 'what the hell.' Just so *happened* that a 'Starski and Hutch' rerun was on the TV over the bar when we shook hands on our enlistment."

"Then the *Navy* said, 'oh, *how* would *you* like to go to Explosive Ordnance Disposal School, too?'" Betty finished her beer. "We said, 'how can *that* be more dangerous than salvage,' and signed on the line. *Now* we're bomb disposers who, ironically, learned to *operate* robots."

"Yeah," Laura said. "Ain't *that* a kick in the head."

* * *

"Geez," JJ shouted over the music, patting an uncle on the back, "ain't seen *you* in a dog's age. How've you been faring?"

"Good, good," Andy McMullen beamed. "Looks like *you've* done well for yourself, John." Andy was an eternally-chapped redhead who was probably cute as a young man, but he just looked weathered and worn in middle age.

"I get by," JJ answered. "The bar's open; get yourself something. Those are Charlie's sons over there…"

"Hear *he's* not well," Doug Barker— another uncle, a big man with a round face—added off-hand.

"No, he's not."

"Stroke, Stella said," Andy mumbled.

"Bad one," JJ agreed.

Doug added, "he's *not* one of my favorite people, but I don't wish ill on anyone."

"Ah, Andy; Doug; Charlie's *not* walking out of there, and *Mom...*"

"She only has to call, John," Andy replied.

"I know that Barb and June don't *like* Mom much…"

"They'll be *fine*, John," Doug nodded.

* * *

Donna edged painfully on her stool. "You ever *have* to pull a gun, Leigh?"

"Twice. Never fired one off the range before yesterday. I've Maced people,

148

used a stick a few times. I've had taser training, but I never used one."

"You use your karate?"

"It's discouraged because MPs always need a solid edge over a perpetrator. Even my black belt may not be good enough to take down a 300-pound drunk swinging a fire extinguisher."

"Might be handy to learn a little of *that* in real estate," Jenny grinned.

"*Or* special ed," Clare agreed. "But doesn't the constant relocation *get* to you?"

All the servicewomen—including Alice—sighed as if on cue. "They're *trying*," Leigh finally declared. "They realize that they have to make accommodations these days…"

"But are they *enough*," Wendy asked. "Dennis reenlisted for the Reserves just so we *might* stay together because he was due for another overseas tour *if* he stayed in the Active." She shrugged. "He's not throwing his fifteen years *away*, but there'll be less at the end if he can't find a Reserve slot everywhere *I* go."

The party wound down, and the pictures were taken. Leigh cornered Wendy in as friendly a manner as she could muster under the circumstances. "So, Wendy, where are you *from*? I understand you're up here on leave."

"Yeah. Dennis has family in Pontiac, but mine's in the UP." She smiled winningly. "My *aunt* was a Leigh Taylor."

"Really," Leigh smiled.

"Yeah, my mom's oldest sister—Leigh Elizabeth Taylor—died in '30."

Leigh felt she'd left her body. *Leigh Elizabeth Taylor; died the year Dad was born...* "Do you *know*…I mean, the *circumstances*…?"

"In childbirth."

*CAN'T be.* "WHERE?" *TOO LOUD, and I'm attracting attention...*

"Albany. She was only *fifteen*."

*NO! FREAKING! WAY!* "Um," Leigh mumbled, *barely* keeping her interrogator's composure, "do you have any *proof* of this?"

"The family Bible. My mom…hey, are *you* OK?"

Leigh had flushed white; Betty sat her down and handed her a bottle of water. "Thanks. *MOM!* Um, Wendy: if *you're* right, you're my *cousin*, and I've never *had* a cousin before." She turned as Cathy walked up. "Mom: Meet *Cousin* Wendy…your *niece*."

Cathy blinked. "*How?*" Leigh told her; she shuddered. "Well, Wendy, if *this* checks out…" she glanced at Leigh, "*we* will have a *great* deal to talk about."

*** 

"Well, Johnny," George, Ann's eldest brother, quietly said just outside the door, "I'm glad you and Claudia can finally be together."

"Thanks, George. Brenda's in town. I could give you her number if you…"

"*That* might be awkward. Did she go into nursing like she wanted?"

"Yeah. She'll be *happy* to see you." *Why the look?* "You didn't *call* her, *did* you? Your wife doesn't know anything *about* you and Bren, *does* she?"

"No." Silence. "I suppose she will *very soon*."

"Did your wife go to *Ann's* party?"

"Ah," George breathed deeply. *"Yes*, of *course*."

"So much for *that* cat in *that* bag, George."

***

"Dad, you're *not* going to *believe* this." Leigh, breathless, wide-eyed, and beaming like a little kid on Christmas morning, rushed in the cottage door, her surprised father standing in the small living room. *"We...have...cousins*," she declared. "This *woman* I was *talking* to..." He listened for the next few minutes, blinking in astonishment. "So, if she's *right* and her *aunt* was your *mother*—my *grandmother*; *wow!*—then *she's*..."

"Wendy would be *our niece*, Ed," Cathy declared. "And her *mother* would be..."

"My *aunt*," Ed whispered. "And there's *more*? *More people?*"

"Yeah," Leigh declared. "Two aunts and an uncle on her mom's side; three uncles on her dad's—*they're* in Nebraska and Iowa. And...*Dad?*"

Ed seemed to simply fold into the floor until he sat cross-legged, smiling wistfully. "I had *finally* come to terms with the fact that, but for you two, I was alone. Now...*we're* not just *us*."

"It's a lot to take in, Eddie," Cathy soothed, rubbing his shoulders. "Best we all *try* to get some rest. This Bible...?"

"We'll see it tomorrow."

## *Friday*

"Think there's a necktie on that doorknob," Ann mused. They were lounging in their favorite atrium corner, with a view of their old 2$^{nd}$ Level room door, where the mermaids and Tom were staying.

*"Could* be. Their future together...gotta wonder." The Semitone's were feeding little Gabrielle—nearly 20 pounds—near a fountain; she was distracted by the water. Liz and Nancy shared a table with Betty and Laura; Tom and Kristin were nowhere in sight.

"Yeah. *Ours*...what's going to happen?"

JJ sighed. "You *could* have a job here: so could *I*." He stretched painfully. "I've *gotta* get out of the field. I *can't* jump anymore..."

Ann murmured, "Could do *worse* than here."

"Money's not the issue. Here's just a lot of less-than-good associations for me."

"There are good ones too, Johnny. And Charlie won't last forever."

"I know, honey, I know." He watched the suite door open; Kristin came out dressed for swimming. "PT time."

*"We* should get ours."

150

"Yeah." *Swimming with Cloud AND Kristin? Let's see what happens.*

***

"Haven't you guys got *other* things to do the morning before your wedding?" Charlie Junior asked. His father's monitors blinked unceasingly, the oxygen hydrator bubbling like a Lawrence Welk show on speed...all of which Charlie Junior watched...distracted.

"*I'm* making sure *he* isn't going to crash the party," JJ said. Charlie's room was crowded. JJ and Stella sat in the love seat; Lois and Brenda sat in stacking chairs. Charlie's sons sat in stacking chairs on the door side; Lew Rockland and August Sherith sat at the foot of the bed; Simon and Roy stood in front of the door, arms across their chests. "Ann's getting her *hair*...something."

Suddenly there was a jerky movement on Charlie's bed, and everyone stared blankly. "Saw this before," Stella sighed. "Wait." Soon it stopped. "Doctors think it's like a dream."

"Happen often?"

"About once a day. It means that either his brain's rewiring itself or it's trying to wake up. A nurse will be here in a minute." Presently a young woman with dusty blonde hair came in, looked at a monitor, smiled at them, took Charlie's blood pressure, charted it, and left. Stella shrugged.

Charlie Junior looked at his father in the bed. "Now, just stay there, Dad, and we'll take care of everything." He smiled at JJ. "Can't help but think that he'll jump up and start screwing things up like he always does."

"That's why Kurt and I eloped," Will declared. "Dad made such a mess of *your* wedding we swore we wouldn't let him do it to us."

"*Mrs.* Parkinson," Lew began, "we have a *great* deal to..."

"You have *not* been given permission to speak, *Mr.* Rockland," Lois snapped.

"Well, I..." Lew sputtered.

"*Shaddap*," Kurt snarled. "You'll *speak* when *spoken* to." Lew moved to get up. "My daughter's firm found your *billing records* at Dad's dealership. You'll *stay put,* or *Fabian O'Bannon* will have you before his committee."

Chastened and pale at the chairman of the Michigan Bar's Ethics Committee's mere mention, Lew sat unsteadily.

At great length, JJ declared. "*Your* services are no longer required, *Mr.* Rockland."

"I work for your parents, *Mr.* Elrath," Lew squeaked with obvious sarcasm. "Your father has been a..."

"*Stepfather*," Brenda grumbled. "Don't confuse *this* scab with *our* father."

"Nonetheless," Lew continued, "I'm here because Charlie's been a long-term client and friend..."

"Dad never *liked* you, Lew," Kurt declared, "you just did *what* he wanted *when* he wanted it, like any good bag-man. Mom has *other* representation now." JJ saw Stella startle, then smile.

151

"Well, *I* need to speak to *her* about that," Lew declared unsteadily. "If you all will *excuse* us…"

"Why," Will asked, innocent-faced, "did you *both* fart?"

Nearly everyone but Lew and August suppressed chuckles, painfully. Lew stared at Will, then Charlie Junior. "Insults? At a time like *this*?"

Kurt yawned. "You've been terminated."

"I don't *have* to sit for *this*," Lew sniffed. "Mrs. Parkinson and I…"

"The firm of Dietz, O'Bannon represents *us* now, Lew," Stella intoned, not looking at him. "Mr. Mordechai Dietz is at your offices at this very moment collecting *all our* files."

"And *your* files, Mr. Sherith," JJ sighed, "are to be turned over to Evans and Towne today. *Please* cooperate with Mr. Evans—yeah, *that* one. Eddie's an *old* friend of mine."

"Evans and…" August whipped around, blinked, surprised; Lew stared. "*Evans* and…but there's nowhere *near* that much…"

"*Do* it, Augie," Will snapped, "and *get out*." With Simon and Roy swinging like doors, their quiet departures caused barely a ripple in time and space. "Could have knocked *them* over with a feather, JJ," he quipped. "You *really know* Evans and Towne?"

"Yeah, I *really* do," JJ answered. "They've got *a lot* of my money."

"Now, a lot of *mine*. John," Stella sighed. "Ladies, *we* have a *date* with a *dress*." She gazed around. "I've wanted to fire *those* toadies for years…*thank* you, *all* of you, for giving me the strength."

✳✳✳

"Wendy, this is my father, Edward Taylor," Leigh smiled. "Dad: your *niece*, Wendy Corey." The little home with a dollhouse-like interior, just off Maple Street in Pontiac, belonged to Dennis's family. Ed shook hands with Wendy and with Dennis's mother, Shirley Oakes, a rounded woman.

"Mr. Taylor," Wendy began, smiled, and added, "*Uncle* Ed."

"Just…*Ed* for now, please. This has been a *lot* for me to take in. I've been *alone* all my life…until last night. But you *have* some documentation?"

"Yes. This Bible has *been* in my mom's family for generations. I believe *this* is your mother."

*Leigh Elizabeth Taylor; born January 5th, 1915, in Albany, NY, to Mildred Inez McGowan Taylor and Oscar Mitchell Taylor*

"Place and date are right," Ed said. "I *have* her birth certificate."

"Oh! Mom would *love* a copy. Here she is *again*…"

*Leigh Elizabeth Taylor; died in childbirth May 4th, 1930, in Albany, NY*

"And, here's *you*?"

*Edward Addison Taylor, born May 4th, 1930, in Albany, to Leigh Elizabeth*

*Taylor and NONE.*

Ed blinked furiously. "That's *me,* alright. I was either going to be Edward Addison or Elizabeth Mildred— Mother chose those names; I *have* the slip of paper she wrote them on. And father...*none.* No one *wanted* to *know* who my father was. Wow. After *all* these years..."

Leigh stared at the entry for her father as Wendy spoke. "Never knew about *that,* Ed. Mom said it was important to keep this stuff up, and I've *tried,* but I've got some gaps."

"Huh," Leigh looked up, barely able to think. "Gaps, Wendy?" She looked at the pages; many were glued into the old book. "Who *started* this?"

"My great-great-grandmother Eppie Reed. She started it during the Civil War. Her family was long-lived...look; this is the earliest date: she wasn't sure of it:

*Joshua Michael Reed; born Effin, County Cork, January 9th, 1771?*

"*This* info came from Joshua's granddaughter, Mom said. Followed by..."

*Joshua Reed married Elizabeth Honor Pegram in Albany, NY, on June 25th, 1801.*

"My great-great-great-grandfather. But the Newhouse connections from the 1950s are weak; I've been trying to make some *sense* of them. *That* branch of *their* family's estranged..."

"Wait: you're *related* to the Newhouse family?"

"By marriage via adoption. Here:

*Charity Francis Taylor married Edward Newhouse on October 22nd, 1948, in Albany, NY.*

"Followed by...

*Charity Taylor Newhouse divorced Edward Newhouse on 19 December 1960 in Lansing, MI.*

"But from *there,* we don't know much else."

"I married *Randy* Newhouse in '73."

"That's the *Randy branch*; there's *four* Randy's. Edward—our uncle—was the *younger* Newhouse brother who passed in '64; Aunt Charity in '69: here, in the notes. Once I get some dates, I'll make proper entries for them. There are only a few Newhouse's who know about *that* branch. Their two girls went into foster care when Uncle Edward died because Aunt Charity was very ill. But...though you look like cousins on paper, you're only Randy's cousin by adoption. Here:"

*Infant girl adopted by Oscar and Mildred Taylor 23 January 1923, named Charity Francis Taylor.*

"Before we go *any* further," Wendy grinned, passing a note. "Ed, Mom is *expecting* to hear from her *nephew* this morning."

***

"May I *help* you, sir?" A slightly worn yet bright 40-something brunette with soft brown eyes at the Gift Suggestions desk smiled. Wandering the mall somewhat aimlessly, JJ wondered at the early-holiday sales traffic…and what to do about a bridal gift.

"I'm getting married tomorrow, and I'm told I should get her a gift, but I have no *idea* what."

"Bridal gifts are either small and personal, or romantic, or both," she declared, "anything from favorite food to a room full of flowers. But the *best* gifts are those *she* can use—and can *appreciate*—but no one *else* can. Have you known her long?"

"Most of our lives; long story."

"And a lively one, I'll bet. Something of a journey."

"You *could* say that. Detroit to Japan to Germany to Italy to Grenada to Florida."

"Oh, you're in the service?"

"We *both* are."

"How about romantic and *practical*? Bob gave me thick knee socks for a bridal gift on *our* way to Germany. Kept *me* warm even in Baumholder in January."

*She complains about being cold all the time.* "*That* might work."

"Down this branch and hang a right," she pointed, "on your left about halfway to Montgomery Ward's is the REI store."

"Thanks, ma'am." He walked down to the REI, dodging the occasional kid running this way or that. Though he'd only ever been in one once, the feel of the place was familiar as he went down one aisle and turned around to see "hi, Jo! What…you *following* me?"

"Not…well, *yeah*," she blushed. "I stopped to find shoes for your party and saw you come in *here,* and…yeah, I need to talk to you. *Personal.*"

"Oh, OK: I'll *trade* ya. I need warm socks for my bride as a wedding present. *You're* a woman: Advise me."

"Um…nobody ever asked *me* for *that* kind of…well, OK, a *smidgeon* of estrogen for *Unka* John…over *here.*" Two aisles over was a rack loaded with colorful footwear. "She's got dark hair, light skin, yeah? OK. Here: red with yellow and white hearts."

"*Perfect,*" he smiled. *No idea if she'd wear them, but she'd love 'em anyway.* He checked out before they found a coffee cart out in the mall. Sitting down together, he asked, "so…personal?"

"You're the only *other* guy I know who's my age and still talking to me. I drove the rest away."

"What about that deputy?"

154

She sighed. "Yeah, *about* him." She looked away briefly and craned her neck. "I once saw your gender as the enemy. Last week a guy said my eyes were pretty. I didn't know what to say! My response *would* have been 'drop dead, Neanderthal' until a year ago, but *this* guy was *cute!*"

"So…what'd ya do?"

"I just smiled, and he went away." She sipped her coffee. "What did I do *wrong*?"

"A guy who says something nice and doesn't follow up is doing just *that*: paying you a compliment. If you had thanked him, he might have taken that as a signal to say something *else*. You didn't, so he was satisfied with that. The old Jo reaction would have stung him like a slap in the face."

She sighed. "I'll be thirty-one at the end of the month; I've had sex with *two* guys in *my life*." She looked forlorn. "I'm *lonely* and *tired* of it. What's wrong with *me*?"

"You drank too much of the women's lib Kool-Aid. You took it too seriously."

"Too *seriously*?"

"You *can't* expect to erase thousands of years of tradition and outlook overnight. We open doors to be polite to *everyone*, not to degrade or belittle. The ladies' tees are there so you *can* use them; you don't *have to*."

She looked stern for a moment as if to disagree before she smiled. "I had *real* conversations with Dan. He doesn't *seem* repelled by me." She cleared her throat theatrically. "I got a suite at Dad's hotel while they patch the house up. I asked *Dan* to come with me to your wedding." She inhaled deeply. "He *said* yes."

"Did you tell him about your suite?"

She cleared her throat. "Not *yet*." She made a squinty face. "I *should*, shouldn't I?"

"A wedding followed by a rendezvous in a hotel suite owned by your *father*. Yeah, *lots* of *first* dates are like *that*. I think it would be *advisable* to tell him that you *had* to get out of the house, and your dad *owns* the joint. It's *true, and* it prepares him for a 'come on up to *my* place' proposition after the cake and coffee. And he *may* have to work…"

"Yeah, *you're* right. He can pick me up *there*. And if he *wants* to *stay*…"

"Think he *might*?"

"A girl can *dream*, can't she?" She smiled slyly. "If we go *that* far, he'd damn-well *better* be ready for a sleepover." She winked unexpectedly. "I get to kiss the groom?"

"Oh, *sure*, *now* you want to cozy up to me."

"Oh! *Take* me *now*, you *handsome savage*," she loudly proclaimed with a *beautiful* grin, spreading her arms wide, turning several heads.

***

"This'll *work*," Ann admired Donna's blouse that enhanced the delicate

155

filigree of the dress.

"Looks *fabulous*, Ann," Barbara said. "You'll knock him dead."

"*I* can do *that* stepping out of the *shower*," Ann said to general hilarity.

"Hem is good," Donna announced. "Formal below-the-knee yet *fashionable*. Hips are…"

"*Glad you* approve," Hillary smiled.

"I wore this on *my* first wedding day," Stella presented a hatbox. "I lent it to your mother on *hers*." She pulled out a white lace birdcage headpiece. "I thought *you* might want to wear it."

"*Oh*, Stella," Ann grinned, putting it on. "It's…" *dusty and old-fashioned and yellowed with age but* "…beautiful." *Something old.*

"Allow me," Anita lifted it off. "We can clean it up."

"*I* have something, too." Barbara opened a small box. "If you would *want* to wear *this*."

"I *remember* this," Ann smiled at the sight of the Celtic-pattern gold wire pendant on a serpentine chain.

"*I* wore it on *both* of *my* wedding days," Barbara grinned. "It's been in my family for over a century."

"I'll be *honored*, Barbara," Ann sniffed.

Brenda studied Ann's dress critically. "Somehow, not very…*wedding*."

"What would *I* do with a *gown* after tomorrow, Brenda," Ann grinned. "Store it in Dad's basement watching it molder? *This,* I can at least wear more than once."

"There's this *cape* thing," Lois draped it on Ann's shoulders. "Looks more formal." She studied Ann in the mirror. "Dad always *liked* you."

"I don't remember *him* well," Ann replied.

"Mm," Brenda agreed. "He remembered *you*. Mom…"

"Wanted to keep Johnny and me apart; yeah, we figured *that* out." Ann glanced at her new sisters in turn. "It was because of *my* mom, Stella said."

"Makes sense," Brenda nodded. "Is *your* mom coming?"

"Complicated but…*WOW!* Look at *that*, will ya?" Ann gaped at the pantsuit Donna modeled, a dull bronze lamé creation that *her* figure filled beautifully.

"It fits well enough," Donna said, "but…*hello?*" She gazed at Brenda, who looked like someone had goosed her.

"Sorry," Brenda shook her head. "Never *saw* an outfit like that in *that* fabric."

"And you're not *supposed* to upstage the bride," Lois said.

"Lois: the first thing you *have* to know about Donna is that she upstages *every* woman in *every* room." Ann smiled. "She *always has*."

"Ann, *come* on," Donna scowled, grinning. "That outfit *you* wore for senior prom: you were *practically* indecent…"

"I was *cold* in that skimpy thing, and you *were* indecent," Ann laughed. "That *flaming red* thing with *no* back and *practically* no front that *you* put on with a *brush*…"

156

"I'll have you know I worked on *that* costume with a floor-length skirt for *four months…*"

"You guys can remember each other's prom dresses," Lois asked. "I can barely remember my *prom*. You must be *terrific* friends."

"*Sort* of," Donna said, "but we *have* good memories." She regarded Ann carefully. "Henna?"

"A *little*," Ann said, starting to take off her dress, "*and* I got my ears pierced again."

"Wow," Leigh said. "Wonder if JJ will notice."

"He'd better," Stella said, "or he'll be in the *big* doghouse."

***

"OK: first step, prelude; second step, Ann steps off; third step, the chorus…" Kurt explained; the *fifth* plan in an hour. Traditionally, a wedding rehearsal is an informal event where the bridal party goes through the motions of coming up the aisle, going back down, and so on.

"Ah, Kurt, hold it," Ann frowned. "If *I'm* that far, the bridesmaids are…where?" *This* ceremony was starting to look a *great* deal like trying to herd kittens.

"Yeah, OK. So, who's the *first* bridesmaid?" Also, the middle bridesmaid was in a walking cast, so *nothing* was pacing correctly.

"Me," Jenna mumbled. Finally, the pregnant matron of honor had to go to the ladies' room in the basement every twenty minutes or so, which slowed *everything*.

"*Still* doesn't address how *we* get the high sign to start," Liz interjected from the choir loft. Before this afternoon, the chorus imagined that wedding maneuvers—like close-order drill—came down on the stone tablets with Moses.

"OK," Leigh interrupted. "How *long* is your piece, ladies?"

They conferred briefly. "No more than a minute," Nancy answered.

"OK. Ann, start back at the inner doors and come up the aisle."

"Time it by thinking 'two…pew' for every *four* paces and advancing *one* pew every repetition." Pastor Lew suggested.

"*Fifty* seconds this time. You've *done* this before," Howard declared.

"All right," Leigh went on. "Think of the pastor as a traffic light. He signals for the prelude—the chorus can cue the organ—when JJ and the ushers come up the side. Then when the prelude *ends…*"

"*Ninety* seconds," Alice declared, "marked by *this…*long chord."

"Good…*Pastor* nods for Jenna and the Wagner to start at the same time."

"Same timing, ladies," Pastor Lew said, "'two…pew; two…pew…'" but was interrupted by a *disturbing* sound from the loft…

*Dum da da DAH dum! Dum da da DAH dum! Dum da da DAHH dum! Dum da da DAHHH!*

"*Send 'em to school, and they eat the books*," Pastor Lou declared. "*Not* 'Ride

157

of the Valkyries:' 'Here Comes the Bride!' Try being *original* next time." He shook his head. "Ever since that *Apocalypse Now* movie, I get *that every* time I say '*cue* the *Wagner*'…"

After the giggling died down, JJ declared, "but *you're* slow as *molasses*, Leigh. Could *she* just start in front?"

"How about a wheelchair," Pastor Lew asked. "We keep one in the closet."

"But *that's* even slower," Leigh complained.

"Not if I *push* it," Mike shrugged. "I *cross over* while Debbie comes up."

"*That* might work," Leigh nodded. "Then, when Deb gets up *here* and *turns*, Pastor cues the aria, and the bride starts."

"And I raise my hands…*so*," Pastor Lew announced.

Even though the choreography *seemed* to work as they practiced and refined it, as *everyone* knows, only a *lousy* rehearsal can result in an excellent performance.

*** 

"We were stuck up here on display," JJ recalled to Lois. The rehearsal dinner at River Hollow Golf Club was on the same elevated dais/dance floor that the bridal table was on for Lois's wedding.

"And *you* didn't want to dance with Melinda," she shot back, grinning bitterly in her unique way. "Embarrassing."

"*You* didn't have to stare at her chest while she glared at *you*," JJ replied. "She was a head taller, seven years older, and didn't have a *civil* word for me."

"True that," Simon replied. "Mel *was* in a mood for some reason."

"She *was*," she asked. "Thought she was *always* like that."

*** 

"So, you two are cousins," Ann smiled, bemused. The big horseshoe seating arrangement on the dais ensured that two sides would be by windows, and the third would have their backs to the main dining room.

"Sure looks like it," Wendy agreed, patting Leigh's shoulder. Leigh and Mike, Wendy, and Dennis sat on the corner by both windows, watching the golden sun setting.

"Never *had* one before," Leigh sighed, "not quite sure how to act around her."

"Don't ask *me*," Ann answered. "*I* never had one, either. Can't wait until somebody surfaces and says, 'oh, your Great-Uncle Jingle Heimer Smith's third cousin's love-child had my step-sister-in-law back in Bug Tussle. You've never *heard* of us?' At which point I'd say…not sure I *need* to."

"Pretty bizarre, yeah," Leigh agreed. "Not like we *looked* for Wendy, though."

"There's *that*," Dennis murmured to Mike. "Might be different under different circumstances."

"My family's so big I don't know that anyone would *notice* there was another

158

branch," Mike smiled. "*You* from a big clan, Dennis?"

"Not especially. Mom, Dad; two brothers and a sister; two nieces, two nephews. Three aunts and three uncles; seven cousins. Both grandmothers are still with us; a great aunt and great uncle will turn a hundred in a few months. I think they're determined to see the *next* world war since they lived through *two* of 'em already."

"Wow: long-lived?"

"My *mom's* family is. My *dad's* clan has a tendency not to make it much past fifty. Except for Grandma Betsy, who seems to be indestructible after two heart attacks, a stroke, and cancer."

* * *

"So, Andy," JJ began, sitting with Andy McMullen close to the windows overlooking the golf course. "Charlie wanted you to take me off his hands?"

"Yeah, he did. We *couldn't*, but he did." In that very room, Andy and June angrily stormed out of Lois's wedding after a *very* loud conversation/argument with Charlie.

"Couldn't, or *wouldn't?*" The reason for the abrupt departure had been a mystery to JJ until recently, but Stella would never speak of it.

"Same thing," Sue McMullen, JJ's cousin, two years younger than he, replied. She was apple-cheeked, cute, and a foot shorter than JJ, and like her younger brother Peter, adopted.

"No, it isn't," JJ replied.

"Yeah, it *is*," Andy answered. "As long as Sue—an adopted minor girl—was under our roof, we couldn't have *you* living with us."

"State law," Peter added. Peter looked like a slightly younger and male version of Sue—which he *was*: a year and three days younger and of the same mother.

"Yep," Andy smiled. "We had to go through all kinds of hoops just to adopt *them*. Governor *Romney* couldn't adopt children in Michigan, the law's so restrictive."

"And as much as we care for you, the idea that your stepfather would pay *us* to raise *you* was enraging," June concurred.

"I didn't *need* his money," Doug Barker lamented. "I can buy and *sell* Charlie Parkinson." Jake's half-sister, Brenda, was married to Andy's younger cousin Doug, who had patented an aluminum siding bending brake that revolutionized the industry and made him one of the wealthiest men in Michigan.

"But he wouldn't listen," Aunt Brenda lamented. "He just kept saying 'name your price.' We just *had* to walk away. Not that we don't love *you*, Johnny, but we *chose* not to have children. We just don't have the temperament for it. The idea of taking money for *that* was insulting *and* infuriating."

159

\*\*\*

"How's retirement," Ann asked her Uncle Allen and Aunt Maggie at the end of the horseshoe. Allen was Howard's older brother, Margaret (Maggie) Ann's mother's younger sister. "Running out of things to do?"

"Wish I *was*," Allen, a veteran pilot/airline professional, opined. "My Honey-Do list never *ends*. Never had a home in such good shape, but there's always *something*. Once in a while, an old boss will call me up and want something or other out of me. I tell 'em all to drop dead."

"But he's been offered a job in Washington," Maggie added.

"NTSB has wanted me on *their* payroll for decades," Allen grinned. "I just may take them up on it someday. In the meantime, would your Johnny be interested in talking about a book? Thought I might write about the war before I forget it all."

"I'm sure he'd be thrilled, Uncle Allen," Ann smiled. She knew that Allen— a decade older than his brother—flew in three different air forces under three names. He wasn't sure how many enemy planes he shot down, though he believed it was thirty. He counted four with the RAF during the Battle of Britain, six with the Flying Tigers in China, and twenty with the USAAF in the Solomons and New Guinea.

\*\*\*

"Nice club," Betty said to JJ at the buffet table. "A lot like the club *my* family belongs to in Cape Girardeau."

"Yeah," he said, interested. "You came from money, too?" Though he'd known Ann's unit members for months, he knew only a little about them.

"Yeah: silver spoon kid. Sadowski Snag and Salvage was—*is*—one of the largest salvors on the central Mississippi. But when the water's high, everybody hits the links. *You* golf?"

"*Swung* at and missed; *shit* at and hit. Just never had the knack for it. You?"

"I always thought golf was an *awful* way to waste an afternoon I could spend reading, though I *tried* to learn."

"You finish your thesis yet?"

"Proofing now," she sighed. Betty worked on a Master's degree in sociology *and* psychology; she and JJ had discussed some of her research. "You about done with *your* degree?"

"Spring. Then *maybe* grad school if I stay in one place long enough."

"Ya *know*, sweet-cheeks," she said softly, just before they left the buffet table, "you *should* say *some*thing about her *hair*…"

"Whose?"

"*Eleanor Roosevelt*, dummy!"

"Oh…Ann?"

"Yeah, *Ann! And* she got her ears pierced again…but you didn't notice *that*, either!"

160

"Uh, well…"

"She got henna highlights; diamond studs in her ears." She made a disgusted sound. "And guys wonder what *we* get mad about."

"Thanks for the heads-up, Starski. I'll say something tonight."

"*Good idea,* sweet-cheeks. That *guy* over there, the blonde. Know *him*?"

"My cousin Pete. He's unattached as far as I know."

"Ah,*"* she smiled. "See if I can wrangle a conversation and maybe a ride to *his* place…give Laura some time with *her* snag."

"*He's* staying at the hotel…"

"*Well,*" she grinned like a hunter at a pheasant, "*that* makes this *much* easier."

\*\*\*

"So, Wendy," Mike smiled and flashed his credentials, "*not* the kind of venue I'd *prefer*, but… we've got some business."

Wendy's face suddenly turned serious. "What *kind* of business?" Her delicate features belied a strong personality.

"Counterintelligence business. How much contact have you had with the Newhouse family or business *before* you came up here last week?"

"Practically none. The only thing I *knew* about them before this week was meeting *some* of them when my Aunt Charity died—I was fourteen—and what's in the family Bible. My mom has corresponded with them; that's how I knew they were around here."

"OK, *we've* got this problem," and he laid out a short version of the perceived threat. "So, if you told *anyone* about JJ or Ann…"

"No," she shook her head. "*My* contact with them hasn't been *that* intimate. I haven't used their names in *any* correspondence with my family or friends."

"Can we talk to your mother?"

"She'll be in town next week to meet Leigh and her family." She sighed. "*Official* business? *Really?*" He nodded; she sighed, "OK, I can set it up."

"Do you know *anything* about your Newhouse cousins on the *Edward* side?"

"We haven't had contact with *them* since their mother died." She shrugged. "My *Dad* thinks *that* part of the family tree looks like a telephone pole."

"You mean…"

"Not *enough* branches."

\*\*\*

"*Hey*, Blue-Eyes." She pulled her new coat on as they left the party.

"*Hey*, Green-Eyes." He shrugged his old parka on. "How's the foot?"

"My *hip* and *shoulder* are worse now. You feel like a groom yet?"

"Not sure what that's *supposed* to feel like. A little trepidation, more nervous that something will change with Charlie that'll bollox the whole thing."

"John: I *wish* you *well*. Really. We *blew* our chance; *everything* got in the way."

"First, Randy, *then* Mike, then the Army. *Still,* I think…*sometimes*…"

"Me, too." She bumped his hip. "If *we'd* made love *just* once…"

"Just *once*. It would have been *beautiful*."

"Would have been *clumsy*. The first time *always* is."

"You've had *how many* 'first-times?'"

"Yeah, OK." She turned to him. "But ours *would* have been in that hotel room on that sack-of-rocks bed."

"I never told you before, Leigh, but the *feel* of your bare breasts on my chest was *spectacular*, even if I couldn't *see* you."

"I never told *you* before, John, but the *feel* of *your* chest on *my* bare breasts was *spectacular* and *sweaty*, and you left those curtains *open*: you could see *more* than *you* let on."

"True." They giggled as the valet pulled her Citation up. "*You* were *beautiful*—you *still* are. And we'll *always* have *that night*."

"We *will*, Blue-Eyes."

✳✳✳

"*Hey*, Legs, I *like* your hair. Can't *remember* you wearing earrings."

"*Hey*, Sandy. I needed a change; I thought I'd keep it simple. I haven't *worn* earrings in *ages*."

"Diamond studs suit you."

She watched JJ and Leigh. "I *think* our friends are content with the way things are."

"She *says* she is. Still…" they stared with small smiles, "we can't *really* blame them."

"No, not if *we…you* know."

"They've gotta figure it out themselves…like *we* do."

# *Ann and JJ*

"*Hey*, groom," Kristin sputtered, having swum three laps—at least twenty yards—underwater as the wind and drizzle battered the skylight, "nervous?" In a suit like Ann's, she was already swimming laps when JJ got to the pool at five that morning.

*Like I want to jump out of my skin.* "Some."

"*Don't* be. All you have to do is sign the papers, say *I do* in front of everyone you know, and kiss her." She smiled *ever*-so-sweetly. "Then, we get to kiss *you* with Ann *watching*."

"*You* tried to *seduce* me once or twice."

"I *knew you* were too devoted to her to expect much. It was fun *sort-of* trying." She slid back underwater, swirled around like a seal, and popped up again. "Yours is the fourth wedding I've ever been to: two sisters and a brother. I keep wondering if, *some*day…"

"What about Tom?"

"He's getting orders for Fort Bliss in February."

*I didn't know that.* "Sorry."

"Don't be, buddy." She nodded. "I'm putting in for recruiter duty. I *want to* go with him, and I *love* the Navy. We'll *make* the Blue and Green Machines figure it out." She smiled her seductress smile, stepping slowly in his direction until they were a yard apart. "Johnny—*sweetie*—if I offered myself to *you* here, *now*, would you *think* about it?" As if to punctuate, she started to peel her top up.

"You *know* I'm marrying *OUR* best friend in about five hours."

She kept peeling *very slowly.* "But she's not *here,* and I'm lonely *now.* It's the way I'm *wired*, lover."

"We missed *our* chance long ago, *lover.*"

"We never *had* a chance, *lover*," she answered, creeping closer, still peeling. "As long as Ann was around, *we* were hopeless." She stood close, her top *very* high up on her breasts, and placed her hands softly on his shoulders. "But what fun we *might* have had." She leaned into him, smiling. "Kiss me like you *mean* it, Johnny." She planted her lips, and he parted his. They lingered for a long moment before she pulled back. "Ooh, yeah, we *would* have."

"I'll have to *tell* her…"

"*I'll* tell her *first*," she grunted, pulling her top down and herself out of the pool, "*Now* I have to wake *Tom* up since *you've* made *me* all hot and bothered."

"I saw Betty *go in* a few *minutes* ago."

"Yeah; so?"

*** 

*I put on a dress; I walk down an aisle. Simple...couldn't be simpler.*

The battering wind outside the condo seemed loud when Ann woke up at 5. She shambled into the dark kitchen and ate an apple and some grapes, wondering about their next duty stations more than what would happen in a few hours.

Howard turned on the lights and pecked her cheek. "I'm glad to see *you* can eat. I'm giving away my only daughter in a few hours and nervous as a cat in a room full of rocking chairs."

Suddenly a wave of nausea made her run for the kitchen sink. *Oh, God, I don't know where THAT came from.* "Sorry."

"I should be apologizing to *you*, honey," he murmured. "I made you bring up breakfast. You OK?"

"Yeah. I was just thinking about how nervous I *wasn't*." She sipped water out of the tap. "What is it about weddings that make the principals so nervous?"

"Fear of the unknown," Barbara answered, bussing Howard's temple. "*My* first, I threw up in Uncle Rubin's Lincoln twice before I got to the church. My *second*, I kicked Howard out of bed, said 'let's do this,' and that was that."

"I was *here*, Barbara," Ann grinned. "You stayed at your friend's house that night."

"Never let facts get in the way of a good story," Barbara snapped. "Point is I drove myself to the church, got in a blue dress, and got on with it. There was no *mystery* at all."

"I suppose. Well," Ann glanced at the clock. "I'm going to try to eat something else. Breakfast, everyone?"

Barbara stretched, her washboard stomach showing under the edge of her sweatsuit. "Breakfast, sure. May as well get going."

*The woman hasn't put on an ounce since '71.* "That's affirm; I'll get on it..."

"*Don't* you dare," Howard declared, regarding his daughter for a moment. "The henna looks...*radiant*, honey. *Your* duties today are to look beautiful and not trip on the carpet."

"Thanks, Dad. Don't say I didn't offer." As Howard and Barbara brought out the pans, eggs, bacon, and bread, Ann thought *I still don't know what a Sea Frontier is... I don't know what Johnny's future looks like...* She realized her father was talking to her. "Sorry, say again?"

"I asked how *many* eggs, honey."

"Oh, just a couple. No bacon, dry toast. Don't want to give anything a chance to come up again."

***

*What's that noise out there?*

Mike listened to the wind howling across the breezeway, his eyes on Leigh's, smiling. *It's barely five, but we're awake.* "Morning, *oytzer*."

"Cuddle, Sandy," she turned her back to him as he wrapped his arms around her, nuzzling her neck. A few minutes later, she felt a hand on her belly and glanced at the clock again. "Let's get going."

"Morning, children," Monica chirped, eating breakfast. "I'm *always* in a good mood when I go to a wedding, aren't you?"

"Sure, Mama."

"My first one, *I* was terrified." Leigh shrugged. "It's a little ironic that Ann was left off the guest list... I don't know *why* and I was too busy. But a week before..." She smiled. "The first time I *ever* kissed JJ." *And that was SOME first kiss.*

"I should *speak* with him," Mike mumbled, "trying to horn in on another guy's girl..."

"It was *Randy* he was horning in on, not *you*."

"*That's* so. We need to hustle."

***

"*Listen* up," Tom announced as everyone piled out of the van in the parking lot. "You all have your search assignments," Tom ordered, "let's get *to* them. Rendezvous at the front of the church NLT 0930."

"Check;" "who died and left *you* in charge;" "roger;" "he *is* the lead rating;" "three bells, aye;" "ranking NCO for *us*," were among the replies he got as they paired off and fanned out.

***

"*He* looks familiar," Tom muttered as he walked around the perimeter of the church with Mike, trying to look nothing more than curious as they swayed around heaps of broken concrete.

"Billy Reidy," Mike answered *sotto-voce*. The pimply-faced young man leaning against a stair rail near the basement emergency exit quickly hid a lit cigarette. "Relax, *we're* not gonna bust ya."

Billy relaxed slightly but still hid the butt. "You guys..."

"Friends," Tom smiled. "Got *another* one of those? You're...*who*?"

"Jenna's friend. Ann invited me."

"Uh-huh," Mike muttered. "Jenna's..."

"Ann's sister."

"You enjoy yourself today." The two kept walking around the building, finding it hard going around the construction debris. They met Liz and Nancy at the church's back, struggling over the same kind of terrain. Mike thought he'd try his Spanish. "*Hola, señoritas. ¿Ver cualquier cosa?*"

"*Nada*," Liz said, surprised. "*¿Has visto algo?*"

"*Nada. That's* about *all* the Spanish I remember, but I didn't *think* you'd know Russian or German."

"I *don't*, but your *Spanish* isn't bad," Liz said, glancing at her watch, "...a-a-and, *we* have to get to the loft."

165

*** 

"*I* wouldn't know *most* of these people if I tripped over their name tags," Leigh declared, "and I'm getting cold in this wind. Let's go in." She and Gary were making a slow round of the parking lot as cars rolled in. They peered between the immense pine trees that lined one side of the lot and the driveway all the way up to the church. *Wonder if...* A man in a jumpsuit with a red kerchief appeared between the trees, nodded, and disappeared again.

"*I* wouldn't know anybody either," Gary mumbled. "You OK on that foot?" The church's circular drive contained three vehicles: two black Lincoln stretch-limousines—one bedecked with crepe streamers—and Howard's nondescript Buick.

"My hip's killing me, but I'll live. *Your* connection, again, is...?"

"JJ was in my unit. My wife and Ann went on shopping sprees. You?"

"I've known *them* since junior high."

He side-glanced again. "Your weapon's not well hidden from this angle, Sarge."

"Since the *holster's* between my *thighs* and the *gun's* in my *purse, that's* an interesting observation, Sarge. *But,*" she opened the back door of the second limo, "I'm *not* going to take a *gun* into a *church*...," nodding to the driver and dropping her purse.

Just inside the church doors, Alex and Jenna identified *their* family members. Next to them, Brenda and Lois did the same for JJ's family. Leigh stopped and waited for *her* family and Mike's while Mike picked out the Brookfield crowd.

In the wings, Dave and Morgan, Ellen and Ernie watched passively, occasionally glancing outside. Dave's red tie almost matched Morgan's scarf, while Ellen's dark red hat clashed with Ernie's scarlet vest. Their credentials were discretely hidden, but the lanyards poked out around their necks.

At last, Donna appeared at the door. "Mrs. Mueller *knew* Dad right away. When they're *all* seated, she *wants* to be *here now.*" A few minutes later, Evan pushed Claudia into the sanctuary, seating her with Barbara.

*** 

"*Nothing* to it, Alex," JJ grinned at Alex as he brushed his coat and pushed back his unruly cowlick. "The hardest part is dancing at the reception."

"*That's* about it," Ernie murmured. "Done it *three times* myself."

"*Not* very complicated," Ellen agreed. "If you don't *lift* your feet, you *can't* step on hers."

"*You* ready, buddy?" Kurt brushed JJ's jacket, sweeping off the last traces of dust while glancing at the FBI.

"I think so. You?"

"All I *had* to do was sign the license, and I've already done that. *You've* got a *lot* more to do." Kurt stopped, smiled. "Here's your tie," he straightened the knot briefly.

"The last thing my father ever taught me was how to tie these things."

Kurt grinned wryly as Mike nodded while dropping the wheelchair's footrests. "I *never* met him but have no doubt he'd be proud of you today…as proud as *I* am. And I'll give you the same advice I gave my *sons*, and I *hope* to give my daughters. Today is the beginning of an adventure, but *nothing* like you'll expect it to be." He raised his arm and dropped it, signaling Pastor Lou; moments later, the organ began the prelude. "Let's *go*."

✳✳✳

"Mag*nif*icent, honey," Howard said. "Your mother's veil…and she *just* arrived." He looked her up and down in the choir loft as Jenna placed the cape over her shoulders, and Debbie fastened it before they went downstairs.

"This was Stella's *first*, Dad." *Smells of lavender and bleach.*

"And Barbara's pendant. Ann, honey," he listened to the organ as it faded to silence, "I'm never prouder of my children than I am on their wedding day. But for *you*…that you *found* Johnny again…"

"*Dad*," Ann said, looping her rosary around her wrist, "I *know*; let's *go*."

He offered his arm, "let's get this road on the show." Mike/Leigh and Debbie, carrying *their* flowers, lined up as Howard and Ann stepped down. The pastor nodded; the organ began "Here Comes the Bride," and Jenna, wearing a *perfect* blue dress and carrying a bundle of white mums, glided forward.

✳✳✳

*Sixteen years after Lo and Simon…remember?*

JJ gazed up the aisle that seemed *so* long at Lois's wedding. He smiled at his sister; she smiled back as Leigh/Mike kept perfect pace behind Jenna. Debbie, six months pregnant and with short legs anyway, paced behind with grace. *A pregnant bridesmaid, Mom. Could you have imagined?* He nodded to Stella; she smiled back.

The pastor nodded again and raised his arms, and the organ faded as the people stood. The haunting notes of Schubert's "Ave Maria" swelled from the loft, with Laura and Betty providing bass and baritone, and Kristin added an *astonishing* tenor between Liz and Nancy's sopranos.

*And there…Oh…My…God!*

✳✳✳

*This is happening?*

Ann and Howard paced up that flower-bedecked aisle, Ann's feet carrying her mysteriously. Dutifully, absently, she genuflected before the altar.

"Who gives this woman to this man," Pastor Lew asked—the first that she realized the ceremony had started. *This! IS! Happening!*

"Her *mother* and *I* do," Howard croaked loudly, placing her hand in JJ's before he stepped back and took a seat next to Claudia.

The next few minutes were a blur and would be remembered later in bits and

167

pieces. "Claudia Ann, do you *take* this man…to love, honor, and obey…?"

*He was supposed to leave the 'obey' out…* "I *do*."

"John Jacob, do you *take* this woman…in sickness and in health…?"

*I hope you meant the 'sickness' part…* "I *do*."

"You may kiss your bride."

*Will I see it, Cloud?* He looked for the solemn-to-joyful change in her face, the one he'd seen in his sisters when *their* vows ended. He saw her light up as they came together, a burning fire of happiness in her eyes.

*And now I know WHY…*

"May I introduce *Mr.* and *Mrs.* John Elrath," Pastor Lou declared, to the applause of the crowd—and *cheers* from the loft.

"*Mr.* Elrath," she whispered as Mendelssohn's "Wedding March" started.

"*Mrs.* Mueller-Elrath," he smiled as they marched arm-in-arm down the aisle.

"Don't you *forget* it, Johnny."

\*\*\*

"Pres*ent…ARMS!*" Tom gave the order as JJ and Ann exited the church and beamed widely as they passed, and the rice flew.

Mike watched as Howard opened his trunk; JJ moved a suitcase to the creped limousine's trunk before he got in the back with Ann. "What was *that*," he asked.

"*No* idea," Leigh answered. "Never *saw* it before."

"Might I ask, Mrs. Parkinson, can you explain the suitcase?" Ben asked.

"Howard did that with Claudia's *father* in '45," Stella replied. "Symbolic of taking the bride's possessions."

"Ah: quaint," Cathy sighed. Wendy, you *have* a ride?"

"Yes, ma'am…"

"Call your aunt 'ma'am' again, and you'll *regret* it," Cathy snapped mildly.

"OK, everybody," Roy announced loudly. "Please make your way to the reception at Telegraph and Northwestern Highway on the west side of the street by noon so we can clean up here. If you need guidance, follow someone who knows the area, but *do not* follow the bridal limos unless you want to go to Beaumont Hospital."

\*\*\*

"Congratulations, Mr. and Mrs. Elrath. My name is Stephen; I'll be your driver today." The driver keyed the intercom as the limousine rolled onto Big Beaver, behind Ernie's car.

"*Thank* you, Stephan," JJ replied, squeezing Ann's hand. "You work for Adam?"

"Yessir."

"*Congrats*, guys," Dave added from the front seat.

Stephan double-parked the limo near the front entrance as Ernie, credentials out, stood by. The couple raised a few eyebrows and turned a few heads as they brushed off rice, Ann still in her headpiece. Several people wished them well on their way to Charlie's room, including one woman in scrubs with a red scarf.

"We just got married, Charlie," JJ told him. "Thought you'd want to know."

Ann kissed his cheek; JJ grabbed his cool hand. As they turned to go, he coughed and mumbled, "Ann." They turned again to see his eyes open, tearing. "Ann," he growled again, "Johnny-cake...Johnny..." before his eyes closed.

*Something's working in there.* They stopped by the nurse's station, telling them that he seemed to recognize people—a new and hopeful development.

\*\*\*

"What's *here?*" In the other limousine, Alex and Jenna found the waiting difficult.

"My *father*," Kurt mumbled. "JJ's stepfather."

"Stella's husband?"

"That's *right*," Leigh added. "They're paying their respects whether he sees them or not."

"Well," Debbie sighed, "this *pregnant* woman needs a bathroom, and *now*."

"*I'll* go with you; *wait* one," Leigh offered. She moved her pistol from her purse to her holster as *discretely* as possible. Kurt and Alex made an unconvincing show of *not* watching her in the confines of the limo.

"Yep, this is *Michigan* all right," Mike grinned, holding the door as a lash of rain—wet *and* frozen—whipped across the roof.

Morgan, who had been seated next to the driver, followed the women into the building, waving at Ellen by the hospital doors.

\*\*\*

"*Thank* you; thanks," they waved genially at the well-wishing strangers as they strode through in the hotel lobby with FBI Dave in the lead and Chauffeur Stephan in tow. The rest of the wedding party followed; Morgan, Ernie, and Ellen brought up the rear.

Ann opened the bridal suite door a few minutes later, where her mother sat in the oversized recliner by the fireplace. The nurse on the loveseat—a pleasant-looking middle-aged stereotype—smiled; Evan stood up from an armchair; Donna, standing at the kitchen counter, smiled.

"*Hi*, Mom," Ann whispered, "it's Claudia Ann."

"*My* dear," Claudia muttered scratchily, a smile slowly crossing her face, "you look *lovely*."

"Thanks, Mom. Look," she took the headpiece off, "it's the same one you and Stella wore."

Recognition was slow, but come it did. "Beautiful, beautiful."

"Mom," she waved JJ in, "*you* remember Johnny Elrath?"

"Closer, young man; my eyes aren't what they were."

"Mrs. Mueller," he whispered. "Remember *me*?"

169

Slowly she smiled. "Your eyes, young man, your eyes. Yes, yes, I do. My, Johnny, how you've *grown*. Claudia married you this morning?"

"Yes, ma'am."

"She's in the *Navy*?"

"Yeah, Mom," Ann added.

"But *you're* in the *Army*. I can see *that* well."

"Mrs. Mueller, we're going to *make* it work."

Claudia reached forward. "Help me up." They hoisted her up by her arms, surprised at how tall she was: nearly 5 feet 10. She smiled and embraced them both, murmuring, "be well, kids; be well. Good luck to both of you. And Johnny?"

"Yes, ma'am?"

"Hurt my Claudia, and my sons will tear you apart."

"You remember them, Mom?"

"I know I have *two* of them—one's George; the other...not sure. Now my *third* is the one I didn't raise." She admired Barbara's pendant for several moments. "Sorry, children, but it's time for my nap."

"OK, Mom. We'll see you later."

The nurse stood up. "She'll rest for a few hours and be fine. My schedule says 4 this afternoon?"

"Yes," JJ answered. "*My* mom wants to come and visit. You can come down for brunch and cake."

"Thank you, and congratulations."

Ann smiled at Evan. "Mr. Hammerfest, I *can't* thank you enough. Come on down to the party, please."

"*Proud* to," Evan smiled, extending his hand to JJ. "Congratulations." He reached for Ann's hands. "You're a *beautiful* bride, my dear."

"Thanks. And *Blondie*; Nick's *been* waiting for you."

✳✳✳

"Never *saw* a wedding brunch," George Mueller claimed while standing in the buffet line. The beef and ham were as popular as the eggs Benedict and the biscuits and gravy.

"My Uncle Fred had a wedding *breakfast*," Mary Parkinson behind him declared, "he got married by a JP near midnight in '41." The symbolic round cake was on display on an angled wire holder above the bridal purse at the buffet line's start.

"Always thought *that* only happened in the movies," Bob Bell grinned. "Never heard of it in real life." Though they emphasized *no gifts* to everyone, gifting instincts would *not* be denied. Soon the envelopes and small packages buried the sequined purse—itself a gift from Anita.

"We had a wedding *snack*," Marie DeHaven said. "On the ship back from England in '46 at two in the morning."

"Did they let you share quarters," Betty asked.

"*One* night in a *single* bunk," Dave DeHaven sighed. "She was an officer; I was an enlisted man."

"They *did* make us a wedding *cupcake*," Marie added. "Our sugar ration for the voyage. That, and they gave us a couple of apples and an orange."

"Our *first* one was small," Cathy said. "My mom stood up for me, and there were Ed's foster parents and us. That was *it*."

"Best restaurant in Albany," Ed claimed. "We pooled our resources…"

"Our families *split* the *check*, Ed," Cathy intoned. "*We* could barely afford the license, the preacher, and the drinks; Mom and your foster parents picked up the rest." She smiled, "*my* law degree and *your* architect's license were the *rest* of *our* wedding presents."

* * *

"We want to thank everyone who made an effort to be here." As the champagne toast came, JJ stood up. Like clockwork, the buffet line closed at 1, announced with *another* ringing of glasses that only stopped after *another* bride-groom smooch. "If you can find it in your hearts, pray for my stepfather, Charlie, who couldn't join us today." He paused ever-so-briefly. *NO response at all.* "We want you all to remember *us* on 15 November before you remember, say, the passing of the Articles of Confederation on this day in 1777…"

"*Real* romantic, pal," Ann stage-whispered, followed by giggles.

"…and the proximity to *other* Elrath family events."

"Amen to *that*," Stella and Brenda both declared, as Lois smiled wryly.

"But raise your glasses, please, to the *miracle* that was our chance meeting just over a year ago—a meeting we had *both* given up on *ever* being possible. Here's to *miracles*!"

*To MIRACLES!*

Kurt stood up, motioning for quiet among the clanging glasses. "As the best man, I'm supposed to say something funny about the bride and groom. I hardly *know* the bride, so: I first met *this* skinny little kid JJ in '69…"

"And he was *terrified* of us," Will shouted to general laughter.

"He *was*. He came to work for me in the summer of '71 and put in the hours, didn't complain, took his money, and came back for more." He stopped, smiled at JJ. "But as steady as he was, there was *always* something missing. Last winter, when I met Ann—who knows more about using bottle-jacks to bend steel than *I* do—I *knew* she was the gal for him. So, raise your glasses, please, to the *finally* completed couple: JJ and Ann."

*JJ and Ann!*

Leigh stood as more glasses rang, clearing her throat. "Deb asked me to say a few words since nobody beyond the first two yards could hear *her*." Laughter. "The three of us were on the 400-meter-medley squad that took first in the state finals in '70, the same year Ann became the *second*-fastest 400-meter freestyle

171

swimmer in the *world*."

"I've still *got* that trophy," Ann smiled amid the applause.

"But Ann was always looking for *someone* in *every* crowd," Leigh continued. "*I* knew both JJ *and* Ann at the same time: JJ from church and Ann from school…only I didn't know *then* that they were looking for *each other*.

"Ann, honey, I love you, but…*damnit*, girl; did you *have* to *love my Blue-Eyes?*" Louder laughter, especially from the ladies. "Girls…really, huh? Is it *fair* that *those* baby-blues of his *really only* belong to *one* woman?" She smiled at Ann. "Yeah, you *did*. And yes, they *do* now. Blue-Eyes, we *all* love you. Good luck, really. And Ann, I've *thought* about it, and…*no*, I would *not* have shared *my* Blue-Eyes with you if I *had* known." More laughter. "But he's yours, now, honey. Take *good* care of him…for all of us!"

*For all of us!*

Lois stood up and smiled broadly. "I have to announce for *my* family that we welcome a *new* member: Claudia Mueller." Applause. "Seeing Claudia—uh, *Ann*—for the first time in *eighteen* years, I was reminded of how Dad *always* liked her." Stella and Brenda smiled and nodded. "So, Ann, today you joined yourself to my brother. That means we're sisters, so welcome, sister, to the Elrath family." Applause.

Tom and Kristin rose near the back of the table area. "As the happy couple's comrades-in-arms," Tom began, "Kristin and I have only one thing to say: *YES!*"

*"He proposed,"* Ann exclaimed.

*"No, I* did." Kristin shouted, *"this morning!"*

"At the *top* of her *lungs*," Betty added.

"On *top* of *him*," Laura laughed.

JJ smiled amid the applause, laughter, ringing glasses, and good wishes.

* * *

"OK, now," Simon said, taking aim at the tableau of the bride and groom and their combined families. "Everybody…stand…*still*…" and stepped quickly between Lois and Brenda and grinned, "say *Budweiser!*" as the light flashed. "Good. OK, next shot?" Simon, a freelance photographer when he wasn't working as a packaging engineer, had been clicking throughout the day.

"We've done the rest," Ann sighed, "but *I* want *all* current uniform personnel—Active and Reserve, Navy, Army whatever—in or out of uniform, report up here *chop-chop!* C'mon; *all hands*." The resulting photo included all but one member of the Florida delegation, Major George Mueller, USAFR, Army Major Ramdas "Ram" Brahmaputra-Reynolds—a Brookfield classmate, and Navy Lieutenant Dan Tanner.

"Ah, brother," Ram knelt between Ann and JJ as the cake and coffee were served, "we *need* to talk, but *first*," he bussed Ann's cheek, "I kiss the bride. Chief, *you'll* get a call soon."

JJ looked up at Clare. "Hey, Ware," he smiled. "Having fun?"

"I *am*," she smiled and touched Ram's shoulder. "Catching up. Stand up so I can kiss you, too. *You*, too, Ann."

Sherry and Roger drifted by. "We *have* to fade out," Sherry grinned. "feeding time pretty soon, and *I'm* not 100% yet."

Roger mumbled as he bussed Ann and shook JJ's hand, "Something's in the works..."

***

"Well, *hell*," Leigh grinned slyly, "he *did* make it."

"Who," Mike asked, "*who* made what?"

"Ann's buddy from high school."

"Who would be... *him*?"

"Yeah." They watched as a short red-headed man and a taller, dark red-headed woman found their way around the edge of the party.

Ann, hobnobbing with the McMullen's, happened to turn her head just in time and "*Christ ALMIGHTY! Sam?!*"

"*Potts*," JJ grinned, standing up, "Well, *WOW*, Sam!"

If he hadn't been so short, Sam could have passed for Andy's brother with his perennially chapped skin. With him was Darla Templeton, a willowy woman almost as tall as Ann but much thinner. "Ann," Sam smiled, walking up to her, "wanted to come by and say congrats. I brought Darla...JJ: you ever *meet* Darla?"

"*Hi*, Darla," Ann smiled. "Long time."

"Yes, it *has* been, Ann. Congratulations."

"Never had the pleasure," JJ said to Darla. "I knew your *brother*, my sister's ex-boyfriend."

"Oh...*Ed's* Lois...yes, I remember. He's got four kids now."

"He still came by when my dad died. But you can tell *Lois* yourself— she's right over there." Turning to Sam, JJ grinned. "So, *who* told you about *this*, Sam? It's *not* in the papers yet..."

"Leigh Taylor," Sam said. "Thought I'd come down and kiss the *bride*..."

"*Leigh*, huh," Ann chuckled, looking around. "Wonder why she'd...oh, *I* know why."

"Probably," JJ smiled, waving slightly at Leigh. "Wanted *your* naked-friend from high school here since *mine* is. And I can...Jenny! Look who's *here*!"

A look of surprised consternation crossed Jenny's face before she broke out into a bright smile, grabbing Jesse's hand and dragging him with her. "*Sam?*"

"*Jenny Jacobs*," Sam beamed. "My *God*, you haven't changed in *twenty* years!"

"Neither have *you*, Sam," Jenny sighed. "This is my husband...." As the old neighbors greeted each other, a woman clearly not dressed for the event appeared. Distracted, Leigh watched Mike get up to meet her, signing; she smiled and signed back. *He learned ASL years ago. But who's SHE?*

Mike led the woman to JJ; he stopped. "*Kat?!*" It was a surprised and instinctively *loud* question for Katherine Wanamaker, a girl/woman he *knew* was deaf.

"Hi, Johnny," she smiled, her nasal intonations hard to make out.

"It *is* you," he exclaimed. "How...?" He didn't have a chance to say more before she threw her arms around him.

"Mike," she smiled, letting go.

"*Oh*, OK," he glanced at her hearing aids. "How *well* can you..."

"Well *enough*, Johnny. I came to say 'hi' and congratulations. That's Gordy, my husband," she waved to him.

"This is Ann," JJ added as the bride smiled.

"*She's* the girl you always looked for when you were with me," Kat asked.

"*Yeah*, she is, Kat."

"She's *beautiful*," Kat smiled. He was full of questions for her, especially those that would fill the holes in his memory about what *really* happened when everyone *said* he threw one of her attackers over a stair railing. They would stay unasked. They talked about her family and his career before Kat declared, "My cousin Sid's over there; I need to say *hi*."

"Sid *Jackwell*?" Ann made a hard-to-describe face. "He's your *cousin*?"

"My mom's sister married his father when we were three."

"*That's* what Sid meant by *personal service*," JJ breathed.

Kat smiled, leaned forward, kissed him sweetly on the lips and Ann on the cheek. "*Yes*, Johnny. Be *well*, my friend."

As the band was setting up, Jo tugged on JJ's sleeve. "Thanks for having me, guys," she mewed, hard to hear. "Had a *great* time."

"Leaving so *soon*," Ann asked. "Party's just getting..."

"Not *leaving*: taking a break," she winked and beckoned to Dan, who was chatting with Kurt and Mary...who were grinning widely. "You said to *be sociable*." She reached up to JJ for a kiss, whispering, "we *found* the *current* offices of Parkinson Title and Trust last night."

***

Gabe struck up a keyboard note, calling for attention. "*Good* afternoon, everyone, I'm Gabe Knowles, and we're the Sweet-Tones. We're here to play for our classmate Ann Mueller, who is now Ann *Elrath*...wait...sorry, JJ, but..."

"Tell me something I *don't* know," JJ shouted.

"OK: Ann went to senior prom with..."

"Steve Hole," JJ answered.

"OK: her *inseam* is..."

"None of *your* business," Ann laughed as the party joined in.

*Electronic rim shot.* "Moving *on*: the bride's brother and sister have a song." Alex and Jenna, with Billy and Brianna, and Ann's niece Adriana and her *fetching* redhead friend, and Adriana's cousins Howie and Nettie all took to the microphone.

174

"We wanted to express how much we *love* you both," Jenna announced, "and this is the *best* way *we* know. With apologies, because we've only been rehearsing *this* since Tuesday." With that, they sang an *A Capella* rendition of the last verse of Simon and Garfunkel's "Bridge Over Troubled Water."

As they sang the last notes, Gabe single-keyed the un-vocalized ending as Alex stepped forward. "Johnny, you are *our* brother now."

The applause was deafening as Adriana, Howie, and Nettie bravely added, "*and our* uncle."

After a few minutes, Gabe played a riff on his keyboard. *"That's* a hard act to follow. Beautiful; *well done*; memorable. As I understand it, if things had been a *little* different, we *might* have had this party a long time ago. Good things come to those who wait, and today, we play for Ann and JJ. And, for *you*…this is *your* song." As the band started, the plaintive and sweet chords of the *only* tune that they had *ever* danced to—"Up Where We Belong," filled the atrium.

"Keep your bloody great boots *off* my feet," she giggled as they swayed clumsily—neither had been a dancer, ever.

"Keep your feet out from *under* my boots," he smiled, turning her steadily.

"And *Kat*," she sighed. "Didn't expect *her*."

"Like *you* expected Sam. Looks like we pulled *this* off."

"Like *clockwork. So* glad Mom could make it."

"Me, too. I haven't seen *her* since '67."

As Joe Cocker faded, "Unchained Melody" struck up, and Ann was seized by her father, while Stella, with *perfectly* coifed hair so stiff it couldn't be moved by a hurricane, grabbed JJ. "He recognized us, Mom," JJ smiled.

"Good for *him*," Stella smiled back, "but this is *your* party, Johnny."

"Having a good time, Mom?" He smiled at Clare dancing with her father.

"I *am*, thank you. Who *was* that woman?"

"Remember 9th Grade? *She* was the reason I was suspended for three days."

"Oh." She puzzled for a moment. "And Charlie *didn't* explode. *Never* understood that." She sighed. "Not sure I ever understood *him*."

"Sorry, Mom."

"Not *your* fault." She gazed up at him. "I married him for his money, *not* his personality."

"As good a reason as *any*, Mom. Apparently, Claudia recognized Evan."

"Oh, *good*. I'll go up there in a few minutes. I hope you're as happy for yourself as *I* am for *you*, John."

"I *am*, Mom."

When The Righteous Brothers ended, "The Long and Winding Road" began, and Barbara cut in. "Act *normal*, buddy," she grinned mischievously.

"Ain't this what you were waiting for, pal?"

"Yup, ever since I *met* ya." She pulled him closer, resting her chin on his shoulder. "You two have a great future ahead of you. Wanna cop a feel?"

"Cop a feel on my new step-mother-in-law, at *my* wedding reception, on the dance floor…you *are* a vixen, girl."

"I'm in *lust* with the guy who just married my step-daughter, who will make her happier than anyone else *could*." She drew back a few inches. "*And* a little drunk. But she's *yours*, and I won't get between you…*even* at play. She *is* the luckiest girl in the world today." She nodded to where Mike and Ann were swaying to the music and squeezed close together, "*he* might go for *her*."

"Mike? *They've* known each other forever." He waited for a beat. "Thanks for being Ann's pal."

"She was *easy*; the daughter I *never* had," she grinned, holding him even closer. "You and Ann will be *so* happy together."

"We *plan* to be," he declared, "as soon as Uncle Sam decides what they're going to *do* with us."

The Beatles faded, and "Lady" began; Cathy placed a firm hand on his shoulder and declared, "dance *now*, young man." As they swayed slowly, she stated, "I find it *interesting* that Leigh was *that* attracted to you." He found it amusing to see Betty dancing with Pete and Nancy with Alex.

"I suppose *interesting* is one way to put it."

"I never *knew*, not for sure." She stared into his face; she was inches shorter than Leigh, which meant she was as high as JJ's upper lip. "Your eyes *are* adorable. I can see why she wouldn't want to *share* you." She smiled enigmatically. "Friend-lovers are different, aren't they? Not lover-*friends*, but…"

"Yeah, they are. And Mrs. Taylor, I…"

"Oh, for *Chrissakes*, boy; call me Cathy. We've known each other for *half your life* and a *third* of *mine*."

"Cathy, then. Leigh and I…"

"Depended on each other. I could see *that* every Sunday we picked you up. I just never thought *you* were *that* close, and I *should* have. That Sunday before her wedding, she *blubbered* when I dragged her away. Thought it was just pre-wedding jitters, but…sorry: I just didn't *know*." He was a *little* surprised to see Laura taking a turn with Bob Bell.

As Kenny Rogers ended, Lionel Richie's "Say You, Say Me" started. Julia grabbed his elbow before he could get off the dance floor. "Thought you'd get away without *one* dance with me, big guy?"

"I was sort of *hoping*…" he smiled, both at her and at Liz, swaying to the music with Tony Junior.

"We danced—badly—at *Brenda's* wedding; we'll dance *just* as badly at *yours*. This time I *won't* shake my ass at Gramps. Too bad we can't *do it* to the old bastard again."

"Yeah. Too *cold* for skinny-dipping. I see Tony Junior made *one* friend."

"TJ's like me: bold when he needs to be. Just glad he found a girl *willing*…"

"Liz is a paratrooper surrounded by Rangers; not much fazes her. Jo said she found the old man's trust company down on Fenkell."

Julia smiled sweetly, pecked him on the cheek. "Thanks, buddy."

He *thought* he could escape on Julia's arm, but Leigh wrested him back. "Blue-Eyes," she sighed over Etta James's "At Last," "we don't want anything *this* big." She smiled, seeing Mike dance with Monica.

"This *ain't* big, Green-Eyes. Smaller than both my sister's weddings." They didn't really *dance* but stood in one place, swaying vaguely to the music. Next to them, Howard and Donna gently did the same.

"My *last* one was…*ugh*, don't want to think about it. *We* never *had* a chance."

"Your mom and I were just discussing that. You had Randy, *and* you had Mike—one of my *only* friends. I only ever had *your* best friend, and I didn't know where she was." He smiled, watching Clare and Ram sway similarly.

"You had *Clare*," she pointed her chin in their direction. "You brought her to church once."

"She was just getting out of the house."

"She was more than *that*, Blue-Eyes, but *you* couldn't *see* it. I wish we'd had more fun then. If we *had*, I *might* have introduced you to Ann, eventually." He thought it only vaguely curious to see Brenda dancing with George, while Lois shared a giggling dance—*finally*—with Jim.

✳✳✳

"*Wait* a minute," Gabe put the microphone back on the stand. "We have *one* last song from…who? The Conch Republic Chorus? *No idea* on this one, folks, but…"

The Florida delegation *all* gathered around the microphone. "*One more time*, brother," Tom grinned, stepping back…and the *ladies* skillfully *vamped* a song to the tune of "Strangers in the Night." First, Liz…

> *Rangers in the night, exchanging passwords;*
> *Wandering in the night, who said the last word?*
> *Looking for a fight; we're Rangers in the night!*

… echoing in the atrium in a manner reminiscent of Marylin Monroe crooning "Happy Birthday" to JFK. Nancy followed…

> *Biting snakes in two; oh, how tasty,*
> *Eat the earthworms too; let's not be wastey;*
> *Ambush on the right, for Rangers in the night!*

Though *intended* as humor, the tune also has a serious side, as Betty and Laura loudly *whispering* the bridge, sounding a *lot* like Julie London doing "Cry Me a River:"

> *Rangers in the night! We're out here scared and tired and*
> *Waiting for the light! We need love too, but we're here!*
> *Fighting for the right! Crawling out of sight!*
> *Lonely, cold and hungry, dirty!*
> *We're still out here, doing our duty!*

The party-goers seemed to be enjoying it—even Gabe's band—Gabe single-keyed along. Many guests on the upper tiers stopped to listen as all *five* women joined in the last verse, a four-part-harmony wrap-up that had to be *heard* to be believed…

> *Never in the light! We're all alone here!*
> *Friends are out of sight! We had girls once, but no more!*
> *Waiting just to fight! We're Rangers in…the…niiight!*

But Kristin *had* to simply solo, in her *deepest, purest* alto…

> *SCOOOOBY-dooooobie-DOOO!*

*That* got a laugh from everyone.

Gabe stepped up to the microphone, sighed, and declared. "If you guys are in the union, you're *hired*. Congratulations, Ann and JJ! We're the Sweet-Tones, and that's all for today, everyone! Thank you, *mazel tov* to the bride and groom, and *good day to all!*"

***

*Why does that bartender just look…wrong?*

Mike tried *not* to stare at the paunchy barkeep who replaced the young woman who'd done yeoman duty since noon. It was now nearly four; the party was thinning by the minute, the staff waiting to clean up. He glanced around, seeing Sid standing off in the wings, watching as Ann tossed her bouquet from the 2nd Level: Betty caught it, just above Leigh's outstretched arms.

Ram, too, had been staring at the new barkeep from time to time, even as he lined up for the garter: Alex was just a smidgeon faster than Tom and jumped higher. Sidling up to Sid, Mike mumbled, "*that* bartender: what do you know of him?"

"Couldn't vet the hotel staff, Mike; just not enough time." Mike made his way to where Ram and some other classmates milled around. "Ram: that booze-slinger looks…?"

"*Familiar*, yeah," Ram said, his dark face even darker. "And *not* with a good vibe." He glanced at Dave near the pool door. "*FBI's* here?"

*I was just gonna say wrong.* "Yeah," Mike said. "You *know* him?"

"Talked to *him* a few years ago," pointing his chin at Dave, "about Wolverine. I need to get Clare home."

Dave and Morgan, hanging out around the pool enclosure, mumbled something at Ellen and Ernie nearby, who acknowledged with a collective nod.

About to depart with Ann, JJ glanced at Dave, then the barkeep, then back at Dave with a tilt of his head, and mouthed *Chuck Wier.* Dave nodded and waved Mike and Leigh away.

Morgan and Ellen, shark-like, approached the bar as JJ and Ann boarded the elevator…

\*\*\*

The newlyweds slipped into bed quietly, watching the rain pelt the skylight.
"Why, John? *Why* were you looking for me for so long?"

"Because *you* are the *only* person who makes me *feel*."

"Feel *what*?"

"*Love, dear*."

"But you loved Leigh and Jenny…and Clare. *Kat*, even."

"Kat was platonic: I never even *thought* about doing anything with her, and you and I were still in touch. Green-Eyes?" He smiled. "We *may* have *wanted* to, but..." He shook his head and grinned again. "Couldn't do that to Mike. Jenny: *you* were always there *with* us…she said so, and I couldn't argue." He sighed deeply. "Clare held my heart from the moment we met because I couldn't *feel you* anymore. Then I found *you* again, and *your* hands took her place."

"You *still* love her. And she loves *you*. You love *Leigh*, too."

"Neither of *them* was the girl of my dreams. My occasional *wet* dreams, maybe, but *you* have *always* been the girl of my dreams. I felt like I was betraying you when I was with *anyone* else. *Why* were *you* looking for *me* for so long?"

"You loved me for *me*, not for what I can *do* or what I can *give*. I never thought I could *have* kids; guys I've been with *wanted* them. I *loved* Cable, but he wanted me to quit the Navy. Roger…I was just his piece of ass on the side. Figured *that* out *when* I found you." She curled into his side, shifting a pillow. "*You* never wanted anything from me but love. You were always the *one* person in my life who didn't speak unless you had something to say, who knew when I was sad or tired or happy or angry, and what to do about it, including when to do or say *nothing*."

"You were the only one I could always count on," he kissed her forehead, "no matter what."

\*\*\*

You OK?" Mike brushed her breast lightly as he stretched his arm across her.

"I *will* be." Leigh sighed deeply, massaging her screaming hip in bed, her removable cast on the floor. "Finding that woman; was it hard?"

"Her parents still attend *our* temple, but she goes to one in Livonia with a signing rabbi. I didn't *know* Sid's connection…"

"No, didn't see *that* coming."

She turned to face him. "*Smaller*, Sandy. I want *smaller*. Your family's *so* big…" She paused, listening. "Is *that your* parents or *mine*?"

"It's… BOTH!?"

She reached for him and smiled widely. "Let's join *this* chorus."

"Roger *that*."

179

# *After...*

## *Sunday*

*I can hardly believe this is real.*

The sun filtered softly through the skylight, illuminating her sleeping face. He stretched his back and legs stiffly, not wanting to disturb her or his feeling of peace and contentment.

The idyllic image shattered when she rolled on her back and started her *uniquely* gentle, quiet, and *very* lady-like snoring, followed by...*WHEW! Boy, we ARE married NOW, Cloud.*

He got up and pulled on his sweats, glancing at the clock. *0750; she wanted to be up by 0900, start dinner by 1200; guests at 1700 or thereabouts, but Mom's never on time. Plenty of time.*

He shuffled into the kitchen and started sorting through the treasure trove they'd dumped on the table, propping his glasses on his nose. *What ho! Cards from DeHavens! That's Lois; Ram, I think; Brenda; that's Mike's scrawl; that's maybe Cathy; haven't seen Aunt Brenda's handwriting for a while. Mom—I know what THAT is. Jenny, I think. Company C—nice of 'em. Big envelope from Florida. Great Lakes Sea Frontier...?*

Wrapped in her big fuzzy robe, she crept in minutes later, starting the coffee. "*Good* morning, Mr. Elrath."

"Good *morning*, Mrs. *Mueller*-Elrath."

She smiled, reaching for her glasses. "Let's look at our *loot*." From Florida, a touching card, some cash, and several checks from officers *and* enlisted, adding up to about a month's take-home pay for an E-7. *Everyone* gave cards; a few gave gift certificates for chain restaurants—one for REI from Jo. Leigh's small package contained a framed watercolor-and-pastel drawing of their faces, capturing their eyes in brown and blue, JJ's half-grin, and Ann's whole-face smile. "Beautiful."

"She *is* good. Here's from Dave and Marie. *Aww...*" He showed her a framed needlepoint of their names over a pair of hearts. "Marie probably worked on it all week. The card says, 'For Our Friday's Child on his Wedding Day: May you always feel as blessed as you do today.'"

She opened the small box from Brenda: a framed photograph of all the Mueller and Elrath kids together in '67. "Were we ever *that* young?"

"We *had* to have been once to have gotten this *old*," he mused, rubbing his burning neck as he glanced at his 12-year-old self, smiling for the camera.

She sighed. "I guess. Card from Nick and Donna; Deb and Bob; Clare—*she* looked good yesterday. And *this* is from *my* dad." It was a large envelope with a card, a check, and another envelope. "What's *this?*" She held a yellowed envelope marked:

*To John on his Wedding Day.*

"*My dad's* writing. Wonder if Lois and Brenda got one."
She shrugged. "What's it say?"

*Oct. 15<sup>th</sup>, 1968*

"A *month* before he died," he mumbled. "He was running out of steam."

> *Dear John*
> *Congratulations, son, on your marriage. May you always be as happy as you feel today.*
> *I watched your heart dying without Claudia. I lack the physical strength now to fight your mother about your seeing her. I hope you found her, or could finally be happy without her.*
> *John, you have a talent unique in my experience: even as a young man, you can <u>think</u> more clearly than any adult I ever knew. Now, as a married man, you're going to have to <u>feel</u> as well as think. She will need your mind and heart, and I hope you have learned to <u>use</u> both.*
> *I know you did a fine job taking care of the girls—all three of them— like I asked you to, and I thank you for that. Now, take good care of the woman you've chosen for a wife because now it's <u>her</u> turn, and your <u>children's</u> turn, for all the power of your loving heart and clear mind.*
> *You are the best son any father could ask for. I'm writing to tell you what you wouldn't understand if I told you before I pass away.*
> *I love you, son.*
> *Your father,*
> *Jake*

Wordlessly, he handed her the letter, carefully removed his glasses, and went out to the balcony.

*The grown-up version of what I found eighteen years ago.* On the afternoon of Jake's funeral, thirteen-year-old Johnny cried into his Cloud's lap in his cold and drafty bedroom. As she reread the letter, she glimpsed JJ hugging himself, making those same, small, pitiful sounds he made on that sad day years ago.

When she came up behind him, he turned and buried his head in her shoulder, sobbing as she stroked his neck, a slight breeze blowing her robe around. "New *husband*," she murmured at length, "your new *wife* has *nothing on* under her robe, and the wind *might* pick up."

He sniffled, and she felt him smile. "So, should I sell tickets?"

"Only if *I* get a cut. Five stories up, I don't think we'll get many takers."

\*\*\*

"*Morning*, sleepy," Leigh smiled and offered Mike a cheek in the kitchen, where she was sharing coffee with Monica. Brilliant light reflecting off the Hammerfest's windows streamed in over the sink.

"Morning," he groaned, bussing her cheek and pouring coffee. "*You're* up early."

"Nearly eight o'clock, Michael," Monica chided. "Not *that* early."

"Suppose," he plopped on a stool. "*Great* party."

"Fabulous," Leigh smiled. "A hopeful preview of ours."

"Could be," he nodded. "*Ours*, though, would have *how many*, Mama?"

"Two hundred fifty, give or take a dozen," Monica declared. "Invitations will go out next week, but I've spoken to *most*…"

"Mama," Mike interrupted, "*we're* thinking family and hard-*not*-to-invite friends." Leigh held her breath when Monica stared.

"Friends?" Monica's eyes bored into him.

"Bridal party; *immediate* family." Mike's face changed, pleading. "Leigh's family is *so* tiny, Mama: they'd be *buried* in Dietz's. Let's use Thanksgiving for a quasi-reception: that's *still*…"

"*Nearly* everyone on the list." Monica looked away. The Dietz's catered Thanksgiving feast always included hundreds of people. "Leigh's family is not as tiny *now* as it was last week."

"True, Mama, but we don't *know* them," Leigh moaned. "We want to spend our energy on where we're going to *live*…"

"The cottage," Monica declared. "You're *here* for a year, yeah?"

"Don't know, Mama," Mike frowned. "But *that* might be a solution." Mike touched her arm. "We don't *need* big, Mama. I'm sure you can make the family understand."

Monica looked at him sidelong. "The gentiles are wondering if Thanksgiving, your wedding, and Christmas *are* too much in the space of five weeks," she smiled. "If I tell *them* that your wedding and reception are *private*, it lets them off *that* hook…and the *rest* are easy enough to persuade. Won't keep anyone from sending gifts." She smiled again. "Very well, children, it's *your* wedding; we'll do it *your* way. There are enough people for a *hora* on Thanksgiving."

\*\*\*

"Here's the list, babe," she handed him a scrap of notepaper at about 10. "*I'll* manage the salad and vegetables, but the *roast*…get back *most* Rikki-tick if we're going to eat before 2000." In addition to the suitcase exchange, a Mueller family wedding tradition held that the bride should prepare a meal for *both* sets of parents as soon as conditions permitted.

*Basil, scallions, dinner rolls…* "Anything *else*?" *This* bride decided to do it the *next* day *and* prepare it in the honeymoon suite's minimally-equipped kitchen.

"Nope: Callie sent everything else. The roast looks good, but I have to go down and sharpen this knife." The little kitchen *had* all the essential tools, but it was still small. Two people working simultaneously—his culinary skills were adequate for salads and vegetables—would be dangerously cramped. Besides, there was but one *good* kitchen knife and a tiny cutting board.

"I'll be back directly. How about another cutting board and something to carve that roast with?"

"Babe, if *you* bring back something bigger than this wooden postage stamp, we'll do last night all over again. Bring a carving knife *and* fork with it, and we'll do it right here in the kitchen before our guests arrive."

\*\*\*

"*This* is the dinner menu," Monica declared just after 10 as breakfast was being cleaned up. Somewhere between the savagery of Wednesday's gun battle and the joy of Saturday's wedding, Monica, Cathy and Mary agreed on a three-family dinner that Sunday at the Parkinson's. During Ann and JJ's reception, the ladies decided upon the menu. "Mary's providing a small steamship round; *I'm* making my parsley-boiled redskins; Cathy is making her cinnamon-and-apple *kuchen*. Leigh, dear, *you* said…?"

"Korean sourdough bread; I made the starter last week; the dough last night. Just need an hour or so for kneading and baking. It's got a *rye* starter, but it's what I learned to make."

"Good," Monica said. "Now, Father? *Your* three-bean soup?" The gentlemen were never quite sure exactly *how* the agreement came about but come about, it apparently *had*. The men's *only* hapless choice was to acquiesce or find dinner—and *possibly* accommodations for the night—elsewhere.

"You need only *ask*, Mother. The beans have been soaking since last night."

"Splendid. Now, Michael? I *taught* you *how* to cook. Can *you* make the squash?"

"I *can*, Mama. Frozen or fresh?"

"*Fresh*, Michael; *don't* be insulting. Ed, I don't know where *your* culinary skills lie, but Cathy *did* say…"

"Tossed romaine salad *with* or *without* croutons and celery, Monica?"

"Oh, *with* croutons but *not* celery; gives me gas. Very well, you have your assignments."

"I can make the salad in the cottage," Ed added, "Just need a bowl about that big," holding his hands about two-and-a-half feet apart.

"I can bake the squash in the cottage, too," Mike put in. "But, I need to get into the pantry…"

"Once you've got all that started, go watch the Lions get *killed* again," Cathy finished. "Who are they playing?"

"They're in Philadelphia," Ed declared. "They stand a *chance* today."

***

*Water will have to do.*

Ann found a quiet corner of the atrium near a small fountain surrounded by a knee-high, flat stone wall to *not* draw attention to herself. She occasionally glanced at Nancy and her family in the atrium as she whetted her knife. Nancy hailed from suburban Chicago, only six hours away by car.

Sharpening the long, stiff blade was a familiar chore. The boatswains traditionally—though *unofficially*—taught working sailors how to sharpen any working knife. She was just about done when someone came up behind her. "May I *help* you," the voice said.

She turned and looked up at the beefy face of the relief bartender from the reception. "Just about done here," she smiled, testing the eight-inch blade with a thumb. "They don't provide sharpening stones in the honeymoon suite."

"I'll make a note of it," the barkeep sighed. The rest of him was about as hefty and round as his face and with some muscle tone. "Anything *else*? My shift's just starting."

"No, I'm fine, thanks." She stood up, taller than he was by about half a foot. He had unusual grey eyes, a little like Mike's.

"Well, if there *is*, just ask for Chuck." To leave, he didn't actually turn away so much as he just, sort of, *moved off.*

Not ten feet away, Morgan, sitting with *her* friend, watched.

***

*Never been to a Meijer's store, but it's just another...* "Hey, Tom: what's up?"

"I could ask *you* the same thing." Tom had a half-full cart in a cross-aisle.

"Just fetching some stuff for Ann's culinary masterpiece this afternoon." JJ suddenly saw what he'd been looking for: an electric knife carving set with a fork and a giant cutting board. "Con*grats*, by the way."

"Thanks." Tom smiled and sighed. "We're *engaged*, but Uncle Sam's gonna object when *I'm* an E-8 in February, and she's *still* an E-6."

"*Are* they?" Rank disparity was often more of an issue to the services than anything else. The term *fraternization*—the mingling of persons of a different rank, though the Army was less rigid than the Navy—was a charge more used in disciplinary actions than *adultery* or *harassment*.

"*Probably*, but there's not much they can do since there are no chain-of-command issues." Tom looked down in his cart: beer, pretzels, a couple of magazines, soda pop, an "I Love Southfield" sweatshirt, apples, disposable diapers, ladies' underwear, wipes, a map of the Detroit area, and tampons. "I might go to the Reserves rather than take those orders for Bliss. Or I *could* just pull the pin and call it a career."

"Can you *afford*...?"

"Depending on where we settle and where *she* gets sent, yeah, we *can*. Alice and Dustin are around here somewhere. We've got to *get*."

\*\*\*

"We about ready," Monica asked, folding foil over her potatoes.

"Another ten minutes," Cathy answered, checking the big oven. "Leigh is your bread…?"

"Nearly. If *you* guys are ready, we'll follow you."

Cathy and Leigh watched the Dietz's and Ed go out, juggling their food before settling at the counter with some chardonnay. "The Parkinson's are *lovely* people," Cathy murmured, "*quite* unlike that Charlie."

"They *are*. How's Dad been now that *he* has a family?"

Cathy smiled enigmatically. "*Different*, a little. He's always been a little *hollow* around the Dietz's, maybe a little jealous. But now…we have a family of our own."

"Yeah," Leigh said, "if they're *anything* like Wendy, they're terrific people."

"Wild coincidence, you meeting *her*; her having her family history handy. They're related by *marriage* and *adoption* to Randy's family?"

"So it seems. I *hate* to do it, but I'm gonna *have* to flash my badge at my new-found family and ask some *official* questions."

"Just don't do it as *soon* as you *meet* them, honey."

\*\*\*

"So, the knife and cutting board were…" They sat in the bubbling jacuzzi with their clothes scattered around, gazing up at the skylight as the rich aromas of the roast wafted in the suite.

"*Better* bridal present than the socks, babe." She kissed his neck. "Think those glasses will work?"

"They *should*." She got him a pair of *tactical glasses*; large-frame, ruggedized eyewear with interchangeable polarized lenses, and dummy cords/head straps for a wedding gift. Like many sarcoidosis sufferers, bright sunlight, like Alaska's arctic conditions, often gave him a headache. "Company C *is* an infantry outfit."

"True, but…" she reached for him under the warm, swirling water, "Michigan's *not* as cold and bright as Alaska."

"Yeah." He moved his hand down her belly. "But cold *is* cold." *OH!*

"Uh-huh." *AH!*

"*Mm*…I should shop for you more *often*."

"You…*should!*" *OHH!*

\*\*\*

"Never saw JJ so *settled* as he is when Ann's around," Mary grinned in her living room. "Known him since he was a teenager, and he always seemed…"

"Lost," Leigh agreed, gazing at the boarded-up window. "I met him just after his father died. How *did* he die, anyway?"

"Heart attack, I understand," Kurt explained, only slightly distracted by the football game. "Young, too; only 46."

185

"He said something last week about he just found out that his father *knew* he was dying." Mike made a face.

"Odd thing to find out just before you get married," Cathy mumbled. "Wonder how *that* happened. You'd *think*..."

She was interrupted by the telephone that Kurt went to answer. He came back, somewhat shaken. "*That* was Charlie. Dad's had another stroke."

\*\*\*

"But his heart's still strong," JJ went on, trying to feel *something* for Charlie other than disdain. The honeymooners and their guests shared a before-dinner drink outside the suite when Charlie Junior called.

"Huh," Stella sniffed. "Wish he'd just get *on* with it. Despite what you saw yesterday, there's been no real change as of this morning...isn't that *Jo*?"

They looked where she looked—3rd Level across the atrium—and saw Jo in a casual sweatsuit on Dan's arm, similarly attired. "Yes," Ann smiled. "And that's *Donna*," she blurted, surprised. "And there's Nick, so...*they* stayed here."

"Beautiful girls," Howard sighed, watching the two couples greet each other. "Where did *those* two meet up?"

"Neighbors," JJ mumbled.

Barbara asked, "she's working for *you* now, Stella?"

"Yes. She and her partner are finding Charlie's money."

"There's Ram," JJ added, looking down. "Wonder how long *he's* here for?"

"Go and ask *before* dinner, Johnny," Ann muttered. "Otherwise, it will distract you all night. Be back in three-zero mikes."

\*\*\*

"I used Charlie Parkinson's title and trust company *before* I got to Detroit," Ed said. "He could *really* put the booze away. We did lunch, dinner a few times. Cath, *you* met him, too. I remember once he got *so* bombed that he tried to..."

"That *was him* at River Run." Cathy shuddered. "I'd *just* got promoted in the county attorney's office. He cornered me by the bar, and I just pushed him off."

"JJ's stepfather," Mike said. "Really? *Groped* my future mother-in-law?"

"More like a *pass*, Mike," Cathy corrected.

"Yeah, that's *good ol' Charlie*," Mary shook her head. "*Not* one of my favorite people. And to think we didn't *believe* Mary and Jo when *they*..."

"We did *after* JJ caught him peeping on Julia," Kurt interrupted. "Brave and lucky at the same time, that boy."

"Survived a double malfunction; won a Silver Star...*yeah,* you could say that," Mike grinned.

"And one of the best iron-sight rifle shots in the Army," Leigh smiled. "The only person to max the rifle marksmanship pop-up target range four *years* running at two *different* ranges."

"You say that like a *fan*," Monica frowned.

"I *am*," Leigh admitted. "*Have* been since we met."

"I'll attest to that," Cathy giggled. "She talked me into letting her go to some church function with a bunch of girls I *knew* she didn't care for, but there was this *one* boy…"

\*\*\*

"*Hey*, man," Ram's dusky but bright face smiled. "Congratulations again." JJ had made his way to the small lounge area on the 3rd Level, where Ram was reading.

"Thanks. How long are you *here* for?" Ram was a Special Forces major who worked in the Washington area. JJ didn't ask *how* he finessed emergency leave/liberty for the Florida gang

"Two weeks at least," Ram smiled. "I have business—Army and personal— and I *might* get extended. I'm going to stay *here* from now on."

"Well, glad you came. And you brought *Clare*." When the tribal drums of Brookfield/Greenbrier thundered: *Spread the word; come one, come all* moments after JJ told Clare, *everyone* knew about the event.

"Got to see *her* without Ernie around." Ernie had been Clare's *official* boyfriend in school. "But after today, I've got work."

"Oh? Anything I can do to help?"

"There's a *crisis*…can't *talk* about it yet."

"Let me know, buddy," JJ grinned, watching Nancy introduce the Florida gang to her family in the atrium. "Chuck Wier down there."

"Yeah; *thought* so." Ram had also gone to Wolverine the year before JJ.

"FBI's been looking for him for a while, and he turned up here last winter."

"Why *here*? Why *now*?"

"*That*, I believe, is what the *FBI* wants to know."

\*\*\*

"Where's your daughter this evening," Ben asked, forking beef onto his plate.

"Ah," Kurt answered, helping himself to the potatoes. "She has a suite at the hotel, said she'd be *indisposed* until Tuesday." He shook his head. "She hasn't *had* a date since she moved back."

"We worry about our daughters, unlike our sons," Ben grinned. "Sons can make their own way; *daughters*…"

"*That's* so," Kurt agreed.

"*Why* are daughters different," Leigh asked loudly, buttering her squash. "We're *just* the same as…"

"Ah, *no*, honey," Ed interrupted, passing the beef. "Daughters can get in different *kinds* of trouble."

"The kind that needs *diapers*," Ben agreed.

"*And* that *can* and *will* be around for a couple of decades," Kurt added. "It's a father's privilege—and *duty*—to worry about his daughters. Jo was struggling;

187

she all her time working. But *yesterday*…"

"She seemed…free," Mike said, "Don't *know* her from Eve, but she was…"

"Unrestrained," Mary agreed. "I haven't seen her like that since she was little."

"Is she any good at what she does?"

"*Very* good," Kurt proudly said. "And she's been a bulldog when it comes to Dad's money."

"Why's that," Leigh asked.

"She loves Stella," Mary answered, "and she *detests* Charlie." She calmly sliced off a piece of Leigh's bread. "*Wonderful* sourdough, Leigh: I *must* get your recipe." She sighed heavily. "If it's to be *found, she'll* find that bastard's money."

***

"Glad I caught you; we spoke with Wier last night," Dave said. That he and JJ met was a happy accident, enabled by the elevators' peculiar arrangements. Only two ground floor elevators went up to the 5ᵗʰ Level, meaning JJ had to go back down to the atrium from Ram's suite to get back up to his. JJ was just stepping out of the elevator when he saw Dave and his family coming in from the lobby. JJ smiled benignly…but Dave signaled that he wanted to *chat*. "He *wasn't* particularly chatty."

"Uh-huh," JJ said. "Why is he *here*? Why *now* and last winter?"

"He's *not* saying, and we've got nothing to arrest him on other than he's been in parts unknown for a decade. Um," Dave shifted, signaling an even *less* pleasant subject, "your brother *co*-owns this place, yeah? Know *anything* about his partners?"

"Nope. You?"

"One's *been* associated with some persons of interest, but it's hard *not* to in the real estate game." He clucked his tongue. "What interests *us* is the general manager, Max DeVere. Know *him*?"

"Nope. Never heard of him. I have *guests* waiting for dinner…"

"And *I* have a *wife and son* waiting for a swimming lesson…"

The Mueller-Elrath family dinner was warm despite their knowledge of Charlie's imminent passing. The fact of it seemed to hang not so much *over*, but somewhere *behind* Stella and JJ, who knew with every glance what would happen sooner or later. At the same time, Ann, Howard, and Barbara were unfailingly cheery.

As their guests were leaving, JJ was troubled. *How do I thank Howard for keeping Dad's letter all that time?* "I read Dad's letter," he whispered, "Thanks."

"One of the last things I was asked to do for him, John."

***

"So the Lions *finally* won one," Cathy sniffed as they headed back towards the Dietz's near dark.

"Eh, it's their *fourth* win this season," Ed replied. "They've had a tough schedule…" Juggling the plates and trays across the rutted grass was out of the question; they took the longer paved route.

"Isn't *that* code for 'they've got no bench," Mike sighed. "Always looks like they're plagued by injuries."

"That's *so*, Michael," Ben replied, "even though they do well in their division. They…" He stopped, staring at the little park. "Is someone *there*?"

"Yessir," a voice replied. "Block Associates. There are three of us."

"Very well," Ben answered. "Thank you."

## *Monday*

*One more day here before we move.*

He slipped out of the big bed and looked around the dimly-lit honeymoon suite bedroom, still in awe. He looked up at the soft sunlight through the skylight, then back at Ann, half-asleep in the soft light. *TOO tempting.*

He smiled, and her eyes rolled. "Stop *thinking that*, babe."

"Thinking what?"

"*Once* more on this big, *beautiful* bed," she sighed as she threw the covers off. "Quit *thinking* and *c'mere*."

\*\*\*

*Beautiful morning.*

He stretched luxuriously, feeling the same odd kink in his back that he'd felt a couple weeks before, on top of the persistent stiffness. *I wish I knew what that was.* He looked over at Leigh, then stared out the window. "Morning, *oytzer*."

"Morning, Sandy. Today, I meet some of *my* family." She furrowed her brow. "Weird."

"I grew up with an enormous family, so I've got *nothing* to compare it to." He stretched again and bumped her shoulder. "Sorry."

"No walking cast today, either," she smiled. "Hope my *hip* recovers soon."

"Me too." He stretched an arm across her. "Wendy's gonna set something up so we can talk to her family about…*OOOH!*"

She grabbed him under the sheets. "NOT now, Sandy."

\*\*\*

"We need to split this," Ann declared, scanning her *long* list of thank-you's as they shared coffee.

"How about I do *your* family, and *you* do mine."

"How about mutual friends?"

"Eenie-Meenie…*We* need to do laundry, too."

"Yeah. *And* we're taking the gang to Brookfield this morning. Let's get *lazy* and let Callie the Concierge do our laundry."

"*Fabulous* idea."

**\*\*\***

"Mom, Dad," Wendy smiled, "*this* is..." They met at Judge Oakes's home, mutually beneficial since the Corey's hadn't met *Dennis's* family, either.

"I'm Ed," he grinned at the tall, angular woman only five years older than he. "And this is my wife, Cathy, and my daughter, Leigh."

"I'm *your* Aunt Faith," the woman grinned, "but if you *call* me 'Aunt,' Ed, *we'll* have words."

"Matt Corey," the big, raw-boned man with thinning hair boomed. "The family's been wondering about *you* for as long as *I've* known them."

Sitting in the small living room with coffee and sweet-cakes, Faith said, "I was five when...." She reached into a shopping bag she'd brought with her. "*This* was taken when she was fourteen."

"*Never* thought I'd *see*..." Ed's fingertips lightly grazed his mother's image. His eyes welled before he passed the oval-matted photo to Cathy. "*Never imagined...*"

"*We* never imagined we'd meet *you*," Matt said. "Faith told me about you when I first *saw* that picture. *Once* in a while, someone would ask about you aloud, as long as Oscar and Millie weren't around."

"Mother and Dad *never* wanted to talk about you," Faith added.

"Do you know *anything* about my father," Ed asked.

"A transient working on a neighbor's farm. By the time we knew Leigh was in trouble, the guy was *long* gone. Mother said that he *forced* her."

Matt shrugged. "Credible on its face. *My* research over the years..."

"*Your* research," Ed was surprised. "What do *you* do?"

"Family law attorney. Semi-retired now, but I still snoop around sometimes."

"You looked like *her*, honey," Cathy passed the photo to Leigh. "Your *grandmother*."

*Never had one of Dad's family look back at me.*

**\*\*\***

"You *have* something for the class," Ernie asked Julia in the Troy agency early Monday morning.

"Yessir," she answered. "My cousin and her partner found the *current* offices of Parkinson Title and Trust."

Everyone turned to look. "I *see*," Ernie said, interested. "If you would *introduce* yourselves, ladies?"

"My name is Josephine Parkinson: Just *Jo* is fine."

"I'm Roberta—*Bobbi*—Eldon. We form the Bobbi/Jo Partnership. We have been contracted by Mrs. Parkinson to look into her husband's finances."

"I see," Ernie said. "And what skills do *you* bring to the party?"

"I have a business intelligence degree from Wayne State," Bobbi answered, "and I have a Michigan private investigator's license. Jo is an attorney and a CPA and *also* has a PI license."

190

"*Huh*," Ernie declared with a nod that, together, *somehow* meant *very interesting*. "*How* did you come to even be looking for this?"

"Because Gramma Stella needs money," Jo said.

"JJ's mother," Dave asked.

"Yes," Jo declared. "Her financial arrangements with Grampa Charlie are out of the 19th Century: she gets enough for groceries and not much more. We were given permission to search Grampa Charlie's financial records." She pulled a contract out of a folder. "Under Michigan law, Gramma Stella is his sole heir and has authority over his businesses because Grampa never incorporated. We found traces of the trust firm at his truck dealership and followed the bread crumbs to Telegraph and Fenkell."

"Very well, Jo," Ernie said. "I *have* to make you aware that what we are doing may uncover important, *life-threatening* information. Do you understand?"

Jo nodded. "We *get* it."

"We could *hire* them," Dave shrugged. "That would make them *legally* liable. That or, when we're *done*, cut off their heads and stick them in a safe…"

"The latter is *melodramatic*," Ernie grunted. "Jules…"

"Jo," Julia said, "let's make a *contract*. *You guys* are joining the FBI."

"*Ladies*," Ernie announced an hour later. "Hold up your right hand and repeat after me: I—state your name—solemnly swear that I shall never divulge anything of what I learn having to do with the Wolverine Working Group or the Special Projects Division, so *help* me, *Hanna*."

Despite the apparent absurdity of the *oath*, the women swore to it just like Mike and Leigh had a week before. *Feels like hazing…but these guys think it's serious.*

"Now, we need to get inside that office," Ernie declared, "but without a criminal referral, we can't get a subpoena or a warrant. Therefore, we need the owner's permission."

"First, we need to *verify* ownership," Dave nodded. "Mike, that's *your* cue."

* * *

"Brookfield class of '73," JJ told the gate guard. The gate went up, and he drove the Suburban through, *still* unfamiliar with the new entrance and guarded security. "This entrance is new," he explained, turning towards the Science Institute. "They had to cut down on traffic…"

"What's *that*," Betty asked as they rolled by a field surrounded by trees.

"A *sculpture* of…*something*. We called it the Worm Field, though the Art Institute doesn't *like* that. *They* built it."

"Looks like a bunch of pipes welded together…and there's a stack of beams," Laura declared.

"Pretty much *it*; art appreciation ain't my forte." They drove around the grounds as he pointed out the sights; Brookfield School; the Chinese Dog Ramp; where Moby Pool *had* been; the Slide; Greenbrier School; Brookfield Art

Institute; Faculty Way; the tennis bubble; the Science Institute. Because classes were in session, getting out of the Suburban was *discouraged*, but…"Right over *there* was *my* room: first floor, third from *that* end."

"*Wow*, Sarge," Liz marveled. "Ivy-covered walls…"

"Yeah. But I wish they'd clean *this* up more often," JJ sighed, staring at the bronze plaque in Brookfield's central brick-lined quad. *To Brookfield's Sons Who Gave Their Lives for Their Country. "Morituri te salutant*: those who are…"

"*Ave Imperator*—Hail Emperor," Gary said. "Those who are about to die, salute you! You forgot the *first* part, JJ."

"*We* didn't use it," JJ answered. "The three of us: me, Mike, Ram; saluted those guys with, I *think*, some Mateus the night before we graduated."

"Huh," Liz added. "Where have I heard *that* from?"

"It's what the gladiators said before they fought," Gary explained. "It's in all the movies. But it *should* have been *morituri te salutamus* if they weren't saluting the emperor…what?"

Ann stared at him. "You *speak* Latin?"

"Took four years of it in high school. I thought it would come in handy; it *has*, on occasion."

"You probably win a *lot* of bar bets with it," Betty grumbled. "Is there a plaque like this over at the girl's school?"

"Not that I *know* of, and there *should* be. That school started in '55, so…" For the rest of the tour, the thought haunted him. *There should be one at Greenbrier…*

✳✳✳

"*Good* afternoon," the sixty-something woman sighed at Mike as she came out from behind the *cleanest* reception desk he'd ever seen.

"Ma'am, I'm Mike Greenhow with Harold's Register." Mike gave his *most* convincing smile. "Is the owner in? We need to update this listing." The nondescript, three-story concrete and glass structure with a modest sign near Dale Street in Redford looked more like a builder's creation than an architect's.

"Mr. Parkinson is *not* in," the woman replied, hand on hip. "Harold's Register? Never heard of it." Her voice was hard to classify, somewhere between honey and gravel.

*I hope this legend isn't too thin.* "We're the national register of real estate service professionals, providing comprehensive services for…"

"We *don't* advertise," the woman blinked. "Now, if you'll *excuse* me…"

"*Yes*, ma'am, I *know* you don't." *If you can't dazzle 'em, baffle 'em…* "And you don't *have to* in Harold's. All we need is the principal's name and contact information, and our index will do *all* the work for you. See, our *marketing* people just put your *name* in front of likely professionals who *need your services* in the area. Your phone will be ringing off the hook, and *you* won't *spend* a *cent*."

"Well…" she looked dubious, "Charlie Parkinson is the owner," but seemed to light up. "He *also* owns a truck dealership. I haven't seen or heard from him

192

in three weeks; he's usually *here* Mondays. Wonder if something happened…I'm Ingrid Torgensen, the office manager." Ingrid pursed her lips, knitted her brows, and rubbed her hands together. "We could *use* some more traffic around here…"

"Of *course*," Mike agreed, smiling like any good salesman. "Now, if I could just get a *few* particulars…"

A phone rang. "Parkinson Title…yes…OK." She hung up and looked stern. "I have to leave for the day."

"Why?"

"Because they pay me double for *not* being here after I get *that* call."

"*Who is it* that calls?"

"I don't *know who*. I just *know* I have to be gone."

\*\*\*

"So, Leigh, you're engaged?" Faith looked up from her depleted salad plate. Some people *eat* to *live*; others *live* to *eat*. Faith Corey seemed to *eat* as a *race*.

"We're getting married on 6 December."

"Oh, splendid," Matt cried, still not half-done with his salad…like the rest of the table. "Have you known him long?"

"Seventh Grade," Leigh answered.

"*How* romantic," Faith smiled, a dribble of salad dressing on her lip. "But I thought you were in the Army?"

"We *both* are: he's in counterintelligence; I'm in the MPs."

"Oh, *really*," Matt replied. "CIC, huh? I was in the CIC in '46 in Germany. Mostly de-Nazification work then. Where are you stationed?"

"Here in Detroit."

"Huh? How did *that* happen?"

"They needed our skills here in town, so, here we are." Leigh sighed, glancing at Wendy.

"And, *about* that…" Wendy began. "Mike and Leigh need to *talk* to you…professionally."

\*\*\*

"OK," Mike explained later. "Charlie Parkinson, who also owns a truck shop, is the *owner* of the business. He's in the office Mondays but hasn't been *seen* for three weeks. Ingrid Torgensen calls herself the office manager."

"Fits," Dave nodded. "What does *she* do?"

"She seems to be like a caretaker."

"He's *got* several real estate investment trusts," Bobbi offered. "Saw traces of them at his dealership."

"When *I* was there, she got a phone call, said she had to leave for the rest of the day."

"Why?"

"All *she* knows is she gets paid for the day for *not* being there *after* she gets that call."

"Let's watch tonight and see why," Dave said. "Mike: *take* the night off."

* * *

"We'll have to get together later," Ed smiled, his voice a little shaky. "Not *every* day a guy meets the family he never knew he *had*."

"And my long-lost nephew doesn't materialize every day, either," Faith smiled, leaning for a kiss. "Really, Ed: we've been *hoping* you were well. I didn't ever expect to *see* you. I didn't tell the rest of the family about you until I'd had a look at you. *That* picture…and your *daughter*…yes, *you're* Leigh's son, all right; I have *no* doubt." She switched her gaze to Leigh. "Never knew our limited associations with the Newhouse's would interest Army intelligence."

"Somehow, however," Matt grumbled, "it does *not* surprise me. We're here until Wednesday."

"You should come down and meet the rest of our family at Thanksgiving," Leigh grinned, "Mike's family numbers in the *hundreds*."

"Oh," Faith said, "then we'll be back next week! Matt, Thanksgiving on the road this year. I'll call Hope and Oscar *tonight*…"

* * *

"Thanks for coming by, Sid," Ann sighed in the atrium. "How's your mom been?"

"Fine, thanks, Claudia—oops! *Mrs. Elrath*. Like I *said*: call any time."

"*Mueller*-Elrath, but Sid, come *on*! We've *known* each other since 1st Grade Catechism, for Chrissake!"

"Claudia, my *dear* friend, I can barely bring myself to think of you as *Ann*, but what I require of my people I *have* to observe myself." He sipped his coffee, grimacing. "That bartender, Chuck; the FBI knows of him. He was Mr. Elrath's roommate at Wolverine for a time. His family is associated with a large criminal enterprise. His role *in* that enterprise is unclear, but," he sighed, "I would caution you to stay clear of him."

* * *

"Dad: you OK?" The family was back home in the cottage trying to relax—undecided about whether to snack or eat a meal—with Ed looking like he wanted to jump out of his skin.

"I'm not *sure*, honey," he confessed. "This time last week, I only had you two in my life. *Now* I have aunts, uncles, cousins…and I know *something* about my mother's family. I've seen my mother's picture for the first time." He sighed. "As if I'd been stuck in a *spaceship* all my life and just landed on another planet, and suddenly, I'm *not* alone."

"*Well*, Eddie," Cathy purred, loosening his tie. "We can parse *all of that* as time goes on." She slipped her own shoes off, glancing at Leigh with a nod to the door. "*Plenty* of time for all of *that*."

194

"*Mrs*. Taylor," Ed side-glanced as she pulled her blouse out of her skirt. "Are you *suggesting*…"

"I *am*, just as soon as *Leigh* skedaddles…unless she wants to *watch*…"

Just then, the phone rang: Cathy answered distractedly. "Yes…oh, *yes*…so, how long…thank you *so* much for calling." She continued taking her blouse off. "They'll start cleaning the townhouse tomorrow. They *think* two weeks." She unzipped her skirt and glanced at Leigh with a look that asked: *why are YOU still here?*

Taking her cue, *that* was the last Leigh saw of her parents that day.

\*\*\*

"So, Dan, you're a sheriff's deputy?" Dan was a seemingly emaciated, brown-eyed man who looked as though a strong wind would blow him away. "Been at it long?"

"Since college, sir," Dan replied with a dimpled grin. "I took criminal justice at Oakland University, went to the police academy in Lansing, put in for a job at Oakland County in '79, and here I am."

"*That* simple," Ann mused. "Did you have to have *all that* to apply?"

"Well, no. I'll tell you my secret: Josie put me in touch with her Aunt Dorothy before high school graduation."

"Ah," JJ replied, trying to look sage while suppressing a grin. "And Dot just said 'do all *that*, and I'll *hire* you? Thought you weren't *talking* to men, *Josie?*"

"Dan *was* the exception, JJ," Jo rolled her eyes, blushing at the sound of *Josie*.

"Have you and *Josie* been in touch a *lot* since school," Ann asked

"I'd call him when I was in town as long as *Mary* wasn't around. First I *saw* him in years was last Wednesday."

"And I was surprised to *see* her," Dan replied. "Then she *called* Friday…"

"Just glad you didn't have any *other* plans, Danny."

"I *did*," Dan smiled, "but alphabetizing my soup cans was a *lot* less interesting than spending a weekend with a beautiful girl…"

"*Danny*, we *talked* about *this*…" Jo rolled her eyes.

"Nothing to *hide*, *Josie*," Ann said. "Your sister isn't around…"

Jo blew out her cheeks briefly. "The *honeyed* words Danny's been pouring into my ear have made me want to *brain* my *dear* womb-mate." She reached for Dan's hand. "I should have listened to *him* before graduation."

"Before…" Ann looked puzzled.

"We had our senior seminar together: life after high school. Mary was in *another* seminar group." The memory seemed painful. "One session called 'breaking your mold' was about trying new things, meeting new people, and studying ideas you'd never *heard* of. Danny said we needed to think about ideas without the same *voices* in our heads all the time. He was looking straight at me: I think I fell in love with him then…but, of course, I *couldn't* do anything about it. *He* was a part of the patriarchal power structure bent on enslaving gyne-kind—

*that* was *Mary* in my head."

"And I *sometimes* wish…" Dan smiled. "But *now…*" they leaned together for a kiss.

"Well," JJ grinned. "Here's to *finally* figuring it out, *Josie*."

*To figuring it out!*

* * *

"So what were *they* doing tonight," Ann called from the bedroom.

"All but Gary and Alice are taking in a movie," JJ answered…and the phone rang. "Elrath."

"Hey, JJ," Julia said. "Listen, buddy: Mike *had* to tell us what Jo told you about Gramp's trust office."

*What? The…?* "*OK*, I suppose. *Why?*"

"We…have our reasons."

"To do with Wolverine?"

"*May*be." A silence. "John; *trust* me, OK?"

"Always, Jules."

"We need to get in, buddy. We need you *and* Gramma Stella to go down there and…"

"We…*the FBI?*"

"Yeah…."

"Sergeant Elrath, Ernie Packard. We've seen too many coincidences to be coincidental, but not enough to get an indictment or a warrant. We have reason to believe that we *may* find something there that would cause trouble for Wolverine."

"Yessir. *What* do you suspect they're into?

"Human trafficking."

*Why am I NOT surprised?* "What do you want *us* to do?"

"Just…open the door."

"Does it affect my *mother?*"

"*No*." Ernie was emphatic.

*Why is THAT reassuring?* "Tomorrow? Be advised, Mom doesn't get up before 9."

"Fine."

*Why am I not surprised…*

# Tuesday

"Morning, Mama," Leigh opened the bathroom door—the bathroom that joined Mike's room—quietly as Monica sorted laundry. "How much do *you* have?"

"*Morning*, dear," Monica chimed. "Three loads." She looked around. "You?"

"I have…ah, *we* have…two loads, probably." *I need to start thinking in terms of two.* "We'll probably do it tonight."

"It *gets* easier, dear," Monica announced. "Doubling *everything*. After your first child, *quadrupling*. Then, the *next* baby will be easier, and after that, *easier still*."

"I'll keep that in mind, Mama."

\*\*\*

"Morning, Cloud." He stretched languorously, reaching for her hand; she clutched his absently, half-asleep. "Moving day."

"Mm. Do we *have* to?"

"Yep."

She slid a hand down his belly and reached for him under the covers. "*One last time* in this *superior* bed."

\*\*\*

"Mary Newhouse? Michael Greenhow, North American International Insurance. I called before?" Mary's once-red hair had faded to dull brass; her once-pert brown eyes were tired; her once-proud frame slightly stooped. Yet, she had a pleasant, mellifluous, and distracting voice.

"Yes," her eyes brightened. "Something about an insurance policy?" Mike's legend was as an insurance underwriter.

"*Yes*, ma'am. Can we talk here?" The little office had no receptionist and no staff, two unused desks, and Mary using a third.

"Sure. What can I do for you?" The mall *had* seen more tenants—about a third of the spaces were vacant—but was busy with pre-Christmas shoppers.

"*Here* we have," he pulled a binder out of his valise, smiling brightly while *covertly-overtly* checking her out, "a copy of the application." He handed it to her. "As you can *see*, your *son*…"

"Nephew," she corrected. According to IRS records, young Randy was fifteen in May, and Mary was a bookkeeper.

"Of *course*, sorry…here…he's named the beneficiary. As this is our first business with Mr. Newhouse, we like to make sure who we're dealing with. You're his guardian? Where's his mother?"

"I don't know." She seemed startled. "Why? Is it important?"

"Only for administrative purposes."

She knitted her brows as she looked the form over. "*This* isn't right. Randall Fred Newhouse IV…oh, wait, yes, *that's* right: sorry. *His* father's Randy Newhouse the *Third*; my ex-husband's the *Forth*. Just got confused…"

"You were *married* to Randy Newhouse the Fourth?"

"Briefly, for the kids, in '72: but it was a *disaster*. This is all confidential, right? Like with lawyers?"

"Absolutely. The children's *mother* was…?"

"My sister. She got poor Randy *drunk* in '70 and seduced him. In the spring of '71, she gave birth and just *took off*. I assumed guardianship."

"I see. What contact do you *have* with the Newhouse family?"

"Very little, though they pay the mortgage here. That's why *this* is a little surprising."

"I see. How often…well, *that* doesn't matter. And have there been any efforts to contact your sister?"

"The Newhouse family has *tried*."

"So, your *maiden* name is…?"

"*Newhouse*. We're cousins. We got married in Tennessee."

"I see. Well, thank you, Mrs. Newhouse. I think I have enough information to complete the application. You'll be informed when it's approved."

*But why would Newhouse still be footing the bills…?*

***

"Elrath," he answered the phone, distracted from his keep-or-toss pile-sorting for their move across the atrium.

"Hello, Lieutenant Brookhaven calling for Chief Mueller."

*Military mode on.* "*Roger, wait* one." He blocked the receiver on his chest. "*Honey*: it's the *Navy!*" …*Sergeant Ward Cleaver called…*

"Chief Mueller-Elrath speaking."

"Chief: Yeoman Peale calling for Lieutenant Brookhaven. Will you hold the line for *him*, please?"

"Hold the line, aye."

"Chief Mueller? Steve Brookhaven here, commanding Great Lakes Sea Frontier." The voice was low, yet thin and commanding, odd in its way. "Is this a good time to talk? I'm aware you're on liberty."

"Good as any, sir."

"*Out*standing. I asked NAVMILPERSCOM if *I* could talk to you."

"I *see*," she smiled. *Talk to you*, in this context, inevitably led to the *mention* of short-staffing. "First, just what *is* a sea frontier?"

"*Confusion to the enemy*," he chuckled. "Some brass hat came up with it, *I* think, to emphasize the importance of the Great Lakes in our defense posture. We have *three* missions: to conduct freshwater undersea warfare research, support the A-Phase dive school at Great Lakes Naval Station, *and* the Coast Guard's Great Lakes and Saint Lawrence Seaway divers. We mustered in…let's see…eighteen *days* ago now—we haven't even piped *colors* aboard yet, and we lack boatswains to do even *that*. I have 140 officers and sailors authorized, but I only have *ten* enlisted, *two* officers, and *one* chief on board as of this morning. And we have *no one* with *your* storekeeping experience."

"And that's where *I* come in."

"Don't *think* about cutting your liberty short, Chief, but…" he sighed. "I've *got* a *roomful* of stores paperwork because we're busier than one-armed paper-hangers doing everything else. *I* haven't done any *storekeeping* since *I* was an ensign. Can you at least help with *that* until you *get* new orders? Just a few *hours* might turn the tide for now."

"I *can*, sir. If you've got a personnel technician, I need to get my records updated, *and* I need a new name tag."

"We *have* one. *When* can you come down? Just *in*formally, to give *us* a hand up."

*He might be my new boss soon...never leave a wrong impression.* "Well, sir, this *is* something of a surprise. Let me check with *my* Gunny: *wait* one." She smiled; he grinned. "Would *tomorrow* be acceptable?"

She hung up and made a face. "Though I've taunted you and flayed you..."

"It's the life we *chose*, honey," he replied. "In the meantime, *I* have to go. You OK here?"

"Sure. Let's finish moving before *you* go. I've *got* to get started on the thank-you's."

***

"Mr. Dietz," JJ smiled, extending his hand.

"*Good* morning, John." In addition to Mordechai and Stella, Bobbi and Jo had arrived. Set back from Fenkell by a large, uneven parking lot, the front of the building sported well-groomed yews in a yard-wide bed, with Japanese maples on the corners.

"I'm grateful that you chose to help my mother..."

"Yes, we *are*, Mr. Dietz," Stella added. "Now, if we can get *on* with this."

"Certainly." Uncle Mort led Stella into the building and through the office's front door.

Ingrid appeared, seemingly tired. "May I *help*..." she stared at Stella, surprised, "...*you!*"

"It's *me*, Ingrid," Stella gave her disingenuous, I-know-what-you're-up-to smile. "You left the dealership and came *here*. This is my son, John, and my attorney, Mordechai Dietz. These young women are here to find his money."

"I see," she answered. "*Pleased* to meet you all. Is he *dead*?"

"No, not *yet*," Stella deadpanned.

"Too bad." Ingrid's graying hair was unfashionably long for her age but pinned back and tidy.

"What do you mean 'too bad,'" Stella asked

"Because once he's gone, I can put a *match* to this mausoleum," Ingrid sniffed. "I've been the only one *here* for years, except *him* once a week."

"Oh? Business slow?"

"*Slow*? To be *slow*, it would have to *move*. Been practically *stationary* for a decade. Lots of *other* goings-on, but nothing to do with titles."

"What do you do with your time?"

"I *open* the mail; I *file* the mail; I make deposits; I answer the phones; I write a few checks. *Most* of what I do is *filing*. It takes about ten hours a week except at the end of the month when I write the checks. The *rest* of my time, I just sit here and watch the dust accumulate." She paused as if waiting to make a decision. "Come on in."

Ingrid led them past the reception area, past row after row of neatly labeled filing cabinets, with tables and desk, piled high with files and file boxes. "Most of *this*," she waved vaguely to her left, "is from his trust business, his REITs and other properties, and his old title work. *This*," she waved to her right, "is stuff I don't know *anything* about, and I'm not *supposed* to." She pointed to a side table piled high with mail. "That's *some more* of the stuff I know nothing about." JJ perused the pile of large envelopes addressed to Parkinson Title and Trust.

She led them to Charlie's office, an untidy place with a faux wood steel desk and dilapidated vinyl-covered chair. A side table was covered with file folders and seemingly unorganized papers. "*There*," she pointed to a framed picture of JJ in '73 when he first joined the Army. "I remember when he hung it, said he'd put it on a dartboard if he *had* one."

"Really," It was Stella's turn to be surprised. "We married in January 1970."

"Huh," Ingrid added. "I stopped screwing him *before* that." She shook her head. "I remember when he got the news about his *first* wife: hung up the phone and kept on working." She shook all over. "We had our first, ah, *encounter* a couple weeks later, in that chair over there."

"Ah, ma'am," Jo interrupted, "the deposits you mentioned? What *banks…?*"

"Several," Ingrid sighed. "I'll get his desk keys."

"And all the *rest* of the keys," Uncle Mort said authoritatively, "and the combinations to those *vaults*." He pointed to three large steel vaults six feet high and eight wide. "Just what *is* your payroll status?"

"I'm salaried; I review myself," Ingrid declared. "I keep my own timesheets; give myself a 4% raise every December. Charlie signs off on them when he comes in. Since I haven't *seen* him…"

"I see," Uncle Mort declared. "Then, as co-owner of the business, Mrs. Parkinson, it's up to *you* to decide about…"

Stella seemed startled. "I'm…I'll approve the past weeks, but the FBI is looking for…something." She glanced at JJ. "Just…give Mr. Dietz your details, and he'll let you know. For *now*, consider yourself on paid furlough."

"*We'll* decide *weekly* on what you'll be doing," Uncle Mort declared as she handed over the large key ring and handed Stella a small bound book.

Jo and Bobbi descended on the desk like wolves on a flock.

***

"Our business here is concluded," Uncle Mort handed the keys and combination book over to Ernie as he entered the office an hour later. "Miss Parkinson is…"

Ernie nodded at Jo as Stella and Uncle Mort left. "Any luck?"

"*Yes*," Jo grinned.

"Then, *please*," Ernie smiled, "we'll take *this* from here." He looked around quickly. "We'll *have* to move this," he grunted, "*can't* secure it here…"

"May I ask *where*," JJ asked.

"Just *don't* expect an answer," Ernie smiled. "The fewer people who *know*, the *better*."

"I get it," JJ answered. "I appreciate you letting Jo…"

"My dad was killed on the job when I was fifteen," Ernie said quietly. "Small, rural sheriff's department; no pension. My brothers and I had to scramble just to keep a roof over Mom's head. I won't allow *another* family to suffer like that if I can help it."

"Even if you have to bend the rules?"

Ernie grinned wistfully. "*We're* the Special Projects Division. We *make* a lot of our *own* rules that *don't* violate either *procedure* or the *law*. Allowing the removal of some personal financial information that had nothing—*to our knowledge*—to do with our investigation isn't bending *any* rules." He cocked his head. "*Shatters* a few but doesn't *bend* any."

"And your bosses?"

Ernie chuckled lightly. "Sarge, the SPD answers *only* to the Director. We only work on two things: what the Director *tells* us to work on and the yellowing mass of Liberty Bell files. *Those* were created because J. Edgar thought there were monsters under his bed. We're here, in *part*, *because* of some of those files." He cleared his throat theatrically. "I know that you and your wife are the wealthiest NCOs in the service and can support your mother well enough. But I *also* know that your physical limitations may put you *both* out of the Active component before you're eligible for retirement. *That* would put a financial strain on you *all*, yes?"

"You *know* a *lot*."

"*That's* our *business*, Sarge."

***

"Well, sir," Mike grinned, shaking Matt's hand, "I'm sure *this* won't take long. I don't have to read you any rights because you're not a military member." The Sheraton Hotel on Woodward was a well-appointed establishment, with a small bar on the first floor just off the lobby.

"Glad to meet you, Mike," Matt said. "I'm *not* sure what we can tell you."

"This is Dave Clawson, with the FBI," Mike said. "*He's* here…different reason." Matt nodded. "We'll start simple: How often do you have *any* contact with the Newhouse family?"

"We get a ham every Christmas from Newhouse Properties," Faith answered.

"*Ugh*," Leigh groaned, "I remember *them*. When did *you* start getting them?"

"Um…sometime in the '50s. We got a Christmas card in '59 from Phyllis…*might* have been the last." Faith thought for a moment. "Got our last card from Ed *and* Charity in '59. Got one or two from Charity after the divorce."

"Then there was Ed's funeral in '64," Matt said.

"*That* funeral, yes. Poor little girls, going into foster care at nine and thirteen…"

"But their *mother*…?" Mike started.

"Charity was enduring her *first* round of breast cancer treatment, and she was *so* sick." Matt declared. "So, into foster care both little girls went."

"No thought of any of *you* taking them home," Leigh asked.

"*That* would have been hard," Faith sighed. "Your cousin Rob was born with spinal Bifida in '63—he passed in '70—and was already taking most of *our* time and energy. Our other kids were seven, nine, and twelve—*they* sucked up the rest. Hope and John were expecting Herb at any moment, and your Uncle Mitch had just lost his job at Studebaker and had three kids of his own. Oscar *wanted* to take them in, but Glynnis already *had* two kids, so *she* nixed *that* idea." She grimaced. "Glynnis is a difficult woman. When you meet *her*, you'll see."

"Phyllis was in *no shape* to take on more kids," Matt declared. "Ultimately, no one in the family *could* or would."

"So we lost touch," Wendy prompted. "I remember the older one wouldn't let go of the younger one's hand all that day, even when they went to the bathroom."

"They were taken in by a lovely foster family, the Adamski's," Matt said. "Ran a grocery store in Hell…"

"My *neighbors*, I *think*," Dave said.

"Indeed? When Charity died in '69, RF moved them."

"And that's the last we knew of *them*," Faith said.

"What *are* the girl's names," Leigh asked.

"You know, we *don't* really know," Matt declared. "I never *saw* their birth certificates—couldn't *find* them anywhere—so, they went into the system without them. The older one called herself Marylin—bleached her hair like Marylin Monroe and wouldn't *give* another name. The younger one was either Lettie or Lizzie. When I filled out the paperwork for their foster care, Charity *wanted* them to be 'Taylor,' so they became Marylin and Elizabeth *Taylor*."

"They were Mary and Lizzie when I knew them," Dave said. "Mary *called* herself Marylin; Elizabeth was Lizzie's *middle* name; I heard *that* in school."

"And that was the last *we* saw or heard of *any* Newhouse's," Faith said, "except for the annual ham."

"We've been giving them to the food pantry here lately," Matt sighed.

"That's what *we* did with them," Leigh declared. *Wonder if we still get them? Wonder if Marylin/Mary does?* "Um…this is going to be awkward," Leigh started, "but…why didn't the family take *Dad* in?"

"Arrangements were made for *him* before he was born," Faith declared with a sad smile. "For Father, there was *no* debate on the subject. Leigh wrote out what she wanted for the baby's name—after her grandparents—before she went into labor, *knowing* she'd be giving him up. When she started labor, Father went for the doctor, then the social worker. While Leigh was screaming in the kitchen, Mother gathered everything the baby was to take *with* him, including Leigh's birth certificate, for whatever reason, and the Christmas tree ornaments *Leigh* made. Even as a child, she was a talented artist." She looked away. "After almost a day listening, the doctor came out, said '*I* can't save *her*.' Mother cried; Father gave *your* father *and* his bundle to the social worker. *That* was the last..."

"*Never* tell Dad."

"I wouldn't *dream* of it."

***

"She seems to be actually *believing* what she's *saying*," Mike sighed that evening. "But *no contact* from the Newhouse family..."

"Nope," Julia declared. "*Not* that surprising if she's who Dave *thinks* she is..."

Morgan smiled. "*Too* coincidental to be a coincidence. But Mary mentioned 'kids,' plural?"

"Yes," Mike frowned. "No names, no mention of a relationship...just 'kids.'"

"Huh," Leigh sighed. "A look at a birth certificate might help. Might confirm..."

"All we know for sure about *that* is that *both* parent's names *are not* on the boy's," Dorothy nodded. "That locks it down by Michigan law, so we can't see it without a court order unless a parent *or* the child consents."

"But we *know*..." Mike started.

"*No*: we've been *told*," Leigh corrected, raising a finger to emphasize the distinction. "Randy *said* Mary was the kid's mom. Now *she's* saying it was her *sister's* kid and that *she*—Mary—was married to Randy in '72, a year *later*. He turned seventeen that May. Without parental *consent*...?"

Mike frowned. "I *should* have asked what her *sister's* name was, but there was no reason to ask *that*; nothing to do with the policy if Mary's the legal guardian."

"How common *is* the Newhouse name in Michigan," Julia asked.

"There are *two* residences listed in Oakland County," Ellen said, "and *one* in Bay County, which includes Essexville."

"Mortgage on that house: did she declare it on her taxes," Amy asked.

"Nope," Dave said. "Her tax return says 'owned by a family member.'"

"Phyllis Newhouse referred to her *grandson* in '73," Ernie asked.

"If they *were* paying for this out of *household* funds, that *might* have been how Phyllis *found out*. They're keeping the boy away because...*still* not sure." Leigh shook her head. "But why do they want to hurt *us*?"

Mike cleared his throat. "The violence doesn't make *any* sense *if* it's just because of a teenage indiscretion. Pay an international terrorist to shoot up a Michigan residential neighborhood? *Why?* Chuck Weir's been in the wind for years, and he shows up *here*. Coincidence? Mary's working for Parkinson Title and Trust, owned by Charlie Parkinson, who is *currently*..."

"In a *coma*." Ellen finished.

"Yeah," Leigh sighed. *"But..."*

"The *original* issue," Ernie declared, "was *who owns Wolverine.*" He paused as if searching for words. "We can only pray that Parkinson *isn't involved* in Wolverine." He drummed his fingers; the FBI agents around him looked at each other, curious. *"Huh,"* Ernie grunted and shrugged...that *somehow* said, *let's not let this poor woman get screwed.*

"If Mary's working for Parkinson, who *may* be involved in Wolverine," Ellen said, "then *she's* of interest. And Randy..."

"Oh, Randy's *involved*, all right," Morgan added. "He's been transporting people to Wolverine for *years.*" She sighed. "What we *don't* know..."

Ernie interrupted, "we *don't* know *for whom.* Indeed; someone who can get an international terrorist on every watchlist in the Western world to attack a house in the Detroit suburbs has a very *long* reach." He hunched his shoulders, frowned slightly. "Leigh, go up to Bay City and see those kids *and* Mary at the same time."

Leigh nodded. "Mary's legend that he's not *hers has* to have *some* reason. Asking them about Mom *might* tell us something more about Mary's legend and what they know about the Newhouse's."

Ernie grunted, somehow that meant *exactly.* "That legend that will open any door..."

"...a *lawyer* executing a *will,*" Leigh finished. *"That* way, I can ask all *kinds* of family questions to establish the legitimacy of *their* claim."

Ernie nodded. "Saturday morning, when we know they're all likely to be home. Now, we've got some preliminary findings from that little phone book. Julia?"

"There's a *lot* of redundancy: of 612 entries, only 325 are unique *numbers*, and nearly all are in Michigan. There're 326 unique *names* in the book: can't account for the anomaly. Now, 35 of those numbers are—or were *once*—Newhouse family members; 41 are known business associates."

Ernie nodded. "Morgan, the traps on the Parkinson Title office?"

"At 10:15 yesterday morning, we trapped a six-minute call to the law offices of Fisher and Ally in Ferndale."

"Newhouse house counsel," Ellen said.

"Yes," Morgan agreed. "Next call of interest out of Fisher and Ally was at 11:01, to a Newhouse Properties office in Pontiac that lasted for two minutes. Then, a four-minute call from Newhouse Properties to a private residence in Bloomfield Hills."

"You've got traps on *all* those..." Mike was dubious.

"We've got traps on all the numbers in that *book,*" Morgan nodded. "Policy is to collect everything we can *without* intrusion. That *last* trap was..."

"RF Newhouse," Leigh declared.

*"Bingo."*

\*\*\*

"Hi, Ann, it's Deb. An out-of-town neurologist is examining Mr. Parkinson. From what I've *heard*, he's *not* cheap, and he's here with support staff." Ann had spent the afternoon showing the Florida gang the sights around Detroit. That evening, JJ was dining with Brenda…alone.

*What the…?* She quickly called Stella's condo. "Stella: Ann. Did you *ask* for a second opinion…?"

"No, I did *not*," Stella declared, "and I'm on my way to the hospital *now*; *Donna* called me a few minutes ago."

"I'll meet you there."

"Dear: hurry!"

*No answer at Sid's…how about…* "Cathy? Ann. Got a crisis at the hospital; Stella might need a lawyer and *fast*…"

Ann, rushing out of the elevator, found Morgan and Julia waiting. "*Come* with *me*," she said, hooking both their arms. "I'll explain on the way."

\*\*\*

"Just *what* does this *mean*, 'a *third party* authorizes?'" Cathy snapped. The document she read was an authorization to move Charlie to a hospital in Ann Arbor, where a cryogenic procedure on his brain was scheduled. "*No* third party is *legally* able to authorize medical treatment—especially something *this* invasive *and* expensive—for Mr. Parkinson or anyone else! Who *is* this 'third party,' anyway?"

"I'm not *about* to disclose that." Dr. Hennessey was a small man with thinning hair and a pencil mustache that reminded Ann of Gilbert Roland. "*I* am *generally* regarded as the world's *leading* practitioner of cryogenic neurosurgery, and it is *imperative* that I treat…"

"You're not *about* to treat anyone," Cathy declared again. "I don't care *what* your medical credentials are, and I don't care what this *New York court* says. I'm an officer of the 48th District Court of the State of Michigan, and *I* declare that you have no valid authorization to treat this patient without the *express* consent of his lawful wife."

"That is not *exactly* true.," the lawyer who identified himself as Attorney Fischer smiled. "As Mrs. Parkinson is *unable* to meet his *financial* obligations…"

*Oh, mister, you have just barked up the WRONG tree.* "*AND WHO* told you *that lie*," Julia asked. "Her bills *will* be met…"

"Not soon *enough*, miss," Attorney Fischer smiled, an oily look. "Your grandmother is *clearly too* infirm and destitute to manage her ailing husband's affairs. *Another* sponsor—and old and *dear* friend—has come to the *aid* of *poor* Mr. Parkinson…"

Ann cringed as Julia smiled like a shark might regard a mackerel. "My grandmother is *not* infirm." She flashed her badge. "Marital rights *cannot* be denied without an open hearing…"

"Wait," Cathy squinted. "Fischer...*Fischer and Ally* Fischer, the *Newhouse* lawyers?"

"The Newhouse's are among our clients, yes. Now, as I have *stated clearly...*"

"As *I* have stated," Cathy declared. "YOU are not *treating, you* are not *touching, you* are not *breathing the same air* as Mr. Parkinson without *Mrs.* Parkinson's *express* permission."

Stella sighed, "and I *don't* grant it. Now, if you will, please *leave...*"

"*Well,* you see," Attorney Fischer pushed Stella by the shoulders—gently— towards a wall, "it's not *up* to you anymore. Now, if *you* will, *please* just *step away...*"

"*You'll* need to step *nowhere,* ma'am," Donna boomed. "The *lady* said *no.*"

"And just *who* do...young *woman,*" Attorney Fischer started. "This is none of *your* affair...wait...*what*...what are you *DOING? LET GO OF ME!*"

"*Now,* sir," Ellen rolled her eyes as she bent Attorney Fischer's arm behind his back and pushed him out of the room. "*Thank* you."

"This is a *hospital* matter," Donna pointed at Dr. Hennessey. "*I* am of this hospital: YOU are clearly *not. OUT,*" she snarled, with a sharp jab of her thumb over her shoulder.

"Saved by the cavalry," Ann smiled.

"Just *thought* I should look in," Donna winked.

"Good thing you did," Cathy nodded, "and *someone* did *something* to the hospital's security because we called *them* twenty minutes ago."

"I'll look into *that,*" Donna nodded.

"*Barbara* can look into it more effectively," Ann said.

"True," Cathy answered. "Now, the Parkinson's need their rest."

"*Tonight,* Cathy," Stella sighed, "*we* are going to get *slightly* sloshed at the nearest saloon. *Who's* going to join us, girls?"

As they waited for the elevator, Ann noticed a redheaded man with yellow glasses and a round hat. "Hi, Randy," she smiled, "haven't seen *you* since graduation."

Randal Fred Newhouse IV turned slightly to look...but it seemed like he didn't *see* her. "Hi," he grunted and turned away again.

*Did he recognize me...there were more than six hundred of us...we didn't hang out...but...* As the elevator door opened and the ladies walked in, a man she didn't know nudged Randy slightly before he stepped—hesitantly—into the elevator.

*Could he even see me?*

\*\*\*

"Hey, babe. How was dinner?" Ann was not surprised to see JJ back before her.

"Informative," he sighed as she slipped into bed. "You went to the hospital?"

"Yeah. Somebody wanted to move Charlie; he had a court order and everything. Cathy *dissuaded* them. So, *dinner…*"

"Brenda and Roy want to move down here when Charlie kicks, be closer to Mom and Roy's family…"

"Closer to Charlie's *money. How much* did Jo find?"

"Five million and change in a dozen different accounts."

"Huh. Pays Charlie's bills easily enough. Your mom *can* drink."

"She's been *known* to. *This* bed's pretty comfy."

"*Not* as big as the honeymoon suite's, but a *big* one. Want to try it out?"

"Thought you'd *never* ask…"

## Wednesday

"Sandy, honey, come *on. Full* day." She had started awake to a brilliant reflection off the Hammerfest's windows after a strange dream.

"Just five more minutes, Mommy," he groaned. She responded by throwing the sheets off.

"Hey," he cried, "that's *cold!*"

"Get *going*, mister: we've got stuff to *do* today."

\*\*\*

"Morning, sunshine," he mumbled sleepily, kissing her ear. "*Time* to *git*." Bright light reflected off the office tower across the street.

"Morning *yourself*, lover-boy," she sighed. "I wanna stay *here* where it's *warm*."

"*Obey*, wife," he slapped her behind gently.

"I *lied* on *that* part of our vows," she answered, throwing the sheets over his head. "You'll not keep *me* barefoot and pregnant, you brute!"

"Even if *pregnant* can't happen, wife, we will *still* go through the *motions*."

"*YOU…*" There followed a weary exchange of pillows-hits before he surrendered to the inevitable and flopped on the bed as she plopped on top of him. "No lovemaking the morning I put on a uniform and meet a new unit. Rain check?"

"I *intend* to *collect* on those one day."

"I'll keep count."

\*\*\*

"Aren't you *cold*, Mom," Leigh frowned. Cathy poured coffee while poaching eggs—stark naked—in the cottage's little kitchen.

"You *kidding*? After the workout your *father* just…"

"That's *enough*, Mom," Leigh interrupted.

"Stella can *put* it away." Cathy blew out her cheeks wearily and bussed Leigh's cheek on her way to their bedroom and came back in a loose, leotard-like outfit. "Your father's getting himself decent for *you*…such *prudes* you kids are."

"*How* kind," Leigh grinned. "You going in to work today?"

"Clearing up things before the holiday. The best thing about government jobs is how we call it quits long before the major holidays."

"I've *got* a government job, Mom. Can't *count* the number of holidays *I've* worked."

"Different," Ed added, coming out of the bedroom. "Bankers are overworked compared to government lawyers."

***

*Probably not a lot of uniformed women come here.*

The Patrick V. McNamara Federal Building on Michigan Avenue was a new concrete, steel, and glass structure with decorative stone planters and polished bronze railings on the broad steps leading up to the entrance. The blustery weather didn't affect her choice of uniform. For the *first* visit to a unit for *any* reason, service dress uniforms were *heartily suggested.*

She studied the directory: *Great Lakes Sea Frontier: USN—Room 1901.* Just off the elevator, a hand-drawn cardboard sign pointed down a long corridor: *GLSF Rm. 1901.* A dot-matrix-printed sign on the glass door announced the Headquarters, Great Lakes Sea Frontier.

She pushed the door open, where a yeoman in jumper and bellbottoms answered the phone at a table just inside. He barely looked at her but smiled and nodded, spoke into the phone, and hung up. "Art Peale, Chief. *Pleased* to meet you." he smiled, standing and extending his hand. Art was a swarthy, short man with incongruous blue eyes and light brown hair.

"Peale, pleased to meet *you.*"

"I *hope* we can get to know each other *better*, chief. I'll ring you in." He picked up the phone again, punched a number, and mumbled, "sir, Chief Mueller's here...aye, sir," and hung up. "He'll be right out. Have a seat; there's coffee over there. We're *usually* this disorganized. The mailman and the UPS guys have it *in* for us."

*Barren walls; folding furniture.* "So Mr. Brookhaven said." Boxes lined the walls.

"New outfits aren't..." Peale began but was interrupted by a spindly lieutenant in BDUs emerging through a door. "Chief Petty Officer Mueller; Lieutenant Brookhaven."

She stood up, not sure whether to salute-as-in-report or what, but the officer offered his hand. *A strong, friendly smile.* "Sir; Ann Mueller-*Elrath.* Pleased to meet you."

"Steve Brookhaven, pleased to meet *you.* Come on back." He led her down a floor-to-ceiling glass-walled corridor, past a large room full of boxes, field desks, and folding tables and chairs. Two sailors in dungarees—one of whom glanced up at her—were shifting boxes; two others worked at tables.

"GSA stuck us *here* rather than in tents on the State Fair Grounds. At least we've got indoor plumbing and central heat." When they entered a small glass-walled office, Steve gestured to a stacking chair in front of a field desk—a gray box that transformed into a crude desk—littered with folders. He rolled an office chair around and sat. "That's nearly *half* my current compliment out there. The other half is *trying* to set up our annex by the river." He made an amused, tired face. "I'm a salvager by trade, so I know *about* you."

"Yessir. Now, how can I *help* you?"

"Well, *first*, you can tell my wife that Detroit is *not* Siberia, that the streets aren't running with blood."

"Where *is* she, sir?"

"Packing the kids and us up in Bremerton, but we talk every other night."

"*I'll* speak to her if you'd like, sir; we can start a *kaffeeklatsch*."

"I'm *sure* you *would*, Chief." He had a child-like giggle. "I've hauled that poor woman *and* our kids from Palermo to Yokohama, and she's protested more about *here* than *anywhere* else. See *that*," he hitched a thumb over his shoulder at a glass-walled room filled with stacks of paper. "*That's* the stores paperwork that's come in since I *got* here, and I haven't caught up with it *since*. We put our shoulders to it when we *can*, but it just seems to keep growing." He looked around at it, then back at her. "All for fewer than a hundred fifty people…eventually. *Most* of my compliment will be reservists."

"A *lot* of *that* would be duplicates and acknowledgments, sir," she explained. "*Half* of it will be new stores invoices and shipping notices. Every new unit and ship gets a disproportional volume of paperwork. Where's your storeroom?"

"You *passed* it. You sound confident. Want a look?"

"It's what I came here for, sir. But do you *have* a personnel tech?"

"We *do*. I'll have Pokhran fit you in; she's getting our muster straight. We'll be taking on three or four warm bodies every day starting next week."

"Does *this* outfit seem unusual, sir? By the time a unit musters in, they're usually squared away."

"It's the *timing*, Chief, with a lot of *now*," he shrugged. "They've got the money *now*, so they cut the orders *now*; then found the space *now*; then started rounding up people *now*." He sighed with a contagious grin. "That's why they sent *me*, I think: salvagers are used to organizing disasters. The Chief Storekeeper they *were* sending *ain't comin'*. You *want* the job; it's *yours*."

*That easy?* "I need to take it up with *my* gunny, sir. If you *would*, have Peale call down to the lobby for my reinforcements."

He looked blank. "Reinforcements?"

"There are *seven* NCOs—three *Navy* and four *Army*—waiting to come up and help me sort your paperwork. Sorry, but they're *not* in uniform—just came up for our wedding—and I only have them for four hours. It was all *I* could ask for."

"Chief, I'll take *any* help I can *get*. Make sense of *that* mess, and lunch is on *me* for your whole compliment."

\*\*\*

"Been great, really," Gary beamed, pecking Ann on the cheek. "Never *been* to Detroit before, but I can *tell*…" The Gulfstream jet which would take them back—with stops in Cincinnati and Nashville—awaited them.

"It's seen *better* days," JJ grimaced. "I've *seen* it in better days."

"I did, too," Nancy grinned, reaching up for a kiss. "I was here for the state fair in '70. Still remember the *beautiful* Fisher Building, even though I was five."

"And that *school*, Sarge," Liz beamed, getting a kiss, "*beautiful* place."

"I *love that hotel*, too," Betty claimed. "*Absolutely* beautiful."

"Yeah," Laura added. "And that *guy* you picked up…*what* was his name?"

"*Honey*…I *think*. Do *you* remember *your* guy's name?"

"*Must* be a common name around here…"

"But we must part," Kristin frowned, "*again*."

"All good things," JJ told her, "*must*…" She interrupted him when she jumped up, threw her arms around his neck, and planted her lips on his. *OOMYNECK!*

"And *now we end*, Johnny," she whispered, smiling.

"I'll *thank yew* to put ma fiancée down," Tom affected some sort of accent, seizing Ann's arm and planting a wet one on her surprised lips.

"*And* to unhand my *husband*, Kristin," Ann chided gently.

"And *one thing* more," Alice smiled, smooching JJ gently, sweetly. "This *CloudWays?*"

"I have an *interest* in the firm," JJ said as two baggage handlers loaded blood coolers in the aircraft. "Primarily medical transport, but they help service members when needed."

"Better, but not *good*, mister," Alice answered. "It'll *have* to do."

\*\*\*

"As of the first of the month, Mrs. Parkinson," Bobbi grinned, "*your* income from your husband's dealership should *clear* $400,000 annually."

"I don't *want* to be *in* business," Stella declared quickly, dealing cards in her living room. "Mr. Dietz, what would it take to liquidate it?"

"Several months at least," Uncle Mort said, tentatively raking his cards. "*I* find this game fascinating."

"There's a steady income of about $4,600 a month from several investment trusts," Jo added, pouring a soft drink. "And we found $5,276,900 in cash, specie, savings, and checking accounts."

Stella stared into space briefly, then glanced at her *second* wedding photo in the living room. "*Three times* what Mr. Evans *says* he has." She finished dealing and turned over a five of clubs. "How long would it take to liquidate the business and the investment trusts, Mr. Dietz? Move *everything* to Evans and Towne?"

Mordechai frowned at his hand. "Your sons have consulted with General Motors. I have a contact there, see what I can do to expedite matters. The bank accounts, investment trusts, and all the cash can be moved in a few weeks. Evans

210

and Towne can handle it all."

"*Sooner* the *better*, Mr. Dietz," Stella sighed.

JJ glanced at Ann, grinning. *She'll be fine.*

# *Thursday*

He fluttered himself awake, feeling for her. *Up already.* He swung his feet off the bed, and as he reached for his sweatshirt, something *POPPED* in his neck. Instantly, he could barely move either his head or left arm. A burning, painful stiffness, unlike *anything* he'd *ever* experienced, engulfed his upper body. *What...The...HELL?*

With difficulty, he *slowly* made his way to the front room, where she was pouring coffee. "Johnny, are *you*...?"

"No, I'm *not* OK. Call your dad for me?"

***

The Dietz household had just got up when there came a knock on the front door; Mike went to answer it...and took a step back. *"Randy?"*

"Mike," Randy replied stiffly, seeming to look at a spot over Mike's head. "Is *Leigh* here?" His broad-brimmed hat put his face in shadow. Donna—holding his arm—was in scrubs.

"*Yeah*, sure...um, *come* in." Donna guided Randy through the door. "Have a seat."

"Thanks, Mike. Can I *speak* with Leigh, please? I won't *take* long." Donna nodded, her eyes serious.

"Sure...let me get her." Mike rushed into the kitchen, grabbed the phone, and called the cottage. "Cathy: I need Leigh *now*...oytzer, *Randy's* here; wants to talk to *you*...no, I'm *not bullshitting*...yeah, NOW...OK, in the living room." Ben and Monica looked stunned. "Yeah. *Me, too.*"

As Mike returned to the living room, the phone rang. Randy and Donna had settled on the big sectional by the fireplace. Donna held both an arm *and* a hand—she looked both tired and solicitous. "She'll be here in a minute; caught her at breakfast with her folks. Can I *get* you anything?"

"No, thanks, Mike," Randy sighed and smiled. "Beautiful place, Mike." He cocked his head towards the window. "Mr. Block's *people* have arrived."

"Probably," Mike answered. "Your visit *is* unexpected."

"Yeah," Randy grinned and *seemed* to look up. *"Mr.* Dietz, I believe," he stood, offering a hand as Mike's parents entered. *"We've* never met. I'm Randy Newhouse."

"Benjamin Dietz," Ben answered. "May I introduce my wife, Monica."

"Ma'am," Randy smiled without turning. For all the introductions, it didn't look like Randy looked directly *at* anyone. Just...over their heads.

"Mr. Newhouse," Monica smiled, "we *finally* meet. Donna, dear, good morning. May I offer you both some refreshments? Coffee, tea?"

"No thanks, ma'am," Randy answered. "I have to apologize for that rudeness on the phone, Mr. Dietz."

Ben shrugged. "Apology accepted."

Randy pivoted towards the stairs. "Leigh: *you* look as *fabulous* as ever."

"Randy." She was in her sweats; her hair bundled behind her head as she came down the stairs, followed by her parents. "What can I do for you?"

"Mr. and Mrs. Taylor: *good* to see you again. Can *Leigh and I* have a moment alone, please?" He sighed, felt behind him, and sat. "Sit down, *please*, honey; you're in a bad light."

"Something wrong with your eyes, Randy?" Leigh tried to sound more solicitous than curious as the room cleared out.

***

"What the *HELL* is *HE*..." Cathy grunted in the kitchen, grabbing Donna's arm.

"*SHH*," Donna hissed. "His *hearing* is extraordinary. He *just* wants a word with Leigh; *that's* all."

"What's *wrong* with him," Mike asked. "Something with his eyes?"

"I *can't* tell you; he's a *patient*. Besides, I really don't know his history. But, he's *not* dangerous."

***

"Is everyone...?" Randy *seemed* to look around.

"We're alone."

"I have Stargardt's disease, honey: been getting worse, slowly. *Accelerating* now, they say."

"I *thought* there was *something* last year. I've never *heard* of...*what* was it?"

"Stargardt's blows holes and cracks in the retina. I've been *going* blind since we were sixteen."

"*That's* why you never learned to drive...."

"Yeah. *Blondie* runs into me at Beaumont often enough. But *that's* not what I'm *here* for. Ann Mueller saw me there last night. She might start asking why *I* was *there* that late."

"Maybe. She's *not*..."

"Mom's in end-stage multiple organ failure; on the same floor as JJ's step-father."

"Oh, *Randy*," she reached for his hand, adding, "I'm *so* sorry," sincerely. He took her hand, squeezing hard.

"Thanks: I *know* you mean it." He sighed, a sad, heart-breaking sound, the kind that makes you want to grab someone and hold them. "When I was born, Dad thought the sun shone out my ass. But *then* came the mumps in 9th Grade—remember? *You* had to get vaccinated. *Then* the Stargardt's in 10th, same day the baby.... Leukemia will finish me soon enough."

*Oh...shit!* "You *were* going to be a lawyer?"

"I *did* that." He sighed and squeezed her hand again. "Yeah, I did *that*. I did *get* a Harvard law degree. Dad paid *a lot* for all those guys to take my exams so *he* could hang *my* diploma on *his* wall like a lion's head.

"They're searching through our dirty linen from the Parkinson's place." His voice was hollow and deep, more resonating than she remembered. "I don't know exactly *what* they'll find, but they'll find *some* things. *That* much, I know." He wiped his suddenly-runny nose. "I don't have *anything* to do with most of *that. I* just run errands."

He squeezed her hand again and inhaled deeply. "Can you *try* to keep *our personal family* secrets—those you know—secret; ask your pal Ann to do the same? You *know* Mom *drank* herself to oblivion, but *that* doesn't *have* to be made public. *My* conditions don't *have* to be, either. And, if you *ever* meet my so-called son...Stargardt's is genetic. Tell *him, or* Mary?"

"I *will.* Ann *won't*...but I'll talk to her."

"And *one* more thing?"

"What?"

"Hold me just *once* more? Even after all *this* time, I can only remember *really* feeling good in *your* arms."

And she did.

***

"You look like you got rode hard and put up wet, brother. Long day?" Ram was perversely cheery by the time JJ and Ann made it to happy hour in the atrium.

"Sick call," JJ sighed. "I pinched a nerve in my neck this morning, and I *suddenly* couldn't move. They gave me a jolt of cortisone with a xylocaine and Demerol chaser." He had managed to gather a plateful of toothpick chow and grab a seat, completely winded, *more* than a little stoned, and *still* stiff, though, with the dope, he no longer *cared*.

"Sorry. Listen: I *may* have a proposition for you, but first: how hot *are* you on going to Alaska?"

With great effort, JJ shoved food into his mouth, chewing slowly. "Well," he replied at length, "Ann's gig dried up, and frankly, I'd rather *not* go to Alaska." He felt more thirsty than hungry, downing a cup of lukewarm coffee quickly.

"Yeah, we figured."

"We...who," JJ paused, squinting. "I've *seen* that look before. You're *thinking*..."

"It's what I do for a living."

"Ramdas, ol' buddy: you're choking on something. Spit it out."

"Can't. Not *yet*, anyway."

They were interrupted by Chuck, who brought fresh coffee and another plate of eggs. Both JJ and Ram stared at him; he smiled back. "*Chuck,*" Ram declared, "where've you *been*?"

"*Around*, Reynolds," Chuck smiled before he passed gas loudly.

"Still your *only* talent, Weir," JJ growled.

"That's where you're *wrong*, Elrath," Chuck sneered before he turned and walked away.

*** 

"Well," Dave declared, sitting in the Dietz's living room, "*we've* got a problem…"

"What," Mike asked, sitting across from him.

"We've got IDs on everyone from that shootout last week." Dave pushed file folders across the glass table. "Two are who their IDs *say* they are: Testa and Harriman. The rest…one's a *local* thug; another's a hitter from LA; three *others* are associated with Testa's cartel protection racket. What's *more* interesting is *this*." He pushed another folder. "Three images of Cliff Eyerdam: one driving a truck that attacked the Parkinson's office Monday night. The second, last night in Beaumont Hospital with Randy Newhouse. Then, this morning, right outside here, driving a Newhouse limo. And we've been *looking* for Eyerdam for *five years*."

"And he surfaces *now*," Mike frowned. "What do *you* think?"

"*I* think we need to talk to him. Tomorrow morning, Leigh and I will ask Randy Newhouse—*politely*, of course—just *where* Cliff is."

# Friday

"Morning, Cloud," he murmured, sitting up.

"Morning, Johnny," she smiled. "Feeling better?" She was pulling on her swimsuit in front of the bedroom mirror.

"*Still* a little stoned. They *said* it could be a few days before it took full effect, *and* I got used to it. Yesterday was just the effects of the chasers. *And* they gave me a bunch of meds…"

"A bunch of *what?*"

"Valium, Wygesic. Take 'em if I *need* 'em, they said." He craned his head around stiffly, finding a hotspot at a certain angle to the right. "*Only* if I need 'em."

"Good," she turned. "*Only if.* PT?"

"Gotta *try*."

***

"OW! OW! *OW!*" she cried, elbowing him in the back as he turned over uncomfortably, inadvertently pulling her hair.

"Sorry."

She blinked, the sun struggling to rise behind a modest but ugly cloud deck. "We need a bigger bed," she moaned.

"*First* thing *after* we get married," he sighed.

She elbowed him again. "And why not *now?*"

"Because neither of us has any clothes on *right now*."

She elbowed him again. "Come on: busy day."

***

"So, *full* day at work today," JJ asked, perusing the breakfast menu. They decided on a sit-down breakfast at the hotel restaurant, which was warmer than the buffet, and offered things the buffet didn't.

"*Sort* of," Ann answered, fussing with the sleeve of her borrowed sweater and not even *looking* at her menu. "The skipper talked me into *another* day on liberty, wants me to buy office supplies on the economy. I'm *also* supposed to meet the other officer and chief." She ordered the eggs Benedict; he went for a ham-and-mushroom omelet. "I need to start trading for filing cabinets, desks, chairs, tables—*lamps*, even—*now*."

"Trading for *furniture*?"

"Yep. I'll trade orders for *new* furniture for what other units have sitting in storage; they'll get the *new* stuff when it comes, then put what they're using *now* in storage." Even during the breakfast rush, their meals were on the table in a few minutes.

"I thought supply trading was weird when we did it in Colorado." He had spent three months in a supply room as a part of the Rangers' *whole NCO* program that required practical experience in non-combat-arms subjects.

"Storekeepers were trading before Noah built a raft. Sherry Marsh referred me to the others in *that* building, and they'll refer me to *other* units. By the end of the month, I'll have at *least* half of what they need."

"You don't *care* if you trade with the Army? We were just trading toilet paper for pencils with other *Army* units."

"Storekeepers only know invoices and inventories when it comes to general stores." She finished her coffee. "I'll trade with *Russians* if it gets me what I need. What are *you* up to today?"

"Hardly anything at all. I'm not *supposed* to do much for three days."

"Well, see you tonight, then, babe." She thought for a moment. "Tell Kurt the Suburban's fine, but get his price down to $4,000 if you can...*and* ask what *else* he's got on his lot in the same general vein; we're *both* gonna need wheels." She cocked her head. "Then...ask about monthly rates in a 5th Level suite."

"You *want* to take the Navy up on this job?"

"We *could* do worse, babe. Call your Ranger company..."

***

"What can *I* do for the FBI," Randy asked expansively. "My business is all above-board." The small, somewhat barren office was lit by valence lights along the walls, casting the room in a diffused glow.

"I'm sure it is," Dave said. "Mr. Newhouse, is there *something* wrong with your vision?" Leigh thought Dave's voice was surprisingly gentle yet forceful.

215

*Just the right tone for Randy.*

"I suffer from a degenerative disease," Randy said lightly. "I can see you around jagged little cracks and holes." He side-glanced at Leigh, winked slowly.

"*What*, exactly, is it that you *do*, Mr. Newhouse," Dave asked. The small office in a glass-front building on a Birmingham side street was hardly noticeable. Only a little sign on the door that read *Newhouse Properties* indicated who worked there.

"I'm a sort-of gopher, Agent Clawson. Please call me Randy: it would save time."

"Very well, Randy. For whom do you *gopher*?"

"For my father's business."

"I see. Gophering…what?"

"As an attorney, I handle legal documents and chores. I'm also a notary…"

"Really, Randy," Leigh interjected. "Can you *see* well enough?"

"I *can* read, Leigh," Randy answered patiently without looking at her.

"Uh-huh," Dave nodded. "How often do you *gopher* between Berryville and Greenville?"

Randy was still, his face impassive. "Where…"

"We've *talked* to a few people, Mr. Newhouse." Dave sat absolutely still. "Where can we find Cliff Eyerdam?"

"Who?" Randy managed a puzzled look.

Leigh blinked. *Perfectly orchestrated. Man, this guy's good.* "The guy driving you around yesterday, Randy," she interjected. "We have him on videotape."

Randy turned his head at her. "Mr. *Block's* cameras, honey?" He sounded like Caesar might have when Brutus finished him off.

"*Yes*, Randy. It's…"

"I *get* it, honey. I won't *live* long enough to hold a grudge." He turned back towards Dave. "I don't *know* where he lives *or* hangs out."

"How long's he been driving you?"

"Um…maybe three months? Joe's had *other* things on his mind, and now poor Dave…." He fiddled with his tie. "I don't get to pick who works for me; haven't for some years."

"Who *does*?"

"I don't know for *sure*, but I *think* Joe Dryden."

"Americans for a Democratic Society, Randy: ever *heard* of them?"

Randy blinked distinctively: he blinked *a lot*, but *this* was different. "No."

"We have a Greenville parade permit with your signature on it from 1972," Dave said. "Americans for a Democratic Society; Randal F. Newhouse IV, Secretary."

Randy switched on a high-intensity light, putting the paper under it and covering one eye. "Ah, *that*," he smiled. "Yeah, I made *that* up, got a permit to counter the *rah-rah* Fourth of July parade."

"*I* see." Dave pushed a picture of Chuck Wier across the table at him.

"Familiar?"

"No," Randy said at length after peering at it under his light, "don't recognize him."

"Funny," Dave smiled. "He recognized *you* from when you *led* that parade. Said you were screaming about how the capitalists were destroying civilization. Kinda funny for a *rich* kid," Dave sighed, pushing *another* picture across the desk. "Remember *him*?"

Randy looked carefully. "No."

"*He* remembers when *you* and Sid and Dave took him to Wolverine in September of '70." Dave leaned forward carefully. "*Try* again. ADS."

Randy's eyes seemed to dart around like moths on a candle. He swallowed hard before he spoke. "ADS was one of my *great* schemes to get away from Dad. Too bad it *couldn't* work the way I needed it to; you know, get under the old man's skin, make him disown me, then wait till Mom dragged me back into the fold." He blew out his cheeks. "No, *not* after the *baby* was born."

"Yeah, *about* him," Leigh said, leaning forward and smiling widely. "*I'm not* that kid's mom, Randy: you and I both *know* that."

"*Yeah*," Randy smiled querulously. "Look," he reached into a drawer and pulled out...

### Certificate of Live Birth
**Child's Name: Randall Fred Newhouse V Born: 15 May 1971**
**Mother: Leigh Elizabeth Taylor Born 12 April 1955, Albany, NY**
**Father:**

"The father's blank," Dave observed flatly. "Why?"

"That's the way *you* wanted it, *darling. Don't you remember? I* do. Until we got married, you said, and we made it *all*...."

"The medical authorities *all* say I've never *given* birth, Randy," Leigh murmured quietly. "And there are tons of people who *saw* me in '70-'71 who say..."

"They are all *lying*," Randy declared, snatching the paper back. "*All* lying." He sighed heavily. "Look, I have a *lot* of important work to do, so unless you have something *urgent,* you'll *have* to excuse me."

As they left, Dave and Leigh met Mike and Morgan outside, huddling against a blustery wind as Ellen listened to a radiophone. "*C'mon*, c'mon," she mumbled, "*make* the call..."

"Who's this ADS outfit," Leigh asked.

"Bunch of mad dogs from the '60s," Dave sighed. "Blew up a draft office in '70, according to one account."

"And *Randy* started it," Leigh asked, incredulous.

"We *don't* think so," Morgan said. "But we *think* whoever's calling Randy's shots *did*...or knows *who* did."

"*There*," Ellen smiled. After several minutes, she smiled, "yeah...good." She hung up. "Newhouse Properties in Bloomfield Hills; three and a half minutes."

217

Dave keyed a radio. "Fed Four: *trap* on one."

"Sierra Two: roger," came the answer.

They waited; Dave mumbled, "Let's hope these people are just *that* stupid…"

"Sierra Two," the radio announced ten minutes later. "Eyerdam in custody."

"Yep," Ellen sighed, "they *are*."

Dave nodded. "Let's wait for Randy to figure out who to call next. Let Cliff stew for a while. You guys can go by Sid's place if you want, but *I* have to go to Bay City, see if it *is* Marilyn."

"Sid's," Mike asked.

"An empty department store in Southfield," Dave grinned. "It's where we moved the contents of the Parkinson Title office. SPD's leasing it."

Leigh murmured to Dave, "Randy as much as admitted that his role in the business is minimal Thursday morning. This façade is just busy-work."

"Not entirely," Dave said. "His name's on some very damning paperwork…"

***

"Elrath," he answered the phone. He'd been *trying* to read—it was hard to concentrate because of the painkillers. For once, he was grateful for the distraction.

"Hi, JJ," Julia replied. "Got a few minutes?"

"Sure; c'mon up." After a few minutes, he opened the door. "Hey. Come on in."

"I've been going through *these*," Julia began, plopping a half-dozen two-foot by two-foot leather-bound books on the kitchen table. "Grampa kept *meticulous* company *and* personal records."

"Where'd you *find* these, Jules?" He put on his reading glasses, examining the heavy leather bindings.

"There were vaults full of 'em in his trust office. He recorded *everything*, even the cost of these ledgers. I never *heard* of anyone doing this, *like* this."

"Funny," JJ mused. "The first book report I ever did for him was called *Fundamentals of Accounting* from the '20s."

"Well," she sighed, "the entries are just cash-out: like diaries. Every *month* has a total; the last page in every *year* has a total, but he adds a cash-*in* from elsewhere." She opened the *Title 1959* ledger book and went swiftly to a sticky note. "I wanted *you* to see *this* for *yourself*."

*May 31ˢᵗ—Final Payment for Wolverine Military Academy: $1,265,000*

"He *owns* the joint," JJ sighed before he started yelling, "he *owns* it! *The BASTARD OWNS THE JOINT!*" He pounded the table—painfully—making the heavy ledgers bounce. "*THAT SONOFABITCH!*"

Julia looked on calmly. "*Looks* like," she muttered as she opened the *Personal 1962* volume to the first of several sticky notes. "Here. Any idea what *this* is? There's a payment about every quarter starting *here*…"

*January 2nd—Greenville PD: $2,600*

He stared at the entry. "*Looks* like he was paying the Greenville police to look the other way when better-*paying* monsters misbehaved."

"That fits with *our* information, yes. And there's *this*, same year:"

*September 10th—Will school expenses: $100*

"Yeah: *Will* went there for three years."

"He *said* that. Then there's this:"

*December1st—Final Payment for Francis Hartmann: $1,542,000*

"The schools *said* they had the same owners."

She opened the *Personal 1970* ledger and flipped to the end. "Here. Any ideas?"

*December 21st—Hartmann Tuition for Lizzie: $5,600*

"Huh," JJ said, surprised. "*She* probably came to those compulsory parties when I was there. They called it a *completion* academy. But…Lizzie *who?*"

"We've got an *idea*," Julia said cryptically. "Can't *say* for sure. But, the *Title 1974* ledger is *most* remarkable. Is *this* what we *think* it was?"

*September 15th—Escrow for Wolverine Lawsuit Settlement: $7,000,000*
*December 16th—Escrow for Wolverine Lawsuit Settlement: $5,000,000*

JJ sighed, smiling malevolently. "Those apes *literally* didn't know *who* they were *screwing* with when they did *that* to Eddie." He heaved a heavy sigh. "I got a million out of it from Eddie's family—from *Charlie*—because I wouldn't deny what I *saw* them *do* to him." *How's THAT for irony…*

"The *Personal 1979* ledger starts an odd pattern. There's an entry like it about every three months until 1983."

*December 1st—Rockland, to find where the Rat got his money: $2000*

"He opened *my* mail from Eddie's firm when I was home on leave in '79, saw some paperwork setting up my accounts. *I* must be the Rat because the paperwork he saw showed *his money!* HAH!" He started to laugh, but his neck hurt too much to get *too* wild.

"Then, there's *this* payment, first of every month since May '71. Any ideas?"

*March 1st—Dr. Leonard Best—$500*

"Who's *he?*"

"A *new* name to us. *Title 1985* is interesting."

> *December 24th—Jimenez plane ticket: $309.60*
> *December 27th—Weir relocation: $450*

He giggled mirthlessly. "Ann and I were up here on *leave* during that time.

Herman Jimenez was my roommate at Wolverine; he tried to burn Ann and me out of our suite. Chuck Weir; *another* roommate—he tends bar here now."

He had no sooner said *that* than the phone rang. "Elrath," he answered.

"*Johnny-Cake*," a voice growled, "we took *another* vote, and *you lost*."

*That was what someone told me when he sat on me that night.* "Get *bent*, asshole," he spat and slammed the phone down.

"Who was *that*," she asked.

"No one important." Then…*what? Charlie called me Johnny-Cake when he wanted to get under my skin. Just how many people would KNOW that?* "I *think* it was one of the surviving Four Horsemen."

"*Not* Eyerdam," she sighed, "we've had him in custody for hours." She shrugged. "*Might* have been another. *We'll* find out where it came from."

***

"Astonishing," Ann shook her head, popping chicken livers in her mouth. "I thought *I* was productive finding five desks and chairs and three filing cabinets today." JJ, Leigh, and Mike spent the evening sharing their information in the atrium. "That and a crate of office supplies…red-letter day for a storekeeper."

"We've got one helluva After-Action Report to write, Sandy," Leigh sighed, "and *I've still* got a full day tomorrow."

"I can get our AAR drafted tomorrow, *oytzer*," Mike groaned, throwing back more peanuts before glancing at JJ. "Brother, I *never* thought *that* about your stepfather."

"I've known the sonofabitch *was* a sonofabitch for years."

A few minutes later, Dave walked past them in the atrium, gave them a thumbs-up, and got in the elevator.

"It's *his* Marilyn, all right," Leigh sighed. "Which means…"

"*She* says his *Lizzie's* those kid's mother," Mike finished.

## Saturday

"Hi! I'm looking for either Randy or Mary Newhouse." A redheaded teenage girl who looked a great deal like Randy's youngest sister answered the door when Leigh rang the doorbell. The modest ranch house on Pell Drive had a small front yard and a bigger side yard. A newer Chevrolet sat in front of the small garage. A disused swing and slide sat rusting near the garage.

"Aunt *Mary*! *Ra*ndy!" the girl called, turning away. That bleak morning Leigh had her pistol in her purse and her briefcase full of non-descript and irrelevant forms and official-looking papers.

"Yes?" The middle-aged woman looked startlingly like Randy's oldest sister.

"Mary Newhouse? I'm Leigh Ingle, attorney for the McGowan estate. May we talk for a few moments? It's about the Agatha McGowan legacy." It was an old ruse: you've come into an inheritance! Money for the asking! Just answer these questions, and a *fat check* with be all *yours*! *Any* answers are right!

"*Who?*"

"Agatha McGowan was Randal Newhouse, the Fourth's great-great-grandmother on his mother's side. She left her *youngest* living descendant, her great-great-*great*-grandchild, a legacy. Can we...?"

"*Randy* but *not Renée*? Typical. You'd better come in."

They went through the living room and into a small dining room just off the kitchen. The house was well-furnished, and the girl had returned to her sofa and TV. A teenage boy sat at the far end of the dining room table, scattered with school books and supplies. "*You* must be Randy," Leigh smiled.

"Ma'am," he nodded, looking up. He had a long and fair face showing some chapping, as Randy's often did, with fading freckles and light brown eyes.

"Well, *pleased* to meet you. Your great-great-*great*-grandmother has left you a legacy."

"OK," Mary interrupted. "Again, *who* is this?"

"Agatha McGowan, Randy Newhouse the Fourth's mother's-mother's-mother. She has left her only great-great-great-grandchild..."

"Renée is his twin sister," Mary stated flatly.

"I see. Well, we knew *nothing* of a sister." Leigh stopped, feeling the full impact of Mary's disarming sneer. "Is there a *problem*?"

"You could *say* that," came a shout from the living room. "*They* never recognized *both of us*."

"I *see*. Well, the *legacy*..." Leigh went on, hurriedly explaining the fake estate and bogus will and the non-existent dollars therein. Randy would come into his non-inheritance when he turned 21. By the time she finished, Renée had joined them, sitting opposite Randy. Her face was the same shape and roughly the same color, though Renée had better skin. "So, if you have *any* questions..."

"What about Renée," Mary asked. "She's two minutes *older* than Randy is. My sister abandoned them the day after they were born, May 15$^{th}$, 1971." She looked away. "Complicated."

"Ah," Leigh replied. "*Well*, if..."

"Who do we talk to about Renée," Randy asked. "I'd think that she'd be entitled to *some*thing."

"The estate was probated years ago."

"*Where* did she pass," Mary asked. "When?"

"Agatha McGowan passed in Ireland in '71; it's taken *this* long to track *you* down." If anyone read the Cork *Examiner* for 20 October 1971, they would find *an* Agatha McGowan's obituary:

*Born February the 14$^{th}$ in the year 1871. Went to her Heavenly Home on October the 15$^{th}$ last in Munster. Preceded in death by her husband, Declan, and her nine children.*

Though their names matched, it was hard to say if there was *any* relation. When the FBI worked up *this* part of her legend, it was hoped that Mary wouldn't have the resources—or the interest—to look it up because there simply wasn't *time* to make it air-tight. "You, Randy, *and* I guess Renée are her youngest *surviving minor* descendants."

"Well," Randy declared, "I'll share it with Renée when I get it if *you* don't mind." Brother and sister smiled at each other, the secret, trusting smile of friends.

"It will be yours to do with as you wish. For *our* records, if we *can*, Miss Newhouse…"

"Mrs., I'm divorced."

"*Mrs.* Newhouse. Can I ask for *your* details? Date, place of birth? Parents?"

Mary shrugged. "Mary Francis Newhouse, born March 16th, 1951. My parents were Charity and Edward Newhouse, both deceased."

*You ARE my cousin.* "How long have you had custody of the twins?"

"Since two days after they were born."

"You would have been twenty?"

"Yes. I was working my way through accounting school. My uncle's family was generous enough to pay for child care, *this* place, *and* an allowance while I was in school. I *married* his son—my *cousin*—in Tennessee in '72; didn't work out; divorced in '74."

"*Very* generous, I must say. Do you know *anything* about their mother's whereabouts?"

"Liz? No. Every year, the kids get birthday and Christmas cards, postmarked Detroit, with a Detroit PO box for a return address. We've *tried* writing back; never get a reply."

"I see. I'm obliged to tell you that Stargardt's disease runs in the McGowan family…"

***

"Bless me, Father, for I have sinned." Ann kept her mother's faith as insurance: what's the harm in taking a few hours a month to go through the ritual? She believed in God, but the rest was up for grabs, and, like most military members, she tolerated the practices—or refutations—of others and didn't argue about it. Having participated in Kristin's Passover Seders with the other mermaids, she considered herself open-minded. "My last confession was four weeks ago."

"Bless you, my child," the priest mumbled, bored. The Saturday confession line at St. Sebastian the Martyr was long. "What are your sins *this* month?"

She suppressed a snicker. "I married outside the Church last Saturday. My husband is a Protestant."

"Did you obtain a dispensation?"

"I *knew* I forgot *something*."

He chuckled. "*Yes*, you *did*. Did you marry *in a* church?"

"We did. *That* church means a great deal to him; that's *why* we did it."

"Ah. Is he a *good* Christian?"

"He's a good *man*, a member of that Congregational church."

"Christianity *lite*. At least he's *not* a Unitarian. Still, you need a dispensation for the Church to consider your union valid. Contact Bishop Hollister's office…"

"Can we get one quickly? We're *from* here, but we're in the military. We *may* have to ship out in a few weeks."

"It's *not* quick, so contact *any* bishop when you stop moving. Are you sorry for this sin of omission?"

"I *am* most *heartily* sorry, Father."

"For your penance, you shall perform two Acts of Contrition, three Hail Marys, drag your *heretic husband* to Mass every Sunday for a solid month, and put $35 in the box *today*. Go ye forth and sin no more, *at least* until the morrow."

"*Yes*, Father; *thank* you, Father. In the *Name* of the *Father…*"

As she knelt in the sanctuary to do that part of her penance, Sid came up next to her, rosary in hand, kneeling. She continued until she hit *now and at the hour of our death, Amen,* for the third time. "Hi, Sid," she mumbled, crossing herself.

He finished *his* Rosary and crossed himself. "Claudia, my *dearest* friend," he whispered, passing a note. "I've been asked to help *resolve* this matter. Just do *this* for *the Church and me?*" He left. The note read:

*You and Leigh Taylor: call…@ 9AM MON for the answers to many questions.*

***

"So, Cliff, didn't *know* you were dead, *did* you?" Mike flashed his credentials. "Army counterintelligence. *You're* in *deep* shit, my friend." Mike had spent the night reading everything he could lay his hands on about Cliff Eyerdam. Through the two-way mirror, Mike watched Cliff answer Dave and Ellen's questions about Cliff's fake ID, what he was doing in Detroit, and a long list of other queries going back years. The interview had left Cliff weary but not bent.

"Like I told the FBI: somebody *stole* my wallet a couple weeks ago." Cliff— a big man—was *not* easily intimidated. "What's the *Army*…?"

"How about Estavo Testa? Seen *him* lately?"

"Who?"

"One of the four guys you were thrown out of Wolverine with."

Cliff blinked. "Ain't seen *him* in years."

Mike pushed a picture at him. "This is you *and him* at the Detroit Bank and Trust branch at Gratiot and Harper on 30 October. You each cashed traveler's checks totaling $30,000 that had been purchased by Randal Newhouse IV. So, *when* was the *last time* you saw Testa?" The last was a bluff: they were still looking into who bought them.

Cliff stared at the pictures. "*That* was the last *I* saw him," he mumbled, sighing. "They *bought* our IDs then. They told me to *drive*."

*Once they start…* "They *who* bought *your* IDs?"

"They…a *guy*."

"*What* brought you to Detroit?"

Cliff suddenly flashed angrily. "Two guys showed up in the club last summer, showed me a picture of that *Elrath* snitch getting a *medal,* said 'we want *him* dead. You in?'"

Mike pushed three pictures at Cliff. "*Which* guys?"

Cliff sat, mute, motionless. "What am I buying myself?"

"You're only facing conspiracy charges so far, so, *maybe* a walk."

"I get it in writing, or we're done." Cliff crossed his arms. "Nothing else until I talk to the state's attorney…*and* a lawyer."

***

"He doesn't seem to wake up anymore," Stella sighed, watching Charlie's monitors with their monotonous traces. "Hasn't since Wednesday."

"Sorry, Mom," JJ said, he hoped earnestly.

"Just wish he'd get it over with," Kurt declared.

"He *will*," Stella declared. "They *say* it won't be long now." They watched blips on the screens, numbers that rarely changed, paying little attention to the patient. "The finance office is happy now." Stella looked resigned. "I've got money enough to keep him here for *years* if I have to, *bury* him, and retire in Miami. I paid off *all* the other bills."

"Let's get some lunch, Mom."

Stella's sons took her to Boesky's Deli just up 10 Mile, lining up with the late lunch crowd in the cafeteria line. Their lunch—sandwiches for the guys; fish for Stella—was quiet except for polite "how's yours" questions until JJ asked, "did you know that Charlie's first wife was a Newhouse, Mom?" More *personal* papers had been filtered out of the FBI's search of the old trust office—courtesy of Ernie, according to Jo—including Charlie's first marriage license and an avalanche of other documents.

"I found out later; it didn't seem *important* then. Now…I don't know. He's so *secretive* about family."

"Why does he *hate me* so much, Mom? He's been mad at me since I caught him peeping on Julia."

Stella was silent as Kurt glanced back and forth. "Want *my* take?"

She frowned. "Go ahead," forking in more fish.

"Before *we* met *you*…" Kurt told *his* version of Jo and Mary's story of *their* peeping incident in '68. "You and Julia was a *repeat*. The old man said the same thing *then* as he did *later*: they were doing *something,* and he *caught* them. *And* when we refused to believe him…*that* was high treason. You two that afternoon, standing next to each other by the car, all casual-like? *We* knew, and *Dad knew* we knew, too: *you* just interrupted *his* fun, *not* the other way around." He went silent for a moment. "When I *asked* if you could stay with *us* Christmas '71 because he and Stella were leaving town …"

"Charlie screamed *'NO'* at the top of his lungs." Stella made a face that JJ saw only when she had to make a hard choice: a thoughtful and worried look. She cut more fish, speared a little potato, and set her knife down. "How important *is* the answer, John?"

"I'd *like* to *know.*"

She ate the fish and potato, chewing slowly before she sipped her tea. "Kurt: how old were the girls the *first* time?"

"July '68…twelve and a half."

She sipped more tea. "And, John, in July '70, Julia was…"

"Just short of fifteen. 14 August is her birthday."

She looked surprised briefly. "Not going to ask *how* you remember *that.*" She went back to her hard-choice face. "He *prefers* young women," she mumbled, barely audible, "but I *won't* speak ill of the dead." She ate more fish as the guys finished their sandwiches and coffee, thinking the whole matter closed.

After they clambered into Kurt's '78 GMC Jimmy, Stella still had her hard-choice face on. "Boys," she finally drawled, "he's not dead *yet*, so fasten your seat belts: it's going to be a *bumpy* night."

"Don't like the suspension on this one, Stella," Kurt asked from the back seat.

"Truck's *fine*, Kurt. Just *listen* and rent *All About Eve* some time. When *that thing* happened at the house, what worried *me* wasn't what *he* said about you and Julia, Johnny; it was *why* he crept back there *knowing* there was a girl there, changing clothes. That night, he and I *discussed that.* He still *insisted* that he *knew* you two were…*well*…"

"We *weren't*, Mom," JJ said, driving through rain squalls.

"I *never* thought so. Your date with Julia later: it was all I could do to keep him from taking a swing at you before you left. Then, Brenda's wedding. *Julia* got *you* to dance, pulled *you* into *her*, danced around *in front* of him—and don't *try* to tell me *that* was *your* idea, though you *didn't* fight it." She chuckled lightly. "If *anything* happened back there that day, you *both* wanted it to happen."

"Nothing *did* happen, Mom."

"If you two weren't just *pals,* you would have done *more* than skinny-dipping that night…"

"You…" JJ choked, "you *saw*…?"

"From our bedroom window. I could see you in the light from that boathouse next door. I was *proud* that you'd become such a fine young man. I thought how proud your *father* would have been of you…though *Jake might* have taken exception to your skinny-dipping with a young woman."

"*Naked* with my *niece*," Kurt harrumphed from the back seat. "I should *tell* my *brother*…"

"He knew *then*," JJ giggled. "Julia came home *wet.*"

"*That* was the easy part, boys," Stella continued. "Charlie likes to *look* at women's bodies; *young* ones. He's a *man*: I'd be worried if he didn't *want* to look. But there were absences—sometimes whole weekends. There are ledgers and invoices, and checks that I was *forbidden* to *look* at. But, no phone hang-ups or mysterious notes in the mail." She sighed deeply, changing her tone. "Your wife *knows* when you've been *with* other women, boys: *know that*. If he wasn't *such* a good provider, I'd have ditched him when you left for the Army, Johnny. But now he's left me a wealthy woman…wealthier than I *would* have been in '73, *that's* for sure.

"When you came back from Wolverine, Johnny, and showed us those marks, those bruises…something in *him* just *deflated. Now* I know *why*.

"He doesn't like *you*, my son, because *you* have *always been* what *HE is NOT and can NEVER be*: a courageous, principled gentleman. You will do what needs doing regardless of what it costs *you*: he will do what *he wants* to do regardless of what it costs *everyone but him*." She turned slightly towards Kurt. "*Sound* right, Kurt?"

"It *does*, Mom."

✻✻✻

"Let's *hear* it," Dave said finally. The US Attorney for Eastern Michigan had produced the paperwork for Cliff's deal without a word. Cliff's court-appointed lawyer—an older woman—perused the two pages silently, nodded, and proffered a pen. Cliff signed; she left. "Who got you *here*?"

"Like I said, a couple of guys came to my club," Cliff sighed, "said *wait to be contacted*. Then I got a call from a guy at the end of July who says I can have a hundred grand for six month's work."

"Who's the *guy*?" Ellen studied her nails.

"I only know him as Neitelsmidt."

On the other side of the window, Mike felt a chill as Morgan whispered, "*click*."

"Where *were* you," Dave asked, "when this call came?"

"El Paso."

"OK: *what* work?" Ellen shifted in her chair.

"I didn't ask. The next day I got an envelope with ten grand and an address."

"Then what?" Dave sighed mildly.

"Then I went up to this little house just off the tollway a spit from the Michigan border…"

"Berryville," Morgan cleared her throat quietly.

"…Berryville, and I met *another* guy who gave me *another* ten grand. I drove a guy to Wolverine the next morning."

"*What* guy?" Ellen shifted.

"*Can't* say."

"Just him?" Dave leaned back.

"No. Joe Dryden and Randy Newhouse were with him."

"*Bingo*," Morgan smiled. "*Got* the bastards."

"*Then* what?" Dave scratched down a note.

"Then we came down here."

"OK." Dave yawned ostentatiously; Ellen stretched. "So, you're here…when? September? *Then* what?"

"I drove to *another* wide spot in the road in Minnesota, just short of the Canadian line, where I met Testa and *his* guys. Then, I start driving Joe and Testa and some other guys around back here."

"Ever drive Randy Newhouse around here?" Ellen tried to look bored.

"Yeah, a couple of times a week."

"OK," Dave glanced over at Ellen and nodded. She pulled another file out of a valise. "We ran your prints; came back this morning."

Suddenly, Cliff's entire demeanor changed. "*Shit.*"

"Uh-huh," Ellen sighed. "Your deal's *gone*. Want to make another?"

"Bring the lawyer back." A few minutes later, the woman and the state's attorney were back in the room. Another two-page document had already been compiled. Cliff signed.

"So, *Mario*," Ellen smiled. "Let's start. You were twenty-two when you started at to Wolverine…" And she laid out the story of Mario Constantine Kosta—Cliff's *real* identity—who was wanted in connection with a Pittsburgh car bombing that killed seven people, including two children. "What *we* want to know is *who* set up your new identity? *Who* sent you to Wolverine?"

"I wish I *knew*," Cliff answered. "My Uncle Feodor just told me to go to a house and wait. I got picked up after a couple of days."

"By *who*?"

"Some guys in a Lincoln limo. They gave me a driver's permit and a Social Security card, told me I was Cliff Eyerdam and fourteen again, and to keep my head down at Wolverine for four years. I'd be shacked up on long holidays and in the summer."

"Shacked up…where?"

"I went to a cabin in Minnesota in the summer; a trailer park in Tennessee in the winter. They provided everything; food, money, transportation, broads. All *I* had to do was not draw any attention or they'd turn me over to the Pittsburgh PD."

"Then *you* screwed up…"

"Yeah. They sent me to Texas, handed me a high school diploma and a thousand in cash, and said get lost and *not* to go back to Pennsylvania."

"Didn't know *how* to turn him in to Pittsburgh without exposing themselves," Morgan murmured. "They had a *lot* to learn."

"*We* need a break: been a *long* night. *Want* anything?" Dave and Ellen strolled out of the interview room, quietly closed the door, and engaged in a *scandalous* lip-lock…scandalous for two people *not* married to each other, that is. "*We got the bastards*, Nancy," Dave smiled at *great* length, "we *got* 'em!"

"Davie, we *finally* did it," Ellen whispered, swooping in once more.

Morgan tapped Mike on the shoulder; he turned his head and met her lips,

227

softly, *startlingly sweetly*, before he drew back, sensing there was *much more* going on here. "You're a *pretty*..." he started before she smacked him again, "...*girl*," he continued, "...but..."

"*Had* to," Morgan sighed. "Need *release. Hope* you didn't *mind.*"

*Not really, but...* "I'm getting married in a few weeks," Mike started.

"Me, too," she smiled sweetly, "but we've been *five years* trying to get *this* much on Newhouse and Wolverine *and* verify what they're doing."

"Yeah," Dave said, squeezing Ellen before letting her go. "*Now*, we sort the evidence to burn them down and hopefully figure out who they're doing it *for.*"

"Doing *what*," Mike frowned.

"Enabling interstate flight. Now, *maybe* illegal entry. *Wish* we could talk to the uncle," Ellen sighed, sweeping her hair back. "He was gunned down in '77."

Morgan stared at Cliff through the observation mirror. "Mike: how about you and me try for some straight answers about last Wednesday?"

*I could turn that down?*

"Your fingerprints are all over two cars at a crime scene where people died last week, Cliff...or do you prefer Mario?" Morgan began, sitting down. "Care to explain *that*?"

"I've got used to Cliff. I *stole* the Crown Vics that he *told* me to steal. He *loved* those tanks."

"Who's *he*?" Mike tried to be nonchalant. *Those sugar-sweet kisses didn't help my concentration.*

"Testa. He was *definitely* calling the shots."

"I got *hit*," Mike declared mildly.

Cliff made a face. "I watched *that* go down."

Mike pushed copies of all four IDs across the table. "Any idea why *these* IDs would have been found in those two cars?"

"Testa said, 'if *this* don't mess with their heads, *nothing* will.' He told those guys, 'you get *caught, this* is who you *are.*'"

"*Then* what?" Morgan leaned forward. Though not well-endowed, she could *look* like she was.

"Then *I* thought everything went to Hell when those people started shooting *back*, but *Joe* just cackled '*better* than I thought! They'll think *you're dead,* and *I'm* in charge again!'"

"What about Dave Harriman?" Mike *tried* to stay focused but found Morgan more distracting than Venus...*or* Leigh.

"Joe didn't shed a *tear* when *he* got clobbered. Joe told me to drive around and make sure everyone *thought* they *knew* who gave the orders, said, 'the other guys will finish *Elrath* off when he gets here.'"

"What 'other guys?'" Morgan reached forward, across the table, stretching.

"The Hammer and Pale Face, two of the *dumbest*..."

"*Huh*," Morgan sniffed, crossing her legs alongside the table. Even though it was about thirty degrees outside, she wore a skirt more suited for the tropics.

"What was all this *for?*"

Cliff sighed. "Testa was told to get Elrath to Detroit. Killing his step-brother's family was *his* way."

"But the Dietz's and the Taylor's…" Morgan pressed.

"Insurance. As I understand it, *they* were to draw the Taylor broad back, figuring that Elrath would follow *her* if knocking off the brother didn't work."

"The fire at California Circle…" Mike asked. He was distracted as Morgan unbuttoned the top of her sweater. Chills ran up her sweater-covered arms as she put her elbows on the table, her chin in a palm, grinning brightly. Mike put *his* elbows on the table.

"*That* gang-bang. " Cliff sniffed, disgusted. "The way *I* got it, the week before last, a phone rang at the Newhouse office that was unpublished, unlisted, undistributed, un-*everything* and was never *supposed* to ring unless...I *dunno.* Then they started looking *all over* for one of those little address books that *somebody* lost *years* ago, saying, 'if Randy left it in *her* shit and *they* put *that* together, *we're* dead. Last week it rang *again*, and everybody's *freaked.* Then, somebody went into the hospital, and Dryden tells me to burn the Taylor place down. I drove Jimenez and Harriman there. Jimenez threw a lot of gas around the electrical gear, saying 'electric fire better.' Then the *first* building lit up, and I saw it was the *wrong* one, but Herman started shooting his .22 for whatever reason. I wrestled it away from him before he did too much damage. Well, *Testa* didn't know *anything* about it, got pissed because it drew attention. Joe *tried* to tell him it was part of *his* plan. Somebody called the office a couple hours later, and Joe shut up." He shook his head. "Joe thought *he* was in charge; he wasn't, not *then.*"

"So, what do *you* think the Newhouse game plan is *now?*" Morgan ran her fingers *oh-so-casually* through her hair, her sweater creeping up her belly.

"Dunno about *Newhouse*, but *Dryden's* got *something* cooking."

"What's *his* game?" Mike was determined to act professionally, but the memory of Morgan's *sweet* lips and that washboard belly next to him was *not* helping.

"All *I* know is…Elrath."

***

"All of *that* was to bait JJ *here*," Leigh gasped when Mike explained it.

"*Looks* like it," Morgan shook her head. "And the fire was because they wanted to burn that phone book. So, they *are* twins?"

"Yeah," Leigh mumbled. "Randy has *no* idea."

"I think, *oytzer*, we showed that *that* family hasn't *seen* a Newhouse in a *long* time."

Leigh shook her head. "Randy said he expected to *adopt* his son… *why?* He's in Mary's *custody*, his *wife*. It's a *custody* matter, *not* a matter for adoption."

"A whole *lot* of things aren't adding up here," Ellen said.

"No," Leigh sighed. "Our ONE source on *all* of *that* was my five-second verbal exchange with Randy, which I can *barely* remember," she declared. "I'm not sure I even got *that* straight."

"Are you suggesting, my dear, that you could have got *any* element of *that* story *wrong*," Mike asked.

"Even if I only got the *basics* right, we never *verified any* of it."

"We've got something *else* to think about," Dave said. "You left their house at 11:10. At 11:15, s line at *that* residence—one you called the other day, Mike—called the private residence of Ingrid Torgensen. The call lasted 49 minutes."

"They *both* work for Parkinson Title and Trust." Mike looked cross. "What...?"

"Give Julia and *her* team a few more days; they'll figure it out," Ellen declared.

Morgan winked at Mike, then smiled at Leigh. "I *kissed* your Mike." Mike nodded, looked guilty.

Leigh looked back and forth at them, then at Dave and Ellen, who were smiling vaguely. "Kiss her *back*, Sandy?" He looked even more sheepish. "*Yeah*, you *did*." She glared at Morgan. "Do that *often* on your job?"

"*Some*times," Ellen grinned. "We don't *actually arrest that* often, so we celebrate..."

"This *was*..." Morgan smiled.

"*Very, very special*," Dave agreed.

Leigh glared mildly at all of them. "You guys owe *me*."

"Collect *now* if you want," Dave shrugged.

So...she...*did*.

### * * *

"So now *I* gotta go to Mass for a month because *you* forgot to get a dispensation?" He stretched painfully on the sofa.

"Part of my penance." She shifted off her bad hip. "OK: I didn't *forget*, but it was the *only* sin I could *think* of other than fornication with my future husband before Saturday."

"*That* I'll buy."

"*What's* in that gun case again?" Kurt had brought it with the Jimmy.

"A Mini-14; a smaller version of the M-14 that fires the same ammo as an M-16."

"You expecting trouble?"

"I want to be ready for it. Eyerdam might be in custody, but Joe's still out there, and he's still got troops."

*Waiting*...

"I need to call Leigh and them," she said. "Leigh: hi...listen; I've got this phone call I've got to make Monday; *you're* supposed to be there with me...I don't *know*, honey...it says 'for the answers to many questions.'...yeah, I figured that…OK, honey; *see* ya." She sighed. "She'll find out *where* that number is…*what* it is." She looked bleak. "Be *with* us?"

"Try to keep me away."

There was a knock on the door. "*Room* service." He let her in; Callie herself pushed the service cart. "*Short*-short handed now," she sighed. "Short two housekeepers, and two waitstaff…*and* a general manager that *I'm* also filling in for."

"They give you *his* pay," Ann quipped, handing her cash and a huge tip.

"Don't I *wish*? No, he was a minor partner in this place…"

"Max DeVere," JJ blurted. "*Left*…?"

"*Fired*," Callie sighed. "One housekeeper and a waiter didn't show up for their shifts yesterday *or* today…not *that* unusual." She stopped. "I heard that a couple of our guests started asking Max questions. An hour later, Kurt and the other partners bought him out and *fired* him. *That* was Friday…" She glanced at JJ. "You know *anything* about that?"

"Not…specifically, no," JJ said. "*Little* surprised myself."

## Sunday

"What?" He awoke to her staring at him, enigmatically. The sky was typically ambiguous for a late November Michigan morning: roiling, streaking, high-altitude clouds of white and grey, and glinting gold in the intermittent sunbeams that flashed off the Hammerfest's windows.

"Come to church with me today."

"OK. Pops and Mamma, too?"

"No: just you and me."

"What's the occasion?"

"Just…come."

*And wait to find out what that number is…*

*** 

"Morning, Johnny. Mass today." She got up in her flannel nightie and flexed her hip stiffly.

"Morning, Cloud. Time for a PT and breakfast?" He stretched painfully as he stepped out of bed, watching clouds scudding across the sun between the sheer curtains.

"PT, affirm; chow, negative."

"Why *don't* you do chow before Mass?"

"*Not* before Communion."

"Why?"

"Because that's what they *told* us in Catechism."

"*OK*, then. So, what's *after* brunch?"

"I promised Barbara and the kids they could come swim today. Then maybe dinner?"

231

"Maybe."
*And wait to find out what that number is...*

***

"All, right, then," Pastor Lou smiled, offering his hand as he swept into his office, "*you* must be the groom." They had been gazing at pictures of the pastors, most of whom Leigh didn't know, some she'd never *heard* of.

"I *am*," Mike confirmed. "My sister says you two seem to agree."

"We *do*. You'll make your obligations in *your* temple. They'd be longer than a Protestant service. We'll synchronize *my* English with *her* Hebrew; my simple Protestant vows with your more elaborate Jewish ones."

"But, doesn't *that* defeat the purpose of..." Leigh started.

"No, *oytzer*," Mike explained. "The obligations we can make any time. So, you *don't* have a problem with a *chuppah*," Mike asked.

"*That's* why we're here, Sandy," Leigh sighed. "*Someone* does."

"*One* of our deacons isn't very open-minded," Pastor Lou agreed. "Wants to take a vote on it with the full church membership."

Mike gazed at Leigh. "Oh."

"Mike, we can..." Leigh started.

"No," Mike interrupted. "This is *your* party *this time*. *Chuppah* or no, you get it *your* way. My family will understand."

"I'm glad you think that way, Mike," Pastor Lou beamed, "because *he* was in the minority. You can have a canopy as you wish."

"I just wanted you to be aware, *zeeskeit*, that there's *some* here..."

"*They* won't be attending, though, will they, *oytzer*?"

"And there's something else," Pastor Lou looked both concerned and amused. "The date: I *have* to be out of town unexpectedly the first weekend in December. But Margaret has a solution: *this* Wednesday morning. No school; the cleaners will be in in the afternoon to get ready for Thanksgiving service. We'll let you have the church for free since your family is such long-standing members. I spoke with your sister; *she'll* make it happen."

"Is there any *sense* to waiting, *oytzer*?"

"Well," she began, staring at the church calendar. "We're *small*..." She stared at Pastor Lou and sighed, "*this* Wednesday morning, it shall be."

***

"JJ," Ram announced on the phone. "I *may* have a new gig for you."

"Yeah? Ann's with her family by the pool. Want to meet down there?"

"Better not. *This* is classified."

"So, my place or yours?"

***

"Jenna, *you* swim well," Ann smiled, catching her breath on the side of the pool after some sprints. "You compete?"

232

"I'm on the school's medley relay team, but we're *nothing* like your squad," Jenna said, pulling out of the pool. "Your team's state record still stands."

"So, I hear." Ann pulled herself out. "*What* do you swim in the medley?"

"I'm the closer: freestyle. *You* still hold the state record for the 400-meter freestyle, you know."

"Huh. Billy, do *you* swim much?"

"Not in the winter," he answered, standing in the water. "I'm not good enough for the team."

"Not *ambitious* enough," Barbara sneered, shaking water off. "You've *got* good *form…*"

"He twists," both Ann and Jenna said simultaneously. Jenna continued, "he kicks too hard and can't stay straight in the water."

"I kick to keep from drowning," Billy complained.

"Then you've got no buoyancy, Billy-babe," Jenna chided. "No good for a *varsity* swimmer."

"Yeah," he grabbed her ankle as she giggled and fell in.

"Good kids," Ann mused as she wrapped in a towel and sat next to Barbara.

"He's good for her," Barbara agreed, gazing around. "Who's the guy staring at us over there?"

"Chuck. A former roommate of JJ's."

"He's been staring at *you.*"

"You, *too*, girl. *You're* easy on male eyes in *that* suit."

"*This* old thing?" Barbara stuck her chest out, the suit's deep-vee opening. "If I *flashed* him, think he'd go away?"

"I *don't…*" Ann began, but it was too late: Chuck got an eyeful of Barbara's bare breast *just* long enough to pop his eyes out and make him leave swiftly. "OK: you've had *enough* for today."

"I haven't done *that* since college," Barbara chuckled, "and all I've had to drink today was at communion." She glanced at the kids splashing in the pool. "Hope *Billy* didn't see that."

"What would he *think* of his future mother-in-law who flashes her tit at strangers?"

"Future…" Barbara watched the teenagers fall into an embrace in the warm water. "Now I know what *my mother* felt when she saw *me* with boys."

\*\*\*

"Who's *that*," Mike murmured as he pulled into the driveway after their leisurely brunch. Since the last Wednesday, they'd seen many cars and trucks on Baroque Circle, but *this* Dodge was new.

"Julia." They parked in the garage and walked out onto the drive as she walked up, smiling slightly. "Visiting your family?"

"Yeah; *that* too." Julia looked puzzled. "We ran the number. It's *billed* to the Archdiocese of Northern Michigan. It *rings* at both St. Catherine's Church *and* the St. Perpetua School and Clinic in Copper Harbor, up in the Keweenaw Peninsula, closer to Canada than us."

*Someplace to hide…*

\*\*\*

"I gotta say, brother, this hotel is *better* than the average." Ram pulled a white soda out of his little refrigerator and set it in front of JJ.

"It *is*." JJ tried to get comfortable in one of the semi-padded chairs in the kitchenette, looking around at the generic surroundings. "How's *Clare* doing?"

"She's *good*; she says so, anyway. I know she was sick…"

"Yeah. She looks a *lot* better now." JJ's eyes lit on a ladies' scarf—*parachute* silk with parachute motif—bunched on the kitchenette counter. "She saved my heart, you know."

Ram glanced at the counter, smiling. "You saved *hers*, she says."

*I gave her that scarf.* "Don't *hurt* her, Ram, *please*. Don't *make* me choose between you."

Ram grinned sadly. "My brother, *we*'re old classmates who peck each other's cheeks. She'll be coming by *Tuesday* night if you want to have dinner or something." His face changed as he pulled a file out of his briefcase and handed it over. "Now, to *business*."

The file's label read RED SUNSET/BLACK LANTERN: TOP SECRET. Inside was some *very* interesting material on Soviet withdrawal planning in Afghanistan, civil disturbance training in Moscow being stepped up, an alarming rise in desertions from border posts, and a startling jump in defections. "*This* is top-level stuff, brother," JJ grunted. "*way* above *my* pay grade."

"It's *proof* of what *we* predicted in '73, man." At Brookfield, Ram and JJ argued that the West was in a long struggle to find the limits to Soviet power: it wasn't a *war* that any *side* could *win*, but that one *faction could lose*. The West, they argued, could *prevail* because they *could outspend* the Reds. "Between Afghanistan and the SDI, we're wearing them out, and they're falling apart. But we *can't* exploit this material from Anacostia."

"Defense Intelligence Agency can't handle it?"

"If Congress got wind of *this* stuff—and they *would*—defense funding overall would dry up in a fiscal quarter."

"So, what's *your* solution?"

"What *I'm* proposing is to have the more than 4,000 trained intelligence specialists between the Army Guard and Reserve, Navy and Marine Reserves, and the Air Guard and Reserves: analysts, linguists, CI agents, imagery interpreters, traffic analysts. Put them to work on this material, *far* removed from the flagpole. *That* way, there's very *little* chance Congress would hear of it— *truly* compartmented. They'll be forecasting the *end* of the Soviet Union and the *end* of the Cold War." He smiled—a beautiful look on a handsome face. "*As we predicted.* I'm suggesting *you* manage the *first* studies from your new gig as training NCO of Company C, 4/75th Infantry. *When* you need it, there's a new secure facility at Selfridge AFB that a Reserve MI battalion in Lansing and Toledo uses."

"You can get my orders changed?"

"Already in the works. All I need to do is make a phone call when I get the word on funding…and I'll know about *that* Monday or Tuesday."

"You know, *Ann's* job…"

"*That's* a done deal, according to my sources."

*Trust your sources…*

*** 

"*Hi, Ann: change of plans.*" Leigh's voice on the phone was perversely cheery. Ann and JJ had been discussing what to do about dinner.

"OK: *what* plans?"

"We're getting married Wednesday."

"*THIS* Wednesday?"

"*That* a problem?"

"No, not for *me*, but…*wow*! *Why* the change?"

"Pastor's availability, and since the wedding is small, so is the reception. We can see *all* of our family's on Thanksgiving for a *real* party. The Corey's are coming down *then*."

"Oh, OK, that makes sense. Same place?"

"That's affirm."

"You've got a *dress*?"

"*Mom's*. Donna's hemming it, letting the hips out. We're booking the honeymoon suite downstairs now…"

"We'll come down. Will *your* family need rooms, too?"

Leigh chuckled. "*My* family. It sounds a little strange now that I *have* one. *Maybe*; I'll let you know."

"We're on our way." Ann hung up and reached for a sweater. "Hear *that?*"

"Yeah," JJ smiled and shrugged, pulling his shoes on. "It's *their* party."

"Uh-huh. Wonder if there's *another* reason."

"You mean…?" He shrugged again. "She's always wanted kids."

"And you know *this* how?"

"I've had more than *one* real conversation with Green-Eyes, honey." They met at the front desk; it took only a few minutes to get the honeymoon suite for a week over Thanksgiving. "C'mon, I'll buy dinner," JJ suggested.

"Naw," Leigh grinned, "Sandy owes *me*."

"Owes you *what*," Ann asked.

"I kissed another girl," Mike said, downcast. "But *she* kissed *me* first."

"Who," JJ asked, puzzled.

"That FBI agent, Morgan." Mike explained the circumstances of the sneaky smooch. "They apparently do it when they do something big."

"Huh," Ann frowned. "Would be a *problem* in the Navy. Wonder why it isn't in the FBI?"

Leigh sighed, *"they* know each other *pretty* well."

*"That* well?" JJ and Ann shared glances.

"I think maybe," Mike agreed. "Would sure as *hell* make for a *lot* of paperwork in the Army."

***

"Last week, he said he had a problem: I asked if I could help. He said maybe." He told her what he *could* of what Ram had said, listening to the rain pelting the windows as they shared wine and schnapps, the room dark but for the fireplace.

"Maybe *this* is *that* maybe."

"A toast to maybe."

"To *maybe.*"

"Whatever happens, Cloud: you and me."

"You and me, buddy."

And they kissed on it.

***

"How's the ankle?" He scratched his healing wound as they listened to the wind from the bed, watched the tree shadows on the window.

"Sore."

"Disappointed in me, *oytzer?*"

"For kissing another girl?" She was quiet. "Was it good for *you?*"

*"Very* sweet. She said she needed *release*. Dave and Ellen were in a *real* lip-lock."

"They know each other pretty well."

"Uh-huh." She reached for him under the sheets. "I'll *hide* my disappointment in you if you make me laugh…*this* way. I'm in a *mood*, and I need a distraction."

## *Monday*

*Hello, Sunshine! So glad to see you this morning!*

She stretched luxuriously, belly-down in the bed, slightly alarmed that there *was* no sunshine out the window—just another dull cloud deck. She got up on her elbows and looked around. *Oh, yeah. Late November; Michigan. It must have been a dream.*

She pulled her big fluffy robe on and shuffled into the living room, finding him dozing in the recliner. She kissed his forehead and started coffee.

*"Ugg,"* he grunted, looking around slowly. "Morning, Cloud."

"Morning, Johnny. Bad night? Remember, they're doing the room early."

"Dreamed of Jason Samson again, saw whoever pulled the plug walk away."

"Are you sure *that* actually happened? The guy walking away, I mean."

"No, but I *do* wonder *who* pulled that plug: he had to have stuck his arm in bloody water up to his elbow."

236

\*\*\*

"*What* do we *do* when *nothing* makes sense," she mumbled, gazing out the window at another overcast and gray morning.

"Huh," he groaned, half-asleep. "You're *dreaming* about this stuff now?"

"Sometimes. *Why* would Mary *deny* maternity? She wouldn't have been the *first* twenty-year-old to get knocked up by a fifteen-year-old."

"Statutory rape works both ways: they *are* cousins, making it incest in Michigan. She would open herself up to criminal charges."

"*Not* convincing. RF could make that a *boast*, not a *charge*. And it's not *quite* incest if they're married."

"What if Mary's *not* their mom? What if Randy's *not* the father? What was it that Randy said: 'my so-called son?' What if *Dave's* Liz *is* their mom?"

"Again: *what* do we *do* when *nothing* makes sense?"

He stroked her hip gently. "We think about something *else* for a while."

She slid a hand down his belly. "*That's* a start…but we'd better hurry up."

\*\*\*

"Any *idea* who's at the other end," Ann asked, shifting off her bad hip. They sat in the semi-comfortable chairs of Ann and JJ's suite, sipping coffee around the table where Kurt had set up an office-style speakerphone.

"Nothing solid," Leigh replied, bundling her hair and rolling her shoulder.

Ann dialed the number…and there came… "Blessed morning. Who *is* this, please," an older woman's voice asked.

"Claudia Ann Mueller-Elrath. I'm putting you on speaker. Who is *this*, please?"

"Blessed morning, Ms. Mueller-Elrath: you too are on the speaker. I am the Reverend Mother Pauline Maria of the St. Perpetua Sisters of the Blessed Oubliette." At that, Ann started, surprised. "Who *else* is listening, please?"

"Leigh Elizabeth Taylor, ma'am."

"Michael Ethan Dietz, ma'am."

"John Jacob Elrath, ma'am."

"And Special Agent Clawson and Mr. Jackwell are *here,* on the other side of the screen."

"*Dave,*" Mike and Leigh asked.

"Yep," Dave answered. "Official *and* personal."

"*Sid?*"

"Here, Claudia Ann. *Strictly* personal."

"Is anyone *else* present?"

"No, Reverend Mother," Ann answered, then said, "the Sisters are cloistered." It was a *statement*, not a *question*.

"Yes."

"Reverend Mother, may I tell my friends about your little place of forgetting? It may help *them* understand."

"Please *do*, Ms. Mueller-Elrath," the Reverend Mother answered.

"*Please* call me Ann. We *heard* about your order as kids, but the nuns *told* us it was a *myth*. Your *order* runs a women's shelter. *You* have more secrets than the Jesuits." They heard giggles—*two* voices—on the speaker. "How am I doing, Reverend Mother?"

"*Fine*, Ann, just *fine*," the Reverend Mother answered. "That's as good an explanation as *I* could give. We provide a sanctuary of faith, serving God with prayer and meditation undisturbed by the outside as our charges heal their souls, and sometimes their *bodies* and *minds*." Silence followed for several moments. "Ms. Taylor, what was your father's mother's name?"

"Same as mine: Leigh Elizabeth Taylor." She scratched out a note and held it up: *Confirm your ID.* Everyone nodded. "Call *me* Leigh."

"Very well. Mr. Elrath, what was your maternal grandmother's maiden name?"

"Helen Marion Burgess. Call me JJ, ma'am."

"Mr. Dietz, when was your *bar-mitzvah*?"

"April 1968; I'm Mike, ma'am."

"Ann, *when* were you confirmed?"

"June 1967."

"*Very* good. Sister Evangeline Marie is here."

Silence again before a younger voice spoke. "Hello." She cleared her throat. "I'm under instructions to tell you about my circumstances and why I came *here*. My *birth* name is Leigh Elizabeth Newhouse; Mom changed it to *Taylor* after the divorce."

*She should play the game, too.* "Sister, *who* were your parents?" Leigh asked.

"Charity Taylor and Edward Newhouse. Mom's *sister* was your *grandmother*, Leigh."

Leigh smiled and grabbed Mike's hand on the table. *Nearly there.* "Sister, where *is* your family?"

"Mom took *Mary and me* away from Dad in '60. Dad died in 1964, and Mary and I went into foster care in Pickney—Hell—because Mom was *so* sick. *Dave* here was our neighbor. We were taken away from there right around the Moon landing."

*All the right answers.* "Pleased to *meet* you, cousin," Leigh answered, lighting up. "But, as a military cop, I have to know: *why* are you talking to us *now*, Leigh?"

"Call *me* Lizzie, please; it's what my family called me. Dad *hated* the name Leigh." There was a great inhalation before Lizzie answered. "The Church has grown weary of the *Newhouse's* irritation." She cleared her throat.

"Where did you go *first*, Lizzie," they heard Dave's voice ask.

"Chicago. We saw the astronauts on a hotel room TV. That fall, Uncle RF put us in a big house in Essexville and came by every week. A man named Charlie Parkinson came by maybe twice a month—usually during the week. Some boys—Joe, *Sid* here, and Dave—came around sometimes, usually with my cousin Randy. I *tried* to dodge *them*, but, as Charlie said *all the time*, they *were* paying the bills. Mary's part-time job didn't come *close*, and they *were* paying for her school..."

"That's *Charlie*, all right," JJ muttered. "He's my stepfather, Lizzie."

"My condolences to his wife...and *you*, JJ. I thought he was an *awful* man."

"A view many people share, Lizzie," Ann said. "What were these visits *for*?"

"They brought groceries *or* cash, or *both*." She paused, then came back quieter. "My friends, the Church is *ordering* me to tell you this." A muffled conversation followed before they heard, "Very *well*, Reverend Mother, I'll *say it*. My sister and I were *prostitutes for our keep*. New Year's Eve 1969 was the first *night I* slept with Randy." Silence. "But *he* was frustrated, and so was *I*."

"He *couldn't...*?" Leigh whispered, making a face.

"*No*." Silence again, more profound. "*RF* and *Randy* traded beds the next morning. I can still smell Mary's perfume on him." Ann scribbled: *14? Uncle?* Leigh nodded and looked down; Mike and JJ closed their eyes and shook their heads slowly.

"Go on, Lizzie?" Mike scribbled: *Crimes 1 & 2?*

Another silence; a *deep* swallow. "*Charlie* only wanted to *watch*."

"Watch *what*," JJ asked; the others glared at him.

"*Me* while I ate, watched TV, slept, studied, what*ever* as long as I had *nothing on*. He *paid* a hundred for an *hour* or a thousand for a *day;* what he called *shows*."

"Lizzie, would you like to pause; collect yourself?" Ann tried to sound solicitous. *Crime 3?* her note read; Mike and Leigh shrugged, JJ crossed his arms and looked disgusted.

"Thank you, Ann. I *would like* some refreshment. Reverend Mother brought tea." They heard a sudden sucking of breath and mild choking. "*That's not tea*, Reverend Mother!"

"Medicinal *whiskey*, my dear. We can *both* use some bracing this morning." JJ fetched his schnapps and four glasses; everyone threw a slug back.

"A *week* of novenas for us both," Lizzie laughed. "In the summer of '70, RF staked *me* out as *his*, said Mary was *Randy's* because she *said she* could get him *done*. She *lied*, but we both felt sorry for poor Randy because RF demanded that *he*...and Randy was frustrated *every* time. I was fifteen when I became pregnant and went to a school in Greenville..."

"Francis Hartmann," JJ declared.

"*Yes*."

"Lizzie," Leigh interrupted, "*when* did you get to Hartmann?"

"Sid drove me from Bay City to Greenville on the Saturday before Christmas in 1970; I was twelve weeks pregnant."

"You *might* have tried to meet me at the Wolverine Spring Fling that April."

"That's *possible*, JJ; I *was* there." There was a long pause. "Have *any* of you *seen* my children? I *think* of them *constantly*, but I *never speak* of them as an act of obedience."

"I saw them Saturday, Lizzie," Leigh declared.

"Is Renée a *good girl*? I'm looking at pictures here…*my*, they *are*…"

"The twins are well, strong. Randy is a scholar; Renée is his best friend. She *seems* like a fine young woman. Her brother said *she* was born first?"

"Yes. When Dr. Best delivered her, Mary took *her* away; I was devastated that I couldn't *see* her, but I could *hear* her. I named her Renée the moment the doctor said, 'it's a girl,' but RF *demanded* a son.

"Then came Randy, and a girl my age I didn't know took *him* to RF in the waiting room. *His* name—Randall Fred Newhouse, the Fifth—*I* didn't choose. RF was overjoyed, but *I* could only cry. Excuse me." There followed some wracking sobs and clinking of glass before Lizzie came back. "*Two* weeks of novenas."

"You were *still* at Hartmann, Lizzie," Leigh asked as *everyone* downed another generous slug.

"Their maternity clinic." She cleared her throat. "Oh, I'll do a *month* of novenas." A cough before she came back. "Now I'm tipsy for the first time since I was fifteen—*whew*. The next day was a *perfect* spring day, and Sid came. I was no longer pregnant, but I had *no* babies, and I wanted to *die*. He handed me an envelope containing a one-way bus ticket to San Francisco and $100. Then, he drove me *here*. We prayed the Rosary all the way from Greenville. Sid never *touched* us though he *had* many opportunities. I even *offered*, but he wasn't—*isn't*—*like* the others." She was quiet. "I still *have* that bus ticket."

"Lizzie," Ann smiled after downing another slug. "Are *you* OK?"

"I'm *fine*, Ann. I haven't spoken of *any* of this since I was preparing for my vows. When I turned eighteen, I decided to stay here to help other women in this little place of forgetting."

"Did you ever *see* their birth certificates, Lizzie," Leigh asked.

"Sid filched Renée's. Leigh Elizabeth *Taylor* is recorded as their mother—even *though* that *wasn't* my legal name; the father is blank."

"*Randy* has the other one," Dave added.

Ann asked, "Lizzie: how would the *Newhouses* have known *you* were *there*?"

"I believe *I* can answer that," the Reverend Mother declared. "Several women left between the time Lizzie came to us and when she took her new name. Our charges live together, go to school together, pray together. Any one of them might have told *someone* about Lizzie. *They* are under no obligation of silence, though we *ask* for it."

Leigh scribbled *secure as a fishbowl*. "Mary says they write to you, but you *don't* write back?"

"I never know what to *say*. My order sends them cards, but *responding?* I *just*…"

"Just *answer*, Lizzie," JJ murmured. "You don't *have* to tell them *where* you are or *what*, but you *should* tell them that you're OK and that you love them. *Any answer* is better than *no answer*. You *wait*; you *wonder*, you *pray* they haven't forgotten you, that they can *recall* your name. Your soul *empties out* waiting. There's *nothing* worse than feeling forgotten by someone *you* love." He and Ann shared a glance and smile—and a slug; Leigh winked and slammed another back; Mike winked back and downed another.

Another deep silence. "I believe you are right, JJ. I sense that you *know* what *that* feels like. May God bless you for your *patience* with my sex."

"Lizzie," Ann sighed. "Did you seek shelter because of *what* their father is?"

"Because of my *mortal sins*, Ann. I can't *say* enough novenas for those."

"You were a *girl*, Lizzie," Mike answered, "from what you've *said*, you were a sex slave. You had no *choice*. RF should have been *protecting* you, *not* exploiting you."

"I *thank* you for saying that, Mike," Lizzie replied. "Dave's given me pictures of my children...and a *note* from Mary. Oh, *how* I would love to *see* them..."

"You *may*, dear," Mother Superior interrupted. "You *can* transfer to Bay City. It's *possible*."

"*May I*," Lizzie gasped. "*Oh...oh, how I...*"

"We'll discuss it with the bishop, dear."

"I should *go*...."

"Lizzie, please," Leigh added. "Our cousin Wendy Corey has a family Bible that has generations of Taylors recorded in it; it's how we knew *you* even existed. Can *she*..."

"I would be pleased to *hear from* Cousin Wendy. Have her write; Sid will bring you my address." Silence before she added, "may God bless you all. Perhaps we shall *meet*, cousin?"

"Yes," Leigh answered before the phone went dead.

They simply stared at each other before JJ had the courage to speak. "Incest *and* statutory rape *and* pandering. My *God*. I *knew* that *bastard was* a *bastard*, but..."

"And RF violated of the Mann Act," Leigh mumbled. "A federal crime with *no* statute of limitations. FBI will crucify him *and* Charlie if he had *anything* to do with it. As she described it, it's statutory rape for Charlie."

"*She* atones for *their* sins with a life of service," Ann sighed, shaking her head.

"She's *happy*; might *meet* her kids; she's seen *pictures*," JJ sighed.

"She's been *given* permission," Ann said.

"That *Dave*..." Leigh smiled.

"That *Sid*," Ann sighed.

After a few moments of *utter* silence, JJ leaned back in his chair, gazing at Ann. "*How* the *hell* many shots *did* we down?"

"*Not* enough." Leigh poured four *LARGE* slugs, emptying the bottle and glancing at the label. "This is...*hundred proof...hell*...how much was *in* there?"

"It was nearly full," JJ sighed.

They downed them, anyway.

241

Mike cleared his throat, staring at his glass. "Time is it?"

"Not…quite…10." Leigh planted her chin in her hand, her elbow on the table.

"Last time I was drunk *before* noon…" Ann's head lolled back.

"*Never*," JJ blew out his cheeks. "I'm gonna pay for this…"

"Pay…*what*," Leigh asked.

"Pass blood for a few days."

"Huh," Mike grunted. "*Why*…?"

"That *beating* I took at Wolverine. That's what the medics tell me."

They were quiet…meditative. Ann looked drowsy.

"Is there a *law* against drunk elevator operating," Mike asked.

"Don't know if I could *crawl* as far as the car, let alone drive," Leigh sighed

"I'm…going…to…go…lie…down," Ann sighed. She stood…wobbly…and *slowly* tottered into the bedroom.

JJ stood. "I'm…going…with…*her*. You guys…there's a pull-out…*there*."

"Pull it *out*, Sandy," Leigh moaned, tossing the sofa cushions on the floor.

Soon, the only sounds they heard were those of the storm raging outside.

\*\*\*

"*Ho-ly shit*." The storm had passed; bright sunshine poured in through the skylight and the window at the foot of the bed.

"Are *we*…" "Starkers and *still* drunk." "*Yep*." "At *least* two sheets to the wind *and* buck naked."

Leigh reached behind her. "*Hand*," she whispered. JJ complied.

"*When* did…?" "It was still raining." "*Somebody* told me to *scoot over*." "*You* guys didn't *seem* to mind."

Ann raised her head slightly. "Sandy, give *me* your *hand*." He raised his head and reached over Leigh and JJ.

"Have we *just* remade a bad '60s movie?" "*Hope* not." "I *hated* that movie." "I couldn't figure out what the *plot* was."

"This *feels* better."

"And *you* have a *sweaty butt*, Blue-Eyes. *ANY* idea what *time* it is?"

"Night sweats, Green-Eyes. Clock's on *your* side."

"Honey, *look*…"

"*Ugh*…15…50."

"Is anyone but *me* hungry?" "*Famished*, truth be told." "Definitely." "I could eat a *horse*."

"I feel…like I want to go back to sleep."

Deep breathing, hands *softly* clutching, resting comfortably on bare skin beneath the sheets.

\*\*\*

All are awake; all *know* they're awake. "Time is it *now*?"

"17…45."

"*Some* nap."

Quiet breathing until… "I *have* to get off this shoulder." "Me, too." "Thought *nobody'd* mention *that*." "*Ugh!*"

Quiet, hands clutching each other until… "We've *slept* together, Sandy."

"We *have*, Legs. Was it good for *you*?"

"*Fabulous*; restful. I'm *almost* sober, I think."

"So did *we*, Blue-Eyes."

"Yeah. *Not* what I *expected.*"

And they all cracked up.

"So, how are we gonna *do this*?"

"This *what*, Sandy?"

"Get out of this bed and maintain a *shred* of our…"

"Say *modesty,* and *lightning will* strike your ass, brother."

"*Too late* for modesty, Sandy." Bathed in sunlight, Ann got up, flexed her hip, walked to the closet, and reached for her robe.

"You're *right*, Ann," Leigh sighed, crawled out of the covers, and walked off the end of the bed. "Johnny's been waiting half his *life* to see *me* like this," she sashayed *slowly* to the dresser. "Why is my underwear…*here*…and my bra…over *there*…and my sweater…by the *window*?"

"*Can't say*," Mike mumbled as he stood and tottered towards Ann. "*Where's* my…? But my *underwear's* in *here*…*how* did?"

"A mystery for the ages," Ann sighed, watching Leigh—and JJ *finally* up—staring at each other.

"As *far* as *we* go, John." Leigh smiled, glancing at Mike and Ann, panties poised for donning.

"As *far* as *we* go, Leigh." JJ sighed, glancing himself and looking for his pants. "Kiss on it?"

They brushed lips lightly.

"How close is *this* to your dream, Legs?"

"Better, Sandy; *much better.*"

They smiled—naked in the sunlight—and *they* kissed on it.

***

They listened to the wind whistling outside. "The best way I *ever* heard of to end a meeting." He traced her belly with a finger. "Would you *want Mike*?"

"Remember a few months ago when I woke you up, and *we* got busy? I'd *just* had a *dream* about all four of *us* making love in the same place." She stroked his bare hip. "*This* was *better.*"

He rolled towards her. "You *dreamed* of Mike?"

"Yeah. *You* dream of other women; you've *said* as much."

He kissed her nose. "I *hope* you still dream of *me* once in a while."

"You *are* a dream, babe. And we all *slept together—eyes-closed.*"

"More like *passed-out*. I haven't felt *so* peaceful since our wedding."

"Leigh and I promised *not* to go *any* further. What did *you* and *Mike*…?"

"The *same.*"

"'Night, Cloud."

"'Night, Johnny."

\*\*\*

The wind sighed in the eves, rustled in the trees. "She's a beautiful woman, Sandy, and now you *know how* beautiful…"

"*That's* so. So, your little smooch was…"

"A promise *not* to go any further, Sandy, and we did it in front of you *and* Ann. *You* shared one with *Ann*. What did you promise?"

"I *think* the same; *naked intimacy* but no *sex.*"

"Sounds…right. That *was* the most *peaceful* rest I've had since I got back."

"Yeah. *Seductively* peaceful. Night, *oytzer.*"

"Night, *zeeskeit.*"

## Tuesday

"*Ugh*," she moaned, blinking at the skylight, "*rain* again."

"Sorry," he said into his pillow, "I signed off on sunshine today."

"How's your neck in this damp?"

"Hasn't been *dry* enough to feel a difference." He turned towards her. "How's your hip?"

"Same, pretty much." She reached for his arm. "Your chest OK?" Sometimes, when it was raining and damp for a long time, his chest hurt.

He took her hand. "I think the Valium helps *that*, too." They listened to the rain beat the skylight—first *softly*, then *savagely*—with flashes of lightning and rumbles of thunder in between in the predawn light.

"*Let's*," she sighed softly, with her come-hither smile that could make him do *anything*, "*PT.*"

He caressed her with a finger, making her tremble. "Sure. *Gotta* keep moving." He cocked an eyebrow. "*Which* PT?"

"*Swimming*, smartass," she got up. "We'll negotiate the *other* later."

\*\*\*

"Sandy, *wake* up," she groaned. blinking at the lightning in the window. "*Wake up* and hold me."

"'K." He stretched his arm across her belly, an irresistible touch. "Morning."

"Come *on*," she insisted, "like you *mean it*."

He climbed on top. "Like *this*?"

"It'll *do*," she smiled into his *dreamy* grey eyes, moving her hips slightly.

"Anytime *you* want, *oytzer.*"

"*You're* going to the hotel today?"

He kissed her nose as she locked her legs around him. "Yup."

"*One* more practice…"

\*\*\*

"*Hey*, guys," Callie said, entering their suite after JJ opened the door. "I have an answer to *your* question…*and* I have a question for *you*."

"*Which*," Ann asked, shuffling her shoes on. "We're *just* on our way out…"

"Long-term rentals up here. The suites have always been hard to rent, especially the three-bedroom. So, Kurt and I *have a figure* in mind for *this* suite," she scribbled on a pad, "Starting in December with a 12-month lease. Now, *my* question: What do *you* know about Chuck the booze-slinger?"

"His *last* name's Wier; he's an asshole," JJ declared, showing Ann the pad. "Why?"

"He didn't show up for his shift last night; the phone he gave us is a payphone in a bar. Whoever answered this morning says he cleared out of his room. Kurt says, turn him loose."

"*I* would do just *that*." Ann nodded at the pad. "This *includes* maid service?"

"*All* current services and happy hour."

JJ and Ann shared a glance. "*Sold*. But *fire* Chuck first chance you get."

\*\*\*

"*Ahh*," Leigh sighed, towel around her neck in the sauna in the *Spa Nouveau Toi* in Birmingham, "*fabulous* idea."

"Better than another drinking party," Ann agreed.

"The heat *almost* makes me forget how often I have to pee."

"Don't stay *too* long, Debbie," Cathy offered. "Not good for *either* of you."

"Yes, ma'am…"

"Call me 'ma'am' again, and I *won't* come to your baby shower," Cathy snapped. "Not going to sit in a sauna and be called 'ma'am'…"

"Easy, Mom," Leigh offered. "She *was* the best breast-stroker on the team."

"And *without breasts* to speak of then," Deb sighed, "unlike *now*…"

"To be *expected*, dear," Monica added, pouring water on the rocks, "but it *is* permanent." She sat down. "Has the Navy decided what to do with *you*, Ann?"

"I the Great Lakes Sea Frontier wants me to stick around here," Ann answered. "Storekeeper work, maybe a little diving support."

There was quiet for a time before Cathy cleared her throat. "*What* in the *name* of the *taxpayers* is a *sea frontier*?"

"If I knew *that* I'd be an admiral," Ann replied. Leigh started giggling; soon, they all were. "Honestly," Ann gasped, "even *they* don't know what it means."

"Oh, *shit*…you've *made* me *need* to…" Deb squeaked, running out.

"Pregnant women laughing," Monica smiled. "Should have remembered that, Cathy."

"Wasn't *my* joke," Cathy claimed. "Blame *Ann*."

"*Your* setup, Cathy," Ann declared.

"*Your* punchline, pal," Leigh declared, getting up. "*I'm* for the pool. Come on, ladies. *We* need to cool off."

They strode into the luxury of the slightly-swirling warm-ish water of the 10-by-10 yard one-level pool with wide benches on the sides, followed by *another* spa guest.

"Hi, Megan," Leigh announced as she came down the steps.

"Leigh, ladies." Megan had kept herself trim-bordering-on-athletic; her bundled hair was stiff; her suit modest. "Spa day?"

"A party before *my* wedding, Megan." Leigh watched Donna approach Megan slowly. "How about *you*? Early workday, or…?"

Warily, Megan sat. "I'm *not* here to make trouble, guys. I *gave* Randy Mike's number, but it was *Joe* that called, and *he's* got something *else* planned for *your* reception tomorrow."

Leigh sighed. "What?"

"Chuck *something was* one of his guys at that hotel; tipped him off."

"Chuck took off," Ann said. "Callie told us…"

"Yeah," Megan said. "*All* Joe's people there took off after the FBI started snooping around. Joe said, 'I'm gonna finish *that bastard* off' as soon as he heard *you* were finally getting married."

"Finish *who*," Donna asked, walking towards her.

"*JJ Elrath*, that's who! *Joe* is obsessed with him."

"*Joe*," Ann asked. "Who put *him* in charge?"

"He's *been* in charge of *that* mob since high school. *Joe* gets the *money*."

"*What* money, Megan," Leigh asked.

Donna towered over Megan; Megan glanced up at her mildly before she answered. "*Easy*, Blondie: I'm on *your* side. Joe goes to the bank every Monday." Megan glanced at Ann. "*Charlie Parkinson's* Greenville Investment Trust joint account with RF. As of yesterday, it's *closed out*."

"You know this *how*," Leigh asked.

"*I* keep the books, those that *everyone* sees, *and* those that *no one* sees. I *also* get the correspondence from the banks…"

"*You're Sid's source*," Ann declared.

Megan glared. "Since RF put *me* in that delivery room in Greenville."

"*Delivery* room?" Cathy glanced at Monica; Donna and Deb looked confused.

"Tell ya *later*, guys," Leigh murmured.

"Sid and I agreed RF *had* to be stopped," Megan continued. "But the *best* we could do *then* was get that poor girl to that nunnery." She rubbed her face with warmish water. "We put up fronts, Sid and I." Donna sat slowly as Megan looked at Leigh. "*Your* first wedding was *our limit*. RF declared that night that if *you* weren't knocked up in a year, *he'd* do the deed himself. When you stormed out of that hotel room…Sid *caught* you, but *I* got you into Randy's BVDs. He left Randy's crew; I stayed, kept the books, started *seeing* Randy just to keep an eye on him. I feed Sid as much as I can *get* on RF's outfit."

"*Phyllis*, Megan," Leigh asked. "How did *she* find out about her grandson?" *Who isn't her grandson…*

"She found a Christmas card RF was sending up there in '72, with a BIG check in it. RF just told her it was for *Randy's* kid and that *she* had nothing to do with it. Poor woman drank herself into a *stupor*." Megan looked at Leigh desperately. "*Randy* sort-of *sent* me here today, Leigh. Can *we* talk…alone?"

***

"Haven't been *here* in *ages*," Ben said. He took a seat at the big round table in the private dining room at Devon Gables, an old-style sit-down restaurant with cloth napkins, tablecloths, and *real* silverware. Before Detroit's suburbs grew to rival the city itself, the northwest suburbs were known as *summer cottage towns*. Then, Devon Gables was one of the choicest spots in the area.

"Don't know that I've *ever* been here," Ed agreed. Belying its name, Devon Gables had only one architectural feature on its roof that could be *called* a *gable*.

"An odd choice for a bachelor party, Mike," JJ added. Though it was only a few miles from where he lived as a teenager, JJ hadn't been there more than a few times.

"The only time *I* was here was just after Grandfather Mordechai moved to the home, and we moved into the mansion," Mike said. "Their fried clams were out-of-this-world."

"*Your* party, big guy; your choice," Gabe shrugged, sitting down.

"Yeah," Nick agreed. "This place is as dated as Fox and Hounds." Devon Gables' main rival in the area was Fox and Hounds. Neither had seen an interior update in decades.

"So, Mike," Gabe managed to suppress a grin, "got any naked pictures of Leigh on ya?"

"Um, no…"

"*Want* some?" The hilarity over the expected old joke was, to be charitable, subdued. The drinks came, and the appetizers, and the gent's ordered their dinners. To Mike's mild disappointment, fried clams hadn't been on the menu since the '70s.

"So," Ben declared as the dessert dishes were cleared away. "I propose a toast, gentlemen: To my son Michael, who will *finally* marry his old lab partner after nearly eighteen years of courting."

*To Michael!*

"And *I* have a special surprise," Gabe said, moving to the door. "Mike's had a *thing* for my *cousin* for many years, and tonight he shall *have* that itch *scratched* because what's a bachelor party without…*a dancing girl!*"

"*Hi, Sandy*," Donna purred in an elegant split-to-the-hip black sheath. "We *never* danced together, my dear, but *tonight* we *will!*" Ann, right behind her, smiled and shook her head as she handed Gabe a boom box, and he started the tape: Engelbert Humperdinck's "The Last Waltz."

"*Cousin*," JJ asked as Gabe sat down.

"By marriage; more *steps* and *in-laws* than direct relations."

"There's a reason *why* we didn't dance before, Sandy." Donna smiled into Mike's embarrassed face with her arms on his shoulders while they turned and shuffled inexpertly to the music.

"Yeah: neither of us does it well." He held her waist carefully as if she might break…or they might *both* crack up. "Whose idea *was* this, anyway?"

"Since you *didn't* want a more *traditional* bachelor party, *Gabe* and *I* just thought…*you* get it."

"Yeah. I suppose if *I* were a *little* more…"

"Risqué? Making out in *my* kitchen two tugs from naked *before* our first *date* was *plenty* risqué."

"*That* was *your* idea."

"*You* didn't *argue*."

"But *we never*…"

"*No*, Sandy: *we* were never like *that*." The song ended; she kissed him tenderly and smiled. "And I'll *always love* my Boy-Next-Door."

***

"*Hey*, Sandy," Ann huffed, catching her breath after her laps. The pool was *officially* closed and otherwise deserted; the lights in the pool itself the only illumination.

"*Hey*, Legs," he answered, stepping into the pool, swimming towards her underwater. "*That* was *some* bachelor party."

"*My* first. We waited for the waiter's high-sign through three *different* guys trying to pick us up."

"*Different* kind of a dancing girl…"

"Originally, she wanted to wear a pole-dance kinda thing, but *I* said it might be cold in *that* skimpy outfit. Besides, *I* was her hemming model this afternoon, and *that* costume didn't fit *me*."

"Ah." He leaned against the wall next to her. "*You* have a *flawless* form."

"Which *one*, big guy?"

"Both: swimming *and*…"

"I *get* it." She flexed her cranky hip.

"What's with *that*? I see you do it often enough." He stretched his back.

"Sixteen years of diving. *You've* got a bum back; you stretch *it* often enough."

"Fourteen years of Army bunks. *We're* a pair, ain't we?"

"Yeah. That thing between *them*…you *still* OK with that?"

"More OK than *another* guy might be." He sighed. "You?"

"Yeah, I *think* so." She leaned back and floated her legs.

"And they *promised that* was as far as they'd go yesterday."

"They *did*," she grinned. "So did *we*. Sandy, *I'd* like to know what I might have been *missing* since junior high. Donna said you were a *great* kisser."

"*Did* she? OK…" He put his arm around her shoulders, leaning towards her smiling face as she embraced him.

"Leigh shares her *lips* with you and JJ; I should try *that* with *you.*"

"JJ won't mind?"

"Think of it as a *balance*, Sandy. He makes out with Leigh once in a while…"

"Huh."

They pressed closer. "We *promised*, Sandy. *First base* is as far as *we* go, clothes or *no* clothes."

And *that's* as *far* as they *went.*

# Leigh and Mike

"*Morning*, honey," Ed called, shuffling out of the cottage bedroom. "Coffee looks ready."

"Morning, Dad," Leigh answered. She looked out at the rolling clouds. A layer of frost on everything outside didn't come as a surprise. Like most Michigan kids, Leigh could remember trick-or-treating in blizzards *and* having to cut the grass as late as Thanksgiving. Those who live in the Great Lakes State cope with the extreme volatility behind the quip; *if you don't like the weather now, wait half an hour.* "Is *Mom*…?"

"Morning, dear," Cathy mumbled, stretching in the doorway *before* she tied her robe—her *only* garment. "Are you ready *this time*?"

"I *think* so. I knew *Mike* better the first time I *kissed* him than I knew Randy on our wedding night."

"Good thing," Ed mumbled. "Don't want to have to do *this* too often." Cathy stood behind Ed, poised by the stove, opening her robe before wrapping her arms around him. "Eggs, everyone? Last chance I get to cook for my daughter."

"Sure, Dad," Leigh answered absently, still watching the sky. *You said that the last time…*

\*\*\*

"Morning, Johnny." In her big fuzzy robe, Ann watched out the frosty window as the curtains fluttered in the heat rising from the climate unit.

"Morning, Cloud." He flexed his shoulders tentatively as he got up, wincing slightly as he turned his neck stiffly. "Wish it would dry out for a while. *Cold*, too."

"Yeah. Sure glad they're finally doing it."

"Roger that."

"*Roger*," she loudly asked, turning around and opening her robe with a smile. "Wonder whatever happened to him?"

"Who *cares*?" He walked into her embrace.

"Got *that* right, two-timing bastard." Her Key West lover—before she found JJ—turned out to be married with two kids.

They stood by the window in the rising heat as the climate unit quietly started again, thinking of not a lot before she nudged him with her chin. "I made out with Mike in the pool last night."

"*Enjoy* it?"

"*Yeah*."

"First time?"

*"Yup."*

"Last?"

*"Not* if *you* want to share lips with *Leigh* once in a while." They were still, holding each other tight. "Deal?"

"Deal."

And they kissed on it.

"PT?"

"Sure."

***

"Am I *supposed* to feel different today?"

"A *little*." Ann regarded Mike curiously as she peeled a banana. "*I* was nervous, excited...*so* excited I threw up my first breakfast."

"I wish *we'd* been better friends in school. You and I never really..."

"No, we were in different *circles*." She finished her banana. "*Might* have the chance now. I've *seen* you swim."

"Not like *you*, but I've been known *not* to drown."

"Very *few* people swim like me, but *I'm* out of shape." She looked around the atrium. "We'll be renting that suite we're in now for a year." She shrugged. "We *could* swim together. Morning PT is around 0600."

"We *could*," Mike agreed, "but we're only here for a week. *I* was thinking more..."

"Intellectual? I'm no Bertrand Russel, but I can hold my own, and I *will* finish my business degree soon."

"My psych degree...spring. I *may* get warrant officer school." He craned his neck. "Last night was nice." *Your lips are like candy, Legs.*

*You are SOME KISSER, Sandy.* "It *was* a beautiful however-long-it-was, Sandy." They stared at each other. "We'll share lips *once* in a *while*."

"*Once* in a *while*, Legs."

***

*I didn't bring much here for one night. It'll still be here...I'll still be here...*

"Can't remember *what* you forgot, can you," Cathy murmured behind her. "We *all* do that on our way to our wedding. *I* did: *both* times."

"Innocence? Hardly. Girlhood? Hell, I'll be 32 in April. Virginity? Nope. *What* then?"

"Uncertainty," Cathy smiled. "Now, you *know*."

"With Randy, everything was planned for me. There *were* no questions about *anything*, even the wedding night since you made me watch that movie." *A grosser anatomy lesson I never could have gotten than I did in that stinking X-rated movie house.* "*That* uncertainty. Now, I'll never *really* be alone."

"Like you *always* were with Randy."

251

***

"Never looks *quite* right." JJ straightened Mike's US insignia on his uniform again, *not* admiring his handiwork.

"No," Mike agreed. "The pictures always look better."

"Sorry, I don't have patent-leather low-quarters: gold insignia's best I can do, and I have to send *them* back to Tom."

"I put a shine on mine last night. I was too nervous to sleep."

JJ shrugged. "Before Ann and I…there were no mysteries left. We knew each other at least as well as we knew ourselves. So what was *I* so nervous about?" JJ adjusted a medal on the coat's chest. "I think it was because when you form a marriage, you make something new, and new stuff is always kinda scary."

"At least as reasonable as…no," Mike declared. "I think in *our* case…we're *still* not sure we'll be able to stay together. The Army *could* separate us anyway when our tour here is up."

"Not if they want to *keep* you. Well, you…oh, *yeah*," JJ grinned, opening the door to a soft knock. Ram, resplendent in a dapper blue pinstripe, came in with a box containing a dress-uniform-green, stiff-felt *kippah*.

"Never *saw* one before," Mike mumbled absently. "In uniform, I usually wear black." He removed the headgear from its wrapper and put it on his head.

Ram grinned, "It's new; *optional* uniform."

Mike looked at him oddly. "*You* aren't Jewish."

"No, Zoroastrian," Ram answered. "But *we* knew *you* were."

"I'm to give this to *you* before the wedding." JJ pulled a small package out of his coat pocket. The tissue paper wrapping held a silver-inlaid magnetic *mezuzah*. "Made by your old employer."

"Old Meyer *said* he was going to go into these," Mike choked, "didn't know he *had*." In high school, he worked in wood and metal for Meyer's Artisans, makers of Jewish religious objects. "How did *you* know?"

"I work in intelligence, remember?" JJ chuckled. "Adam gave it to *me* to give to *you*. He also said his *wife* will be attending."

"I asked if he could attend off-duty as a friend of the family. Pops *told* him he could." The security arrangements—courtesy of the FBI—were well beyond Adam's control. Ernie told them it would be easier to get close to the President than it would the little church for those who weren't *supposed* to be there.

"OK, brother," Ram intoned, "*we're* under orders to have you at that church dead or alive by 1000, and we've got 45 minutes. So, it's *dusty-trail* time!"

***

"*She's* upstairs," Ann, standing at the choir loft door, declared when JJ, Ram, and Mike walked into the church. "Your *dad's* downstairs." The weather, still ambiguous, lashed windy and chilly.

"Join your dad." JJ helped Sara erect the tent-like portable canopy over the altar as the first guests arrived. Adam and a *very* pretty, large woman entered

252

close to 10 and sat in the last pew. "*Mr.* Block," he smiled, "I'm under *strict* instructions to make sure you're up *in front with* the family. If you *would*, please."

"*Mr.* Elrath," Adam nodded, following his wife.

JJ looked around as if to find something undone before taking up his post at the basement door...*Dad and I installed that coat rack the Saturday before the first service. I put that wall anchor in wrong and had to do it over.*

***

"OK, *today only* until I'm dead," Cathy declared, placing a gold filigree/emerald broach on Leigh's ivory sheath. The jewelry had belonged to Leigh's great-grandmother; Cathy wore it only on *very* special occasions. "Phyllis forbade it *last* time."

"Now *this*," Donna placed a Venetian lace veil on Leigh's head. "You know how *this* works?"

"It's a *veil*. What's so hard about *that*?"

"Well," Monica explained, "you come to your groom with it raised off your face, and the first thing *he* has to do is lower it."

"Because *that's* his *job*," Donna continued, "to protect your *modesty*."

*Like Monday?* "OK. Now, I'm *borrowing* the dress; Mom's *broach* is old; the veil was Mama Monica's..."

"No," Donna said, "it was *my* mother's."

*Oh, I swore I wouldn't cry!* "OK," she sniffed. "I need..."

"Here," Debbie proffered a small box; inside were two blue garters. "New and blue."

"Oh, thanks. I *remember* now. I asked *you* to..."

"Yeah, and *you* forgot."

***

"Are you ready for *this*, my son?" Ben nervously straightened Mike's tie.

"Think so, Pops. *You* nervous about something?"

"Frankly, yes. I've never *been* a best man before; don't know how well I'll *do*."

"I believe *I* have to do most of the work, and *you* just sign the license, Pops."

"Very well, let's...but first: I had little wisdom to pass to your sisters at this moment in *their* lives, and I don't know how much I have for my son *now*, but," he looked curious. "Remember I told you that I wasn't sure I loved your mother until Sara was born? That was *not* true. I knew the *first* time I saw her in San Francisco. It was three in the morning, *pouring* rain, and a thousand or so of us were crammed into a waterfront shed, soaking wet, and it was easily a hundred degrees. A dozen of us followed signs in Hebrew that read 'Jewish Relief' to a little corner. Your mother handed me a cup of warm coffee and a stale cookie and said, 'welcome *home*, Lieutenant' in Yiddish. I thought she was the most beautiful sight I'd *ever* seen; I had *found* the *love* of my *life*. But I didn't *know* until your sister was born that *that* was what it was." He smiled at the memory. "And you? When did *you* know?"

*Third Period Science? No*... "She and Donna asked me what was bothering me in the lunchroom. I was worried about Max in Khe Sanh." The girls barely knew him, but they talked to *that* lost-looking New Boy with sexy grey eyes.

"Funny the things we remember," Ben grinned. "And it was Leigh, *not* Donna?"

"It was *both*, but Donna's always been more of a...a..."

"A *friend* you *loved*, who you walked out with, but not a *lover*."

"You, too, Pops?"

"Every young man *should* be lucky enough to have one. Mine was *Joan*. She had the most remarkable whistle for a girl; hazel eyes, delicate hands. We said goodbye when I enlisted, and I haven't seen her since." He heaved a sigh. "Well, it's *time*, Michael."

\*\*\*

"How's *he*," Ann asked JJ.

"He'll be fine." Pastor Lou met their eyes and nodded as Sara did the same, and Gabe struck the Wagnerian chords. "They're *ready*."

"OK. Get...Hi, Monica."

"*They're* ready," Monica whispered, taking Sara's husband's Oliver's arm.

"Good; get *yours* up here, Johnny."

JJ opened the door; Mike, Ben, and Gabe were just behind it. "Get *moving*." As evenly as he could, Mike led his father, Gabe, and JJ up the sanctuary's side aisle. He took his place under the canopy as Ben and Gabe took hold of canopy poles.

Ann opened *her* door; Donna was behind *it*, with the rest in the stairway. "Come *on*."

Ann and Debbie led the march up the aisle. Then Donna, grinning beatifically, floated up the aisle in a plain blue satin dress. Finally, Leigh and her parents followed. Leigh, alone, stepped under the canopy to face Mike as Donna and Debbie grabbed their poles; Mike gently lowered Leigh's veil.

"Dearly beloved," Pastor Lou began, followed by Sara's "*Libli balibte*." There were surprised giggles when Lou *and* Sara simultaneously asked—in English and Hebrew— "who gives this woman," and Ed and Cathy loudly announced "*we* do" at the same time.

It was finished—as far as Mike and Leigh knew—within minutes, even with Sara's additions, the wine, the circling, and the wreaths. Before they knew it, they each smashed a lightbulb, and there came a shout of *mazel tov!*

*Will I see it?* JJ smiled at Ann as Leigh suddenly glowed brightly as she kissed her groom.

*This time, I know why.*

\*\*\*

"Thanks, everyone, for coming," Mike smiled. Callie and the hotel put on a brunch buffet, not unlike Ann and JJ's but *much* smaller, with tables set in a U for only twenty-two guests.

"Hey, *glad* to do this one, Sandy," Donna beamed widely, squeezing Nick's hand. "That *last* soirée of Leigh's *wasn't* so hot."

"Yeah," Bobbi agreed, bumping Gabe's shoulder. "So many *ugly* characters hanging around. One tried to pick a fight with another one for the 'honor' of sitting next to *me…*"

"Where's JJ, Ann," Ben asked, looking around.

"On the phone with his mom," she sighed. "Some complications with Charlie."

"Hope it's something severe," Cathy made a face.

"Well, everyone," Debbie sighed, "I'm for the bathroom again."

\*\*\*

"That's *Randy,*" Ann blinked as Megan escorted him into the atrium in the middle of the brunch, followed *discretely* by Dave.

"*Who,*" JJ looked. "Never clapped eyes on him…no, wait. Yeah: 3$^{rd}$ Grade, maybe."

"*Mr.* Newhouse," Adam smiled politely, "I *don't* believe you were invited."

"*Mr.* Block," Randy answered, pivoting his head as he removed his hat. "I only want to give my best to Leigh and Mike."

"It's *OK*, Adam," Leigh called, grabbing Mike's hand and walking towards them.

"Leigh," Randy scanned around, turning his head in a swift-but-practiced motion, stopping at an odd angle. "Mike, I just wanted to stop by and say congratulations and good luck." He extended his hand, trembling.

"Thanks, Randy," Mike said, taking it. Megan leaned in for a kiss.

"*Thanks*, Randy," Leigh declared, embracing him lightly.

Megan, offering Leigh a cheek, whispered, "We'll be over *there* by the fountain; RF is in the lobby. Joe *won't* be coming."

Ernie and Morgan, flanking the lobby entrance, were *almost* invisible.

\*\*\*

Taylor's and Bell's chatted with Dietz's and Elrath's and Block's as the buffet was being cleaned up. "Our *second* wedding," Magda Block declared. "Barely remember what *time* it was."

"Early," Adam said, "*or* late, hard to say. We weren't halfway across the Mediterranean, and we were the fifteenth couple the captain was marrying that night."

"You *eloped?*" Debbie made a face.

"Not *exactly*," Adam said. "It was 1954, and we were among a few *hundred* dual citizens who managed passage back to America. We were *sort-of* married in Jerusalem in '49: a *civil* ceremony in a city without a *recognized* civil government at that moment. Like the others, our civil union certificate wasn't *necessarily* lawful. So, we got married again on the ship just to be safe."

"With our *oldest boy* as a witness," Magda smiled, "he was *four*."

"Our second was…*twenty* years after the first, Ed?" Cathy, in a shimmering blue silk dress, looked as young as Leigh.

"Twenty-*one*…but we never signed the divorce papers from the *first*," Ed giggled, "and Leigh stood up for her mother."

"True fact," Leigh agreed.

"And we were at *that* one, too," Ben said, standing up. "*My* friends: as best man, it is my duty to propose a toast *and*, I understand, say something amusing about the bride and groom." He looked puzzled. "But I'm not that *good* at amusing…but I *will* tell you about…Memorial Day in 1968 when Michael asked *Donna* for a date…"

"It was the week *before* Memorial Day, Ben," Donna called.

"Just so. Donna had been *enticing* Michael for a solid week, wearing a swimming costume that even *I* knew was too small…"

"We'll discuss that *later*, Benjamin," Monica stage-growled, causing a ripple of laughter.

"*Yes*, dear," which triggered more guffaws. "As I was *saying*: Michael was *captivated* by Donna, who is as lovely *now* as she was *then*…"

"Careful, sir," Nick called, "that's *my* girlfriend you're talking about…"

"*That* was before *we* even *met*, sweetheart," Donna laughed, which made for more giggles.

"But Michael was unsure," Ben continued. "I said: 'go on *over* there. Not every conversation leads to an altar.'"

"Hell, I just wanted to go to a *movie*," Mike deadpanned, raising more laughs.

"And go he *did*, and to a movie, they went, with *Leigh*, too, if I'm not mistaken."

"Yup," Leigh agreed. "He sat between us. Blondie and I couldn't decide if we should *try* to make out with him or *not*."

"So *neither one* of 'em *tried*," Mike quipped…to another ripple of laughter.

"And so here we are, with Michael and Leigh, and Donna is Leigh's maid of honor." Ben paused. "As an attorney, I must smile at that outcome. As a *father*, I must *puzzle* at it." Another ripple of smiles. "But as best man, I raise my glass in a toast: To Michael and Leigh…who I watched *grow up* together, grow *to love* each other, and who I hope will *always* love as they do today."

*To Michael and Leigh!*

Cathy rose, clearly emotional. "I *should* be better at this than I am, but the first time Mike came to ask *Leigh* for a date…"

"*Mom*," Leigh groaned, smiling.

"Just the *clean* parts, honey. Leigh had *just* broken up with Randy the *first* time; they were sixteen, I think. Mike just *happened* to come over to ask her to some party, and when he knocked on the door, I was a *little* distracted on the phone and went to answer it…"

"Tell the *rest*, Cath," Ed shouted, "the part you *didn't* tell before."

"Yeah: *steal* my punchline, Ed." Laughter. "The part I *never* told before was that I didn't have a *stitch* on when he *knocked*." More laughter. "It was warm, I'd *just* got out of my monkey suit, and so I jerked a one-piece sweatsuit on—and the zipper jammed!" More laughter. "So I put the damn thing on *backward*, figured 'what the hell,' opened the door, said 'you *know* where to go' with my *butt* in the breeze. What an *eyeful* you'd have got if I'd *turned around*!" The atrium reverberated with glee.

"But when I came up later to ask if they wanted anything, I *had* turned that suit around. But with the *zipper* jammed, I just sort of *held* it shut with my hands in the pockets…" A *burst* of giggling. "And I asked if you objected to women who preferred *not* to wear clothes…and I *don't* if I don't *have* to."

"True fact," Ed agreed.

"*Oh*, yeah," Leigh smiled, grabbing Mike's hand. "You sat on the window seat, remember? *I* had nothing on but a robe and some shorts; you handed me another top, and I had you close your eyes while I took my robe off with my feet in your lap."

"Yeah: I peeked!"

"*You…!*" Leigh burst out; Monica was in tears; Donna and Nick clutched at each other in mirth. Even Adam was laughing, and Deb…another beeline to the ladies' room.

"Anyway, Mike," Cathy managed. "You said: 'if my friends want to walk around starkers, who am I to disapprove,' or something like that. *Who* could argue with *that* attitude? Mike, it was then that I decided that *you* were the boy for Leigh…for her *mother*, anyway…only *Leigh* didn't know it yet. So, I raise my glass and toast a *persistent* young man!"

*A persistent young man!*

Then, JJ stood up. "Now…*I'm* not that good at this kind of thing, and I'm not going to *try* to be funny, but *I* met Green-Eyes in church. I can't *remember* what we *talked* about…"

"Me neither," Leigh smiled.

"But I talked her into going to the youth congress that year…I don't know *how*…"

"Your *eyes*, buddy," Leigh declared.

"If *you* say so. Anyway, we had fun together. At the same time, I missed Claudia—and they *knew* each other—but for some unknown reason, I never told *either* of them about the *other*." As if on cue, they shrugged simultaneously. "And I lost track of *both* for a while; it was only through Mike that I got in touch with *Leigh* again. Leigh was winning Mike's heart by then. Up until I believe '79, *I'd* made out with Leigh, but *Mike* hadn't." Leigh looked thoughtful, then nodded.

"*Wasn't* a race, brother, but you *won*." Smiles. "But Leigh and Mike have been *my* friends for a *very* long time, and Ann's been Leigh's for *just* as long. So, if I may, I'd like to raise a toast to *our* lifelong friends: may we *be* friends forever."

*Friends forever!*

When the party broke up hours later, Mike hugged his new mother-in-law, whispering, "there was a mirror inside the *open* closet door, Cath: you *were* beautiful."

She kissed his cheek and smiled, "keep *that* to *yourself,* boy."

* * *

"Hi, Mom," Ann said, hugging Stella. "Any changes?"

"He's slowing down, dear," Stella sighed, pecking her cheek. They sat quietly, watching Charlie's vitals before Stella brightened. "Can you give *this* to Leigh and Mike, please?"

"OK, Mom," JJ smiled. "Just a card?"

"Oh, there's a check," Stella sighed, watching Charlie. "*Every* couple needs a *little.*"

"Thanks, Mom," JJ smiled. "They'll be thrilled. And, Mom, I need to get something out of that photo album of Charlie's that I saw last year."

Stella looked curious. "OK. They're in a box in our storage space." She looked sidelong. "Important?"

"Just…checking *more* boxes, Mom."

* * *

"Is Mike a *better kisser* than me?" They listened to the battering wind, to the canvas flapping on the eaves of their little porch.

"He's more *relaxed* than you *usually* are." Silence. "It *isn't* a competition, babe."

"So, you'd *do it* again?"

"With *your* permission." Silence; wind shifting around. "I love *him* as the husband of my *dear* friend and the buddy of *my* husband. Call it *friend-sharing.*"

"*Friend-sharing*…OK, call it *that.*"

"*You two* can make out." She squeezed his hand. "*We* might, too."

"Maybe we'll do it *together.*" They shifted on the bed. "Donna and Nick seem committed."

"They're going to try *living* together. Tired of falling in and out of *like,* Donna says. What do *you* know about *them*?"

"Just what I *hear.*"

She pushed him over and climbed on top, her hip protesting. "*Now hear this…*"

* * *

"I think the next wedding we go to *might* be Donna's and Nick's," Leigh declared. "She *did* catch my bouquet."

258

"Yeah, but she and Bobbi were the only *single* women there."

"And Gabe caught my garter." They watched the skylight, the scudding clouds rolling over the moon from time to time. "What did you *think* of making out with Ann?"

"She's…can making out be *athletic?*"

"I suppose. But what *else* was she?"

"Sweet; *very* sweet."

"So, you'd do it again?"

"I *might*. You *mind?*"

"Maybe the *four* of us can have make-out parties." Silence. "You *peeked?*"

"A *little*. I was too scared to *look*. *Did* see a *little*, though."

"Huh." She stroked his chest. "Any change since then?"

"I didn't *love* you then…not like *now*."

"You *realize*, Sandy, that JJ has *felt* these, too. If I ask *him*…"

"Just the *once*."

"He's had a good *look-down* view in the pool *more* than once, *believe* me. My thirteen-year-old boobs were *smaller* than my sixteen-year-old ones."

"You'd know that better than *I* would."

"You didn't watch them *grow* over the years?"

He breathed deep. "Only my love for *you, oytzer*."

"*Good* catch," she declared, pulling him on top of her. "You *are* a good catch."

# *Thanksgiving Day*

"It's *supposed* to *feel* different," she whispered.

"Mm. *What* is?"

"Being married."

He reached for her behind him. "*This* feel different?"

"Feels *sweaty. Turn* over."

He rolled to face her, opening a bleary eye. "Morning."

"*Hi*, husband."

"*Hi*, wife." He pulled her closer. "I could *stay* like this…"

"I want to *swim*, then try that jacuzzi."

"What *time* is it?"

"Nearly 7."

"Ann and JJ *might* be down there."

"So?"

"So, let's *go*. Housekeeping's here at 10:30, and *I* want to be *gone*."

\*\*\*

"Look at *this*," JJ showed Ed, Leigh, and Cathy the old and yellowed memo copy in Charlie's sprawling handwriting.

> *Re: Future Plans*
> *Met woman with convenient name and daughter at Albany convention. Approached; interested. More later.*

"February 1967…NP Investors…convention." Cathy knitted her brows. "Yeah, OK. We pressed a *lot* of flesh…" They were in the cottage, away from the party in full swing that they could still hear.

"I'd just started that *first* Detroit branch," Ed added. "*We* were at a convention looking for investors…"

"After *that*, I got a letter from Oakland County offering *double* my salary to move to Michigan." She glanced at the memo again. "*Convenient name?*"

"It's *complicated*, Mom," Leigh replied. "How long have you *got*?"

"Are *we* going to *need* more drinks?"

"You *might*."

\*\*\*

"*Great* party," JJ sighed. "I never knew Mom knew *how* to dance the *hora*." It was late when they got back to the hotel, ears still ringing from the revelry of the full-family reception/Thanksgiving party. Over *300* guests attended, with Gabe's band playing in a tent in the Dietz backyard.

"I never knew *you* could either," Mike grinned.

"Even *I* can hold hands and move in a circle," Ann smiled. "Johnny can...um..."

"*Mr.* Newhouse," Leigh said as she stared past Ann.

"Leigh," RF answered, rising out of a lobby chair. Ellen, not far away, nodded. "*Nice* party?"

"Yes, it *was*, thank you." Leigh glanced at Mike. "My friends, this is Randy's *father*, Randall Fred Newhouse, the Third. I don't know if you ever *met* my husband, Mike Dietz? And these are John Elrath and *his* wife, Ann Mueller-Elrath."

All shook hands silently, waiting. "Can we go somewhere more private?" RF gestured to the bar. "You and I?"

"Whatever you have to say to *me*, sir, you can say to *all* of us." Leigh gestured to the atrium. "There's a corner that doesn't echo all over." Leigh *visibly* moderated her voice—with a *monumental* effort—to keep from screaming *bloody murder* in his face.

RF seemed worn out, but his voice was steady as they sat. "Congratulations, Leigh. I wish you well." Ellen followed discretely.

"Thank you, but you *could* have sent a card for *that*. Sir."

RF sighed, took a deep breath. "I brought Renée and Randy to see Phyllis this morning. She *saw* them, touched their hands. It was a *good* Thanksgiving for her."

"A beautiful gesture, sir," Leigh smiled.

"*You* know the *truth* now, don't you?"

"Yessir, we do."

"*Small* consolation, but now they *all* have trusts. *All* my children can live off of what I built *before* I started taking money from the wrong people." He stared at the atrium's skylight, his head lolling back on the chair. "I got a call from Mr. Paulson, the US attorney for Eastern Michigan; they're looking at my books for the past *twenty years*, a *little* longer than I've been hooked up with those *people*."

"*What* people," JJ asked.

"The DeVere/Wier organization. It was just *too good* to be true."

JJ struggled to remain calm; Ann grabbed his hand. "The old saying," she said, "if it *sounds* too good to be true..."

"Yeah," RF said. "My *legit* businesses were doing well *enough*, but of course, I wanted—*needed*—more. Taking *that* money, providing *that* service was easy with Charlie's help: he had shell businesses protecting *him* already. So, I protected my families—those *everyone* knew, *and* those *no one else* knew—with shell companies Charlie had just *sitting* there.

"Then Charlie told me that *he* was out better than ten million because of *you*, Mr. Elrath." RF gazed steadily at JJ. "But I can't fault *you* for being a better, *braver* man than *anyone* expected, even if *he* blamed you for the loss." He shook his head violently. "It was just a couple months ago that Charlie told me: 'that rat bastard Elrath will be *dead* at my *feet* before the end of the year...and Stella will *know I* did it.' He never *ever* got over what you did...and *he* paid Joe *handsomely* to kill you. *Joe* found *Chuck* and all the *rest* of those beasts..."

He glanced at Leigh. "I *needed* your *name* on a birth certificate to *say* the boy was *Randy's*. That's *all*. Now I can't *remember* just *why that* was *so* important. When I got that letter from the Army Provost Marshal, *that* was a wake-up call. I thought the wrath of GOD was coming down on me. I wished it *had* then; I wouldn't have been in *this* deep."

He turned and gazed at Mike. "Why in the *hell* didn't you just *grab her* and run away? It would have saved me *thousands* in legal fees for the annulment and *trying* to get her *back*."

He turned his gaze to Ann. "Mrs. Mueller-Elrath: *congratulations* on winning that race. *Quite* an achievement. I forbade my daughters from even *joining* the swim team; they wanted to. I needed *them* to be *wives* to my important business partners, *not* strong women." His head sank slowly into his hands, briefly. "Now, I have to *tell* them their mother passed away this afternoon."

"*So* sorry," Leigh whispered. "I *liked* Phyllis when she was sober." "Sorry," "*So* sorry," "Sorry for your loss," came from the others.

"Didn't see her *sober* much, though," RF grinned slightly. "Phil's been drunk since Randy was born. Now I must *find* my daughters and tell them that their mother's gone and that their brother's failing, *and* their father's *probably* going to jail." He sighed again, reached into his coat pocket, pulled out an envelope, and handed it to Leigh. "Here's the payoff for the Essexville mortgage *and* insurance and taxes for the next ten years. Your *father* can handle this."

"Mary, sir," Ann asked. "What does *she* know?"

"Nothing of my shady business; she's a one-way conduit. She never had to lie except about *being* married. That was a joke that Joe came up with—used actors—for what, I don't know."

"When did *you* find out about Renée," Mike asked.

RF smiled wryly. "I heard *her* cry when she was *born*, then silence, then *another* cry. *Not* the same cry; the *first* was a girl. I've had *four* girls; I *know* the difference." He shrugged. "Years later, I saw her picture in the Bay City paper, some dance recital. I was *so* proud...but it broke my heart that I *couldn't* cut it out and keep it."

"Your brother, sir," Mike asked, "why did you..."

"My...*Oh, Eddie*. My mom's teenage *neighbor* had him; Dad took him in when he married Mom, let him use the name. Turned out we had *similar* tastes, but *he* liked *teenage* girls and wasn't above screwing his own. That he died before Lizzie was old enough was a blessing.

"Now, I shall take my leave of you." He looked around at all of them. "We had a few laughs, but we took it too far; *too* far by half. Charlie Parkinson's a rotten bastard but a good businessman who shared my *fondness* for younger women. I'm glad *he's* out of it now, too. Good luck to you all."

They watched him walk away—slowly, carefully—as if shouldering a great weight.

***

"*That's* what all this was *about*," Leigh sighed, twizzling her whiskey in the empty bar.

"They were eyeballing those girls as early as '67," JJ intoned slowly, glancing at Leigh. "They got your mom a job she couldn't refuse because *you* had the right *name...*"

"Knowing that there *might* be an *accident*," Leigh groaned.

"No," Ann declared, "because RF couldn't *depend* on Randy, even though he believed Mary; she *said* Randy *could...*"

"Randy was pissed off that he was being manipulated." Leigh smiled wryly. "He started hormone treatments after he was off RF's health insurance. Then he could *finally...* That's what *Megan* told me. Dynasty went into the toilet because *Mary lied.*"

Silence filled the little corner, as quiet as the empty atrium.

"*Let's* go up." The 5th Level elevator closest to the honeymoon suite was next to the pool enclosure off the atrium. The glass room's lights were off, but the pool lights cast an eerie glow.

"'Swim at your own risk after closing,' the sign says," Ann declared, opening the door, "*that's* where *I'm* going *now.*"

"*Right* behind you." "Me, too." "Anyone *care* about suits?" They looked at each other, the steam wafting out the open door.

*Nope.*

# December 1986

## Monday

*Five in the morning…this better be good.*

The phone's jangling interrupted JJ's dream about golf (which he *didn't* play) and Jackie Gleason (who he *didn't* care for). "Yeah…oh, *hi* Mom…oh, I'm *so* sorry, Mom…OK…I'll call Brenda and Lois…the *boys* too…OK, Mom. A couple of hours, we'll be there."

She sat upright as he hung up the phone, knowing by his tone… "Charlie?"

"Bastard lasted *just* long enough to *not* die in November." He glanced at the clock again, numbly. "I'll get in the shower. Call your dad?"

"Then Leigh and Mike."

\*\*\*

"Morning," Leigh answered the phone. They were *just* getting up.

"Leigh, honey: *Charlie's* gone," Ann said quietly. "We're going over there in an hour. Meet for breakfast?"

"Check. Atrium in three zero mikes."

\*\*\*

"*Sorry*, Mom," Ann smiled after embracing Stella in her apartment. "I *know* you loved him…" The weather that morning matched everyone's moods: thin cloud deck, occasional sun, blustery breeze.

"I did *once*, dear," Stella smiled, "but I fell out of *love* some time ago; the *like* went after that. But, *thank* you, dear; *thank* you."

"If you want, I'll speak to the Monseigneur about the Mass…"

"*That* would be *so* helpful, dear. Father Dukakis gave him the Last Rites Saturday."

JJ answered a knock on the door, expecting one of his brothers, but instead… "Sid! How did *you*…?"

"My *job*, Mr. Elrath," Sid smiled. "Just seeing what may *need* doing. May I *see* your mother?" Sid embraced her gently, politely, before he asked: "Is there *anything* you need, Mrs. Parkinson? I know there are *many* details…"

"Well, there *is* something in *your* line, Mr. Jackwell. If you *can*, locate his family in Berryville, Indiana? They were estranged."

"*Simplicity* itself, Mrs. Parkinson. If there's *anything* else, just call. I've written my *personal* number on the back of my card."

"*So* sorry, Mrs. Parkinson," Leigh declared, lightly embracing Stella an hour later.

"It's a *relief* now, dear," Stella smiled, "and it's time you called me Stella."

"Ma'am," Mike politely smiled, offering flowers and a snack tray. "I know you have had many blessings in your life; Charlie was one of them."

"Thank you, Mike," Stella said, "but *he* was a decidedly *mixed* blessing."

"If I *may*, ma'am, it is my duty as a friend of the family to sing *Kaddish* for your husband. I know you *aren't* Jews, but…"

"A lovely gesture, Mike: thank you."

"Your mom seems to be holding up well." Leigh and Mike sat with JJ in the den as well-wishers filled the condo. The *spare bedroom* was really a crowded *den*. Boxes joined piled papers on the bed—searched by Jo. A surprisingly-tidy desk filled one corner.

"As well as expected," JJ sighed. "Lately, she'd gotten to where she didn't even *like* him much."

"How about *you*, brother," Mike asked. "*You* look a little ragged."

"Not used to early First Calls. Can *you guys* do something for us? We've got to get clothes over to the funeral home."

On the way back from the funeral home, they passed a Newhouse firm's satellite office, where the flag flew at half-mast.

***

"I need to feel for the bastard, Cloud, but I just can't." JJ sat behind the wheel, key in hand, staring out the windshield after a long day of greetings, condolences, visitors, phone calls, and offerings of food and flowers.

"No, you *don't*, Johnny. Feel for your *mom*."

"*She* doesn't either."

"What's *that* tell ya?"

"You're right. The late *unlamented* Charlie Parkinson." He sighed again, "and nobody gives a *damn*," raising her hand to his lips.

## Tuesday

"Johnny," Stella's voice on the phone was weak, quiet. "Could you bring me *that* letter from Charlie?" They were just about to go meet Brenda.

*Letter from…OH!* "Right away, Mom."

***

"And *you* must be *Johnny*," the elderly woman with blue hair and a familiar tone of voice declared as he walked into the condo. "*How* can *you* hold your *head* up?"

"Ma'am," JJ answered blankly. "*You* would be…?"

"Freida Parkinson *Hayes*," Charlie Junior sighed with resignation. "My *aunt*."

"I see," JJ said. "And…"

"That adulterous *hussy* should run away in *shame*," Freida announced,

265

cocking a thumb at the kitchen, where Stella chatted with Charlie Junior and Dorothy. "And these *bastards* of *my brother* are keeping me from taking *him* home. And you, *Johnny*, should be *locked up*. *Raping all* those girls, *attacking* my *nephew* like that for *no good reason...*"

"Hold *on* a minute," Ann, behind JJ, interrupted. "Your *nephew...*?"

"*Who* are *you* to question *me*," Frieda snapped. "Another of *her* poxed *bastard* brats?"

"She's *my wife*," JJ managed with some effort. "But...*what* nephew?"

"*Matt*, you *murderer*," Freida declared. "You pitched him over that stair rail when he was trying to *protect* that young woman from *your* ravages."

"*Here* he is," Stella announced, smiling at JJ as she came into the living room. "He wrote you *off*, Mrs. Hayes."

"He *did*," JJ confirmed, holding the old, fading letter out to Freida.

"*Impossible*," Freida cried, jumping up and seizing the paper. "He *wouldn't...*" She read...and *read*...and reread it. Suddenly she sat down again, muttering to herself. JJ gently took the paper from her hand.

"This is the notarized original." Stella declared. "Charlie *said* you'd come sniffing around when he was gone."

"And there's Lew Rockland's signature as a witness," JJ said. "Bag of guts finally did something useful."

"Johnny," Ann mumbled, grabbing his arm, "come *here*." She led him to the kitchen, crowded with people, then into the bedroom before she turned to face him. "How would *she* have known about all *that*, with Kat and Matt?"

"Well," he sighed, sitting on the bed, "*that's* a good question. *That* version *had* to have come from...she said 'her *nephew*?'"

*What...the...hell?*

"*What* the...?" Kurt answered Stella's door; JJ could barely hear him. "What do *you* want?"

"To offer my condolences to the *widow*, *Mr.* Parkinson," Lew Rockland mewed, "and to present *her* with *your father's* Last Will and Testament."

Kurt stood aside. Stella looked up blankly. "Yes?"

"*Mrs.* Parkinson," Lew began. "*So* sorry for your loss. I know this is a difficult time, but..."

"Spit it out, Rockland," Kurt snapped.

"*Very* well. In executing your husband's will, I *have* to inform you that you have *thirty days* to vacate *these* premises..."

"*What*," Charlie exploded. "*Why?*"

"*Mr.* Parkinson," Lew sneered. "I was *not* addressing *you*. *You* may *leave now* if you wish." Turning to Stella again, Lew continued. "Mr. Parkinson's *sole heir* will take occupancy of *this* residence on the first of January. You may take with you *only...*"

"*Mr.* Parkinson's sole heir is my *mother*," JJ declared. "Who *else* would..."

"*Read this*," Lew interrupted with a most oleaginous smirk, "then *get out*."

JJ read the paper, a Xerox copy, and passed it to Charlie.

*...all my worldly goods, chattels, possessions, money, and investments I leave to my only natural grandson, Joseph Philip Dryden. All other spouses and relations by blood and the issues of bigamous marriages are hereby denied...*

"That *cult* his *family's* in; marriages once made *cannot* be unmade, even by death." Charlie shook his head. "But he *disowned* them: we *have* that statement witnessed by *you*, Rockland."

"A *forgery*," Lew sniffed. "*This* document was registered with the county just last month. *Thirty days*, Mrs. Parkinson; before Mr. Dryden will occupy *these* premises, or you will *be removed* by the sheriffs."

"Not if *I* have anything to do with it," Dorothy declared, scanning the paper. "*Wait*: the signature...November 4$^{th}$...the day *after* he *had* his stroke?"

Lew blinked. "No. We *signed* this document together *that* day..."

"No, you *didn't*, Rockland," JJ smiled. "Mom called me on the *morning of the* 4$^{th}$, said he'd had his event *just after dinner the night before.* He had his stroke on the *evening* of the 3$^{rd}$ of November."

"*That* is a *LIE*, Mr. Elrath. *That* is a *slander* for which you *shall* be *prosecuted* if you *dare repeat* it," Lew spat unsteadily. "You *misremembered*, Mrs. Parkinson. Your husband was in *my office* on the morning of the 4$^{th}$..."

"No, Lew," Stella smiled, a perfect replica of Lew's greasy grin. "I marked it on my calendar. 'Charlie shut up' on the 3$^{rd}$. And the 4$^{th}$, 'Johnny home.' And, of course, there are the *hospital* records..."

"*No* matter," Lew snapped, turning away. "Your mere diary is of *little* moment and *hardly* evidence; the hospital got the *dates* wrong—happens *all* the *time. THIS* is a copy of a *notarized* and *witnessed* document registered with the county. It is, therefore, lawful and enforceable. Be out by the *end of the month*, Mrs. Parkinson." He looked at Charlie and Dorothy disdainfully. "And as we speak, the *lawful owner* is *taking possession* of his dealership."

\*\*\*

"*I'll blow you to HELL, Elrath*," Joe growled, reaching behind him and stopping. "*Freeze right there!*" JJ walked into Charlie's dealership in Ferndale. It was only dimly familiar to him, having visited only a few times.

Will, confused if determined, looked to JJ as if for an explanation. "*Who* the *hell* is *this* clown, and *what's* he *think* he's *doing?*"

"Joe *claims* that he's Charlie's grandson," JJ sighed, entering the sales department, which consisted of four desks with baffled and slightly frightened occupants. "Lew Rockland is waving some bogus..."

"*I SAID FREEZE, ELRATH*," Joe screamed. "*The rest of you GET OUT! I'm calling the cops! You! The big* guy there!" Joe pointed at a large man in a work uniform who had just arrived outside of sales. "*Throw those people* out of here *at once!*"

"Say *what*," the big guy asked—whose shirt read *Oxford*—as Will ducked out a side door. Ox was a rare creature: a huge man blessed with an unwaveringly sunny disposition, maintaining his smiling countenance rain or shine, happy or sad, calm or angry, shaking your hand or crushing it.

*"I SAID THROW THEM ALL OUT!"*

"Now, *why* would I do *that*? I don't know *you*. I worked for Mr. Will afore; I know Mr. JJ since he were a boy. This here's their *Paw's* place." As he did in the sales department, Ox *filled* most doorways and had to duck under many a door jam, including *that* one.

"*He's dead*, moron," Joe shouted. "It's *my place* now, and *I say* throw them *ALL* out!"

"Sorry about your Paw, Mr. JJ," Ox said simply. "I just come up here to see what all the ruckus was with all the *shoutin'*…"

"I SAID THROW THEM OUT OR YOUR FIRED," Joe shouted again, picking up the phone as he punched in 911. "Hello; yes, this is Dryden GMC…*idiot!* You KNOW where it is…just send a squad car over here before I start *shooting* these tress…what? My *name?* JOE DRYDEN, you *imbecile!* I SAID…hello?" He looked stupefied. "They hung *up*…"

"No," Will declared, reentering. "I shut the phone lines off."

"*You*…" Joe barely pulled a pistol out before Ox, with astonishing speed for such a big man, grabbed his arm and shook it *once*. The pistol fell to the floor.

"Now, sir, *you* need to calm down," Ox declared, securing both Joe's wrists in one enormous paw. "There's no *need* for violence; there's enough of *that* in these parts."

"YOU'RE *FIRED*," Joe shouted, struggling. "*YOU…Let go of me, imbecile!*"

The sales secretary, a comely woman with black hair and an amused expression, spoke gently. "Ox: *this* gentleman is *leaving*." Ox spun Joe around like a top and picked him up by the forearms as if he were a rag doll. He carried Joe out through several suddenly-open doors at arm's length and placed him firmly on the sidewalk.

"Now, *sir*," Ox admonished, "*don't* come back in here, or I shall *have* to *hurt* you."

By the time the police arrived, Joe had fled.

# Wednesday

*There's nothing good about this good-bye.*

JJ and Brenda flanked Stella as they marched down the aisle behind Charlie's coffin. Shimmering organ music played, and holy water was sprinkled generously.

"Thank you all for coming," Father Dukakis intoned, signaling the beginning of the service. Charlie's sons and daughters-in-law attended. So did Jo and Julia, Brenda and Roy. To support their friends, Mike and Leigh sat with them. Uncle

Mort and Sid made an appearance, as did Lew Rockland, August Sherith, and, surprisingly, RF. Claiming that the funeral was "a heathen, idolatrous gathering of Popery," Aunt Frieda did *not* attend. Other grandchildren sent their regrets, as did Lois.

The hour-long ritual did *not* include a personal eulogy: no one wanted to speak on Charlie's behalf. Father Dukakis merely recited Charlie's brief biography, naming his wives, sons, and grandchildren. *Stella's* children *were* mentioned.

When the service ended, Leigh spotted Mary Newhouse and another woman dressed in black, leaving the cathedral from the back.

"Mary," Leigh called urgently after her, "Mary Newhouse!"

She stopped, turned, glanced at Mike, and did a double-take. "Who," she started.

"Ingrid," Mike shouted after them. "*Wait* a minute."

"For *what*," Ingrid asked. "Got *another* line you can feed me?"

"No," Mike pulled out his credentials. "*No more* lines to feed you. Just some questions."

"What's going on," Mary asked. "Who *are* you," she stared at Leigh.

"Army CID, *and* your cousin," Leigh flashed her badge and pointed across the street to a small saloon. "Let's talk over there."

"What's this *about*," Mary asked, sitting on a stool. "*I* came to make sure the bastard was *dead*; *that's* all." The only other occupants of the little neighborhood tavern were a rail-thin bartender and an older patron; both seemed like part of the furniture. "You got *another* phony will to talk about?"

"No," Leigh declared, "we have *other, real* business."

"Your *employer* may be dead," Mike smiled, "but his *trust* business...we need to know some details."

"What's it worth to *me*," Ingrid sneered, "or to *Mary*?"

"We don't *know*," Leigh answered. "You're under no criminal indictments, but we *do* know the current *owner* of Parkinson Title and Trust. There *may* be a substantial *severance* in it for you."

The two women looked at each other. "*How* substantial," Ingrid asked.

"Can't say for sure, but *maybe* four weeks' pay for every year you worked for the outfit," Mike offered.

"In *cash*," Leigh added. "*No* 1040s; *no* deductions."

"Ask away, then," Ingrid answered.

"What name is on your paychecks every week," Mike asked.

"Parkinson Title and Trust," both women answered.

"What accounts did you use to pay the bills," Mike continued.

"Second Century Fund," both women answered.

"Who told *you* to pay *what* to *whom*," Mike asked.

Mary and Ingrid looked at each other. "I got a printout every week from Fischer and Ally in Ferndale," Mary said carefully.

"My instructions had always been 'pay *this* to *this* and *don't stop* until I tell you,'" Ingrid declared.

"Until *who* tells you," Mike goaded.

"He's in the coffin."

Mike and Leigh looked at each other. "Just as a curiosity, ladies. The jobs you describe *couldn't* have been full-time work, yet you were paid 40 hours a week. What did you do with your time?"

"I keep books for about half the pushcart businesses in the mall," Mary said. "That may *have* to pay the bills now."

"I did secretarial work for other outfits just to stay awake," Ingrid nodded. "Don't *need* to, now."

"All right, Ingrid," Leigh said, "that's all we have for you. Mary: hang on for a few minutes." Ingrid grabbed her purse, downed her shot of vodka, and shot out the door. Mary waited, curious. Leigh glanced at Mike; cocked her head to the door; he left. "We talked to Lizzie last week. She's in a better place now than where RF *wanted* her to go."

"Uh-huh," Mary shook her head slowly, wiped away a tear. "I *wondered* what happened every time the kids got a card. *Dave* came by the office, took some pictures of the kids with him. RF picked them up on Thanksgiving. *They* said they met their *grandmother*." She shook her head. "That's where *I'll* leave it."

Leigh rolled her bad shoulder. "Your *mother's* family—*my* family—wants to hear from you. Your Aunt Leigh was my grandmother."

Mary looked curious. "Mom never discussed *her* family, but that makes *us*…"

"Cousins. Randy and Renée too."

"Huh," Mary smiled slightly. "Never *had* a cousin before."

"*I* never knew I *had* one before two *weeks* ago."

Mary sighed deeply. "The kids have *wanted* family. Their friends all have *some*."

"My husband has *hundreds* of cousins; you and I have thirteen between us; some in the UP, more elsewhere. I'll get you their contact details."

Mary screwed up her face. "That *insurance*…that *will*…?"

"I got a bundle of cash from RF, $170,000. He also created trusts for you, for Lizzie *and* the kids." Leigh smiled. "But the best thing is the *truth*: they *have* to know sometime."

"That their *uncle* is their *father*? I don't *think* so."

"He's *not* an uncle by blood: *your father* wasn't a blood relation."

Mary shrugged, grinned wryly. "Even so, how do I explain *you*? You were a *lawyer* the last they saw *you*."

"Try a *version* of the *truth*: I needed official information, and I didn't know for sure that *you*—or *they*—were related to me, which is more *true* than *false*."

*And…how did I get HERE?*

## *Thursday*

"Gramma," Julia smiled, "*we* need to talk. This is my partner, Dave Clawson, and my boss, Ernie Packard." They met in Stella's living room…and they brought their own coffee.

"*Pleased* to meet you, Mr. Packard," Stella smiled. "Mr. Clawson and I *have* met. You want to talk about what *Charlie* was into?"

"Yes, Mrs. Parkinson," Dave nodded. "I don't know what your son has shared with you already…"

"Just some vague details," JJ said. "She knows he owned Wolverine, was into some shady business."

"Well, *that's* what we wanted to talk about," Ernie said. "Your husband appears to have been a *facilitator* for shady dealings."

"Right," Julia agreed. "The Newhouse organization had *most* of the hands-on for the *worst* of the unlawful activity."

"I see," Stella said. "And, can you say what that activity *was*…?"

"Hiding felons," Ernie said. "The Newhouse organization moved young men to Wolverine for safekeeping, hiding their identities and creating new ones. But," he grimaced, "then your son stumbled onto an early benefactor of the operation."

"I *did*," JJ said dubiously.

Dave pushed a picture at him. "Remember seeing *him* at Wolverine? In the library…he had no nametag."

JJ looked, squinted, pulled out his glasses. "Um…no. I don't *remember* him. Who *is* he, other than a No-Name?" *No-Names* bunked in what was known as Patton Hall, an elite, 40-bunk barracks.

"Well, *he's one* reason for all that shooting a couple weeks ago." Julia smiled brightly. "To bait *you* back to Detroit…so *you* can be killed *here*."

"Because Charlie wanted me dead *here*," JJ blurted. Stella started but recovered quickly.

"So did others, but that was *part* of it, yes," Ernie said. "But Joe Dryden didn't have the reach to get *Testa* here. The people *this man* once worked for *do. He* is one of the Holy Grails of American law enforcement. In November 1970, he was on his *second* name when *you* saw *him* at Wolverine…and *he* remembered *you*."

"I thought he was such a *nice* boy," Stella said. "He was a neighbor on Franklin Road…"

"Oh!" JJ started. "*Vaguely* familiar…"

"Your *sisters might* remember him better. In the summer of 1975," Ernie said softly, "he transported a package between a house in Bloomfield Hills and a chroming works in Warren. It was the body of one James Riddle Hoffa."

"Then this guy went to his *third* name," Julia continued, "got into *more* trouble and is now serving multiple life sentences." She cleared her throat. "The people who paid him to deliver that body have been terrified that you *might* remember seeing him under that *second* name even if you didn't *know* it. Just knowing *him* might have revealed *their* involvement *and* the Wolverine operation. They've paid Grampa Charlie an *enormous* amount of money to be killed…and Grampa wanted *that*, too. To *that* end," she swallowed hard,

"Grampa's been giving them copies of *your* letters home. *That's* how they knew where you and Mike and Leigh were all the time."

"Why Detroit?"

"That was Mr. Parkinson's condition for his participation," Dave said. "Simple as that, we think. He wanted *you*, ma'am, to know that *he* was responsible for your son's death."

Stella listened passively…though JJ could see her rising fury. "Is he still in danger?"

"The guy that gave the Hoffa orders got killed a few years ago; the acid vats that Hoffa disappeared into are *long* gone. We *know who's* been paying all the money…" Dave shrugged again, "but there are *some* things…"

"How *much*," Stella asked.

"Your husband had been getting as much as $10,000,000 a year for his cooperation since 1967." Ernie folded his hands. "An organization called the Second Century Fund was collecting *four times* that."

"The *good* news, Gramma," Julia added finally, "is that the dealership is, was, and always *has* been not only clean but profitable. So is the *other* school that he—now *you*—own: Francis Hartmann School for Girls."

"Well," Stella declared, "I've no interest in *that*, either."

When the FBI was leaving a few minutes later, JJ went out with them. "How clean *is* Mom, really, Jules?"

"Clean *enough*, Sergeant Elrath," Ernie said. "*We* shall make *certain* of it."

Julia winked, so did Dave…winks that said, *not our first rodeo, buddy.*

***

"*Another* day shot to hell," JJ sighed, leaning back in his chair in the atrium.

"I found four secure filing cabinets today; an Air National Guard warehouse up at Selfridge is parting with them just to be *rid* of them. Learn anything useful," Ann asked, reclining in a chaise.

"Yeah." He gave her a capsule review of what the FBI told Stella.

"Wow. Makes *sense*, somehow. What's she gonna do with what's left."

"She's dumping it all. GM has a dealer ready to slide in next year, one with the capital to buy the land."

"Hey, great. Your mom will be set, then."

"Like she's always wanted to be: a lady of leisure." He was quiet. "Then that *other* thing…"

"About Charlie's body?"

"Yeah. Freida wants to take him back to Berryville; the boys want to bury him with *their* mom…*sort* of. *I* think they're just yanking her chain. Not sure they really care where he *gets* buried as long as he *is* well and truly *buried*."

"Yeah. That and…*Joe's* still out there somewhere." She waved at Leigh and Mike as they came out of the elevator.

"So's Chuck…and *Herman*." *And two of the Four Horsemen.*

# *Sunday*

"So, *next* week is my *last* compulsory Mass to atone for *your* sin of omission?" JJ hung up his coat, got ready to pull off his pants.

"Yup. Forgot how tedious Mass gets when I go every…" Ann picked up the ringing phone. "Chief Mueller-Elrath." *Just…Mueller-Elrath here, kid.*

"*Chief* Mueller-Elrath, this is Dave Clawson. May I speak to your husband, please?"

"Yessir." She held the phone out, a puzzled look on her face.

"Yessir," JJ answered…quizzically.

"JJ, we're serving warrants in Greenville tomorrow morning." Pause. "It might be a *great* deal less *trouble* to gain access to the Wolverine grounds if a representative of the *owner* were present." Pause. "Joe Dryden and Chuck Weir are holed up in there; we *think Herman's* there too." Pause, long, deep. "Want in on the kill?"

"You gotta ask?"

# *The Battle of Greenville*

"What's with the sign," Leigh asked from the back seat of the Suburban.

"Says…Greenville Seat Belt," Mike added. "Largest manufacturer of seat belt hardware in the USA." He took note of several cars lined up on the road nearby.

"What…huh. Never *saw* that before." A large billboard in front of a small factory announced that Greenville was Safety City, USA. "*After* my time." There was a large number of state troopers and sheriff's vehicles on the roads.

Greenville had four industries: Greenville Seat Belt, corn, Wolverine, and Francis Hartmann. The people there mostly worked in or *for* one of the four; teaching, supporting, making, or gathering. Greenville Seat Belt employed a thousand people and did indeed stamp and chrome more seat belt buckles, latches, and anchors than any other firm in the country. In the summer, the nearby Rifle River brought a small body of fisherman and canoeists. In hunting season, the cut fields and woods drew deer hunters.

"*That's* it?" Wolverine was on the other side of the factory. Empty lots like firebreaks with signs of previous structures surrounded the Wolverine compound for two blocks. Four blocks away, lines of cars and trucks waited.

"That's *it*." *And my guts have just turned to water.*

*THAT'S what's been haunting him?* Parked on a small apron ten yards in front of the main gate, they stared at Wolverine Military Academy. The place looked like someone made a half-assed attempt at creating a fortress set for a French Foreign Legion film. They started with a small concrete-and-glass skyscraper but gave up half-done and added a few random windows. The building was surrounded by a low wall topped with barbed wire, with steel light towers at the corners, and a rolling iron gate the only access. All in all, it looked more like a prison. "When were you last *here*?"

"1 June 1971." *And I vowed NEVER to come back.* On his long bus trip home, JJ made two resolves. He was breaking the first by coming back but was obeying the second—that he would always meet threats head-on. "And here I am again. Let's *go*." Glancing in his mirror, a line of vehicles filed into the parking lot twenty yards behind. Light snow greeted them as they climbed out.

A flat CRACK rebounded off the cold ground, and JJ heard a small scream. He turned to see Ann staring at him—surprised—before she dropped out of sight. Another shot, and Mike went *UGH* and dropped himself. Two more quick shots plunged through the Suburban's roof as JJ and Leigh sought cover.

*CLOUD!* JJ looked under the truck, saw Ann's warm brown eyes staring back at him, pleading, blood spattered on her face, her fingers twitching.

"*Ten thousand dollars for the HEAD of Johnny-Cake Elrath,*" Joe's voice called over the loudspeakers.

*SANDY!* Leigh looked over to Mike, saw his head pivoting, his left hand clutching his right arm.

"That's TEN THOUSAND CASH for that *asshole's* head," Joe called again. "*You're dead, Elrath: so's everyone WITH you and everyone you KNOW! I'll KILL you all!*"

*Don't think of HIM now; think about surviving work to do...* "*Where's* that shooter," Leigh shouted, drawing her pistol.

*Shit to do Elrath; pay the hell attention to THIS now...* "That light tower, over on the other side," JJ grunted, skidding to her. "Only one that'll support that much weight. I make it just over two hundred yards. He'll be on the light platform maybe twenty feet up. *Duck down.*" *Neck's screaming and I can barely move my arm wish that key alarm wasn't so persistent need the door open...*

"*OK*, but *what...*" She braced herself, waiting in eerie silence as JJ clambered over her and into the Suburban. *OK foot get over it you too shoulder...*

He emerged moments later with Kurt's Mini-14. "I'm going up front: better angle." He crawled towards the front of the truck, looking back at Leigh; he winked—barely a tic; she smiled. *Don't think about her think about the target; just let me take aim neck and I won't use you for a week...* "Cover fire when I yell." *Deep breath in...hold...half-out...* "*NOW!*"

Leigh stood on the rocker panel, snapping off shots while JJ rolled in front of the Suburban, stopped, aimed, and snapped off two rounds...and Boniface Pale dropped off the platform with two bullets in his head.

"*TEN THOUSAND DOLLARS FOR ELRATH'S HEAD,*" Joe yelled over the loudspeaker.

"*GONNA GET THAT MONEY,*" Rick Stutz yelled as the gate rolled open. "*GONNA RIP YOUR GODDAMN HEAD OFF, ELRATH!*" Stutz was a *monster* of a man, fully six-foot-six and easily three hundred pounds. JJ, his ears ringing and more concerned about the towers and other possible snipers, *didn't* see or hear Rick coming.

*TWENTY THOUSAND DOLLARS FOR THE HEAD OF ELRATH! TWENTY THOUSAND DOLLARS!*

But Leigh *did*, jumping over her Blue-Eyes, delivering a flying kick to Rick's face that smashed Rick's upper teeth, destroyed his nose, and blinded him with pain and blood. Her foot felt as if it were on *fire*, but she twisted around, delivered *another* kick to the side of Rick's head...and *suddenly*, her foot no longer hurt. She followed that with a coiled fist to his abdomen and delivered a final swinging kick to his right knee. Rick fell to the ground in a heap.

*TWENTY THOUSAND DOLLARS FOR THE HEAD OF ELRATH! TWENTY THOUSAND DOLLARS!*

*SHUT THAT SHIT UP!* JJ took aim at the nearest foot-long speaker, 120 yards away, and... "*TWENTY THOUSAND...*" was the last sound *that* one made.

Seconds later, another speaker—225 yards off on Pale's tower—suffered the same fate. A third and fourth at 250 yards and nearly 300—met the same fates.

"Ya know," he sighed after the last shot, "ever since I *left* this place, I imagined *everything* I *aimed* at *was* at some corner of this place…and I don't miss much."

"Good shooting," a small man in a blue nylon jacket with FBI credentials crouching behind him declared.

"Been wanting to shut *that* up for *years*," a sheriff's deputy crouching behind him declared. "You're violating a county firearms ordinance, but I *really* don't give a *shit*…"

"Best iron sight rifle shot in the Army," Leigh grinned as paramedics arrived.

*TWENTY THOUSAND BUCKS for the HEAD of ELRATH!* There were more speakers on the building's roof, hidden from sight but still audible.

"And *who* are *you*," JJ asked.

"Special Agent in Charge Dewitt Harris; I'm the SAIC of the Special Projects Division—your niece's boss's boss." He grimaced tightly. "I haven't been here since '70 when my boy was murdered."

"Don't remember a *Harris*…"

"My *step*son: Jason Samson. Call me *Dusty*," he announced loudly, "and I'm taking *charge* here."

"I have to see to my wife," JJ declared, watching her sit up with a paramedic's help. "She's…"

"We'll *wait*," Dusty declared, standing up warily.

As they loaded Ann onto a litter, JJ reached her side. "Skidded across my *shoulders*, babe," she declared, squeezing his hand. "*Hurts*, but…"

*TWENTY THOUSAND BUCKS for the HEAD of ELRATH!*

*"Go shut that asshole up!"*

"She's in *excellent* hands, Mr. Elrath," Adam replied, wearing a similar windbreaker and flashing an Interpol credential.

"*Thought* you were a something," JJ muttered.

Leigh reached Mike soon after, where his arm was being cleaned up. "Went right through," he grimaced. "But *you've* got work to do. Legs and I will be fine."

JJ led Dusty and the growing mass of law enforcement to the gate, where several uniformed men stood watching. In the thirty-yard empty space between the gate and the main building, many frightened boys watched. JJ stared coldly at the building, then turned his attention to a large man in uniform with the rank of major and a name tag that read *Hardin*, visibly cold in the light breeze.

*TWENTY THOUSAND BUCKS for the HEAD of ELRATH!*

JJ stared at the major briefly, cleared his throat, and announced, "*open up,* Pills."

"*Jesus CHRIST* on a *crutch*," Hardin exclaimed, quickly unlatching the gate and nodding to someone behind the wall. As JJ entered, Hardin extended his hand. "It *IS* you. They *said*…"

JJ ignored it. "Yeah." Men and boys in the courtyard scattered as he and the marshals, followed by sheriff's deputies and state troopers and agents from a score of other agencies, marched towards the big double front doors. The crowd parted like the sea before Moses until a boy with cadet colonel's rank stood in the way. "Battalion commander?"

*TWENTY THOUSAND BUCKS for the HEAD of ELRATH!*

"What's it to *you*?" The lad looked frightened but still defiant.

"I would *advise* that *you* take *charge* of *your* men, *Colonel*," JJ declared. In his peripheral vision, he saw other uniforms spread out around the school's wall.

"I'm under *orders…*"

*TWENTY THOUSAND BUCKS for the HEAD of ELRATH!*

"You're *obliged* to *care* for your *men*, sir. *They* are your *first* duty." *Sotto voce*, JJ mumbled, "take charge *now,* son, or you'll *never* command *again!*"

The boy nodded, coming to grips with his new command structure. "Captain *DeJesus*! Major *Horne*," he shouted. "Fall the men in—two ranks facing the gate." The boys hesitated. *"DO IT NOW!"* Deputies started to herd boys into ranks; cadet officers stood before them, directing.

"Good work," Dusty declared. "Let's try to get inside."

*TWENTY THOUSAND BUCKS for the HEAD of ELRATH!*

JJ marched up and tried the door: locked. He pounded. *"Open up*: I represent the new owner."

A marshal produced a clipboard and began to read. "The United States Court for the District of Western Michigan has issued fugitive warrants for the following individuals: Steven Marchese AKA Steve Markus; Juan DeCastro, AKA Juan Castro de Melancton Felecia; Albert Green AKA…" he went on, reading forty names. "We've come to serve these warrants. If you *fail* to open this door and produce these named individuals, we *will* enter by *force*."

Silence; deafening…until… *TWENTY THOUSAND BUCKS for the HEAD of ELRATH!*

JJ asked Hardin, who had followed them in, "what's *your* function now?"

"*Function*?" Hardin smiled. "I'm *still* the Provost Marshal for all the good *I* do." He looked curious. "What's going *on* with all the badges?"

"This place has been harboring fugitives for nearly two decades, and you *know* it."

*TWENTY THOUSAND BUCKS for the HEAD of ELRATH!*

"I *suspected*. You're from the *new* owner?"

*You chose not to know.* "Yeah. My mother has inherited the place."

"This Dryden character's *not* our newly-appointed Commander-in-Chief?"

"Not even of the latrine," Leigh offered, hanging her credentials around her neck.

*TWENTY THOUSAND BUCKS for the HEAD of ELRATH!*

"You got keys, Pills?"

"Yeah." Hardin inserted his key in the deadbolt, turned it, and withdrew.

"Weir and Jimenez are set up on the balcony. They've each got a *couple* of guns with them."

Dusty turned to JJ. "Balcony?"

*TWENTY THOUSAND BUCKS for the HEAD of ELRATH!*

"Across the drill floor eighty-five paces straight ahead opposite this door, there's an open corridor between Patton Hall on the left and the B Company barracks hall on the right." *I marched around the perimeter of that floor for days...I know those dimensions better than anyone.*

"How *wide*? How *deep*?" By this time, there were easily twenty armed people around the entrance portico. The windows, heavily barred, were about chin-high; deputies and marshals were planning to tear the bars off with trucks and chains.

"Fifty paces from one end to another; three deep. It's enclosed by a heavy wood rail between two wood pillars a pace wide on each end."

"Is there *another* way in?"

"Fire door at each end."

"But," Hardin sighed, "they've barred *those* with boys."

*TWENTY THOUSAND BUCKS for the HEAD of ELRATH!*

"Where's that *PA* coming from," Leigh interrupted.

"Commandant's office," Hardin answered.

"Where's *that?*"

"First *door* on the right," JJ answered. "Thirty-three paces and change from the front door diagonally across the drill floor." Everyone stared at him. "I *marched* that damn drill floor every Saturday and most Sundays for *eight months*. It's 21 paces from *here* right to where Headquarters Company barracks starts; the Commandant's office is 26 paces left from *there*. 21 squared times 26 squared is 1117; the square root of *that* is just over 33 paces." They *still* stared, several affecting puzzled-puppy looks. "I *worked* it *out*, guys. I *know* those dimensions, and *you* don't."

Leigh shook her head, grinning. "If there's anything you'd *know*, buddy, it's *that*. Thirty-three...maybe five seconds' dash." She checked her magazine: *five rounds*.

"*She* any good," a marshal asked.

"As good as she *has* to be," JJ answered, not *really* knowing what skills his Green-Eyes had. *I hope she's good enough.* He winked. She winked back; barely a tic.

"OK," a small deputy shouldered a 12-gauge. "*You* open the door," he nodded at a marshal, "*I* open fire..."

"*We'll* open fire," JJ declared, shouldering his rifle, taking a stance. "the doorknob is on the left..."

"I *can't* authorize..." Dusty grunted.

"I don't give two *shits* what *you authorize*," JJ snarled. "*He* opens the door; then *we all blow* the Commandant's door open, then *we* fire at that balcony at about a 30-degree up-angle from *here*...they'll be behind the pillars on each end…"

"*That's* a plan," Dusty declared, nodding at seven different badges, "and *you* dash through, um…miss?"

"*Sergeant*…but the lights are off in there. You won't be able to see anything for a moment when the door opens."

"Just *run like hell*, Green-Eyes; I know where that *Goddamn door is, then* we'll *fire* at their *flashes*…"

She nodded; he winked…
*Ready…DOOR…NOW!*

\*\*\*

Two rounds whizzed by her head as the thin office door jamb was shot to pieces in front of her. She shouldered through the door as one more round slashed past her. Then, shots roared into the darkness behind her.
*I wish I had a plan for AFTER this.*
*TWENTY THOUSAND BUCKS for the HEAD of ELRATH!*
A thin man with a pencil mustache sat at a desk just inside the office door. The plaque on the desk identified him as Deputy Commandant Gavin Wheatly. He sat with his hands folded on a desk blotter pad as though waiting to be called to give a recitation. He appeared calm but blinked furiously at Leigh. She mouthed *Joe?* He cocked his head slightly towards the door beside him, marked *Commandant*. She could see a lamp on a desk through the office's wavy-glass half-walls and movement through the half-glass door. She could also *hear* Joe, keying a microphone…

\*\*\*

"*THIRTY thousand, boys*! *THIRTY thousand bucks* for Elrath's head. *Who* wants that money, eh? You *cops* out there: that's more than *you* fools make in a *year*. Just *shoot* that stupid bastard, and I'll go with you quietly…*after* I *pay you* to *see him dead*. Get me? *THIRTY thousand*…"

\*\*\*

"Give her a few seconds," JJ murmured in the sudden stillness. "You hear more *shooting, open* that door and rush 'em…if *they're* still *there*…"
She glanced around, seeing a big, heavy trophy cup: *Rifle Marksmanship*…

\*\*\*

Wheatly swung the trophy…
*CRASH! BOOM! BOOM! BOOM!* Leigh fired, shattering picture frames and their glass covers on the wall but missing *Joe* completely…

\*\*\*

"Leigh, meet *Major* Gerald Hardin." *Pills* shook Leigh's hand formally in the Commandant's office. "We called him 'Pills' because he looked like the

Pillsbury Dough Boy then; he's lost weight." JJ sighed. "My last night *here, he* put a bunk adapter under my pillow with a note that read: 'you know what to do and to who.' I bashed Pardon and Jimenez that night."

"You weren't the *only* one I did that for," Pills grunted. "Over a *dozen* that year. *They* would have *killed you* if…"

"Yeah, I know." JJ stared at him. "But *you* know something *else, don't* you?"

Pills blinked, stared at Dusty. "About time somebody *asked* me." He led them to a small office under the balcony, pulling a ledger-like book off a high shelf. "I started keeping a log a few weeks after I got here once I realized that I was just window-dressing." He flipped the ledger open. "Mr. Harris: I believe *this* is what *you* wanted to know."

> *Dec. 24, 11:45 PM: Weir and Jimenez outside Room B-19.*
> *Dec. 25, 7:15 AM: Weir in B Co. Corridor; arm wet, dark.*

"No one ever *asked* me," Pills mumbled. "Weir was in Headquarters Company then and had no *reason* to be in B Company barracks, especially on Christmas Eve *and* Christmas Morning, *and* he lived in town…."

"Then…" Dusty stared, incredulous.

"Then Weir and Jimenez *probably* wrestled Jason—that was *his* room, B-19—into that tub and slashed his arms open." JJ made a face. "Wouldn't have *taken* much. Then Chuck pulled the plug the next morning, and I *saw* him leave. I remember poor Jason in that tub: no *water*, no *blood*, like a wax dummy. And no one thought to *ask* Pills—*Major* Hardin."

"Nope," Pills sighed. "No one *wanted* to know what went on here. *Now*…" he pointed at the scores of ledgers on the top shelf, "now, you can *have* those. I'm *done*."

***

"Hey, Sid," Ann sighed, weakly grasping his offered hand. "*Thought* you might come around." They met in the back of the ambulance in the Wolverine parking lot mid-morning.

"Wouldn't *miss* this," Sid smiled. "*Dearest* Claudia: how *are* you, really?"

"More *blood* than damage—blew across my shoulders—but it'll hurt for a while." She blew out her cheeks. "Morphine eases the pain."

Sid nodded. "Agent Addison is, at this time, arresting Dr. Best for medical records fraud, a *federal* crime that he's been committing for decades. Agent Clawson is arresting the chief of police. But, *I* have a confession to make."

"Oh?"

"In 1924, Charlie Parkinson married Ima Dryden in Berryville, Indiana, and left town soon after. Ima gave birth to David Mercer *Dryden* later in 1924 and died of consumption in 1930."

"That's *interesting*," JJ started, "but Charlie *left* Berryville in '23 when he was fifteen. He *said* so over and over again."

Sid smiled disarmingly. "True. But *that other* story is what the *Berryville* Parkinson's were *told*...and *they* believe it. Your stepfather *left* Berryville, as you said, in *early* 1923, not returning until 1935. The Dryden's only *moved* to Berryville in *late* 1923. Our *Joe's real* father—*also* David Dryden—was born in *Ohio* in 1930 and was a construction contractor who died in 1972."

"So, *where* did Joe get...*how* did...?" JJ was confused; Ann looked amused, but *that* might have been the drugs.

Sid glanced at JJ, inhaling deeply. "*That's* what I'm confessing to. Dave Harriman and I went down to Berryville with Joe in early '73 and contacted Mr. Parkinson's family. I cannot remember if he gave us a reason for that trip or not. All *Dave and I* did was go *with* him." He looked pained. "Until Mrs. Parkinson asked me to *find* the Parkinson's Tuesday, I frankly forgot all *about* it.

"I believe your stepfather told Joe where he *came* from; *when* or *why* is unclear. I suppose Joe claimed that he was Freida's long-lost nephew and concocted his story so he could claim Newhouse relations. I further believe that Joe used Lew Rockland to make *his* fable look good. When Mr. Parkinson had his stroke, they forged the will—Rockland's been forging the gentleman's signature for *years*—but made an error in the date. Joe *probably* promised Rockland a cut of what he could get."

"So, Sid, how...when did you do all this research on...all this stuff on Joe?"

"When I left Randy's orbit in '73, I went to work for Adam's firm...*yes*: keep your enemies *closer*. I told Adam's people all I knew as part of my vetting, *then* did the research on Joe and *his* family, found the *other* Dryden's, and...well, *here* we are."

"So, Rockland..."

"...*will* get called before Fabian O'Bannon soon enough."

"JJ," Leigh called into the ambulance, "they're ready for us."

✳✳✳

They watched as the agents hauled Joe out of the office in handcuffs, his face laced with cuts from glass fragments and wood splinters. "Wait a minute." JJ stood in front of Joe, briefly. "You'd really have let those *kids get killed?*"

Joe's face was a mask of contempt. "*Yeah*, Elrath. YOU could stop me from getting Charlie's fortune."

"I have *three brothers*..."

"THEY don't have *your* determination, your *guts*, your *brains*."

"OK," JJ sighed, grabbing Joe's handcuffs from the agent. "C'mere." He led Joe onto the blood-spattered drill floor, where JJ had spent hours marching in circles for telling the truth. Forty handcuffed youngish-looking men were on their knees there, surrounded by blue nylon jackets. Around the edges and in the barracks halls leading to the drill floor, other blue jackets held back frightened boys and angry teachers. JJ pointed up to the balcony opposite the front door, where Chuck and Herman died in a hail of gunfire and splinters. "That's what *they* died for? *Your* fortune?"

"*Stupid* assholes," Joe sniffed.

Leigh, smiling *ever* so sweetly, mumbled softly. "Joe, Joe, *Joe*," she shook her head. "Do you now, at long last, *finally* realize that you are, without a *doubt, the* most *miserable, inept, complete,* and *utter failure* of a villain?"

"*Bitch,*" Joe growled, "all *you ever* were to *me* was *bait for Elrath.*"

In a flash, she sank a fist into his abdomen, dropping him to his knees. "*This* bait bites *back.*"

"And here," Dave announced, dragging a most uncooperative-yet-uniformed prisoner in handcuffs, "is *another* failed experiment."

"Boehlke," JJ murmured, staring at him.

"Yeah, that was *one* name he had," Dave nodded. "Idiot called *your room* Friday before last; *that's* when we *knew* we had him. He was *born* James Franklin Best, part-time loan shark, part-time pimp. Got himself into a jam that his *daddy* couldn't get him out of, so the Second Century Fund changed his name and stuck him into Wolverine to cool off."

"In '67," Pills nodded. "Same class as Eyerdam and them."

"Yep," Dave said. "Those assholes couldn't keep their noses clean for that last year. But, Jimmy here has a useful skill: loyalty. The Second Century Fund made him their pet police chief—in the town where his *uncle* was medical examiner—so they could cover up the, ah, *accidents* and *suicides* more easily."

"Getting rid of witnesses," Leigh declared.

"That's right," JJ agreed, standing before Boehlke. "Missed *this* one, though, *didn't* ya?"

"*You* are the *luckiest* bastard alive, Elrath," Boehlke mumbled, his face swollen.

"In more ways than one, whoever-the-Hell *you* are," JJ sneered, "in more ways than one."

# New Year's Eve, 1986

"Can't remember ever being around *here*, guys," Mike announced from the Jimmy's back seat. Top Forty countdowns had replaced the ubiquitous Christmas music on the radio.

"Well, now you can't *say* that," JJ declared, turning onto Franklin Road.

"You guys used to *live* here," Leigh asked.

"We *did*…that house there on the left—next to that pool—was where *I* lived until '67. It's an office for that condo complex now." They rolled to a stop. "To the right, through those trees, is where *Ann* grew up."

"We wanted to show you guys the reason *we* think *we're* still here," Ann smiled, opening her door painfully.

They walked onto the grassy two-acre lot where a gnarled old apple tree with an odd split trunk dominated the center. Most years, the field would have been knee-deep in snow, but Michigan winters can be fickle. It *had* snowed, but then it *rained*, followed by weeks of sunny 40s and even 50s. By Christmas, the only snow left in Detroit was the dirty piles under the north side of buildings.

"Our Safe Tree was a wedding present to *us* from Stella," Ann smiled. "My father bought *this* lot with our house—where *that* one is now." Ann pointed to a house behind a line of oaks at the back of the lot. "The day Kennedy was shot, Johnny and I promised to be friends no matter what."

"Mom bought this lot from Howard when he sold that *other* lot." JJ smiled. "She bought it for *me*; used what was left of Dad's estate that Howard managed. *He* said it was the last thing *my* father asked him to do," JJ added, "I can *sort-of* hear him say, 'Howard, keep that lot; Johnny's soul depends on it.'"

"I would like to have met him," Leigh smiled. "He sounds like a good man."

"*I* thought he was. Now we're making *this* lot a park."

"Huh," Mike grunted, pushing on the tree's twisted branch. "Pretty solid for its age."

"Now, my friends, there's a promise *we all* have to make…"

"To *stay* friends, *no matter* what," Ann declared. They each placed their hands on the tree, stacked one on the other.

"And to never hurt each other," JJ grinned.

"And we seal our promise with a kiss just like…" Ann started.

"…Like our *last* promise," Mike finished.

Leigh chuckled. "I've seen *you guys* do it often enough."

"I'm gonna kiss *your* ugly mug *once* for friendship, brother."

"*Once* for friendship, brother."

## *Not That Long Ago*

"This new service is doing a better job," he sighed, stopping the car. They stared at the big lot under a blanket of snow that came the day before.

"Hard to tell now," she declared. "The new markers and corner hedges are better than the ones they tore out. The markers are readable from the road; day-glow-bright and above a foot of snow…"

"Until a snowplow comes through and buries them *and* the hedges," he mumbled. "The arborist says the tree doesn't *have* another year left."

"Yeah." They gazed at the aged, barren tree that hadn't blossomed in *their* lifetimes. "What do we *want* to *do*?"

"Put *another* tree in; hope *it* takes root and…"

"Can't just make *any* old tree our *Safe Tree*, babe."

"We may not have a *choice*, honey: *all* living things die. Somebody *else* will make promises on it, make it *their* Safe Tree."

"On the day *another* president gets shot?"

"Maybe on some *other* auspicious day."

"Maybe it was for someone *else,* maybe on 9/11."

"They closed the schools *then*, too. Part of me hopes *they* were eight. Maybe *they* felt the fear in the air like *we* did; felt better after…like *I* did."

"*I* did, too. So, we plant another tree," she agreed…

And they kissed on it.

\*\*\*

The markers read…

*Safe Tree Park*
*Open to the Public Every Day Except 12 and 19 July*
*Make a promise to another with your hands on this tree.*
*Seal your promise with a kiss, and your promise will last forever.*

Children of all ages still make solemn promises on the new tree—fragrant with blossoms every spring—*and* on the old tree's stump.

And they kiss on those promises, making them good *forever*.

## *For the story behind THIS story, read* The Liberty Bell Files: J Edgar's Demons